SERIAL
KILLER
GAMES

SERIAL KILLER GAMES

Kate Posey

BERKLEY

NEW YORK

BERKLEY
An imprint of Penguin Random House LLC
1745 Broadway, New York, NY 10019
penguinrandomhouse.com

Book design by George Towne

Library of Congress Cataloging-in-Publication Data

Names: Posey, Kate, author.
Title: Serial killer games / Kate Posey.
Description: First edition. | New York : Berkley, 2025.
Identifiers: LCCN 2024045444 (print) | LCCN 2024045445 (ebook) |
ISBN 9780593818510 (trade paperback) | ISBN 9780593818534 (ebook)
Subjects: LCGFT: Thrillers (Fiction). | Romance fiction. | Novels.
Classification: LCC PR9199.4.P67577 S47 2025 (print) |
LCC PR9199.4.P67577 (ebook) | DDC 813/.6--dc23/eng/20241125
LC record available at https://lccn.loc.gov/2024045444
LC ebook record available at https://lccn.loc.gov/2024045445

First Edition: April 2025

Printed in the United States of America
1st Printing

The authorized representative in the EU for product safety and compliance is
Penguin Random House Ireland, Morrison Chambers, 32 Nassau Street,
Dublin D02 YH68, Ireland, https://eu-contact.penguin.ie.

This one's for you, dollface!

SERIAL KILLER GAMES

1

The Serial Killer at Work

THERE'S BEEN ANOTHER MURDER.

"It was a hundred-foot drop," Kara-from-Accounts says as she presses the DOOR CLOSE button at the end of the day.

"One fifty, at least," says Stanley-from-IT. "It's a fifteen-story building."

The elevator lurches as it begins its descent, and everyone goes quiet for a moment, contemplating that fairground feeling of falling, falling.

"Have the police done a press release yet? Do they know for certain it's connected to the others?" Tiffany-from-Project-Management asks. Her commuting sneakers squeak as she rocks back and forth.

"It only happened yesterday. They haven't said anything yet."

"It wasn't a murder," Stanley-from-IT says. "He threw himself off."

Tiffany-from-Project-Management gasps. "How do you know?"

"It's what I wanted to do when I worked there." Stanley-from-IT guffaws.

Kara-from-Accounts doesn't laugh. "Nine falls in five years, each at a different office building downtown," she muses. "There's someone behind it all."

Everyone thinks there's someone behind it all. The existence of the Paper Pusher has been a topic of speculation at every temp job I've had. Every downtown office building I've worked at in the past five years.

I know a little more than most.

"Maybe it was an HR exercise. A trust fall gone wrong, eh? Eh?" Stanley-from-IT doesn't get a laugh from Kara-from-Accounts, so he turns to Tiffany-from-Project-Management. He doesn't get his dues there, either. He frowns. "It's just an urban legend," he says irritably. "You don't *actually* believe someone's going around pushing people off rooftops?"

Kara-from-Accounts sniffs.

The elevator doors open on the fourteenth floor to welcome a newcomer dressed in all black, her red lips a surprising pop of color at the end of this boring, dreary day. She slides in like a shadow, bearing her phone like a talisman that will protect her from small talk, and slinks against one wall of the elevator, the collar of her black trench coat flipped up and her face angled down at the screen. I don't know her name yet, but I make a point of learning names and departments. I'll figure her out soon enough.

"It's a serial killer. I *know* it," says Kara-from-Accounts.

The shadow perks her ears.

Stanley-from-IT sticks his hands in his pockets and gazes up at the grille ceiling, shaking his head with a stupid smirk on his face and sighing indulgently. Stanley is a bit of a bully. "Serial killers don't push their victims off rooftops. They strangle them, or slice them up. They like to watch their victims die."

Tiffany-from-Project-Management turns green.

"Maybe this serial killer is squeamish," Kara-from-Accounts persists. "Maybe he doesn't like to get his hands dirty."

"He? Who says it's a he? It could be a she," Stanley-from-IT says indignantly.

"Are you agreeing with me that this person exists?"

I watch the newcomer from across the elevator. Her eyes gleam, and she presses her lips together like she's heroically restraining herself from joining in the conversation. And normally I wouldn't join in, either. Generally, I prefer to watch and listen. I stick to the fringes. But . . .

"What's the appeal of serial killers?" I ask, and everyone startles. They'd forgotten I was there. Unremarkable, dull, in my gray coat and gray slacks and gray tie, my everyman haircut and glasses. I melt into the walls wherever I work.

"What?" Stanley-from-IT says.

"Why do people enjoy the topic so much?"

There's an awkward little pause while they sit with my accusation that they're *enjoying* this, and the woman in black jumps into the silence.

"Wish fulfillment, obviously."

"Is there someone you want to kill?" I ask.

She holds my gaze, and her lips quiver in a tiny, vicious smile. A good serial killer would never draw attention to her target.

We reach the ground floor and the public transportation cohort spill out when the doors open, nattering all the while. Normally I'd be with them, but I drove today, the first day of my new temp job. I have an errand after work. The doors sigh shut, and I'm left alone with the shadow bundled stiffly in one corner, her black leather bag clamped under one arm. She glances at me—just a quick lizard-brain reflex to scan her environment—but our eyes catch, and I'm surprised to find myself talking again. Chitchat is not something I do.

"What would your MO be? Would you push someone off a roof?"

She answers immediately, as if she's been waiting all day for this question. "I'm a straight razor kind of girl. Small, portable, quick. Wouldn't require much physical exertion. And there's a certain retro classiness to it, don't you think?"

"Very Sweeney Todd."

She frowns and turns to face me properly with dark, inscrutable eyes. One slim hand slides her phone into her pocket.

"I was thinking Black Widow. Kept her first husband's razor as a trophy."

"Sounds messy." I don't like messes myself.

Her red lips twitch. "Why do you think I'm wearing all black? How would you do it?"

I adjust my cuffs while I contemplate my answer.

"Ah. You have strangler gloves," she says.

I flex my fingers in my black leather gloves. "Like Stanley said," I say. "A true serial killer has the good manners to keep it personal. A good firm stranglehold and then eye contact till the end."

She snorts. "Don't threaten me with a good time."

My insides twist pleasantly and unexpectedly. It's not unlike that fairground feeling. "What's your name?"

The amused twist to her lips flattens. She doesn't need a straight razor. She slits my throat with a scowl and returns her attention to her phone.

A moment later the doors open onto the dim basement

parking, and her heels fire a gunshot staccato that echoes in the cavernous space. I follow. She walks to a black car, swings her bag into the front seat, and turns to me.

"You're following me."

"No. This is my car." I lean against the car next to hers.

She considers the sleek car and weighs it against my temp uniform. "That's definitely not your car."

"It is."

"Prove it. Open up the trunk and show me your latest strangle victim."

I don't move.

She twists sinuously on the spot and flicks her eyes up and down, from my head to my toes. "You're a creep," she says, and I can't tell if it's an insult or praise. She hops in her car and I watch as she drives off. She flips me the bird as she vanishes around a cement pillar.

I stare after her, my thoughts twisting this way and that. There was something about how she looked at me and really saw *me*—the faceless office temp who no one normally sees, who no one is supposed to notice. It feels risky, and exhilarating.

I fish my keys out of my pocket and pop the trunk. There's a rolled-up rug inside, blond hair spilling out one end.

I *could* have shown her. Wouldn't that have been hilarious.

2

The Temp

MY LIFE IS LIKE THIS:

My alarm clock says 4:00, or 3:47, or 5:10, or something like that, when consciousness stitches itself together. I never actually rely on my alarm clock to wake me. I don't sleep well. I don't think people tend to sleep well when they're living with the sorts of things I am. Thoughts that go bump in the night. Secrets that scratch away in my head.

Sometimes I drink my coffee in the dark living room while watching the news. The housing crisis. The climate crisis. The crisis crisis. Luckily none of it affects me. Sometimes I watch the sleeping neighborhood from the balcony. Sometimes I stand in my roommate's doorway and watch him snore as Verity lies unnaturally ramrod-straight beside him. No normal woman sleeps like that, although it's been a while since any woman has slept next to me, normal or otherwise. I stand there and wonder what I'll do with him. I wonder what I'll do with *her*, when the time comes. We're going to run out of rugs.

The apartment building grumbles to life, radios and TVs flick on, cars outside start, and I come alive by proxy, a robot humming awake from a pulse of ambient electrical power. When my roommate comes out, I fire a bright shit-eating grin at him, because that is what humans are supposed to do.

"Good morning, Grant," I say.

THE MORNING TRAFFIC SQUEEZES MY BUS DOWN MAIN. I OFFER MY SEAT TO the pregnant women and elderly and mumble "Sorry" and smile self-effacingly when someone steps on my foot. I'm the perfect extra in the background, with my messenger bag and glasses; my hair and clothes neat, appropriate, forgettable; a free city newspaper folded in half in one hand—which I never read. When the credits roll, my part will be Morning Commuter #6. My bus spits me out at Richeson and I catch the SkyTrain to Bylling, then walk the remaining five minutes to one of a hundred skyscrapers rearing up like late-stage capitalism's middle finger held up to humankind. I'm a cog in the corporate machine. I'm one of a billion fruiting bodies on the capitalist fungus that permeates the globe with a fine, hairlike mycelium. I'm no one. A nonentity. I like it that way.

I work for a temp agency, which means I'm a warm body for hire. As long as I have a pulse, I have a job. At the moment, I'm a placeholder for a human with actual value. Harriet is on unpaid leave, and so that some bean counter doesn't decide that her position can be cut since no one is performing her job or taking her salary, her supervisor, a man called Doug, who has been promoted several strata past his zone of competency, has hired me to fill her spot. Her tasks were redistributed to her team members, so my job is to sit at her desk and keep her chair warm. I *am* given work to do: I have an intimate relationship with the photocopier, the coffee machine, the collator, and the rooftop, where I take about twelve breaks a day.

People call me Jacob and Jack and Jonathan. Quite a few people don't bother with my name at all, although *I* make a point of learning everyone's. I always do. A few busybodies patted me down for gossip about a week after I arrived, found me empty-pocketed, and have left me alone since. I'm a little friendless island in the workforce sea. I prefer it. I'd rather watch, and listen, and work on my list to pass the time and ease the boredom. Adding names, removing names. Adding them back again.

At the end of the day, I take public transportation home with my fellow hollow-eyed survivors of the downtown commercial hell zone. I smile vacuously at them. *Good job, team! Same time tomorrow?* I let myself into the apartment and find Grant and his latest consort, Verity, sprawled on the sofa watching reality TV. He cradles her against the side of his body and absently strokes her hair. I know better than to be envious of what he has.

I clean. I restore order. And then I cook. Healthy meals with expensive ingredients—organic vegetables, grass-fed meat, and things like saffron salt and truffle oil—carefully and thoughtfully prepared, all at Grant's request and on his dime. If it were just me, it would be a bowl of cereal. *I'm* not planning to live to a hundred. I make a show of inviting Verity to join us, because Grant likes for me to be polite, but of course she never accepts. Grant doesn't date the sort of woman who eats. Instead, she watches us with wistful eyes too large in her perfect, sculpted face.

Rinse, repeat.

3
Hello, Dolly

UNTIL DOLORES.

It isn't easy figuring out her name. My new place of work is a massive termite colony, each department compartmentalized and unto itself, and it's difficult to find anyone who knows anything about the woman dressed like Satan's shadow, always in black, with long sleeves and high collars; the one with the vibrant lipstick and the cruel heels, who swirls through rooms without others registering her presence. Purposeful but aloof, like a malevolent spirit with shit to do.

"Who was that?" I ask Tricia-from-Marketing after another spotting in the break room.

"Who was what?" Tricia-from-Marketing asks, attempting to eat her yogurt daintily, not realizing she has a smear on her chin.

I trail the shadow down a hallway, round a corner, and she's gone.

Another time, she materializes in a packed elevator next to me. She doesn't acknowledge my existence, and I certainly don't say anything. I watch to see which button she'll push, but she doesn't so much as glance at the numbers. She steps off at the sixteenth floor when it opens to let someone in, and I watch, waiting to see if she'll go left or right, but she does neither. She dawdles, looking at her phone, and just as the doors slip shut, she looks left, then right, and ducks into the stairwell.

"Who was that?" I ask Brennan-the-Intern.

"What was who?" Brennan-the-Intern asks, swiping right ten times in a row on a dating app while waiting for his floor.

Whoever she is, she acts like a secret agent. She gets off at the wrong floor and uses the stairs to throw off anyone who might be watching. She always has her phone out or pressed to her ear to deflect conversation. There's no way to figure out who she is. I decide she must be a consultant, or a freelancer, or maybe even a client representative. Not a Spencer & Sterns employee at all.

Several days go by without any sightings, and then at the end of the day one Thursday, later than usual, I catch the elevator by myself, down, down, down, until it stops at the fifteenth floor. The doors yawn open like the gates to hell, and there she is.

She wears a black dress with a neat white collar under her open coat, and her lipstick makes her look like she's just finished devouring some poor man's heart, raw. She steps into the miasma of elevator Muzak with me, presses B, and turns to face me—a slow, graceful pirouette, her arms extending as she leans back on the handrail. Her sharp nails rasp the metal of the rail and the hairs on the back of my neck stand at attention. Then she cocks her head to one side, exposing the bareness of her own neck, and she looks like a vampire offering herself up to her lover. The elevator doors close, her eyes meet mine, and there's that lurching fairground drop in the bottom of my stomach again, except the elevator hasn't started moving yet.

"Ted Bundy," she says.

I blink. "My name is—"

"Your Halloween costume," she says. "You're dressed as Ted Bundy."

I'm not wearing a costume. I glance down at my arm in its sling. Yesterday I fell, and Grant—well, it was a whole thing. After Verity moved in, the large box she brought with her had to be carried out, and lending a helping hand is the nice, room-matey thing to do. Everyone at the office today was very solicitous. Deb-from-IT, in a disturbing cat costume, parts of which may have been sourced from an adult store, even gave me a double handful of Halloween candy.

"You're the first to guess. But what about you? You're just wearing your usual vampire nun getup."

She narrows her eyes at me. "Vampire nun?"

"You're always in black and covered up like a sister wife, except your legs."

She looks thrown for a moment, like she doesn't know whether she likes that I've made an observation about her. "I told you. I'm going for a Black Widow aesthetic."

I want to know who she is.

"I'm Jake Ripper."

She snorts contemptuously. "That's definitely not your name."

"It is. What's yours?"

She doesn't give me her name. She doesn't say a thing. She is a wall. A stone. A—

The doors slide open, and my clinically stupid supervisor, Doug, enters at the ninth floor. In the jocular voice he uses to disguise the fact he has no idea what's going on, he says, "Jack! And if it isn't the lovely Dolly."

She startles and shoots him a venomous look, but my stomach pinches pleasantly, and I file away my first little bit of data. Her name. I visualize it being typed across the blank screen in my head, the cursor blinking patiently, waiting for a surname.

"That's not my name," she says, and her tone makes it clear this idiot is taking his life into his hands calling her "Dolly."

Backspace, backspace, backspace . . .

"Haha, yes. Yes. Dolores dela Cruz."

Bingo. Entered and saved. I never forget a name. Here, her eyes dart toward me. The game is up.

Doug continues obliviously. "Haha, ¿cómo Esteban?"

She stares at him in disbelief. "'¿Cómo Esteban?'"

His grin slips. "You don't speak Spanish?"

She says, "I'm Filipina."

It's not going well for Doug. He still has no idea what's going on, and his HR-mandated sensitivity training only got far enough into his skull to create a generalized impression that the conversation is turning dangerous. He scurries off at the third floor when the doors open to let someone in. The third floor isn't even leased by our company.

I watch Dolores dela Cruz's profile for the remaining two floors down to Ground, where I get off.

"Good night," I say in my boring human voice.

"Buenos nachos," she says flatly without looking up from her phone.

THE NEXT MORNING, I WAKE AT 4:53 A.M. AND STARE AT THE DIM GRAY SQUARE that is my ceiling and think about Dolores dela Cruz. I drink five cups of coffee in the dark, and I don't even feel annoyed about Verity anymore. I have a name. Now I need to find out where she works. I need to know her department.

At work, after serving two weeks as photocopy bitch, Doug finally gives me some data entry to do.

"How long did this job usually take the last person?" I ask him.

Doug sweats and fidgets. "A week?"

I nod mournfully. "It will take me longer because I'm learning."

Then I request permission to relocate to the empty annex so that I can take advantage of the quiet to *really focus*, i.e., write a script that will automate the entire process, completing one week's work in five minutes, allowing me to spend the rest of the day working on my list. Or staring into space and imagining shoving every person I ever knew off a tall building. Or thinking about a slight figure in a black trench coat.

Permission is granted, and off I gambol to claim a cubicle in the annex, a deserted corporate postapocalypse frozen in time after the chaotic bloodbath of the last round of layoffs two years ago. The conspicuous absence of the warm bodies that left pens and papers scattered about and chairs half turned from their desks pleases me. The fluorescents hum at the edge of hearing, the dry air tickles the throat, and the sensory pleasures of greasy melamine surfaces and polyester upholstery beckon.

I plug in my computer, line up my pens, square my Post-its, purposefully press the power button . . . and as my computer makes the sound of an angel chorus sighing, I look up, and there's Dolores dela Cruz herself.

Ensconced in a corner office, her long blue-black hair twirled into a perfect knot on the nape of her neck, her winged eyeliner like little black knife blades, her lipstick the only splash of color in this monochrome environment, she's been watching me through the floor-to-ceiling window that makes up one wall of her office with a stony expression.

I smile a bright, fake, shit-for-brains grin at her.

Fancy seeing you here!

She doesn't even blink. She holds my gaze for five seconds, then turns back to her computer.

NOW, MY LIFE IS LIKE THIS:

On Monday, Dolores walks in with lips as red and sticky and sweet as a Halloween candied apple with a razor blade inside, plucks up the coffee labeled DOLLY from her desk, and holds my eye while she drops it in the trash. Which is fair. I wouldn't drink a coffee bought by me, either.

On Tuesday, my Post-its and pens are smacked out of order when I arrive at work, and the pervasive pong of fish reveals itself to be one of Jared-from-Accounts's dirty tuna cans, taken from the kitchenette and hidden in my waste basket.

On Wednesday, my user account has been wiped from the computer. I make eye contact with Dolores as I pull a flash drive out of my messenger bag and restore my lost files.

On Thursday, I festoon my cubicle with strings of braided garlic and pour a salt ring onto the carpet around my desk.

On Friday, she cranks up her true crime podcasts to full tilt, daring me with a glance to protest. But the grisly podcasts just make the place feel homier. I decide to stay, and dear old Doug, pleased with my productivity, lets me.

It's clear she isn't happy about my intrusion. She never asks me what I'm doing here or how long I'll stay. In the beginning she doesn't talk to me at all, but some days I look up from my desk, my gaze drawn as if by an industrial magnet, and there she is, staring right at me through the glass window of her office with a bored, dissatisfied expression, like an apex predator considering something quite beneath her on the food chain.

When she's not there, I pick the lock of her office door with a pair of paper clips and snoop her computer. It wakes when I touch the space bar, and she's left open a browser tab for me: a Google search for How to tell the office nutjob you know he's snooping on your computer after hours. I leave a new search for her: How do I gently let down an infatuated co-worker?

There's nothing personal on her computer, and I can't make out anything work related, either. She spends all her time on her laptop, and that goes home with her.

I look up her podcasts and download an episode of *Murderers at Work* on my phone. I press play, and that eerie, now familiar opening jingle tinkles like a mallet sweeping over a skeleton's ribs. I open her drawers and look through each one, just as she did to me, and as I lean back in her chair, I notice that the black stone vase sitting on her desk is angled just right so that she can see my workstation reflected in one of its flat, rectangular sides.

It's a mystery to me what Dolores does. She doesn't participate in any meetings. She doesn't seem to be afflicted with a recurring appearance of paunchy middle management knocking on her door to "check in." I watch her all day, and see nothing.

And all the while, there's *something*. Something irresistible. I feel like a kid who keeps teasing the cat that scratches him. I feel like a cold, rubbery lab frog twitching to life every time she jabs me with an electrode.

AT THE END OF THE FIRST WEEK, WE FIND OURSELVES ALONE IN AN ELEVATOR again.

"Dolores," I say.

"Jake," she says, stiffly.

And in my best imitation of a normal human being, setting aside for the moment that she poured an entire cup of coffee on my messenger bag earlier, I ask, "Plans tonight, Dolores?"

"No. But I know what you're doing."

"What?"

"Putting the finishing touches on your human skin suit. I'm an expert on serial killers. I can always spot one in the wild. It's the stench of bleach and the aura of despair."

"Don't have time tonight," I say. "I'm defrosting my freezer for my next victim."

"Do you use your fake golden retriever to lure them in?"

"My fake golden retriever?"

"The one whose picture you have as your desktop image."

"What makes you think he's fake?"

"You never have any dog hair on your clothes. And because it's a stock image. It's the first picture that comes up when you google 'golden retriever.' I checked."

I would never be that obvious. It's the third image.

"Is this part of your pretending-to-be-normal disguise?" she asks.

"Yes. Is your cat part of yours?"

She swivels on me. "Cat?"

Earlier, I heard her asking her neighbor to feed her cat. I can hear all her phone calls from where I sit, and I'm fascinated by the rare details of Dolores's out-of-office life that come my way. I collect them, polish them up, appraise their value, and sort them into neat, meager piles. Pets resemble their owners, and I can picture the cat: vicious, sharp-fanged, black. Because of course she's black.

She narrows her eyes dangerously at me. "Nothing gets past you, Jake. You're a real bunny boiler, you know that?"

"What?"

"Am I going to come home someday to you making rabbit stew in my kitchen? Wearing my clothes? Blood smeared all over the cabinets? You picked the lock to my office. You went through my drawers."

Just look at this little hypocrite.

"You went through my desk first. Maybe I should file an HR complaint."

The split second of hesitation after my response gives her away. For a fleeting moment her face is afraid. Drawing the attention of HR scares the bejeesus out of her. A tiny, doubtful seed of suspicion morphs rapidly into a plant on time lapse. Her reluctance to tell me her name, her secret agent tactics, her remote office apart from everyone else—it all comes together. Suddenly I understand everything. I know her secret.

"What makes you think I haven't beaten you to it?" she says airily. "I already spoke to HR."

"You haven't. And you won't."

"Don't be so sure. I've been advised to keep a log."

She hasn't, and I've never been so sure about something in my life. I get off at Ground, and one backward glance reveals Dolores staring after me with a small line between her eyebrows.

"'Grief,'" I say over my shoulder. "It's a good name for you."

"A more accurate translation would be 'pain,'" she calls out. She says it like she's cautioning me not to forget it.

The next morning I pull up my list. I create a new one every time I start at a new office. It's my list of expendables, my list of people to be eliminated.

Dolores dela Cruz

I tuck her name in neatly at the bottom, under two dozen other names. My fingers hover over the mouse. What the heck. Why not? I cut her name and paste it at the top.

4

True Crime Aficionado

DOLORES

IT'S 8:30 A.M. ON A FRIDAY, AND AS USUAL I'M CRAMMED INTO ONE CORNER OF the elevator with my face in my phone as I ascend from basement parking to my floor. The doors sweep apart for a pit stop at Ground to welcome the usual crowd, but today . . . today, there's a little ripple in the atmosphere, the universe exhaling its breath on the back of my neck, and I look up to see the back of a head with familiar, neatly trimmed dark hair. Dark gray coat, gray slacks, black gloves. Ted Bundy in the elevator. The dashing stranger strangler.

I don't get off at Fourteen or Fifteen or Sixteen. I stay put and watch from my corner as he reads text messages on nearby phone screens, tilts his head to the conversation around him, studies faces and notes the floors they sort themselves onto.

He steps off at Twenty, and I stay, chewing my lip. And maybe it's the boredom building in my head, making my brain slide out my ear like a piece of charcuterie sliding off a cracker, but a chime tinkles, a prancing little dance of mallets on a xylophone that no one around me hears—a podcast jingle, the soundtrack to my boring little life.

My life was interesting, once.

Tinkle, tinkle, tinkle.

I jab the button just in time to stop at Twenty-one, cross the hall, and glide down the fire escape stairs, my heels snapping violently against the concrete steps. I peer through the door before stepping out onto Twenty. Coast clear.

I've perfected the art of gliding through populated spaces. I've been flying under the radar in this building for years, after all. The trick is to not slow down, to not make eye contact, to keep my face severe enough that the bashful intern is relieved when I pass by without acknowledging him. Down the hallway, past the phone desk, around the corner and into the bullpen, becubicled within an inch of its demonic, corporate, undead life. The sickly drone of industrial air circulation stabbed through with the frantic pulse of phones ringing, everyone murmuring, murmuring, murmuring, except for one loud jackass with the self-awareness of a two-year-old describing his skin fungus over the phone. I prowl the perimeter, my pulse ticking faster—until it stops.

Another sweep of the xylophone.

There he is.

Dark head bowed over his desk, fingers plucking methodically at his keyboard. His movements careful, rehearsed, like a stage actor playing a part.

He stands and pans the room, and I duck behind a pillar. He makes his way to the break area and drinks from a paper cup, *slowly*, definitely not listening in on the watercooler gossip being hashed out by two coworkers nearby, finishing his break a sensible ten seconds after they leave, using that time to monitor the movements of a gaggle of middle managers with studied disinterest. As he returns to his seat, he scans the computer screens of everyone he passes with a bored expression.

I stalk down the main aisle and breeze past where he sits, mere inches from the back of his bare neck, and complete my flash reconnaissance: just a spreadsheet this morning, a list of names; no photos on his desk; murder gloves stuffed in his coat pocket; his shoes aren't filthy with mud from a shallow grave, and they haven't been scrubbed with a toothbrush and bleach, either; fresh shave; bare ring finger.

A creak behind me could be his chair as he turns to watch me walk away. A shiver goes down my spine, but I keep my pace steady.

I leave the bullpen via a long, narrow hall I know leads to a stairwell, but behind me . . . Are those footsteps? It's hard to be certain on commercial carpet, and now I'm in a stretch of office wasteland missing the ubiquitous wall of unnecessary glass that would give me a reflected view of everything behind me. It won't do to allow him to track me back to my lair. But the difference between predator and prey is a predator will calmly allow herself to be stalked by another predator. She doesn't bolt like a silly bunny. Predators understand how to play the long game, how to front, how to employ theory of mind. Predators are artists.

Without changing my pace, I round a corner and duck into an open door. The janitor's closet. It's pitch-black inside, except for a gash of light under the door illuminating my toes. I wait.

My heartbeat slows.

The silence stretches on.

I feel . . . disappointed.

There were no footsteps behind me.

Suddenly two shadows appear in the sliver of light under the door, and my toes disappear.

My stomach folds in half, and in half again—

My heart races—

Tinkle, tinkle, tinkle. The little mallets trill up and down my spine—

And my face—

It's a good thing it's dark in here. I never smile before noon.

The shadows vanish, my toes reappear, and I'm alone again. Just me, the mop bucket, and my heart, beating again after years of flatlining.

He's definitely a murderer. I haven't rotted my brain on true crime for five years for nothing.

AT MY DESK I FISH OUT MY PHONE AND SET TO WORK. HE'S GOT HIS OWN PAGE of notes, and it's filling up faster than the one I keep for the shifty-eyed parking attendant or the new HR consultant with the unsettling, pale gaze.

Jake the Ripper: He's Doug's. He doesn't seem to have any real responsibilities. No particular friends. He wears the exact same clothes, day after day after day, the monotony a form of visual Vaseline to make people's eyes slide right off him. He takes public transit; he definitely does *not* drive the Aston Martin that appeared once in basement parking, and as a matter of fact, no one does. Whoever owns it sits in it and masturbates to the thought of their car's price tag. I know that's what I'd do.

Full points for his mask. He's exactly like everyone else here, a cookie-cutter corporate drone with a number tattooed in his ear. Cheap suit, boring tie, shoes that can't possibly be comfortable. He's a temp, a little sore thumb poking out at odd angles from the corporate body, and that's all part of it. It's easier to sustain an act for short stints. It's handy to point at the challenges of being thrust into a department full of strangers and blame the antisocial behavior on shyness. And when things get weird—when someone notices him stuffing a duffle bag full of plastic sheeting into his trunk or wiping a speck of blood off his shoe—he takes a new job and vanishes. Just like the Paper Pusher, he slinks into offices like vapor curling in from under the door, and then leaves, barely imprinting onto the memories of anyone there. *You remember that temp—what was his name? Jack? Jonathan?*

And all the while, he slinks around, studying people, learning their routines, casing his next victim.

There's a thud behind me. I swivel in my chair to look out the glass wall of my office, and who should happen to be claiming the cubicle opposite but . . . Murder Gloves himself.

He performs his move-in rituals solemnly and fastidiously, wiping down his desk with Clorox wipes before taking a seat. His movements are slow, smooth, careful. He lines up his pens, twists his Post-its *just so*, presses the power button on his computer, folds his hands. And then raises his eyes to mine.

I already knew he was attractive in a neat-hair-and-glasses sort of way. I'd noticed. Good looks give you a leg up in every field, including remote farmer's fields full of unmarked graves. People like you, they trust you, they want to be alone with you. The glasses are a great idea. Thick-framed and dark, they're what you see first when you look at him. He probably looks completely different without them. But if you look past them, he's got a sort of root-cellar paleness, like someone who's been kept in a secret basement all their life—which no doubt he has been. Dark hair and expressive eyebrows. Behind his glasses his lashes are thick, and dark circles give him a debauched, cocaine-weekend, hasn't-slept-in-three-days look. Or hasn't-slept-in-ten-years. He's being eaten from the inside out by a horrific secret—the body hidden under the floor-boards.

I know all about bodies hidden in plain sight.

And then the fucker *smiles* at me. An unhinged smile that doesn't reach his eyes, the sort of smile you see right before Hannibal Lecter bites your face off.

Tinkle fucking tinkle.

I don't smile back. I hit my quota early today.

He's gone by the time I finish for the day. I board the eleva-tor and lodge myself in the corner behind a pair of Spencer & Sterns accountants. That wall of bodies blocks me from view when he steps in at the ninth floor and turns to face the doors. What a pleasure. What a *delight*. So much Jake Ripper in one day. I creep forward until I stand just slightly behind and to one side, close enough to inhale that signature bouquet of so-cial isolation overlaid with the lighter, cloying notes of bleach for wiping away DNA and fingerprints.

Except . . . he doesn't smell like that. His mask is too good, after all. He smells pleasantly mannish—like clean hair and soap and something else, something inviting and red-blooded that would make a woman lean her face right into his shoulder seconds before he reached up and wrapped his hands around her throat.

He raises his chin to watch the numbers—*9, 8, 7*—and I raise my chin to watch him, the neat outline of his head, the contours of his shoulders. His head is angled so that I can see the world through one lens of his glasses, distorted and strange. He turns slightly to let someone off at Four, and I no-tice a patch of stubble that he missed, right over an artery in his neck. I could take care of it myself, quickly, gently, whisking the razor over that tender skin between heartbeats. Maybe I'd be careless, and a ruby of blood would form.

Our greasy reflection comes together as the elevator doors close, and when I look, I can see his eyes were on me first.

I work it out in my head on the drive home. He knew I was there behind him, as I leaned into his space and studied his haircut, his shave, and breathed in his smell—

He was breathing in *my* smell. He knew I was there because he recognized the scent of my perfume.

Three things occur to me. First, *he's* been watching *me*. I made the mistake of drawing his attention. A couple of jokes in an elevator and now he's like a pale, fluttering night bug that glimpses a flash of light and won't go away. Or maybe a mosquito that's sniffed blood and circles around lazily, waiting for its opportunity.

Second, a crooked little part of me *likes* that he's been watching me. My life's come to a pretty pass when I'm lonely enough to be flattered by the attention of a man who wants to carve my face from my skull and wear it.

And finally, this is bad. Nobody is supposed to notice me.

5

Hostile Work Environment

JAKE

I'VE BEEN AT SPENCER & STERNS FOR ONE MONTH. I COULD BE YANKED SUD-denly by my temp agency and placed somewhere new, but for the time being I'm here with Dolores in our little annex, our little cell, our little funny farm.

It's November now, and we are clenched in the white-knuckled death grip of Christmas season hysteria. Holiday music wafts like a bad smell over the elevator sound system, and twining vines of green and silver tinsel metastasize around railings and doorways. Not in our private sanctuary, though. An hour after the decorations go up, Dolores emerges from her office and Grinches the annex from the freckled ceiling tiles down to the shit brindle brown carpet, shoving everything into a big black garbage bag.

"Where's your Christmas spirit?" I ask her, and she ignores me. She's been ignoring me all week, ever since my comment about going to HR, and I miss her little acts of guerrilla terrorism. She returns to her office and flicks on a podcast, and

the now familiar tinkle of a jingle starts. A jaunty waltz across
the minor keys of a xylophone, and—

"*Hellooooo, Killjoys and Murderheads! That's Bex—*"

"*And that's Aya—*"

"*And this—*"

"*—is* Murderers at Work!"

"*Where we pretend to find lessons about society in grisly
true crime stories!*"

"*Um, where we pretend to be appalled and not morbidly
fascinated—*"

"*How's this:* Murderers at Work, *the barometer of an in-
different society's decay.*"

"*Can I get that on a mug?*"

"*Maybe on a Christmas mug with little snowmen and shit,
because this episode of* Murderers *is guaranteed to put the
festive spirit in the cold, empty void where your heart used to
be. But first . . . Bex?*"

"*Tickets to our live event in Las Vegas are selling out! So
get your shit together and buy some!*"

"*Do it! It's Las Vegas, guys!*"

"*Aaaaand on with the show. Today we're going to talk
about . . .*"

"*Arguably my favorite serial killer—*"

"*. . . SECRET SANTA! If you've been with us for any
amount of time, you know that approximately fifty percent of
our inside jokes revolve around killer mall Santas. Today we
discuss the original killer mall Santa—*"

"*The* original *one, guys—not the copycat acts from the
nineties—*"

"*Ugh, no. The nineties were not good for killer mall
Santas—*"

"The one who would hack up his victims and wrap them in Christmas paper, then leave the packages around town. And that's totally not a spoiler. The story gets so much better."

"I told you before we started recording, but I'm going to repeat it now—"

"Absolutely. Do it."

"I looked up the photos in evidence—"

"You always do this—"

"And the wrapping paper this guy used for his victims . . . is the SAME green wrapping paper my grandma used for, like, three Christmases in a row!"

I sit with my chin in my hand as I run my script, once again completing this week's work in a matter of minutes, and I watch Dolores through her window, wondering who she spends Christmas with, who she buys presents for, who will buy *her* a present.

That evening after work, I don't board the SkyTrain. I wander the bustling downtown sidewalks, peering in shop windows, not sure where to find what I'm looking for. Clothing stores. Shoe stores. Stores that identify as "lifestyle stores." I'm swept into a downtown mall on a current of shoppers, and *there*—

I walk into the toy store. I'm used to feeling out of place, but now I feel more out of place than I've ever felt in my entire life. The proprietor smiles at me, and I grimace back, and in the back, on a shelf laden with pink Mattel boxes, I find Dolores's gift.

I WATCH HER OUT OF THE CORNER OF MY EYE WHEN SHE WALKS IN THE NEXT morning. She deposits her purse, hangs her coat, swivels to face her desk, and it's not until she reaches to tap her keyboard that she notices it: my gift.

It's a small package, about the length of her pinkie, wrapped up in shiny green wrapping paper with a tiny filament of gold ribbon. It was too small to tie into a bow, so I dragged the blade of a sharp knife across the ends to make them curl.

She would never lower herself by raising her head to look at me right now. I sit there, watching her out of the corner of my eye, and I know she watches me out of the corner of her eye, too. Two mirrors reflecting each other into infinity.

She slides the loop of ribbon off the package, plucks carefully at the tape, then parts the freed edges of the paper to reveal the thing lying in her palm: a smooth, beige plastic leg, severed neatly at the knee. She touches the toes with one finger and rotates it in her palm.

She's silent and still for a long moment, but then she raises her head and looks right at me—and she doesn't smile, but I *know* from her face that this is the best Christmas gift she's ever been given. A doll for Dolly. And an invitation to play.

I STAGE THE TWELVE DAYS OF CHRISTMAS FOR HER IN NOVEMBER. EVERY DAY, a new gift awaits in a new spot: A severed hand in her coffee mug. A dismembered foot in her paper clip tray. An upper and lower torso, sawed neatly in half, in the print tray and the filing cabinet, respectively. All with the same shiny green paper and gold ribbon.

All except the head. The original killer mall Santa did something fun with the head.

6

Not Like Other Girls

DOLORES

MY LIFE IS LIKE THIS:

Being a card-carrying adult, I wake at an hour that leaves me with such a number of minutes to be at work that every single one is accounted for and there is no room for error. Morning is a blur of ablutions and makeup and hair and dressing and packing and a last-minute search for shoes. If I could mainline caffeine into my veins, I would. If I could get my hands on something stronger, I would.

Some people live to work; others work to live. I don't do either. I exist. I keep my lower lip just above the water as I tread, a slave-driving sense of duty keeping me going. I'm spurred forward by mundane procedures that would not be completed if I didn't take care of them: Car maintenance. Home maintenance. Cat maintenance—just the bare minimum is what it feels like. I'll get no awards there. She'd been a selfish impulse in a difficult moment of my life, a drastic decision to stave off loneliness. A warm, breathing thing to love and cuddle and play with—something to bring purpose into my life. But instead, she makes me feel like a stranger in my own home. I walk in the door, and she watches me with skeptical eyes and scampers off to be by herself.

Every day there must be a breakfast, lunch, and dinner— three problems I get to solve all over again every single day, my personal Groundhog Day, my private ring of hell. Every day I must scrape messes off surfaces anew—or not. If I don't, they sprout and grow legs and become their own ecosystem. Every day, there is a pile of laundry, self-generating, bottomless, gradually gaining sentience, studying me, plotting to destroy me. And the bills. Oh, the bills.

There's no satisfaction in any of it. No sense of a job well done. Only the persistent feeling that I'm doing it wrong, doing not enough, that I'm bailing out a sinking ship.

Late at night, when it's dark out, and the rush has abruptly ended, and my bones sag like a Halloween skeleton that's been taken down and tossed back into its box, I crane my ears and reach past the silence of my apartment for the healthy, normal humming of the families above and below and on either side. They exist in a false sense of permanence and stability, and it agitates me. They have no idea how quickly life can change. I pace my apartment. I pluck at my clutter, picking up a book and setting it down, moving an envelope from here to there, wiping down a counter and then giving up on the others. A baby cries next door, and a woman soothes him, and a man laughs, and I throw my rag into the sink and pour myself another glass of wine and turn on the TV to drown it all out. The sounds, the humming, the silence in my own apartment. I watch an episode of something funny and I don't laugh. I found this shit funny once—I'm sure I did. But laughter is a social behavior, and it's not something you do on your own. Even though I do everything else on my own.

That's what I like about true crime—it doesn't ask me to laugh. That, and the victim blaming. The victim blaming is so . . . *reassuring.* So long as I carry pepper spray in my bra and don't talk to men with their arm in a sling, I'll be fine. Not like those other, *stupider* girls. Ho, no. How different from lung cancer or brain tumors. Can't do a fucking thing about oncogenes.

I find a rerun on the Bottle Factory Killer. Six women over three years. Idiots. When you're a single woman, you have to be smarter than that. *I'm* smarter than that. A serial killer would never get the chance to hunt me because I'd be hunting *him.* I have room for hobbies now, after all. So much room.

The thing about my existence is there's a man-shaped chalk outline sketched all over it, marking out where a body used to be. I roll over it when I get out of bed in the morning. I step over it when I walk out the front door. When I'm walking to my car in a basement parking lot by myself and I notice the sound of a stranger's footsteps behind me—a single woman on her own—the outline is there, the man inside conspicuously absent.

I'm not special. I think we all have hearts like a baby's shape-sorting cube, holes left behind by the people who passed through. If we're lucky, another one that's just the right shape comes along, and we're whole again for a moment. But triangles and squares and circles are common and easy to come by. This very distinct, four-limbed, man-shaped gap is difficult to fill. I'd resigned myself to that.

But when I sit at my desk and hold that unwrapped doll leg in my hand, I reflexively think of that chalk outline, of the unique shape left open in my heart, and although it's a terrible idea—although there is so much more to lose than to gain—I can't help the guiltiest, most shameful fantasy of filling it up again.

THE DAYS PASS AND I COLLECT MY DOLL PIECE BY PIECE. A LEG, A HAND, A foot, a chest . . . I lay the pieces out in my drawer. I carry them in my purse. I rub my thumb over the nubby little toes of a foot in my pocket as I take the elevator down at the end of the day. No one's ever given me a gift like this, and I puzzle over what it means. I want to pry apart the sutures of Jake's skull and trawl my fingers through his brains for answers, but a man like Jake has his guard up. There's no waiting till it comes down. The trick is to make him think his defenses are working and to pick away at the cracks where he's not looking.

It takes two seconds to fish the flash drive out of his messenger bag when he's gone to brownnose Doug. He was so careless about letting me see where he keeps it after I wiped his computer. Some of the files are password protected and some aren't. There's a spreadsheet that is a list of names, with mine at the top. I won't deny the thrill I feel at that. The columns to the right are filled with values that don't make sense to me. I copy it to my desktop, remove the flash drive, and stalk back to his desk. He's nowhere in sight. I return the drive to his bag.

When I straighten, I bump his desk and his computer wakes. The golden retriever has been replaced with a new photo. My heart stumbles, cartwheels, and falls on its face.

There's a beautiful nighttime view of the river behind them. In the foreground, Jake's face is right next to hers, cheek to cheek, and he grins like a fool while she gazes distantly at the camera. She's stunning, in a highlighted, lacquered, lip-filled, paralyzed sort of way that speaks of careless wealth.

It's the Botox. Or maybe the horse tranquilizers kicking in, before he takes her back to his place and decapitates her. I look closely. Dolce & Gabbana sunglasses perched on her head. A Tiffany pendant. I'm a materialistic brand-name hound.

I return to my desk. I feel old and dowdy and cheap. I have heartburn and a headache coming on. I delete my Jake the Ripper notes from my phone. That's that.

He comes back from lunch, and I watch him tinker away at his computer in the reflective surface of the black stone vase on my desk. I watch him push his glasses back up his straight nose and accidentally muss up his neat hair when he scratches his head. He glances over at me, laconic, bored, and I wonder if she's his girlfriend. He's clever and good-looking—even if he is just a temp and his freezer's full of severed heads. I wonder if they have frequent, vigorous sex. I bet she lets him keep his glasses on.

I hate him so much.

At the end of the day, I go home and line up bits of beige plastic on my coffee table. Arms here, legs there. In my head, I line up bits and pieces of Jake.

He placed that flash drive in his messenger bag pocket in front of me while I watched. He wanted me to find that list for some reason.

The golden retriever photo—he was checking to see what I noticed.

And that selfie he replaced it with . . .

He's teasing me. He's still checking to see what I notice. He's . . . bored.

Are you as bored of real life as I am?

A man with a wealthy, beautiful girlfriend doesn't get bored.

She could be anyone. She could be no one. I'm the one he's playing serial killer games with.

Tinkle, tinkle, tinkle.

I consider my deconstructed doll laid out before me, and I realize there's a message here—an offering, if I'm interested in accepting. I'm missing a head, and I need to know: Will this Ken doll have dark hair and glasses?

7

The Ghost on the Roof

JAKE

DOLORES DOESN'T FIND THE HEAD. DEB-FROM-IT DOES, LETTING OUT A SHRIEK when she wanders in to pilfer coffee creamer from the under-utilized fridge in the annex break room. Dolores bolts from her desk, shoves Deb-from-IT out of the way, and stands there basking in the sickly refrigerator light while the head stares out glassy-eyed from one fridge shelf, surrounded by a pool of scarlet blood spilled from some split red ink refills I took from the supply cabinet. Secret Santa had a charming MO.

"What is *wrong* with you two?" Deb-from-IT cries.

I know that something shifts between Dolores and me after that, because that evening her heels clatter up behind me as I wait at the elevator. When the doors open, she steps in with me, but I don't look at her. I stare straight up at the number above the door as it changes. I feel her eyes on me.

"Jake," she says after a few floors.

"Dolores."

"Thank you for the doll."

"I was raised to share my toys."

"Your upbringing is between you and Norma Bates. Plans tonight, Jake?"

"No, but I know what you're doing."

"What?"

"Stropping your straight razor and combing the dating apps for your next husband."

"Close. I'm watching that indie crime documentary on the Paper Pusher tonight."

I was vaguely aware there was a documentary now.

"Do you think he's single?" she drawls.

"Let me know if it's any good," I say as I step out into the main floor foyer. "Hasta banana," I say, and I walk away without turning back.

FROM THE COFFEE CREAMER INCIDENT RADIATES A LITTLE RIPPLE TO DISTURB our peace in the annex. The next day Cynthia-from-HR appears, cat earrings and pathological humorlessness and all. As she stalks toward me I smoothly press three keys to hide my open windows: my list, of course, but also payroll, the email server, and everything else I'm not supposed to look at.

She peers at me over her cherry red reading glasses. "That's Dolores dela Cruz in there?"

I nod helpfully, and she frowns at the sheaf of papers in her hand.

Cynthia is in her fifties, tall and hale, with short gray hair and sensible footwear, and a way of speaking with emotionless precision at all times. I'm certain the inside of Cynthia's house is filled with stacks of cozy murder mysteries and framed puzzles she's glued together. A litter of kittens in a wheelbarrow. A duckling poking its head out of a watering can. She collects her cat's fur in a bag to eventually knit into a sweater.

"And you're Jake Ripper?"

I dust off smile number three for her: cheerful and charmingly rueful—*Yes, I'm afraid that's me.*

"Jacob *Ripper*," she repeats, staring at me with pale, ice-cube eyes. Something toggles in my brain. She's . . . familiar. And I'm familiar to her, too.

She peers at me like I'm a disgusting little boy with dirt under my fingernails. Before I can place her, she tucks the papers under one arm concealed in a frumpy cardigan and opens Dolores's door without knocking. "Dolores?"

On the other side of the office window, Dolores snaps her laptop shut with one hand and cranks down the volume on the desktop computer speaker with the other. I've never seen her flustered before.

"I'm Cynthia Cutts. HR has brought me in as a consultant. I wanted to meet with you in person."

Dolores stares, unblinking, and slowly clasps her hands over her closed laptop in a protective gesture. I've listened to too many of her podcasts, because right now she looks to me like a murderess with blood spattered on her clothes, casually adjusting her long skirt to conceal the murder weapon at her feet.

"What about?"

"I'm just checking in."

It's one of those harmless-sounding phrases that is utterly ominous in an office setting. Cynthia glances dourly in my direction, then shuts the door. I, however, have the hearing of a nocturnal predator, and I move to stand directly outside to eavesdrop. Cynthia can't see me, but Dolores looks up and shoots me a peeved expression through her window.

"I'm getting ahead of a potential harassment situation. I heard there was an incident here with a doll."

Cynthia is a corporate veteran. As usual, I've had my ear to the ground. She's rattled around between companies, a hospital or two, even the Catholic school board—going where she's needed like a frumpy, pickle-faced Mary Poppins sniffing out workplace harassment, and right now the east wind is blowing her into our annex.

I've probably seen her at one of my past temp jobs. That must be it.

Dolores is silent for a split second. "Yes?"

"A *dismembered* doll?"

"Yes."

"It's a hostile gesture. Your colleague left a dismembered Barbie doll in your office."

"It was a Ken doll."

"Are you interested in putting anything on record?"

A longer pause.

"No, thank you."

"I've already made some notes in your file."

Dolores's voice changes subtly. "That wasn't necessary."

"Which caused me to notice, it's been well over a year since you've had a performance review."

"It's all right."

"It isn't. I'm not familiar with your department. What is your chain of command?"

"I really am busy right now," Dolores says, walking the fine line between pleasant and crisp. "Perhaps we can schedule something—"

It's exactly as I suspected. Dolores has reasons to be terrified of drawing the attention of HR.

"I apologize," Cynthia says, not sounding apologetic, "but I will be leaving for a conference soon, and it will take as long to arrange a meeting as it will to sort this out now. I've taken a special interest in you, Dolores."

And for some inscrutable reason, the apex predator's dark eyes dart toward me, the little rodent, for help. Before I know it, my arm is raised and I'm knocking two sharp raps on Dolores's door. I open the door without waiting.

Smile number five: roguishly apologetic and definitely not lying.

"I'm afraid Dolores is needed upstairs for a top-floor meeting," I say. "Now."

Dolores stares at me for a beat, then locks her laptop in a drawer and pushes past me without a backward glance.

"They can't tie their shoelaces on their own," she huffs as she passes.

"They really can't. Sorry, Cynthia," I say.

She narrows her eyes at me. I wonder what she caught me doing at that previous temp job.

In the elevator Dolores swivels to face me.

"Why did you do that?" she asks.

"Because I was bored."

She nods knowingly. "Boredom's a chronic problem for sociopaths. Where are we going?"

I hadn't thought that far.

Dolores cocks her head and prowls, catlike, to the buttons. She runs her fingertips deliberately from top to bottom, circles the B, then looks over her shoulder at me. She presses 50, the top floor.

"I have a top-floor meeting," she explains.

That fairground feeling, except we're moving upward. "Me too. On the roof."

When the doors heave open onto the top floor, she trails after me to the stairwell that takes us the rest of the way.

It's chilly when we step out. The skyscrapers press close all around, and to our left is the dull, metallic glint of the harbor.

I've been wanting to bring her here, wondering how to lure her up, and here we are. She deposits her phone on a rickety outdoor table that the janitorial staff keep up here for their smoke breaks.

It's such a part of my routine, I light a cigarette without even thinking.

"You *smoke?*"

Fuck no, but a lit cigarette is an essential prop if I want to spend time up here.

"Aren't you worried about dying from cancer?" she prods.

"I'm not going to die of cancer."

I hold out the pack, and she hesitates for only a second. I light her cigarette, and she puffs prettily at it, but she doesn't really draw. She holds it like a fifties movie star, hand cocked carelessly, her sharp fingernails scraping the air, the blue veins in her wrist a surprising glimpse of vulnerability.

"Dying of something else, then? I don't think you worry much about your future."

My heart beats a little faster. She *thinks* about me. "What do you mean?"

"Apart from the fact that you're working a go-nowhere temp job? That you didn't finish your degree?"

She's put at least a few minutes of effort into rifling through my LinkedIn profile. I haven't searched her online. It's the main rule of my list that I have to harvest my data at the office, to prevent the muddling of the personal and the professional. I do have standards. But here she is, admitting she's googled me.

I'm not enough to hold her interest, because she changes the subject.

"Look at this insect colony," she sighs, panning the city view. She leans up against the concrete wall just a foot in front of me, hips pressing flat against it, and tilts her head to one side in her vampire lover pose. I watch her like that. She's dressed as she's always dressed—covered from neck to wrist to knee in black, her outfit today a stretchy black pencil skirt and a soft black sweater that blots up the sunlight. The wind tugs at a few fine strands of hair escaped from the glossy knot on her nape. I could reach out and twirl my finger in those strands. She leans over the wall and looks down, down.

A cold current kicks up, and I stub out my cigarette and tug the black leather gloves from my pocket. I always have them on hand so I'm never caught short in moments like these. She turns just in time to see me pull them on.

"Oh, goody," she says, looking up at me with watchful eyes. "You going to strangle me now?"

And there's something about her voice as she says this, and the poison-apple redness of her lips, and the way she looked at *me* for help just a few minutes ago. My body feels like a guitar string that was strummed. I vibrate. I resonate with whatever energy she puts out.

There's a feeling she's been stirring up in me these past weeks that I haven't felt in a long time. It's the desire to be in another person's company. A desire to hold eye contact with another human being, a desire to *touch* another human being—

She holds my eyes and leans sinuously against the wall, her arms folded across her chest, and then she *shivers* from the November cold—and without really understanding how it happens, I'm suddenly standing just inches away from her. She smells like coffee and cigarettes and herself.

"What the fuck do you think you're doing?" she whispers, her breath steaming in the cold air between us.

I drift a little closer. "The gloves aren't for strangling," I say.

Her lips quirk in a sharp little smile, like she knew this all along. "They're for pushing."

She wraps her hand once, then twice in my tie, and pulls me in. I grip her by her waist and pick her up—I've never done anything like this before, so I'm almost surprised when it works—and I place her on top of the wall, the only thing keeping hapless humans from wandering off the edge of this building. Her bare knees press against me, and I wrap my hand behind one calf and hold her like that. Her face is now above mine, and she stares down at me breathlessly, lips parted, close enough to bite. I can see fine lines around the corners of her lips and the edges of her eyes—smile lines, though I never see her truly, properly smile. She turns and drops her cigarette over the edge, and we watch it fall toward the street below until it vanishes from sight, a little white pixel blinking out.

She turns back to me, eyes dark and fearless, and she wraps her little hands around my neck to hold on for dear life—or to choke me.

"Are you going to push me off now?" Her voice is a whisper, a little puff of air against my lips.

"Not today." I slide my hands around to her back to demonstrate.

Her breath is warm when she pulls me in by my neck, and our lips brush. Her lips are warm, too—all of her is *warm*, and it's something I think I forgot about other human beings. They're warm to the touch. I lean into her. A wet slide, and the tickle of her breath, and the softness of her skin. The kiss is like slipping into a steaming bath, and I'm thawing. My body flares to life at her touch.

I step closer still, until we're as close as two people can get without breaking any public indecency laws. There's a certain logic to the way we fit together that makes me wonder why I never imagined doing this before. Her leg shifts against my hip, and my hand finds the smooth skin there. I wish I wasn't wearing gloves. She doesn't protest when my fingertips touch the hem of her skirt—

And then she bites my lip—gentle at first, and then slowly increasing the pressure until it stings, until I can feel my pulse in every part of my body—

"What the hell are you doing?" a voice bellows. "We're in the Cascadia Subduction Zone! What if there's an earthquake?"

It's the elderly caretaker whose smoke breaks sometimes overlap mine. Dolores slips to the ground and tugs her skirt down, swearing under her breath. Her lipstick has left a pink smudge on her lips, and I wipe my own mouth with my gloved hand.

"Idiots!" he hollers at us. He lights a cigarette and stomps to the far side of the roof, where he glares at us from under bushy eyebrows.

I cough, and Dolores coughs, and she can't seem to look at my face. She stares at the city view instead, and I stare at her profile, wondering if that kiss was as surprising to her as it was to me.

And then another feeling creeps in after the surprise: apprehension. It's a terrible risk to let anyone in.

She clears her throat one more time.

"You're not as bad at that as I thought you'd be," she says, casually shanking me with her words, her voice back to normal—bored. "But you should quit smoking. If you want to kill yourself, I can help you think of some more creative ways to do it. In fact, I'll do it for you."

And to her it's just a little insult, but it's something com-plenty different to me. She turns to walk past me, but I side-step in front of her.

"Would you?"

Surprise, for a split second, before her habitual sarcasm rallies. "What sort of loose floozy do you take me for? If you want to see my straight razor, you're going to have to put a ring on it first."

She's already turning away, back toward the rickety table with her phone. I'm desperate to stop her. All I want is for her to keep looking at me like she actually sees me.

I blurt out the first thing I can think of. "How was the Paper Pusher documentary last night?"

She stops in her tracks at the abrupt subject change. "It was delightful," she says over her shoulder. "An ethical serial killer who goes after corporate perverts with a long HR trail. Doing God's work. And *local*, too. So important to appreciate home-grown talent."

"I ended up watching *Ghost Hunters*," I tell her. I did no such thing.

She turns and narrows her eyes at me. She can't make me out. "So you're into that paranormal shit."

"Well, I wasn't. Until I started seeing a ghost."

She snorts contemptuously. She turns away from me again, and I add, "Here. At work."

Dolores stops and slowly revolves on the spot to face me once more. "Really."

Her voice is bored again, but I know she's not bored. If she were bored, she'd leave.

"At first I didn't understand what I was seeing. I thought she was just like everyone else. But after a while, I noticed it's almost like no one else sees her. Just me."

She peers at me.

"She shows up at work every day like a normal, living, breathing worker bee. She sticks to the annex, which is perfect because it's been a ghost town since the layoffs."

Her expression has changed.

"She goes through the motions of a normal workday. Ghosts are like that—they'll carry on with whatever routines they had before."

"Is this a story about a ghost, or her stalker?"

"Just a ghost."

Dolores flinches against a gust of wind whipping across the rooftop. She glances at the caretaker across the way.

"This is a very boring story," she says, and I know she's hooked.

"Well, I think there's a clever twist."

"And what would that be?"

"The twist is, ghosts don't know they're ghosts. But she knows *exactly* what she's doing."

Dolores's eyes are fixed on me, unblinking. She actually sees me, the dull temp who vanishes into his surroundings. I want her to know I see her, too. Both of us in stark relief on the top of this skyscraper, the city at our feet.

"And what is she doing?"

What is she doing, she asks.

This company is like a great, purring, half-slumbering creature. Unseeing, unfeeling, intent on one thing only: feeding itself, expanding, growing. Increasing profits every year. More. *More.* Chomping down on its employees, sucking the juices out of them, chewing them to a pulp and spitting them out.

I applaud anyone who gets the better of it, and what Dolores is doing is getting the better of it. Every day she strolls into work, stands in an elevator full of Spencer & Sterns minions, glides past supervisors and HR henchmen, and locks herself in a cushy stolen corner office to dick around all day in peace. All so that every two weeks she can collect her paycheck without having done a lick of work, courtesy of the disastrous, chaotic layoffs, like a cool, collected sociopath. She knows I know. I can see it. And she's not the least bit concerned. She stares me down.

She's clever. She's fearless. She's irresistible.

But in answer to her question, I say, "She's haunting the living. Lingering over unfinished business." I think of the laptop she was so careful to conceal from Cynthia. "Keeping her secrets in plain sight on her desk."

Dolores's eyes are strangely glassy. "I'm not so great at elaborate metaphors. You're a creep."

"*You're* the creep." *She's* the one who made a sexual innuendo about strangling when we first met. She's the one who threw my peace offering in the trash and snooped through my things and fucked with my computer.

She cuts across me. "I found your list, you know."

This is interesting. She's most certainly seen the desktop image by now. I changed it after her idle question about the Paper Pusher's dating status.

"Maybe Cynthia will want to know you spend your days adding your coworkers' names to a spreadsheet labeled 'Terminate.'"

"Maybe she'll want to know you're gray-rocking from paycheck to paycheck hoping nobody notices you weren't reassigned to a new supervisor after your entire department was laid off."

Whiplash. Dolores stiffens, and I have to wonder what our conversation about ghosts meant to her if my words surprised her.

"Or maybe we call a truce," I say.

She watches me with suspicion. We're a pair of poker players holding our cards tight to our chests. I toss mine down first.

"Because I like you a lot more than I like Cynthia," I add, "even if you are a creep."

She holds out for two seconds, and then her sharp edges soften. The quills go down. She takes one half step toward me, and my phone buzzes.

"You going to get that?" she says impatiently on the second buzz.

I fish it out of my pocket and pick up.

"Jacob?" a familiar voice says on the other end of the line. Normally I wouldn't have answered. Normally, I would have glanced at the screen properly first instead of trying to hold Dolores's eyes.

I pinch the bridge of my nose. "Yes?"

Dolores turns on her heel and is gone in a flash. It's just me, the amateur geologist caretaker, and my uncle.

It's the usual. The birthday dinner tonight. He guilt-trips me by invoking my aunt, and I agree, and we both hang up, and that's that.

I look out at the harbor one last time and debate tossing myself over the edge.

8

Death by Family Dinner

JAKE

"YOUR PARENTS ARE ALREADY HERE," THE HOSTESS SAYS, GESTURING ACROSS the trendy restaurant with its uncomfortable chairs and narrow tables.

I spot them: two graying heads stooped over their menus, practically off-gassing straitlaced, affluent suburbia. They're not my parents, but the family resemblance is there.

"Jake," Aunt Laura says with her sunshine smile when I approach. My only living blood relative—at least, the only one who knows about me. She has the same dark hair as mine, but with white streaks at the temples, and large, dark eyes, like a gentle fawn. Pearl ear studs and a shell-pink cardigan complete the look. Laura is warm and sweet, at first impression the sort of person a child would want to bury their face in so they can huff the smell of home-baked cookies. Well, not a child like me. Not after what I'd been through by the time they took me in.

Next to her sits Uncle Andrew, judgmental as God, in a midrange suit, his shirt as crisply starched as his soul. He simply grunts when he notices me. Andrew has always made me think of some great, scaly, leathery dragon, spiteful and quick to anger, lolling on a great hoard of every single thing I've ever done to earn his disapproval. He sifts bullion and jewels through his fingers as he asks about my life.

I wonder why they still bother with me, what sort of obligation to my mother compels them to meet with me like this, every year. Do they feel good about themselves after? Relieved that it will be another year before they have to do it again? Is it a seasonal routine that anchors them to the passage of time? Do they go home and change the batteries in their smoke detectors after?

I avoid Laura's gaze as I take my seat. How long has it been since we talked? A month? Two? Some aunts would make sure I was aware of it, but Laura's not like that. And for some reason my brain slithers to thoughts of Dolores. Does she have deeply unsatisfying family relationships? What hilarious, insulting little comment will she prick me with tomorrow when I mention this dinner? I'm lowering myself into my chair with the enthusiasm of a convict walking to the gallows when a flash of bright, arterial red out of the corner of my eye catches my attention—

Dolores sits at a table for two not twenty feet from us.

But it's Dolores as I've never seen her before. Instead of black, she's wearing scarlet. Instead of a smooth knot, her hair tumbles down past her shoulders in careless waves. Instead of covering up from chin to kneecap to wrist, her arms and collarbones are bare, and it's obvious now why she dresses like a corporate sister wife from nine to five.

"She must have spent a fortune to ruin her looks," my uncle says, following my gaze. "What is that on her chest? A pair of skulls? It looks Satanic."

"I think the roses look lovely," my aunt says sweetly.

Bright, bold American traditional tattoos cover her arms and chest. Roses, spiderwebs, a skeleton, a dagger. Below her collarbones are two skulls, facing each other, one dressed as a bride with a veil, the other a groom. Her face is different, too. Her lipstick has smudged off, and I realize I've never seen her without her office war paint on—always some shade of vivid pink, screaming crimson, or a deep blood red. Her bare lips are almost indecent.

She must feel my gaze on her, because she lowers the menu and her eyes skim up the length of my body, from my shoes to my face. She doesn't smile, but one eyebrow slides up at the sight of me. Coming from Dolores, it's an enthusiastic invitation. I stand without giving an explanation to my aunt and uncle and go to her.

"Dolores."

Dolores is silent for a long moment. She's been silent with me ever since the rooftop this morning.

At last, she says in a bored voice, "Jacob."

I put my robust sleuthing skills on demo. "You're on a date," I say.

"Yes."

Yet there's no coat draped over the back of the chair opposite her. Her decanter of wine is empty, her appetizer plate wiped clean.

"Where is he?"

She stares me down with the withering gaze of a woman scorned. She was stood up, and to make a shitty evening even shittier, I'm here to witness it.

"He's dead to me."

I direct away from the missing date. "Cat's home alone tonight with a tin of Fancy Feast and the TV on to keep her company?"

"Had your face pressed against my living room window, I see. Are those your boomers?" she asks with a chin jerk toward my aunt and uncle.

"They seem to think so."

"They've been staring at me like I'm a zoo creature."

"I'll discipline them later. No Facebook or Olive Garden for a week."

"They seem so normal. The apple fell far. Unless . . . the real Jacob Ripper is buried in a shallow grave somewhere, and you have assumed his identity and are holding his family hostage to perpetuate the charade?"

"You know me better than anyone."

Her eyes slide from my aunt and uncle to my face when I say that. "I don't know you. I don't know anything about you, Jake."

I wonder if I sound aloof and mysterious or just plain idiotic when I say, "Do you want to?" And then it occurs to me that I haven't cared in a long time if anyone thinks I sound like an idiot. Office Idiot is a useful disguise.

She tips her head to one side. "Maybe, for the sake of adding to your case file." She slings back the dregs in her wineglass and rises, ungracefully. She's *tipsy*.

"What are you doing?" I ask.

"I'm bored. It's a common problem for sociopaths."

And then, as she passes me, she hooks one finger into my belt loop and gives me a little tug. A shiver ripples down my spine. It's a performative gesture, one I feel like everyone in the room must have seen. When I glance at my aunt and uncle, I can see that *they've* seen it. And then, when she saunters over to their table, I realize she meant for them to see it.

"I was early, and I didn't know what name the reservation was under," Dolores tells my aunt and uncle in the breezy tone of a compulsive liar cutting the first silk thread of her web of lies. "So I just got a table for myself and got started. But it's so nice to finally meet you."

My uncle's mouth falls open, and my aunt's face blossoms into another sunny smile.

"How wonderful, Jake," she says sincerely. Her eyes dart to my uncle, cautiously. He stares as Dolores sits down across from my aunt and hooks her purse on the back of the chair. In her red dress she looks like a little bomb about to detonate in the midst of my family dinner. A scarlet stick of ACME TNT.

"So you were the host body," she says conversationally to Aunt Laura, helping herself to a pour of wine from the bottle sitting on the table. "I know Morse code. You can blink a help signal to me."

She's funny, but I don't laugh. I don't ever laugh in front of Andrew.

"I don't know Morse code," Laura says, shooting me a confused look, but then the waiter arrives to take our order.

"Medium rare," Dolores requests of her steak dinner.

"Rare," I say for mine.

"Actually, I'd like the steak tartare," she says, holding my gaze. She wins. When I look back at Laura, there's a strange crinkle around her eyes.

"You have a girlfriend?" my uncle asks stupidly when the server leaves.

There's a fleeting pause while Dolores levels her X-ray vision at him to read the whorls in his brain and determine exactly what to say to annoy him the most. "We don't like *labels*."

To be fair, there's no label for two people who antagonize the shit out of each other and make out on the roof, anyway. And that's when I realize the nature of Dolores's drunk. She's not a slurring, giggly drunk. She's a waspish, clever drunk. A filters-off drunk. A power-crazed drunk. And as a mark of how drunk she is, her lips curl in a smile at me over the rim of her wineglass. An actual smile. Evil, and enjoying my discomfort, but a smile.

There's that strange twist in my chest, as usual when I'm around her. The motor clunking over from idle, the default setting to get me through the day, into gear.

Andrew frowns at me. "What's that supposed to mean? This isn't serious?"

It's my turn to fuck with Dolores. "It's very serious. We're getting married."

Andrew's eyebrows vanish into his hairline. Laura lets out a gasp, and for a brief second, I feel bad. Next to me, Dolores doesn't even flinch.

"Which church?" Andrew asks with a stern look. I haven't been to any sort of church since I lived with them.

"We're still looking at venues," Dolores says smoothly. "He wants his golden retriever to be the ring bearer, but I want to be married by Elvis in Las Vegas, and I can't picture getting him on a plane. The golden retriever, that is."

By now Andrew has realized there's a joke somewhere here, and if he's not in on it, he must be the butt of it. He has no problem flipping it back onto me. He makes bored, lazy eye contact with Dolores and says, "When did you and that man end things, Jake?"

Dolores cocks one eyebrow at me prettily, unfazed.

"Who?" I ask blandly.

"That man you lived with—"

"My *roommate*." It's a conversation we've had a dozen times. He always says *that man*. My uncle thinks I get up to all sorts of sordid, ungodly things with Grant.

Well. I *do*. But it's different from what he thinks.

"*Roommate*," my uncle echoes.

Laura interrupts. "Girlfriend, or fiancée, or neither, we're both so happy to meet someone special to you, Jake." She hadn't believed Grant was just a roommate, either, in the beginning, and she'd sported a jaunty rainbow sticker on her bumper for a whole week before Andrew ripped it off. Now she's pivoted quickly to latch onto this good news of a real, live *someone special*. She glows, and I feel another twinge of guilt in the pit of my stomach. Laura deserves better than the version of me that comes out when Andrew's around. But he's always around when I see her. Bossy and possessive, a fiercely jealous third wheel.

"Hopefully this one sticks," my uncle replies, resurrecting another one of his favorite subjects: my charming, beautiful university girlfriend, the one who got away. Well, the one I broke up with when I decided someone like me shouldn't be in a relationship. I would give my left nut not to have this conversation again in front of Dolores—I consider hoisting her over my shoulder and physically removing her—but then I see her expression. She's fascinated by all of this. And that's the only leverage I've ever had with her—her curiosity.

She's getting to know me, all right.

"*She* moved on quickly enough, after. And we just got a Christmas card from them. Did you get one?"

Dolores's eyes flash back and forth amongst us all, like she's hanging on every word.

"No," I say, nettled. No one knows my address. I never shared it after I moved in with Grant.

"Engaged," my uncle says, like he's been sharpening that word to a keen point and was looking forward to stabbing me with it.

My aunt purses her lips and glances at me, concern creasing her forehead. "Lovely girl! It's nice to know she's happy! And you're happy, too!" Her voice is brittle, like a cracked windshield about to give way. "All ancient history," she says to Dolores in a loud whisper. "It's *so* good to meet you."

There's an awkward pause at the table, punctuated by Dolores slinging back the rest of her glass of wine. She smiles sweetly at my aunt. "Likewise. Now tell me, did Jacob torture animals as a small child?"

My aunt stares at her with an expression of alarm. "He was good with animals. He wanted to be a vet."

My uncle snorts at this. "He had more drive as a child than he does now."

"Andrew," my aunt says, but my uncle carries on.

"A veterinarian would be a step up from a 'temp.'" He says it like it's an experimental word that hasn't been accepted into common usage. He uses the same invisible bunny ears he puts on words and phrases like "mental health" and "feelings."

Dolores eyes me.

Laura ignores him. "How did the two of you meet?"

Dolores shoots me a dreamy, sickly smile and takes my hand in hers. My fingers start to tingle, but I notice Laura twinkles at our grasped hands. She's *so* happy. She's a reflective substance, requiring that I be happy in order for her to be happy. No pressure at all. I leave my hand where it is.

"It was a chance meeting. I'd stopped looking, to be honest. Do you know how hard it is to find a man who gets what a modern, equitable relationship is supposed to look like? I'm talking splitting the load. I bumped into him at a hardware store—Jake was in front of me buying rope and a hunting knife, but he was *also* buying bleach and a tarpaulin. I thought, here's a guy who cleans up his own messes. No weaponized male incompetence here. We got to talking, and what do you know? He knows his way around a kitchen knife, how to clean fingerprints off walls, get bloodstains out of his own laundry. If he fills the bathtub full of lye, he'll drain the sludge out himself when he's finished."

My aunt laughs and says, "Oh, you like that stuff, too. Jake was always so interested in it. He used to spin theories with me about the best way to off someone." She smiles fondly at me, like plotting murder was our alternative to I Spy for long car rides. Because it was.

Dolores stares between the two of us.

"For a while I thought he'd follow in my footsteps," my aunt continues. "It takes a strong stomach, I suppose, being that close to death every day. At any rate, you figure out the best laundry stain removers on the market pretty quick. But it's an *interesting* career. Every day is different. The *variety*! The number of ways a person can be killed! It's fascinating." My aunt prattles on pleasantly like that, like she's participating in book club conversation. "My favorite murder weapon so far has to be the fake leg—"

"Laura!" my uncle hisses. "We're in a restaurant. There are people around."

Laura turtles in on herself and glances around nervously.

For the first time, Dolores looks like she's at a complete loss. I allow her to feel uncomfortable for ten seconds while I slowly sip my wine.

"She's a mortician," I explain. "An excellent one, so she winds up with the most grisly cases. Accidents. Murders. She makes them . . . presentable."

Laura beams at my praise.

Dolores is fascinated. "And him?" she asks, gesturing to Andrew.

"Catholic school superintendent."

There's a certain logic to it if you know how to look for it. Catholics display their dead. I've imagined their meeting: Laura lurking behind a floral wreath with a paint palette in her purse for last-minute touch-ups on a cadaver she really got invested in; across the room, Andrew, only tangentially related to the stiff in the casket but present nevertheless for the recreational experience of pouncing on the grieving and helpfully rationalizing their loss as God's plan. Andrew and Laura raise their eyes, connect gazes over the top of the casket, and nothing is ever the same. Laura has a romantic streak. All the white flowers, the sunlight slanting through the stained glass onto the pews, the muted sobbing into handkerchiefs—it must have felt almost bridal.

Dolores sips her wine thoughtfully. "In a Catholic school and a mortuary you were raised," she says archly. "So much about you makes sense now."

"Funeral *home*," Laura corrects with a warm smile. "I try to emphasize family and human connection in my business. You know, I actually come across a lot of tattoos through my job. Nobody has secrets from me. And—I just noticed you have someone's dates on that tombstone tattoo—"

Dolores's right hand twitches over to cover her left forearm, and Andrew makes a noise.

"Why do women these days ruin their bodies with tattoos?"

It bursts out of him so forcefully, it must have been building pressure this whole time. Dolores looks down at her smooth, colorful arms, and I do too. I spot a death moth, a bottle of poison, a claw hammer.

"'Women these days'?" Dolores intones. "My great-grandmother was covered in traditional batok tattoos. I'm very old-fashioned." There's something different in her tone now. She has the better part of a bottle of wine in her system, and her give-a-fuck meter is running on E. "It must be hellish being conservative. To wake up every day terrified of the things you don't understand. Just think of all the interesting people you can't be friends with. And what's it like being a man? Going through life thinking women exist to be decorative elements in the visual landscape?"

She turns to me. "Your dad's a creep. You came by it honestly."

There's a stunned little silence. Laura blinks several times at the tabletop. Andrew's mouth falls open once again, and when his eyes meet mine, there's raw fury in them.

Dolores stands and takes the bottle of wine around the neck and shoves it in her purse. She sways ever so slightly. "I'm not sticking around for the main course. It would interfere with my alcohol absorption. Adios, amoeba," she says to my uncle. "It was lovely meeting you," she says to my aunt. "Maybe next time you can show me pictures of Jake dressed as an altar boy or whatever twisted stuff he used to get up to."

And with that, she stalks off across the restaurant, flames smoldering in her footsteps as she goes.

9

The Girlfriend Removal Expert

JAKE

"I'M SORRY, JAKE," AUNT LAURA SAYS IN A SMALL VOICE. "WE'LL GET THE BILL. Will you call me? I *really* like her."

I realize she thinks I'm going with Dolores, so I do just that, leaving Andrew practically smoking around the edges and Laura resigned to an evening spent placating him. I almost duck to give her a quick hug and kiss—it's been years since I've done that. I've been trying to wean her off me.

I catch up to Dolores in the mezzanine just as she pulls the wine bottle out of her purse. She holds it out to me when she spots me.

"You need it more than me. Your dad—"

"He's not my dad. They're not my parents."

Her face puckers in confusion. "You look like them."

I do, and it's been a source of irritation to my uncle since I went to live with them. They couldn't have children of their own, and I was the disappointing consolation prize. The last thing he wants, ever, is for me to be mistaken for their son.

"I look like my aunt."

"Yes. And you stone-face just like him."

"He would stone-face at me and I had to stone-face right back. They raised me after my parents died."

She doesn't hand out the automatic apology. She just examines my face for tells of emotion and tucks away this bit of information in my case file.

"So that's how you know so much about ghosts," she says.

Her reference to our rooftop talk is random and confusing, and I don't want to get into any of that. Dolores is like a wisp of smoke, and she could slip away into the night at any moment. In her red dress, with her tattoos on display, and truth serum running brightly in her veins, I feel like I have the real Dolores standing in front of me, not the one camouflaged in a monochrome corporate disguise playing an elaborate game of cloak-and-dagger from Monday to Friday. I need to make her linger. I need to hook her in, snag her interest. I need another stroke of brilliance, like I had with that doll.

She looks at me expectantly, and just as I open my mouth, my phone buzzes in my pocket. I send it to voicemail without looking at it. Then it starts buzzing again. I know who it is. There's only one person in my life who feels this entitled to my attention.

"Will you wait for me?" I ask Dolores.

She tips her head to one side, like she's listening to a little devil on her shoulder. "Sure. Why not." She sits on the lip of the indoor fountain and pulls out her phone, and I step across the mezzanine, out of earshot, to return the missed calls.

The first was not Grant, after all. It was my uncle. He's left a voicemail.

"How *dare* you tell her I'm your father—"

I delete it without finishing. The second was Grant, so I call him back.

"*Jake.*"

We're one syllable in and I can already feel a headache coming on. He cuts right to the chase in anguished tones.

"I need you to get Verity out of here for me. Right now. I can't stand to look at her."

And here we are. The sordid, ungodly things I get up to with my roommate that Uncle Andrew would never guess. I look over at Dolores, across the room. I squeeze my eyes shut.

"Does it have to be tonight?"

When Grant says, "Jump," my job is to say, "How high?" It's the main condition of our arrangement. He's taken aback enough to be rendered mute for a moment.

"Yes, it does have to be tonight," he snaps. A pause, and his voice becomes tragic again. "Verity's not right for me. These feelings aren't real. None of it is *real*. I'm so *lonely*, Jake."

He gasps, close to a sob. He's always like this when the honeymoon phase is over.

"They never stop me from feeling *lonely*. It's like—an ache in a part of my body I can't even identify. Maybe if she wasn't so *fake*. It makes me feel like all of it's fake. Is that all I deserve? A fake relationship? Because it doesn't matter what I feel if she can't love me back—"

"You deserve something real," I say placatingly.

"I do," he agrees, his tone less dramatic by degrees. "I found one of her nails in my bed. It broke off. She's cheap. What do you think of her hair?"

I try to think what color this one's hair is.

"It looks . . ."

"I can always tell the difference between real hair and fake. I want to meet a real, *natural* woman, Jake. But I work too much. So instead I do this. It's a cycle."

It's a cycle he's repeated two dozen times since I moved in: infatuation, creeping disenchantment, and then finally disgust, self-pity, and despair.

It floats up in front of my eyes, the sight of Grant up all night at his computer, desperately clicking away at photos of brunettes, blondes, tall, short, curvy, thin—and then charging his desires to a credit card. The oversized Barbie of a woman shows up, stays a while, and then is shown out, leaving Grant's wallet significantly lighter. The idiot could just hit up a club like a normal person. He has the clothes and the money and the car for it.

I've suggested a psychiatrist. He's told me he's already seen them all.

"I need you to get her out of the apartment for me."

I watch Dolores, sitting there, and I wonder how long until she loses patience and leaves.

"Where is she?"

"She's in the shower right now. Shit. Jake. I feel so disgusted with myself. I'm going to leave. I'm just going to walk out. I'll be back tomorrow. Just . . . just make sure she's gone when I get back. Please."

In four years he's never once asked me what I do with them. He leaves that up to me. It's not like I can just open the door, bow like a butler, and show them out. They won't leave on their own. I wonder if we have another rug we can spare. Shower curtain? Tablecloth? I suppress a sigh.

And that's when I catch sight of my reflection in a mirror panel across the room. I look so normal. Dull, even. Nondescript suit. Boring haircut. Glasses. It's all part of my carefully curated mask. *Don't notice me.* I wonder what Dolores sees. Not much. I know what Grant sees—a chump. The possibility of an evening with Dolores floats away.

"She'll be gone when you get back," I tell Grant. I end the call.

When I go back to her, Dolores is still perched on the edge of the fountain, wearing her black trench coat now. I hold my hand out to her, and after a moment's hesitation she takes it and I pull her to her feet. We spill out onto the dark street, where the rain has petered out to a few random drops. It's a gleaming, water-slicked night, all inky blackness and sparkling traffic lights. A car's sound system vibrates in the background like a big creature's heartbeat. It's the sort of night I could walk for hours in. It's the sort of night I have walked for hours in, when I couldn't sleep. Dolores stands six feet in front of me in her spindly little shoes, her hair flecked with a handful of glittering raindrops, her eyes wide and dark.

"I have to go," she says, preempting me. But she says it in a way that wants to be convinced otherwise.

"Not yet."

I take her by the elbow and swing her into the darkened doorway of a storefront boarded up for renovations. The memory of that rooftop kiss sits between us like a third presence. What I wouldn't give for a rooftop right now.

"Why did you kiss me?" she whispers. "On the roof."

I look at her lips, then her eyes again. She smells like red wine and perfume and herself.

"*You* kissed *me*."

"You grabbed me," she says.

"I was just trying to push you off."

"Fair," she breathes. "I *was* trying to strangle you."

It's a terrible idea to let anyone in, but it's reassuring, the way she looks at me—even in moments like these—like she can barely stand me.

I'm someone else when I take her face in my hands and kiss

hor. At that moment a brisk wind blows in from the harbor, swirling her loose hair around us, but her lips are warm against mine. I imagine what we must look like—red dress, dark coats, a shaft of light from the streetlamp catching reflections in her chaotic hair—but then I stop all thinking, because after a moment's hesitation, she kisses me back. She doesn't kiss me like she thinks I'm boring, and dull, and forgettable. And when she parts her lips against mine, smooth and wet, a terrible idea forms.

We could end this evening on a kiss—or start it.

"Come out with me tonight," I say when I pull away.

Her expression is perfectly blank, a masterful poker face. "To do what?"

I glance between her eyes, back and forth. Dark brown, with scalpel-sharp eyeliner. My hand is still cupping the side of her face, and the black of my glove makes her skin look pale.

"Serial killer stuff?" she asks. "Or a cozy night at home in your footie pajamas dismembering Barbies?"

And when she says that, it's all decided for me. She's every bit as twisted and morbid as me. She's been signaling this whole time, putting out feelers, testing me, and I've been doing it right back. Are we birds of a feather? Do we have matching stripes under our clothes? I want to outdo whatever expectations of crazy she has.

It's impossible not to feel a spasm of nerves. It's that moment before revealing a secret, or executing a prank, or delivering the punchline of a risqué joke. The moment of uncertainty, the fear that this person will *not* get it, after all. It's that moment right before she opened the little green package I left on her keyboard. *Do we laugh at the world in the same way?*

"Yes," I say.

She's silent. "Yes to which?"

"I have a job to do."

"A job? How boring."

I'm not boring.

"I need to dispose of a body."

It's like someone tosses a pebble into the blank surface of her face. Her expression ripples, then settles back into blankness. Fear? Surely not. *Amusement.* Then, one eyebrow, elegantly arched. I've hooked her again. She's mine for the time being.

"So you *are* a murderer? You keep getting more interesting, Jacob."

10

Meat Cute

DOLORES

TODAY OF ALL DAYS. A KISS ON A ROOF, A TRUCE WITH A GLOVED STRANGLER, an introduction to his family to announce our pending nuptials, and now, finally, a first date.

I'm *just* that level of drunk, the level that feels euphoric and consequence-free, the level where I completely forget everything else, where all I want is to get naked and bite a man's shoulder and make terrible choices. It's incredible, because it's been years—*years*—since I felt this way. He brushes my lips with his gloved thumb, and it all comes roaring back like a half-dead ember bursting to flame on a bit of dry tinder. Real life recedes. It's just this moment. I angle my face to his for another kiss.

And he abruptly turns and walks away. I stare after him stupidly.

The shit-heel.

I shiver and wobble a little in my heels. I'm going to walk away too. Fucker. But before I do, Jake walks into a storefront without looking back. **OPEN UNTIL MIDNIGHT,** says a sign in the window of an old-fashioned mom-and-pop hardware store.

I smile. Even serial killers get their meet-cute.

Inside I trail after him, up and down the aisles under the sickly green fluorescents. We must look like two night insects caught in the beam of a flashlight. We're not meant to be seen in such bright light. We're meant to be heard scuttling around in the dark.

I watch the handsome stranger fill his basket slowly. A hunting knife. Rope. Duct tape. A saw. Bleach. A tarp. Extra large, extra sturdy, reinforced garbage bags. This is a man who takes initiative to plan date night. No weaponized incompetence here. *Don't forget protection*, I think. He tosses a pair of safety goggles in the basket.

I have my own shopping to do. I take a basket from the stack.

At checkout I run into the handsome stranger again. Literally.

"I'm sorry," I say in a prim voice, and he turns to see who knocked his elbow with her basket.

"No worries," the stranger says.

"Christmas shopping?" I ask. "What's Santa giving everyone?"

"Homemade gifts, this year. Everyone wants their pound of flesh."

I suppress a smile. "Sounds like you have your work cut out for you. At least it's not going to cost you an arm and a leg."

His lips don't even twitch. He peers in my basket. I have a wrapping paper four-pack, scissors, and tape. "Now that's something I'm not good at," he says. "The presentation."

"Presentation is everything. I'm a very *handy* wrapper. I get my head right into it." I bite my lip. "I know we've only just met . . ."

"Has it really only been thirty seconds?" he says.

". . . but if you needed help wrapping—"

"As a matter of fact—"

"Because it would be no trouble . . ."

"If you're sure . . ."

"It would have to be your place. I have carpet, and my landlord is very tetchy about security deposits."

"Understood."

The doughy teenager behind the register watches, mystified, as I pick up this handsome monster and invite myself to his place. Jake pays up and leads us out. He stops by a shabby Toyota, and I walk around to the passenger side and grip the door handle, waiting. A bobble head stuck to the dash, two empty coffee cups in the console. I'm going to snoop through the glove compartment as soon as he lets me in. The real Jake Ripper waits inside. The lethally funny loner with the dysfunctional family, dead-end job, and—if it's me he's taking home—hopeless dating prospects.

Jake fishes a fob out of his pocket, and the car adjacent purrs to life. The Aston Martin from basement parking. I manage to keep my mouth from falling open, but it's touch and go.

I stare at him, his glasses lit eerily by the headlights of passing cars, concealing his eyes. There's the jingle in my ear.

But then a car pulls up behind us and sits there with its lights on, and in that beam of light, he's just Jake again. I can see his eyes. Behind that perfect mask, he's as uncertain and pleased by this turn of events as I.

"It *is* your car."

He hesitates. "I'm borrowing it. I would never move a body in my own car."

I step closer and peer inside. No bobble heads. No cups.

"Not losing your nerve, are you?" he asks.

There it is again: the uncertainty. I could devour his uncertainty and nervous pleasure crumb by crumb. I could huff them out of a bag for a high.

I shrug nonchalantly. "The entire premise of dating as a straight woman is being alone with men who are potential murderers."

"That's very insulting," he says. "Potential?"

He opens the door for me and there's a tug in my brain, a reason not to get in—real life, waiting at home for me—but I flick it away and duck inside.

We cruise uptown, the city light spilling into the darkened interior and lighting up Jake's gloved hands on the wheel. He parks in a reserved spot in the basement of a tall new building, pulls the goods from the trunk, and leads me to the elevator.

He takes us directly to the top floor and leads me out. When the doors close behind me, I may as well be trapped in the impenetrable dark of a windowless basement, and I wonder if a gloved hand will reach out to guide my face to another kiss. Then the darkness parts. A door. Beyond that, a broad, sweeping view of the city and the ghostlike glow of city lights tracing the contours of furniture. A Christmas tree drawn in string lights blinks stupidly on the side of a high-rise in the distance. The lights come on, and I blink, frozen in the doorway.

White, modern, minimalist—but expensive. So expensive. Brushed steel, glass, white stone. Incomprehensible modern art on the walls. Above the sofa, a big white canvas with a streak of red, rivulets dripping down.

"I forgot vampires need to be invited in," Jake says from inside.

I step into Bluebeard's chamber and spin around. "You can afford this place on a temp salary?"

Jake turns to look, as if it's been a while since he's taken it all in.

"No. This place belongs to my roommate."

"Is your roommate Patrick Bateman?"

"It would explain some things. He's filthy rich. Family money."

I stroll into the center of the living room without taking off my shoes or coat. I touch the soft leather of a chair. I half expect to leave fingerprints. I feel like a dirty black ink smudge in this pristine snow cave. When I turn, Jake stares at me like he's examining a Rorschach test.

What do you see, Jake? A ghost? A vampire? A lonely Black Widow?

It's what my problem with Jake has been all along. He sees me. He notices me. I'm fascinating to him. It's been years since I was fascinating to anyone. And maybe it's the booze, or maybe it's just the way his eyes track me, but even though I'm in strange territory and should feel on the back foot, I've never felt this completely in control of another human being in my entire life.

There's something I need to know. "Is he *just* your roommate?"

Jake's lips almost twitch. "He's just my roommate."

"Why would someone who can afford a place like this want a roommate?"

"He likes the company."

"*Your* company?"

"I'm like a live-in assistant," he answers seriously. "I take care of anything he needs."

"Dirty work?"

"Anything he has an aversion to doing himself. Cooking, shopping . . ." The power flickers on Jake's serial killer simulation, and I see past the mask again. He's just as curious about what I'm thinking as I am about him. He clutches that bag of gag purchases like he doesn't know what comes next.

"Disposing of bodies for him," I prod, and I see something I've never seen before. A pleased smile starts in his eyes and tugs his lips in a shy, asymmetrical twist. It's got to be worth something to be able to make a psychopath smile like that. He's exasperatingly handsome. A jury would let him walk free.

I slink over to him and take the bag from his hands. "Where's the kill room?"

I follow him down a hallway and into a large room, where he turns on the lights, dim and golden and easy on the eyes. A California king bed in the middle. Invisible cabinetry concealing a wardrobe on one side. It's barer than most hotel rooms but oozes luxury.

I place the bag of loot on the bed, and Jake watches me, unmoving. His uneasiness makes me feel enormous, powerful, so even though the crap from the hardware store was never part of my plan, I take the items out and toss them on the bed one by one. The rope, the duct tape, the tarp, the saw, the knife, the goggles, the garbage bags, the wrapping paper—finally they all lie on the expensive white linen coverlet, a twisted tableau. I turn to him to lap up his awkwardness—but it's vanished. Or maybe it was never there.

This is getting fucking weird. It's time to set some ground rules.

I step out of my heels and slink up to him, take his tie in my hand, twirl it once around my list, and pull his head down, close to mine. I can taste his breath on my lips. "I take the lead. I call the shots. If I'm not having fun, I'm leaving."

"We'll follow your MO," he says, and I relax. "How do you want to do this?"

"Hmm. I'm not so sure about the duct tape," I say in a mock-serious voice. "I have sensitive skin."

He considers this like a professional. "I guess that leaves the rope."

"You can show off your Boy Scout knots," I say.

There's something I need to know before we go further. It's been a while for me. "Do you do this often?"

"Maybe every few months. I change it up. Last time I wrapped her up in a rug and took her to the river."

My mistake for thinking he'd break character. I suppress a smile. "Not my preferred approach. I think your bed will work just fine."

Jake's forehead puckers. "That's my roommate's bed."

I freeze. "We're doing this in your roommate's room? Are you the roommate from hell?"

"No. He is."

"Right."

"We could do it in the bathroom," he says, tipping his head in the direction of the en suite. "Easy cleanup."

Exactly how messy are we going to get? Not that I'm . . . opposed. I turn away from him and pull my hair to one side. "Zip."

"What?"

I glance at him over my shoulder and his face is blank.

"I don't want to get blood on my clothes," I say. "Zip."

It takes a long moment, but I watch from the corner of my eye as he removes his gloves and tosses them on the bed. His fingertips are like ice when they brush against the back of my neck. I shiver. My zipper parts, and then my dress forms a red puddle around my feet. I turn to face him in my bra and panties.

His face is red. He swallows, and says nothing, and doesn't allow his eyes to travel lower than my shoulders. He doesn't even breathe.

I've *never* had this effect on a man before. I could expire from the power trip.

"What do you think of my tattoos?"

He opens, closes, and opens his mouth again, and finally looks down. I feel warm everywhere his eyes touch me. "You're going to make a very gaudy lampshade."

Those are some valiant fighting words, but he's lost this round of cat and mouse. He'd eat out of my hand. He *will* eat out of my hand. I win.

"There better be condoms in that bathroom," I say, leading the way.

His expression turns alarmed. "Wait," he says, and I stop. "Don't . . . don't go in there."

"Why not? I was promised easy cleanup."

His mouth swings open and shut again.

"I bet it's one of those fancy waterfall showers," I say, stepping into the doorway, but he remains frozen by the bed. A petrified, horny little mouse. I lean seductively against the jamb and drop into a throaty voice. "You could always slip on Mother's clothes and bring that knife along if it helps you relax."

He glances at the knife on the bed.

I enter the dark bathroom and rake the wall for a light switch. Suddenly there's light, and now there's Jake, inches from me—the fucking *knife* bared in his *fucking* hand—

Tinkle.
Fucking.
Tinkle.

I pluck the pepper spray from my bra, raise it to his face, and spray. He's flattened in a second, coughing and wheezing and dribbling tears and spit and snot all over the bathroom tiles. His lesson is not to fuck with a fellow predator.

My lesson hits me a second later: pepper spray in small spaces fucks everyone.

I can't breathe—I have an inferno in my windpipe, in my lungs, and my entire face is turned on like a faucet. I'm on all fours, coughing uncontrollably, fat black tears of runny eyeliner dripping onto the white tiles in front of me. I spot the knife and grab it.

The shower starts.

"Are you okay?" he hacks from the shower. "Get in here and rinse your face off."

I wheeze, and snarl, "Fuck you, you *fucking* nutjob . . . fucking *knife* . . . What the *fuck* is wrong with you . . ."

"You told me to bring the knife, you kinky *psycho*!"

"You're the fucking psycho!"

I bumble-crawl across the floor, hacking, coughing, raking the walls with my hands to find the door to the bedroom, but I've been spun around. The mist on my skin tells me I've wandered into the entry to the walk-in shower instead. I reach out and my hand collides with—

I freeze there, on all fours, my nails snagged in—

"What—"

My body convulses at the exact moment I recognize the texture of human hair. I topple sideways into the cold spray of the walk-in shower, I shriek, I wipe my eyes with the back of my hand, and force myself to keep them open long enough to take a look. A woman is slumped over, lifeless and naked, at an unnatural angle in the bottom of the shower. Her body is stiff and awkward, her blond hair tousled and wet, her face slack, her mouth forming an O, like she's frozen in a moment of wonder or horror.

I slip backward onto my ass, knocking over Jake. I can't keep my eyes open for more than a split second—I scrub my face madly on his shoulder, my red and black makeup coming off onto his shirt.

"What the fucking *fuck*!" I shriek between coughs. I swipe furiously at my face a few more times, peering at the sight in front of us in between swipes. I cough again, a brutal, never-ending cough.

"Is that—?"

I cough and cough, and my cough resolves into a laugh—a hoarse, cackling witch's laugh. I grasp my shaking sides with my hands, and if I weren't already crying, I'd start.

It's the first time I've laughed in ages.

"It's—Oh my *god*—"

I fall onto my side with my face buried in Jake's chest, heaving and wheezing and laughing, and he brings his arms around me. He's strong and warm, and in spite of my burning eyes, and the screaming cold of the water, and the tiles hard as concrete underneath us, it's strangely nice in here.

I'm being rude, I realize. A man has just come bearing a romantic gift, and I'm leaving him hanging.

"It's—it's—" I lose it. "You *shouldn't* have!"

11

Psycho in the Shower

JAKE

I MISCALCULATED.

I slide out from under her, shut off the water, and get to my feet, dripping. She lies there, boneless on the tiles of the shower floor, hair wild, makeup a mess, laughing. I've never seen her laugh. I don't know what makes her seem more exposed—all that bare skin, or the laugh.

"Do you always carry pepper spray?" I ask, drying my glasses on one of Grant's heavy, luxurious towels.

"Any woman who doesn't is an idiot," she says, coughing and grinding her eyes with the heel of her hand.

"You thought I was going to fillet you." I have no reasonable grounds to feel defensive.

"You scared the *shit* out of me."

"You *told* me to bring the knife."

Dolores ignores this. She hooks her thumb at tonight's project. "Are you going to introduce us?"

"This is Verity."

She loses it over the name. I knew she would. She crawls

over to Verity and does what any normal person would do: she pokes one giant, gravity-defying silicone breast.

She looks up at me with a feral grin. None of our conversation before was a joke. *Serial killer stuff, or dismembering Barbies in your footie pajamas?*

"Why the fuck is there a hyperrealistic sex doll in your shower?"

I don't know about hyperrealistic. She doesn't look like any real woman I ever saw. Impossibly thick blond hair, dense caterpillar eyelashes, bee-stung lips, nipples that could poke an eye out. She sits firmly in the uncanny valley. She'd pass a first and second glance, maybe. But on the third glance, she's off enough to make you do a double take, and real enough to give you nightmares when you do.

"This is Grant's shower. It's Grant's doll."

She bites her lip. "Right."

"It is." I experience a jolt of panic. It hadn't occurred to me that she'd think it was my doll. "It's Grant's doll," I repeat.

"Oh, I believe you. It's definitely your absent roommate's doll."

"It isn't mine."

She cocks one eyebrow. I throw the heavy towel on her and she cackles.

"Why does he want you to get rid of it? Is his parole officer coming to visit or something?"

"He cycles through them. When he gets bored, he needs a new one."

"When the sex gets stale?"

I wouldn't so much as touch one of these dolls if he was having sex with them.

"It's not like that. He thinks sex is disgusting. It's . . . a romantic thing."

Her sharp little fangs show in another smile. "Aren't these things ridiculously expensive? I find rich people fascinating. I also find perverts fascinating. There is a ripe nexus of interests here." She sits back on her heels and narrows her eyes at me. "You said you took the last one to the river."

The day I met Dolores in the elevator. It was a beautiful night. I even took a selfie of the two of us with a view of the river behind us. She saw it on my desktop. "That was Una."

"Were there others?"

"The first one—Anastasia . . ." I hesitate for a second. "I put her in the building's dumpster wrapped in garbage bags." I've never stopped feeling uncomfortable about Anastasia.

She's grinning at me now like I've delivered the filthiest joke she's ever heard. That look makes me continue.

"I bundle them out of here in a rug or a blanket. Then I . . . dispose of them." I get quite creative these days. I've come a long way from dumpsters.

"Boredom's a chronic problem," she says. "Would you get in trouble if someone traced one of them back to you?"

"For what? Littering?"

Her lips quirk. She staggers to her feet and I reach out to steady her, but she gazes at my hand with a confused expression. I look down and my hands are white—completely white—and cold as ice again. It's a recent development, and one I don't want to think about right now. I fold my arms and tuck them from view. She gives me a curious look but doesn't ask. She pulls the towel tight around her and marches through Patrick Bateman's bedroom, stepping over her dress pooled on the floor.

"Where are you going?" I call after her. "Wait. *Wait.*" I trail down the hallway after her, while she sticks her nose into Grant's office, his home gym, his sauna, and finally—

"Here it is," she says triumphantly. "Your lair."

It's smaller than the other bedroom, and it might as well be the inside of a fridge. White walls, surfaces bare and scrupulously dust-free. Not even a sock on the floor or a nickel on the dresser top. I like it like this. I don't like having possessions. If I had possessions, I'd worry about someone rifling through them when I was gone.

She takes it all in. "Did you get your last major depressive episode to do the interior decorating for you? Can I get a business card?"

I've never been depressed. I lurk in the open doorway like a great awkward shadow and watch as she pulls open the drawer of the nightstand next to my bed. Inside the drawer are two earplugs and nothing else. What did she hope to find? Next, she inspects the contents of the top drawer of my dresser: a dozen identical socks, paired and folded. She swings open my closet door next: five identical white button-ups on one side and five pairs of gray slacks on the other. There's nothing else.

Well, except the bathrobe. She drops her towel on the floor and turns to face me, and for the second time tonight ten years of Catholic schooling resurfaces from the deep. I freeze. The devil sighs in disgust, and Dolores lifts one eyebrow at me, unimpressed. She slides on my bathrobe.

I cough. "We have a job to do," I remind her.

But she's not listening. She's finally sniffed out my secrets. She crouches at the foot of my bed, and I'm across the room in an instant—

"What's in it?" she asks when her fingers touch the cardboard banker's box.

"Let go."

I yank the box away, but she leaps to her feet and hooks her fingers into the handle hole nearest her and pulls. We're toe-to-toe, the box between us.

"It's your sewing project," she says. "Do you still need some skin for your skin suit? Is that why I'm here?"

She tugs, and the bathrobe slips down one shoulder to expose her tattoos. I tear my eyes away. "I don't wear bright colors or bold patterns."

She bites her lip. "It's a stack of photos with the eyes cut out."

I look in her eyes, so dark *they* could be holes cut out of her face.

"No . . ." she says thoughtfully. "It's your cannibal recipe cards."

Now I'm looking at her mouth. She worries her lower lip with her teeth again, like she's trying not to smile. I know what those teeth feel like on my own lower lip.

"I know," she purrs. "They're trophies from your sex doll kills."

We've been pulling the box in opposite directions, and now she suddenly shoves it toward me. I topple backward onto the bed, the box lid spilling off, the contents scattering. I close my eyes.

"Paper," she sighs. "How disappointing."

I reach out and swipe up the papers. Important documents, a few letters I've read a hundred times—dull things. Less interesting than a pickled human head, but they're *my* boring secrets.

I start to scramble off the bed, but then she kneels on the coverlet next to me, one bare knee slipping through the front of the bathrobe, and I . . . well. I stay put. She plucks up a handwritten letter at random. Does she see *Jacob* signed at the bottom? A date from thirty years ago at the top? No. She glances at it without reading it and tosses it back in the box. Her eyes connect with mine, and there's an electric pulse in my stomach.

Dolores dela Cruz is in my bed.

Her hair is still wet, her makeup wrecked, and my bathrobe swallows her up and makes her dimensions and angles mysterious. A shoulder peeks out, a knee, two hands. She leans in until I feel her breath on my cheek. I close my eyes.

"We've let ourselves get derailed. Where did we leave off, before the pepper spray?"

She tugs on my tie, but I don't think that's the reason I can't breathe.

"I think we were about to do something awful together in the shower," she breathes into my ear. "Do you still want to do that?"

There's a moth tattooed on her bare shoulder. A stud earring smolders dimly in her ear. Her perfume still clings to her—I notice all of these things. I notice everything about her. And I notice she loves this—me noticing her. Me . . . *wanting* her. I do want her.

She wants to toy with me, like a cat. I have to be cleverer and more interesting than the other mice.

"Maybe," I say. I turn my head so my lips are by her ear. "I just have one question for you." She turns her head to look at me.

"Saw or knife?"

Her lips twist into a beastly little smile.

12

Secret Santa

JAKE

HAND, FOOT, SHIN, FOREARM . . . DOLORES AND I DISMANTLE HER PIECE BY piece. I've never done it this way before. The knife works but requires force. The fret saw is easier but messy. We make a few bad cuts before we find our groove, amputating exactly where the joints bend so the bolts in her titanium skeleton can be unscrewed. We stack her bits up like firewood, and then I vacuum the bathroom floor of silicone crumbs while Dolores spreads out wrapping paper on the plush carpet of the bedroom.

"What do you think, a foot for Billy? Will Johnny be jealous?" she asks.

She sits cross-legged in the middle of Grant's floor in my robe, wearing a pair of yellow dish gloves to safeguard against fingerprints, her hair in a messy knot on top of her head, her sparkly earrings catching the light. She's trash at wrapping gifts, in spite of her brag at the hardware store. I let her boss me around, and I steal glances at her, like I always do, while she works and swigs from a bottle of Grant's wine like a pirate.

She's mine for a few more hours.

She ties one last sloppy bow, stands, stretches, tosses her gloves on the bed, and plucks her dress off the floor.

"I need to get dressed," she says, and I take the garbage bags full of Christmas presents to the front door. But—there's a pair of shoes—and classical music wafts from the kitchen—"The Flight of the Bumblebee"—frantic, frenzied—

"Jake!"

No.

"Grant," I say through my teeth.

"Jaaaake," Grant says pleasantly. I never heard him arrive. He still has his coat on as he pulls a half-full bottle of white from the fridge and pours himself a glass, bouncing a little to the music. "What are you up to tonight?" he asks, as if we never had that conversation on the phone. "Just a regular night in?"

In my head Dolores is a blinking red dot in the floor plan of the apartment. She's moving around in Grant's room, while two dots pulse in the kitchen. I try to visualize an out for her—the window—an air vent—

"Yes."

"You're a creature of habit, Jake. You need to get out more. You need to *meet* people."

He's revved up. Expansive. He's going to start talking about taking over the world any minute. Maybe he'll have a nosebleed, or maybe this is pure Grant tonight. The music whips up, faster and faster, whining, keening.

"What you need, Jake, is to do *therapy*. It's not normal to be so cut off from the world."

"Yes."

"I know a good therapist. She wears pencil skirts. Not every woman can wear a pencil skirt, you know. She pretended not to like *that* compliment when I gave it to her."

"Yes."

"Although"—he frowns—"I don't know about her. She wasn't happy to hear about Verity. She's a very jealous woman. Women are *jealous*, Jake."

"Yes."

"It's unprofessional of her to allow feelings like that to interfere with her doing her job," Grant says, jumping rapidly from thought to thought, faster than a violinist's fingers or a swarm of bees. "There's a code of conduct, you know. There's a board I could report her to."

"Yes."

"I should report her—I'm *going* to report her. Tomorrow. It's so hard to find a good therapist, Jake. Which is terrible, because *everyone* needs to do therapy. I'd be out of business if people looked after their mental health. By the time *I* see them, they've gone off the deep end."

"Yes."

"Look at me: I take my mental health seriously. I'm *very* concerned about my mental health."

I nod. "We're all very concerned about your mental health."

Grant smiles, flattered, and opens his mouth to reply, but no sound comes out. He's frozen in place, staring over my shoulder. The back of my head down to my tailbone prickles and turns cold. *No.*

The music shuts off and, "Hello," Dolores says from the entryway to the kitchen.

I swivel to look, and my stomach drops out onto the floor between my shoes. She's poised with one finger on the power button of Grant's expensive speakers, and she's not wearing her red dress. She's not wearing the bathrobe, either. For a split second I think she's not wearing anything, but then I realize she got into Grant's wardrobe, full of designer dresses and shoes and everything else a spoiled sex doll could want. She wears a formfitting long-sleeved dress the exact color of her skin tone, a dress that looks like tensor bandages stitched neatly together, or maybe strips of leather harvested from someone who was good about rubbing lotion on their skin, and a pair of painfully high nude heels to match. She looks like a Barbie, all her creases and hollows smoothed out, legs a mile long, everything airbrushed tan. Grant's eyes slide all over her, tasting her, leaving invisible slime trails.

No. No, no, no.

"Hello," Grant says, his voice slightly lower and slower than normal. "Grant Velazquez."

Dolores steps into the kitchen and takes the glass of wine from his hands, as if he'd been holding it out to her.

Don't. Don't, don't, don't—

Dolores dela Cruz is no idiot. "You can call me Dolly."

Grant's gaze swings back and forth between the two of us. He wants an explanation, *now.*

Dolly obliges. "Your . . . butler? . . . brought me here to help you," Dolly says over the rim of her wineglass.

That breaks the ice. Grant glances at me and guffaws. "Butler! Ha! Hahahaha!"

"He brought me in for my . . . *services.*"

She means her body disposal services, but Grant's face goes serious—too serious. He shoots me a betrayed look. A *call girl.* A beautiful, sophisticated one, but a *call girl.* How could I do this to him? Don't I remember how it is for him? Don't I remember all those traumatic experiences in the past from bringing real woman back to his penthouse—all those women who expected *sex* when all he wanted was an intellectual connection, a connection of the *soul*—

I know exactly what Grant is saying with his eyes because he's said it out loud to me a million times, late at night, when he couldn't sleep, and therefore wouldn't allow me to.

But Dolly isn't done speaking. She stalks over to the sitting area and says over her shoulder, "I have a very special set of skills, as a matter of fact." She drawls her words slowly, punctuating each one with a step, the red soles of her shoes flashing like she's been traipsing through puddles of blood. She stops in front of the snow-white armchair in the middle of the living room.

"What do you do?" Grant asks grudgingly.

"What do I do? I'm a"—Dolly pirouettes on the spot—"*psychologist.*" She flounces into the armchair and caresses the armrests meaningfully. She's an *armchair* psychologist.

Grant's jaw drops and his eyes light up, and he shoots me a look of pure gratitude. He loves psychologists. Better than psychiatrists, because there's more talking and fewer pills. Better than therapists, too—therapists are lightweights. They get skittish and fire him after a couple of sessions, as Pencil Skirt is about to do. He sweeps Dolly with his eyes again—she can definitely pull off a pencil skirt.

"Are you taking new patients? What's your specialty?"

She cocks her head. "Sociopaths, egomaniacs, garden-variety perverts . . . You'd be amazed at what comes my way. But my roster's quite full. I just took on an aspiring serial killer who has an unhealthy fixation with a coworker. It would have to be *quite* an interesting case to tempt me to take on a new patient." She narrows her eyes appraisingly. "Why, do you have something good for me? You seem so"—she chews her lower lip, then purrs the dirtiest word she can summon—"normal."

"I'm not normal," Grant brags.

"Hmm. I don't believe it." She leans back in the armchair, crossing her legs sinuously, languorously, her movements those of a cat settling into a sunbeam, and the hem of her dress rises slightly to reveal the bottom of a tattoo dangling down her thigh. She scratches her red claws absently on the armrests, and Grant takes it all in, a flush settling on the back of his neck.

"I'm not normal," he insists.

Dolly drinks deeply of her wine. "Tell me everything, Grant."

Grant settles on the white sofa next to her armchair and pulls out the big guns. "I'm a workaholic. I work eighty hours a week. Grisly cases. My favorites are the murders, though—I love a good murder—"

Dolly holds up one hand, a slight furrow to her brow. She glances at me.

"He's a criminal lawyer," I interject.

She raises her eyebrows, amused. "A criminal lawyer or a *criminal* lawyer?"

Grant soldiers on without missing a beat. "I want to find love, but I have no time for relationships—"

Dolly yawns prettily, and Grant's speech becomes more urgent.

"I haven't dated in five years," he says. "No, six. Women are interested," he avers, trying to catch her interest. "Very interested. I mean . . ." Here, Grant waves around at the minimalist opulence of our surroundings. Only extreme poverty and extreme wealth can produce this level of Spartan bareness.

"I could have a lot of women. A *lot* of women are interested in me." He frowns at Dolly, who is examining her nails, not interested in him at all.

"It must be difficult watching your butler enjoy a more vibrant love life than you," Dolly says, deftly manipulating Grant for information about me.

"Jake?" He scoffs, shoots a disbelieving look at me. "Jake doesn't have a . . . significant other." Grant frowns, like perhaps this is the first time he's wondered which way I swing. I have never had a guest over, and I have never been on a date the entire time he's known me. I'm a piece of furniture in his life. A robot. I could be a eunuch for all he knows.

"Hmmm. Maybe not a significant other. But when he has a *date* over—"

Grant laughs at this preposterous image. A giant neon sign reading **LOSER** flickers and hums above my head, and Dolly watches me with a satisfied expression. She dangles the shoe off the tip of her toes, and both Grant and I watch it.

Grant lunges desperately for Dolly's interest. He wants to get things back on track. "I—I don't like sex," he tries. "At all. A sexual connection feels cheap, but that's what all of these women want. Sex. Sex-sex-sex. What I want is the connection of *mind* and *soul*. I want a soulmate, I want my *person*, and I want to be someone else's person." What he wants is to sound poetic and romantic, but nothing piques Dolly's interest. He frowns at her apathy, then bites the ring, yanks, and throws his grenade.

"So I spend about a hundred thousand dollars a year purchasing silicone dolls instead."

He waits for it to explode, but of course Dolly doesn't even flinch. She uncoils her legs and sits up straight, and Grant is finally happy: she's interested in him.

"Is it because you want to be in control?" Dolly asks with thinly veiled excitement. "You want them to stay here in your apartment and never leave? You want to pick their names, and their clothes?"

Grant blinks. "No."

"You like that they don't have personalities and opinions, and families and friends?"

Grant frowns. "No."

Dolly deflates infinitesimally. "So what's the appeal of dolls?"

Grant blinks again. "I feel less lonely with one around."

"Why?"

"Because . . . I feel less misunderstood. I don't need to feel understood, but at least not *misunderstood*."

Surprise, but then Dolly's face settles into a cool, professional expression. She swirls her wineglass thoughtfully. "So where is the problem, Grant?"

Grant stares at her mutely. "What?"

"You've told me that you can't get your needs met by real, live women, and that you've figured out a work-around. Where is the problem?"

Grant has no answer.

"Here's my professional opinion: you don't need to fix anything. You've found a way to be happy without making anyone else unhappy. Do you know how rare that is?"

"But—"

Dolly shakes her head. "Connecting with another human being is difficult. Other people make it look easy, maybe, but some of us . . . some of us are like those endangered mountain cats, who have to live thinly spread out over vast tracts of land

In order to survive, and only encounter another of our species rarely and fleetingly."

Dolly glances at me, her eyes glinting like those of a rangy mountain predator, and maybe she doesn't see a giant flashing sign above my head. She spots a fellow prowler in the distance, just as hungry and starved for company as she.

"I think someday you'll meet her, Grant. We all do, eventually." She gets to her feet and stalks over to me, holding my gaze, and I feel warm.

We all do, eventually. Suck a dick, Grant.

"Thank you for the wine, but Jake and I have to go now."

"What? Where?"

"We have to drop off some Christmas presents," I say, and Dolores smiles for me. "There's a toy drive at the Children's Hospital."

"Oh." Grant frowns.

I grab the sacks of wrapped presents by the door, and Dolores puts on her black trench coat and slips out of Grant's life forever, while he stares after her, his heart ripped from his chest.

WE DON'T GO TO THE CHILDREN'S HOSPITAL. WE DEPOSIT A FOOT ON THE DOORstep of a podiatrist's office. A hand at the YMCA. Dolores clutches her phone in front of her and barks directions at me. I pull up, and she darts out, barefoot, and runs to deposit a gift, and runs back again, over and over and over. Close to one in the morning, she makes me drive left, and left, then right, and we pull up in front of a squat, boring apartment building sprouting from the ground amidst ranks of similar squat, boring apartment buildings.

"Who lives here?"

"I do," she says.

I would never have pictured this, but I don't know what I would have imagined for her. I look at her, and her eyes gleam in the dim light of the interior of the car. She's cradling the last Christmas package in her arms: the head.

"You sure know how to show a girl a good time. It's been a real slice." She makes a slicing motion across her throat. "Sleep tight in that cold, hospital-cornered bed of yours. Is it meant to remind you of the comforts of the asylum for the criminally insane?"

"Yes. And what about you? Are you a coffin sleeper or do you hang by your toes from the rod in the closet?"

She shakes her head. "I usually just spin a web in the corner."

Her hair is still pulled up in a knot on top of her head, and I can admire the shape of her skull, the slenderness of her neck. She bends to slip her stolen shoes back on, and from the side, I can make out the vertebrae of her spine tenting the soft skin where her neck meets her shoulders. Her little ulnar bones, her delicate hands, her carefully articulated ankles, the expressive arch of her foot. Her skeleton would be very beautiful.

And because she reads minds, she says, "You're looking at me like you're imagining picking the meat from my bones."

And so of course I drift in, and I don't think I imagine her drawing nearer too—

"I'm glad you asked for help tonight," she says, and I can almost feel her breath on my face. "It isn't easy for those of us in this line of work. It's just about impossible to stay in the business long enough these days to reach serial status, what with video surveillance, cell phone towers, DNA databases . . ."

"Just one more job being destroyed by technology."

She smiles at me, an actual smile.

"If *you* ever need help disposing of a body . . ." I tell her. Her smile fades away, and she considers me very seriously, but she doesn't seem unhappy with me.

"Good night, Dolores."

"Dodi," she whispers.

"What?"

She holds my eyes and hesitates for a moment. "It's been a long time since anyone called me that."

"Dodi."

She tilts her head, like she's weighing how it sounds in her ear, and her eyes flick down to my lips. But there's a small knot of something in my chest, ever since she psychoanalyzed Grant.

"What did you think of Grant?"

Dolores sighs indulgently. "He's definitely not a serial killer." The way she looks at me says, *He's not part of our little club, is he?*

"You seemed to like him."

Dodi lifts a brow, amused. "He's not weird enough for me." She glances at my mouth again, and now her fingertips find the side of my face. I tingle where she touches me.

"You know, I've been waiting all night for you to come in for the kill," she whispers. "But I know why you haven't."

"Why?"

"You don't have a clue how to finish me off, or what to do with my body."

She's so pleased with her little joke.

"I know exactly what to do with it," I say. "I have a very particular MO of my own."

I absolutely do not.

"Come up and show me?"

"I'm allergic to cats."

Her lips quirk. "My neighbor is borrowing her. Doesn't have one of her own. And it's not like I can leave her alone when I go out. She'll climb the curtains. Leave hairballs in my shoes. It's a whole thing. Come up, Jake."

She leans in close, and now I *know* we're going to kiss . . . but I'm an idiot who still wants reassurance. A different sort of reassurance this time. She notices a change in my face, because she stops an inch from me.

I unglue my tongue. "It's just . . . it must be difficult, being a Black Widow. Breaking your heart on the job every day. What if you develop feelings?"

She pulls back, annoyed. "Don't flatter yourself. I don't get attached to my victims." She frowns at me, like she's seeing me afresh. "Forget I asked. I haven't restocked on lye since my last date, anyway."

She scrabbles with the ridiculous door handle, and before I can stop her, she's slipped out into the night. I watch Dolores—*Dodi*—speed-walk to her apartment, her coat flapping like a cape, Verity's head cradled in her arms. She doesn't look back.

I stay there for a while, the car silent, the street silent, as the inside of the car gets colder and colder.

There was something about the stillness of night, the closeness of her face to mine, the strangeness of our conversation. I felt like we'd unlocked a moment in which I could say anything. I almost told her, then, about the thoughts that go bump in the night. I almost asked her about her offer to do away with me, on the roof. Is she really capable of something like that?

But I didn't ask her. Because there's *something* there.

I've been casing her out, taking her measure, and here we've run aground on something hidden underneath. Her own buried bodies. Something I don't understand yet, a secret she still doesn't trust me with.

And to think I almost told her *my* secret.

13

Solitaire

DODI

HE'S THE FIRST PERSON I'VE TOLD MY SECRET—IN SO MANY WORDS.

I drop my new shoes by the door and the bag containing my red dress slithers to the floor. The apartment is silent as a tomb. *Here lies the sex life of Dolores dela Cruz.* In the darkened living room the TV casts a flickering light, like the votive flames of a funerary altar. I hadn't realized I'd left the TV on. I turn it off, but I'm not ready for sleep. I feel twitchy and edgy. I feel alive.

I could walk down the hall and rap on my neighbor's door. Have a drink. Spill the tea about the date with the wrong man. She wants to be friends, I think. I estimate that I have about two more months of her goodwill before she finally takes offense and stops trying. My estimates are fairly accurate after all these years of the same scenario playing out over and over. But it's too risky, having friends. They clasp their hands around their coffee mugs in their warm, clean kitchens and tilt their heads to one side, eyes dilated wide with concern, and say, *How did he . . . pass?* and *What do you do for a living?*

and *Dolores dela Cruz . . . that sounds familiar.* I can't tolerate any of that. Everything has been so neatly buried.

I chuck Verity's head into my freezer. In the bathroom I reach into the medicine cabinet for my toothbrush, the back of my hand knocking against the men's safety razor that's been sitting, unused, since that last morning when I kissed his smooth cheek good-bye, and he waltzed off to meet destiny.

I feel the phantom of Jake's stubble prickling the pads of my fingers, and I shut the cabinet.

I look different in the bathroom mirror. My hair is piled on top of my head, my makeup is smudged, my lips stained with wine. My cheeks burn pink, and my eyes are glittery and strange. This is what he was looking at when he almost kissed me just now. I wish I'd kissed him. I wish he was here right now, on top of me. I'm so glad he isn't. I still haven't decided if I'm going to let him keep his glasses on.

He had his glasses on tonight, though. I peel off the bandage dress and leave it crumpled on the floor like a deflated potato skin and stare at my reflection in the mirror, sobriety and self-consciousness creeping in. He was stone-cold sober tonight, while I minced around drunkenly in my panties and bra, confidence fueled by the miracle of table wine. I touch my belly, a part of my body I haven't loved in a long while. How much younger than me *is* he?

He . . . rejected me. In the car, just now, didn't he? He didn't want to come up.

I won't be able to meet his eye tomorrow.

And yet, he knows my secret, he knows who I am, and doesn't flinch from meeting *my* eye.

A distraction. Spider, or Pyramid. Maybe a nice game of Yukon. Solitaire is the perfect game for someone like me. I know two dozen ways to play by myself, two dozen different ways to arrive at the same conclusion: hearts to hearts, spades to spades, clubs to clubs, and diamonds to diamonds. Everyone with their own kind. The soft, tender, bleeding ones in one pile, the cold, unfeeling rocks in another. The murder weapons over here, and the shovels for burying the evidence over there. I sit cross-legged in the middle of my bed and take the decks from my bedside table, the ones with the holes punched through the middle, the luck snuffed out of them, and shuffle. Caesar's Palace. *Thwick*. I've always had a knack for shuffling. But as I lay the cards out, they fall into a familiar pattern all on their own. I'm dealing blackjack for someone who isn't there, again.

I wonder if Jake knows how to play. He has the best poker face I ever saw. That perfect deadpan just now as he teased me in his car about allergies. The way he's always talked about my cat has been a coded acknowledgment—cheeky, but respectful in its own way. He's aware of what my life is outside of this fantasy world we've built to contain our flirtation, and he knows we have to keep reality and fantasy separate. This isn't real life.

That's why he didn't come up.

I smooth a crinkle in the bedspread and uncover a decapitated head with dark hair and glasses. She's claimed the dismembered Ken doll as one of her own toys, and the pieces turn up in the strangest places. I carry it down the hallway to where the little musical jewelry box sits on a shelf in the living room. I nestle it in between the severed limbs, and the music tinkles sweetly in the dark for a moment before I shut the lid.

14

Escape to Las Vegas

JAKE

THE NEXT MORNING THE ELEVATOR DOORS GROAN APART AND I STEP IN TO FIND Dolores coming up from the basement: black coat, black bag, black dress, *pink* lipstick. Pale, poisonous, the color of salmonella in your chicken breast. And nude heels with red soles.

"Dolores," I say.

She leans against one wall and peers into her phone, ignoring me. She has shadows under her eyes. I know I do too, but I always do.

"Dodi."

This time when I speak, a muscle in her jaw twitches, and I realize my mistake. We're not alone, but our companion is absorbed in his own phone and could care less about the grifter sneaking around in our midst. We glide to a stop at the second floor and Pat-from-Projects and Sara-from-Accounts bring their conversation in with us.

". . . and Doug's department has a bunch of unused training

money. If he doesn't use it all up they'll allot us less next year—"

"Tell him!"

"I've been *hounding* him. He's avoiding me—"

"He's been avoiding me too!"

"So I've told Doug to just send someone to a conference—"

"Oof. He can send me. I'd take a free trip to a conference destination . . ."

Dodi glares at the two of them. They're too much. Too much action and noise and earnestness for a Wednesday morning. I want to put them on my list. The elevator grunts in sympathy and spits them out at the next floor along with the man, leaving us alone, and when the doors close I take one step closer to Dodi.

"You smell like Clorox wipes and despair," she sighs. "What do you want?"

It's one step forward, two steps back with her. I'm the lowly office rat again. What I want is for her to look at me like she did last night when I introduced her to Verity. Obviously, I need to present another gift. Something better than a mutilated Barbie. Something better than a hyperrealistic sex doll ready for butchering.

"What do *you* want?" I ask.

"I want a fucking aspirin and an espresso for my hangover. I want—" She presses her lips together and closes her eyes. "I want to get the fuck out of here."

"Where would you go?"

She shoots me an exasperated look. "Anywhere."

"Anywhere? Antarctica? Guantánamo Bay?"

She makes a peeved noise, like she's swearing off this interaction, but then she says, surprisingly, "I want to go to Las Vegas."

I almost don't have a response. Bright lights, noise, revelry. People on vacation, people there to gamble, to take in the spectacle, to be a part of the spectacle. Businesspeople on work trips loosening their ties and wallets at the end of a long day cooped up in the frigid conference rooms, making idiots of themselves in the casinos and clubs. Bachelor parties, stagettes, magic shows, circuses. My skin crawls at the thought.

"Isn't Las Vegas the vestibule to hell?"

She frowns and looks away. "Sometimes when I look into your eyes I get a glimpse of the vestibule to hell, Jake."

"Las Vegas is full of people having fun."

"I know. I would *hate* it." She says it like she would relish the hating.

"Why Las Vegas?"

She places her phone in her coat pocket and turns to face me properly, gazing at me with a strange, lazy stare. *"I have a job to do. I need to dispose of a body."* Then her face distorts into a deranged smile.

It takes me a second to realize she's impersonating me. She doesn't have to tell me the real reason, because a memory twigs. Aya and Bex will be hosting their *Murderers at Work* event in Las Vegas.

The doors glide open on the tenth floor, and Doug's square, pink ham-head peers warily around the jamb. When he's satisfied it's just the two of us, he leaps in and jabs the DOOR CLOSE button with one stubby thumb, his eyes trained nervously on the hallway beyond.

"Jack! Haha. Dolly. Are we going up or down?"

"Up."

"Haha. Okay." He cracks his knuckles like a nervous lunatic, then wipes his sweaty forehead with his cuff. He's like a slice of American cheese left out on the counter—always a greasy, damp sheen collecting on his skin.

"What are you two talking about?"

"Travel."

"Oh," Doug says, intimidated. His idea of travel is a nice, safe beach resort, or a Caribbean cruise where his intrepid peregrinations see him migrating between the buffet and the toilet.

I connect eyes with Dodi. "So dreary and gray here in the winter. But . . . the waterboarding in Guantánamo Bay this time of year . . ."

Doug's eyes light up.

"That sounds about right! I love beach vacations—waterboarding, waterskiing—anything in the water, sign me up, eh?"

"I'm sure Jack would be happy to do some waterboarding with you anytime," Dodi says. Always so quick on her feet, dear Dodi is. But not as quick as me. Her next gift has been piecing itself together in my head this whole time. I smile pleasantly at her, and she frowns. Nothing good ever came from one of my smiles.

"As a matter of fact, Dolly's next trip is a work trip," I say.

Dodi makes a small noise and Doug's grin slips. "Oh?" I can see him shuffle through the cluttered, crumb-filled pockets of his brain. *Gas station receipt, candy wrapper, used Q-tip—here we are, list of goings-on that I need to be aware of. Nope, nothing here—*

He coughs.

"The conference in Las Vegas this week? Have to spend all that unused training money, and—well, you know all about it." I give him ass-kissing smile number twenty-three, his favorite. I glance at Dodi, and her expression is blank surprise.

"Oh." Pieces of dried out chewing gum rattle around in Doug's head. "*Oh.*"

"We'll need to get the reservations made today."

"Right. Right! Yes." He claps one damp hand on my shoulder. "Talk to Sara." He squeezes my shoulder and summons a paternal expression. But he can't think of anything else to say. The doors open to allow newcomers, and without checking which floor it is, he bolts out.

"What the fucking fuck," Dodi hisses.

The newcomers are engrossed in their office politics and aren't paying us any attention. Dodi stares at me with wide eyes. That look is back, the one she had when she was sitting in the bottom of Grant's shower, realizing I'd put together a serial killer playdate for her. Disbelief, and some other big suppressed emotion. Some people wear their feelings on their sleeve; Dodi keeps hers shoved under the floorboards beneath her bed.

"So. Las Vegas," I whisper to her.

"What conference is this?"

"Any conference. Las Vegas is a conference destination."

We exit at our floor, and Dodi speed-walks down the hall to the annex, her heels firing like bang snaps as she goes. I lengthen my gait to keep up.

"I can't go to Las Vegas this week."

She doesn't say she can't go to Las Vegas. Just not this week.

"Why not?"

"It's too short notice."

"It's perfect timing. A way to get out of Cynthia's sight line."

Dodi shakes her head and smooths one eyebrow in annoyance.

I tally it finger by finger. "Complete some bogus training seminar. Come back and feed Doug a line about the new 'strategies' you're going to 'implement.' Create a busywork project. Insert yourself into his fold. Get your performance review and raise. Gray-rock Cynthia."

The metronome popping of her heels skips a quarter of a beat as she takes this in. It's the only indication I've said something interesting to her.

"Hire a cat sitter, pack your bags, and come with me to Las Vegas."

She swirls in the doorway to her office, her hand on her doorknob, and faces me. "I'd have to go with *you*?"

"Yes."

There's the slightest flush to her cheeks. "I don't know. My doctor's warned me about picking up parasites during travel."

I've won. I know I've won. I take one step closer to her.

"You might even have fun."

Her lips twitch and her nostrils flare. "Do I look like the sort of person who has fun?"

"I'll make you experience things you've never felt before."

She lifts her chin and tilts her head, and she sways a little closer to me. I take all this in. I take another step closer to her until I'm practically standing in the doorway with her.

"I'm sure most women have felt nauseous and regretful before," she says.

I've won, she's mine, she's coming. I'm humming along in highest gear now. Dodi, all to myself for a few days.

Her cheeks are pink and her eyes bright. I lean in just a little closer, and she leans in just a little closer too—and shuts her office door in my face.

While Dodi ices me out for the rest of the day, furiously

hammering away at her laptop, I book plane tickets with Suru, make hotel reservations, and when I have a private moment at my desk, purchase two tickets to the *Murderers at Work: Dead in Las Vegas* event.

Gifts are overrated. The trick is to give *experiences*.

15

Kill Bill

JAKE

I BORROW ONE OF GRANT'S CARS TO GET TO THE AIRPORT. I TAKE A KEY FOB AT random and click it repeatedly in the basement parking until I find the car it belongs to: red, and fast-looking. Dodi will like it. There's an accident on the way to her apartment building, and after crawling only two blocks in fifteen minutes, I turn onto a side street and coast down a residential road, hang a left, and then drive parallel to the main road.

But then on autopilot, I turn right, past the dog park, the running path that leads to the beach, the weird, artsy private school for the posh kids—and there it is: *his* street.

I have plenty of time. I can indulge myself. I prowl down the quiet lane, all massive chestnut trees and narrow concrete sidewalks shifted around by the roots underneath. In the summer this street is a tunnel, the sky closed off by the branches above, the sunlight sifting through the leaves like green gold. The houses are big and old, brick and cedar shingle and deep verandas and massive shrub roses. The house in question is shabbier than the others. It's been years since he was able to get up on a ladder and strip the creeping ivy off the porch.

I come down here sometimes, just to check. Just to make sure he's still—

I slam the brakes in time to avoid killing the elderly man who has stepped out onto the road from behind an SUV with tinted windows.

"For fuck's sake!" I shout at no one. The old man turns, and it's him, of course. Stooped, white-haired, craggy-faced. He'd have a grandfatherly look if he ever smiled, but I don't think he has much to smile about these days.

"What are you doing out here?" I say through my lowered window. He's not dressed for the weather—a thin bathrobe and slippers. You have to be fucking kidding me.

"My bin's making off," he says, scowling, pointing to where a garbage can is rolling down the road ahead of a strong wind. I park the car and jog after it. When I return with it, he's staring at me, confused, like he recognizes me, but not where from. It's unsettling. I avert my face.

"Where do you want this?"

He opens the tall gate at the side of the house, ushers me in, and I deposit the can next to a recycling bin.

"I have to go," I mutter, still not looking at him. The gate has swung shut, so I push it, but it won't budge. I grip the handle and rattle it. Then I notice the padlock.

I turn, and the old man is staring me down with a grim face. He's eighty if he's a day, frail and shaky. One bare leg is swollen, and his back is stooped, but somehow in his expression I can see him as he was when he was a younger man. Scrappy, bold. Not afraid to get in a fight. One hand is balled into a fist at his side.

"What do you want?" he asks.

"What do *I* want? I want you to unlock this gate."

He shakes his head at me. "I recognize you from the video."

He's not making any sense. Dementia? But then he raises one gnarled hand and points, and I follow his gaze to a camera on the corner of the neighbor's house.

That's new.

"They showed me." He speaks slowly, like he has all the time in the world, although at his age, he really doesn't. "Snooping through my mailbox, prowling around my yard, peering in my windows. Three times in the past two weeks since they set them up. Gave me your plate number, too."

"I have no idea what you're talking about."

"Burglars and murderers case out their targets before striking. Which are you? Might as well make it easy for you. Here's my house, doors unlocked. And here I am, a lonely, doddering old senior with no family. If you kill me, it would be good timing. It will be at least a week before anyone notices that I didn't take my recycling out for pickup."

"You're confused. I don't have time for this." I consider the height of the fence. Six feet at least, but with a foot on top of the weedy flower planter, I could get over.

"Neighbors have a German shepherd," he says, as if reading my mind. "Not a smart idea."

No fence-jumping, then. He and I consider each other, then he stumps up the steps to his side door and points his cane inside. "May as well make a proper visit of this."

A good serial killer has the good manners to keep it personal, and it's an invitation I can't turn down. I follow him inside the house—the house I've been so curious about. A TV is playing somewhere I can't see, and canned laughter erupts as the door closes behind me. It looks different from inside, the clutter and dust more apparent. It hasn't been properly cleaned in a very long time.

Down a little doglegged hall with creaky floors, past an open door—there it is, the TV, in a room that looks like a nest. There's a pillow and a blanket on the armchair, a stack of old books on a table to one side, dirty mugs and plates, a little space heater in lieu of a properly functioning furnace. No wellness checks here.

At the back of the house is the kitchen, and there he heaves himself down into a chair by the table, where there's a new coffee maker fresh out of its Amazon box. He pokes it contemptuously with the handle of his cane.

"Neighbors ordered this for me. I'd offer you coffee before you murder me, but I can't figure it out." The old, battered coffee maker on the counter is from the nineties and has one toggle switch. This one has as many buttons as a graphing calculator.

Next to it a finished crossword rests on the table. A small plate freckled with toast crumbs sits nearby. I bet he uses that same plate every day. I pan around a little, trying to steal just a bit more from this moment while I can. Bottles of medicine in a jumble by the sink. A pair of broken reading glasses on the counter, held together by tape. Is anyone helping him from day to day?

"Help yourself, kid. It's just stuff. It's all going to a landfill when I croak. They'll scrape my remains off the linoleum, and then they'll toss everything into a bin and take it away. I have no family, so the house will revert to the city. In a few years the neighbors won't remember the name of the stooped old wanker who lived by himself and forgot to tie the front of his bathrobe when the postman rang."

He swivels a little in his chair and points through the doorway.

"My TV is twenty years old, and I haven't seen the remote in two years. It's been on this whole time. Mary's jewelry and silverware went to her nieces in the States, so there's none of that here. I have about a hundred dollars cash in that drawer right there. I don't remember if there's anything good upstairs—haven't set foot up there since my knee surgery. So when you're ready, one swift crack to the back of the head, right here—and make it count, please—and then have fun rifling through my stuff."

It's not *his* stuff I want to rifle through. There are probably boxes shoved into an old childhood room, upstairs. My eyes fall onto a yellowed newspaper clipping stuck to the fridge. A picture of a smiling, handsome man with dark hair and glasses, and two paragraphs of text below it: an obituary. He catches me staring.

"That's my son. He was only a little older than you when he died. A bludgeoning on the back of the head would beat how he went. Degenerative neurological condition. It was awful, once it started. Numbness." He raises one gnarled hand and waggles his fingers at me to show where the numbness started. "And then he lost function bit by bit, until he was trapped in his own body. A terrible way to die. You young men think you're indestructible, but you're not—unless you get to my age, and you realize you're one of the unlucky few who are. Hereditary. It's a good thing he never had kids."

On cue, the sitcom audience laughs uproariously in the next room.

He twists his head like an old vulture and peers at the photo. "I wish I had more photos. I never thought I'd live so long I'd forget the color of my son's eyes, but there you go."

"What time do you drink your coffee?"

I press buttons until the coffee maker is programmed to

run at the time. He tells me. When I look up, he's staring at me with a bemused expression.

"Change out the grounds when you're done and it'll be ready the next morning for you," I tell him.

"You're a very helpful murderer." He squints his eyes shut and scratches his hairy ear. "Hazel. They were hazel."

Applause erupts from the TV in the next room.

"What are you really here for?" he asks.

I've stayed too long. Dodi will be wondering where I am.

"I have to go, Bill," I say, and he raises his bushy eyebrows when I use his name. He never told it to me.

I walk out of the kitchen, down the dim hallway. There are faded family photos on the walls—many of them of that young man with the glasses, from babyhood to adulthood—and I let myself out the front door. I lock it from the inside before I close it.

16

Paper Pusher Expert

DODI

JAKE WILL BE HERE ANY MINUTE AND I'M NOT EVEN PACKED. I DUMP THE CON-
tents of my laundry basket onto the sofa and turn down the
volume of the TV to a companionable murmur.

*"He said he was going to the roof for a smoke? I didn't
even know he smoked. That was the last I saw him. Well, until I found him on the pavement . . ."*

It's a two-night trip, so mathematically that's six pairs of
underpants, five socks, and an entire box of condoms, un-
opened, still piping hot from the pharmacy. I imagine a security guard unzipping my bag in full view of Jake. I bury the
box at the bottom of my carry-on and layer it with my underwear.

*". . . from a height of five hundred feet, death would have
been immediate upon impact . . ."*

I decide not to bring pajamas. Sleeping is not on the itinerary. If I need to wear something to bed, I'll borrow one of his
shirts, and I'll leave a giant lipstick smudge on it somewhere.
I'll leave lipstick smudges in a lot of places this trip.

He's so pale. I bet he turns all blotchy and pink during sex.

The outfits are harder to pick. Something understated, corporate, and concealing for the seminar, obviously, but I count two nights on the town. I pad into my bedroom and pull dresses off the hangers and throw them on my bed. He's already seen the red one, and the tan bandage one. The rest are black, black, black, and another black—

"... *the police ruled suicide. The victim had been the target of an internal corporate investigation, which had ultimately found him blameless, but his wife says the stress* ..."

He likes me in black, though. And black is an appropriate color for the purpose of this trip. Somber. Funerary. Sexy. The color of mourners and dominatrices. I select two.

The laptop will stay at home. I finished my last assignment ahead of schedule. Surely I can take a break for two nights. I've been a servant of two masters for long enough. Well, three. My neighbor had been willing enough to reprise the role of sitter.

"... *patently the stupidest theory I've ever heard. The Paper Pusher is an urban legend.*"

It's a compact bag. Just big enough to stuff a dead man into, and a few outfit changes, too.

"*No. That's absurd. It wasn't a murder. You know what they found up there? A paper airplane. The idiot was on the roof test-flying a goddamn paper airplane when he fell. If that's not time theft* ..."

I barely manage to zip my bag closed, and my eyes fall on the entire purpose of this trip, still sitting on the coffee table. *Jesus.* I unzip my bag and start over.

"*Are you telling me people don't fall to their death in other cities too? Maybe you're saying each city has a Paper Pusher. Or maybe the Paper Pusher goes on working vacations. Ha!*"

I press my fingers into my temples. I've waited so long to take this trip. I can't decide if it's better or worse that Jake is coming.

The documentary is almost over. True crime has always been my drug of choice when life gets too real. I sit on the sofa and crank the volume. I've watched it fifty times, but something's been teasing at my brain these past few days. I study the men's faces fading in and out, one after another, studio portraits, clipped family photos, close-ups of obituaries, every one of them a fall death in the downtown core, some dating back fifteen years.

"Police are still reluctant to draw a link between these deaths, but it's impossible to accept they are unrelated. The only thing we know about the Paper Pusher for sure is he's still at work."

The view changes: the foot of a downtown skyscraper appears, and the camera slowly pans up, the building rising proud and erect like a shiny glass phallus.

"You fucking *idiots*," I whisper at the TV. "It's obviously a 'she.'"

17

Departed

JAKE

I PRESS THE BUZZER TO DODI'S APARTMENT. THERE'S A CRACKLING SQUEAL and then—

"Hello?"

It's the most unfriendly hello in the world.

I barely recognize her when she comes down. She's covered up, as usual, but in casual clothes. She seems strangely small in sneakers and joggers, her sweatshirt swallowing her whole. She slings her black weekend bag into the back seat, something hard making a *thunk* when it hits a buckle, and then she curls herself into the door of the car with her phone. I sort through conversation starters. *Someone else thinks I'm a serial killer too.* I wonder what she would think of Bill. I wonder what she'll think of the *Murderers at Work* tickets. I wonder why on earth she agreed to go to Las Vegas with me. I wonder why on earth *I* wanted to go. But I know why. Dodi is a speck

of vibrant color in a gray world. A controlled substance caus-
ing fireworks in a serotonin-depleted brain. I'll keep coming
back to press the lever like an addicted lab rat in a wire cage
until I die of exhaustion.

She doesn't talk to me during the drive. She doesn't talk to
me while I park. She doesn't talk to me during check-in. I almost touch her elbow when we pass the escalator that would
lead to arrivals. I could take her down, show her the chair I
left Katrin in. It would break the spell, and she'd turn to me
with a smile like I'd delivered another dirty joke.

She makes a point of taking the security lane farthest from
me, and I watch from one aisle over as she twitches and chews
her thumb while her bag passes through the scanner. A TSA
agent curls his finger at her and unzips her bag with gloved
hands.

"What do you mean, what is it? What does it look like to
you?" she snaps. And surprisingly, the agent raises his hands
and backs off. She zips her bag furiously and stomps her feet
into her sneakers. She scowls when she sees me watching.

She's a closed fist wrapped around who knows what, and
she's always been a puzzle to pry apart, one finger at a time.
But it occurs to me, slowly, uncomfortably, that maybe she
didn't want to go to Las Vegas *with me*. She wanted to go
badly enough to tolerate me tagging along.

I leave her and find a seat by the gate. I have two more
missed calls from Andrew. I delete the voicemails without listening to them.

I lose track of her until boarding, and she's already seated
at the window when I get to our row, eyes riveted on the tar-
mac. Her bag has been forced into the too-small under-seat
stowage in front of her, like she can't bear to part with it. I

stow my own carry-on above and snap the overhead storage shut. When she hears the click, she startles and looks at me.

I've had time to regroup. I'm the facilitator of work vacations, bearer of mutilated dolls. I bring value to our working partnership.

"What did you do with the last Christmas gift?" I ask when I slide in next to her.

"She needed to cool her head."

"Next to the ice cream?"

"Next to the other decapitated head."

"Did you—"

"Are you going to talk to me for this entire flight?"

Closed fist. She puts in her earbuds and fixes her attention on the window, and there her attention stays as we take off, ascend, and glide through the gathering evening. The sky turns liquid blue outside, then inky, and the lights of the cabin shut off, and a handful of individual reading lights flick on one by one. Our row stays in darkness. And then I realize Dodi is asleep.

I watch her profile. I watch her face when her head lolls toward me. And then I watch our blurry reflection in the seat screen in front of us, when she slumps over and smooshes her face into my shoulder. I stay still as a statue. I can smell her hair, and hear the tinny rattle of a podcast playing in her earbuds. I wonder if this counts as Dodi letting her guard down.

The plane banks lazily just after midnight and I glimpse the sprawling sparkle of Las Vegas through Dodi's window. We circle round and round. And we keep circling. Round and round and round . . . And then a voice rasps over the speaker.

"*There are some issues on the ground at LAS. We're waiting for instructions and we appreciate everyone's patience.*"

Minor murmuring gives way to gasps and groans as everyone consults their phone.

"Bomb threat!"

"We're not going to be able to land. Can we call—"

"The whole airport has been evacuated—"

We circle for another fifteen minutes, and then the voice returns.

"*We're being directed to land at—*"

Howls erupt, and Dodi twitches.

"That's a three-hour drive from Las Vegas. Are you *kidding* me," someone behind me huffs.

When the lights come on as the plane begins its descent, Dodi asks, groggily, "Are we there?"

"No. We're doing an emergency landing at a different airport. We're three hours away."

She stares at me. She pinches sleep out of the corners of her eyes. She looks around the airplane.

"Is this some Podunk little airport in East Jesus Nowhere? Because everyone here is going to need a rental car."

I realize she's right. Her face hardens.

"Get your bag," she says to me, undoing her belt.

"What?"

When the plane rolls to a stop, Dodi slithers across my lap with her bag in a vise grip and darts down the aisle.

"Move it!" she shrieks.

There are other planes landing, too: even more competition for rentals. Dodi sprints through the night, and I kick up my heels to follow. We smash through a pair of double doors, round a corner, pelt past the baggage claim, and there, glimmering like a beacon, is a dingy **Avis** sign. There are other people making their way there too. The groggy agent's eyes widen when he sees us all barreling toward him.

Dodi slams to a stop against the counter like a baseball player stealing home.

BY THE TIME WE HAVE A RENTAL SECURED, THERE'S A LINE FIFTY PEOPLE DEEP. Dodi leads the way out to the parking lot. She's smoldering. She's vibrating. Whatever diabolical energy she packed for this trip is coming out in lashings now.

"It's a silver Nissan Rogue," she barks at me. "What's the license plate number?"

I consult the paperwork.

"P-M—"

"B?"

"No, *P*—"

"Use call signs!"

"Pterodactyl, mnemonic, three—"

"Fuck's sake!" She whirls on me, panting, her hair clinging to her clammy forehead. "Three as in 'T' or the number?"

She's a wreck. A nasty little creature with its foot caught in a bear trap. I reach out and take her heavy bag from her, and her whole body sags with relief when I do. She looks hard at my hand on the handle of her bag.

"Click the key fob."

She stares stupidly at the fob in her hand. She presses a button and the car next to us beeps.

"You need food," I say. "You're too tired to drive. I'm tired too. We can stay in a motel somewhere."

She turns to face me and her eyes glitter dangerously in the night. We've been on the ground for half an hour now, but as I look at her murderous expression, there's that fairground feeling again. Falling, falling, not sure where solid ground is.

"I need to get to Las Vegas," she grinds out.

This is where a normal, boring person asks why.

But I'm not normal. I'm the calm serial killer who doesn't raise an eyebrow at his victim's histrionics. I'm the stranger with secrets who doesn't ask questions. The con artist who procures plane tickets and executes devious plans. The boy who reaches out to hold a girl's hand and is delighted to find a closed fist. *This* is why Dodi is letting me tag along.

"Please," Dodi whispers.

No. She's not just letting me tag along.

She needed me to take her to Las Vegas. She couldn't do it on her own.

My exhaustion vanishes. I stow her bag in the trunk of the car while she peels off her sweaty pullover and throws it on the back seat. I take the keys from her and we hurtle down a dark highway, engine keening, music blaring. She lowers the windows, and the wind assaults her hair, and she screams the lyrics to Johnny Cash and Elvis at the top of her lungs. I feel light. I feel free. I feel like a helium balloon slipping away, and my real life is the shrinking child throwing a tantrum on the ground as I soar up, up, up . . .

I feel *alive*. I always come alive around Dolores. Grant and Andrew and my temp job—and *everything else*—are someone else's problems.

"I will make you *hurt* . . ." she sings.

I press the pedal to the metal and slide into the far left lane, speeding up even faster, passing two cars on our right. We have to pass everyone. We're too full of purpose to tolerate anyone in front of us. We're going to *Las Vegas*.

The sky is dark and starry and huge. We drive for hours, or years, until we spot an unearthly glow on the horizon. It burns brighter, and brighter, until the sprawl of Las Vegas materializes underneath.

18

Dead on Arrival

DODI

I SURFACE BY DEGREES.

Scratchy fabric on my cheek. Light against my face. The stirrings of something warm and living beside me.

Timeless, placeless, a little bubble between sleep and wakefulness, and for a moment I don't know who is lying next to me, or which timeline I'm in.

Jake.

The bubble pops silently.

I'm in a Las Vegas hotel room.

I'm in a Las Vegas hotel room, lying crosswise on a bed in yesterday's clothes, the next afternoon's sunlight shining through my eyelids.

I'm in a Las Vegas hotel room in bed with Jake.

Jake, who brought me here. Jake, who put up with my shit all day yesterday. Jake, who is patient, who understands. It's been a long time since I've had understanding.

I creep up onto one elbow and blink the sleep from my eyes.

He lies beside me with his hands clasped over his chest like a corpse in a coffin, his face pale, peaceful, dreamless.

I touch his cheek, rough with stubble, and I lean close and hover there, a hair's breadth from his lips.

He's not breathing.

My stomach drops out for one second before an almost imperceptible tremor flickers across his closed eyelids, then settles. He's awake. He hasn't opened his eyes yet and he's already playing games.

"Are you dead? I know a trick for that." I give him a slow, deliberate kiss, a kiss to wake Snow White, a kiss to put the pink back into his corpse-pale skin. His eyelids flutter open, and he stares at me from close range. He looks different without his glasses. His face is strangely exposed, his eyes larger. He's stupidly handsome. I want to fillet his face off and wear it myself. Watching a man mince around with cheekbones like that is like watching a toddler play with a steak knife. He has no idea how much damage he can inflict.

"Your eyes are green," I whisper.

"Hazel," he whispers back sleepily. "Like my dad's."

"No," I say. "Green."

He shakes his head. I trail my hand down his face, neck, chest, stomach . . . I slip my hand into his pants . . .

He tenses. "What are you doing?"

I pull out his wallet. "Grave robbing." I slide out his driver's license and inspect it. "Green," I say. "Case settled." I learn his birthdate, finally. The age gap isn't too weird, I suppose. I toss his wallet onto the bed.

He just lies there, watching me.

"You're a real pillow princess, aren't you?" I spread my hand across his throat, and squeeze.

19

Desecration of a Corpse

JAKE

"DEFINITELY A PULSE," SHE SAYS TO THE SIDE OF MY FACE, RELAXING HER hold. "I was worried for a minute."

She's thinking about death now. I'm always thinking about death. I could turn my head slightly and whisper my secret in her ear. But instead she sits up and from this short distance her face is a blur. Everything is a blur. I skim the bedspread for my glasses, but they don't turn up.

"Why are you wearing your gloves, weirdo? We're in the middle of a desert."

I glance down. I have no idea when I put them on. "It's the air conditioning. It's freezing."

"Should be perfect for the Iceman."

She's not cold, apparently. In one fluid motion she slides on top of me and peels off her shirt. She's in soft focus above me.

I feel like we skipped a few steps.

She tugs the tip of each finger, one by one, and removes my gloves for me. I flex my fingers experimentally. I can't read her face without my glasses. I don't know where to put my hands, so I keep them on my chest.

"Is this part of your virginal Catholic schoolboy mystique?" she whispers. "Touch me."

I don't know where to start, so she starts for me. She takes my hand and places it over her heart, and my fingers twitch to life. I trace the contour of her collarbone, out to her shoulder. I can feel better than I can see. I touch a smudge on her deltoid.

"Colder," she says, and I reverse the direction of my stroke. "Warmer," she says, when my fingers collide with her bra strap. I'm holding my breath again. I brush a lock of her hair over her shoulder, and trail my fingers along the strap, down her back . . .

It's both predictable and surprising, the way my body reacts to hers. It's been so long. I keep calling her a vampire, but I feel like the one drawing my energy from her. It's this feeling of being watered after being left to wilt. I've been dried out like a spore for so long, hibernating, waiting for a reason to come to life, and now here's Dolores. Surprising. Interesting. Vibrantly and unapologetically *alive*.

I forfeit my battle with her bra clasp before I've begun. I bring my hand around her rib cage and touch the blurry blown out candles with twisty ropes of smoke billowing from the wicks—and her breath hitches, like it tickles. *Enough of that.* She threads her fingers through mine and presses my hands into the coverlet on either side of my head, pinning me in place, then flops down on top of me, heavily, and plants her mouth on mine and kisses me, long and slow. No one's ever kissed me like this, like a spider sucking the life from its prey.

When she pulls away, she sets to work on the buttons of my shirt, quickly, and it's too fast for me. My brain hasn't caught up with the moment. I wrap my hands around her wrists to slow her down, and I spot a tombstone tattoo on her inner forearm just in front of my face where I can see it, inscribed with dates. The dates Aunt Laura pointed out. I touch them with my thumb.

Dodi recoils and shakes my hands off. When I look up at her face inches above my own, her expression's changed to a frown. The apex predator sniffing disdainfully at the slimy little amphibian.

She slides off the bed and onto her feet, and across the room I hear the rip of a zipper. Her bag clunks loudly when she drops it on top of the dresser.

"Pretty presumptuous of you to book us one room," she says, rooting around inside. I finally find my glasses on the side table and slide them on.

"I booked us two rooms."

Her hand stills inside the bag. She plucks the room cards off the dresser top next to her bag, and I can see the moment she spots the different room numbers on the cardboard sleeves.

"You followed me in here last night—this morning. What time is it?" I ask. It was close to dawn when we arrived.

She stomps into the bathroom, and I lie there, wondering what happened and feeling like an idiot, as usual. The shower starts. Unfortunately I don't have a knife, or Mother's clothes. The clock next to the bed reads one in the afternoon, which means I slept for seven hours. I haven't slept that long in years.

We've missed the first half of the training session. It doesn't matter. I get up and toss our conference lanyards onto the bed. Then I notice Dodi's bag.

The shower is still running. I pick up the bag and weigh it experimentally in my hand. I put it back down on the dresser and it thunks. The zip is open, but the flap conceals the contents. This is different from a retaliatory snoop around someone's work desk. I leave it there.

When she reemerges and barks at me to vacate so she can dress, I have a shower too. When I come back out dressed in the identical, boring white shirt and gray slacks I wear every day, she's turned to the window with her phone pressed to her ear.

"Please make sure she actually eats something. Give her a cuddle for me," she whispers into her phone. A call to her neighbor about her cat. "I'll be home soon." She registers my presence and ends her call without looking at me. She chugs the watery black poison spewed out by the hotel room coffee maker. "What's happening today?"

"The seminar reconvenes in fifteen minutes."

"Reconvenes?"

"We missed the morning."

She doesn't seem to care too much about this. "And then what?"

"And then we go out."

She leans a shoulder against the floor-to-ceiling glass window and peers out. If the glass broke, she'd fall right through.

"Maybe I'll stay in. Get room service. In my room." There's the slightest emphasis on the final two words.

"That would be rude. After I bought you a ticket?"

Her head twitches, as if she catches herself from turning to look at me.

"A ticket?" She says it contemptuously. *A ticket*. Ludicrous.

"It was just something I thought you'd like. An event I thought you'd be interested in."

"Right." She's silent again, still leaning against the glass. I fold yesterday's clothes; zip my bag; put on one shoe; and then the other . . .

"An event," she says spitefully. She slurps her coffee with disdain.

Her curiosity is killing her.

"*Murderers at Work*'s Dead in Las Vegas event." I use a special tone to let her know she's an idiot.

She swivels around and sloshes black dishwater on the carpet. "*Murderers at Work*?"

"Yes. The live event."

She stares at me, uncomprehending. "You listen to *Murderers at Work*?"

"I started."

"Which episodes?"

It's a bizarre question. Am I supposed to list off the numbers of each episode I've listened to? Her harsh angles soften, the line between her eyebrows disappears, and she regards me with an unreadable expression. "Well, this is unexpected. How are we going to incorporate body disposal into our itinerary if you're booking it up with surprises like this?"

But she doesn't seem upset. She's not upset at all. She's a mercurial little monster, and for this split second in time she's on an upswing. I did right. She pushes off from the glass and marches briskly past me in her red-soled shoes. She opens the door and I follow her out, and in the hallway outside we collide with—*Cynthia.*

She blinks owlishly at us. She looks at my damp hair. She takes in the key card in Dodi's hand. She raises one wrist to inspect the time.

Las Vegas hosts thousands of conferences and trade shows each year. So of course Cynthia is here taking her HR conference at the same time we are, in the same hotel that makes its money by stuffing warm bodies into suites and conference rooms to maximum fire-safe capacity. Nature abhors a vacuum. I wonder if she's learning any good tricks. I wonder what the speakers have to say about rooting out and quashing workplace affairs, or handling unprofessional behavior between employees on business trips.

If she's picked up any tips, she doesn't implement them just now. She just stares at me with the same ice-cube eyes as that day in the annex. *Jacob Ripper?* I still can't recollect how we crossed paths before.

Cynthia turns into her room across the hall from ours and the door clicks shut behind her.

Dodi bolts down the hallway and I race to catch up. She smashes the elevator button with one hand.

"What the *fuck*," she hisses.

The doors open and we enter, and I press the button for the second floor.

"She's in the room across from you," Dodi huffs under her breath. "Are you fucking kidding me."

On the second floor there's a crowd—several crowds—all spilling out from different conference rooms, mingling and getting tangled up in one another. A big panel says **Las Vegas 2023 HR Expo**. We're swimming with sharks now. I grab Dodi's hand and tug her across the room. A big menu of lectures on the far wall reads things like **Demystifying the Millennial Employee: Lazy or Under-motivated?** And **Why Work-from-Home Doesn't Work**. We wind down a tortuous hallway, leaving the noise behind, and come to a smaller sign taped to a door:

PIVOT Synergistic Systems Certification

A woman at the door smacks gum and hands us a pamphlet.

WELCOME! This lightweight, custom-tailored and
solution-driven course will equip you with the practical
strategies and problem-solving mindset to confidently
implement transformational change in your
organization within a holistic framework . . .

"What does this mean?" Dodi demands.

"I just hand out the pamphlets," the woman says with the
emotionless eyes of livestock on a transport truck.

Dodi and I take a pair of seats in the back of the room, the
lights dim, and the afternoon session begins. Dodi crosses,
uncrosses, recrosses her legs. She adjusts her purse in her lap.
And then her little elbow presses against mine. She doesn't jerk
away. Slowly, her hand slides from her lap until it rests on the
edge of her chair, pressed close to mine in this packed room,
and a second later, the back of her hand rests against mine
where I've tucked my fingers under my thigh to keep warm.
She keeps her hand there, and I don't register a single thing
said by the speaker for the rest of the afternoon.

20

Paper Plane

DODI

I SMEAR MY LIPSTICK DELIBERATELY, SLOWLY AROUND MY MOUTH, OVERLINING by a hair's breadth, filling the dip in my cupid's bow for a slightly sloppy, sexed-up look. It's easier to kiss a mouth that's already been messed up a bit, and I feel like Jake needs a bit of help. I lean back from the mirror and take a look. I'd fuck me.

I slap my phone and "Goodbye Horses" cuts out. Jake's waiting for me downstairs in the lobby. I'd peered through the crack in the bathroom door as he'd changed his shirt and tie, folded his dirty clothes *just so*, lined up his bag next to the bed *just so*. I bet he has to make the bed and line up the pillows before sex.

It's handy to keep a litany of reasons to reject someone until you're certain they're not going to reject you. But it's a list I might delete after tonight, even if he is the sort of man to sit next to you for three hours without moving his hand a single centimeter to hold yours. Because Jake *is* the sort of man who gifts you a stolen trip to Las Vegas, a ticket to *Murderers at Work*, and a standing offer to dispose of a body. At my point in life, I'm ready for a man who puts in the emotional labor. I slip on my dress and slide my feet into my shoes.

I peer out the window at the writhing city below, and a dark bundle of laundry falls past.

I stare unblinking, ears buzzing. I press myself flat against the glass and try to see down, but I can't.

The bundle of laundry was wearing shoes. I saw shiny patent leather shoes. It was a *man*. A *man* fell past my window.

There's a distant scream—from inside the hotel or out-, I don't know—and my heart jackrabbits delightfully in my chest. I crane to look up, and of course I can't see anything there either. I push off from the glass and I'm out the door in an instant, my heavy purse slapping my hip as I run down to the elevator bank. My finger hovers over the down arrow. An emergency response team will arrive, and I should give a statement—

But where did that man fall from?

How did he fall?

The *Murderers at Work* jingle plays in my head as my finger trails up to the highest number almost on its own, traces the raised metal ring around it, and presses. Hearts to hearts, diamonds to diamonds, and murder weapons to murder weapons. I don't belong downstairs giving a statement. I belong upstairs, making friends with someone even worse than me. The elevator clanks and groans, and I'm launched upward, my guts lagging by a second.

When I step out, I can hear the wail of an ambulance and the indistinct voices of a crowd carrying on down below. The rooftop is poorly lit and I can barely see my own feet as I creep to the north wall and peer over. An emergency response is in full swing on the ground. One floor below me, a woman leans over a balcony, hollering.

"He just went over!" she screams over her shoulder into her hotel room. The drink in her hand sloshes as she swings around. "Did you see him fall?"

He fell off the balcony, not the roof. Some drunk idiot partying in a hotel room met his fate over the edge of a penthouse balcony railing.

I step back from the parapet and stalk across the rooftop to the far side, away from the sirens, and I could be walking across a vast field, gravel crunching underfoot. My shoe collides with something metal—cigarette butts scatter from a can left up here by hotel staff—and I catch myself on the parapet before I stumble. The city sparkles and hums beyond the flat black edge of the rooftop wall. Glitz and seediness, a labyrinth of possibility, a machine that converts money into fun, thrills, and hangovers. Dizzying highs and tragic, careless falls.

In my case, a shot at closure, and a chance to feel alive again. I've always accepted the limitations of this thing between Jake and me. There's no room for him in my real life, and he's made it clear he wouldn't want that anyway. This thing between us is never going to be real life, but it's the most life I've had in years.

I can't believe he got me those tickets. He's really making me face this head-on.

I know exactly how things will play out with Jake tonight. He's been so patient with me. There are things I need to say to him. And, after, there's that thing I need to do. That thing he'll help me do. Something screwed-up, and weird, and definitely not for the faint of heart.

Not everyone is cut out to be an accomplice.

Something scuttles at my feet—and I jump backward when it drags its teeth across the arch of my foot—

I catch my breath when I see it's not some disgusting

American desert roof rodent. It's a piece of folded paper, glowing oddly in the dim light of this city that never goes dark, twitching across the rooftop ahead of the breeze. A bit of trash left out by the rooftop smokers.

I pick it up and trace my finger along the folds, crisp enough to cause a paper cut. I stare out at the beating, glittering heart of this city of chaos and mayhem and, yes, murder, too. I lift my hand above my head and launch the paper airplane into the night.

21

Murderers at Work

JAKE

WHEN DODI STEPS INTO THE LOBBY SHE'S WEARING A DRESS LIKE WIDOW'S weeds—a lacy knee-length black sheath. Her tattoos glimmer dimly through the netting of the sleeves, and her lips are the color of sudden, painful death.

"There's been an accident," I tell her when she's close, jerking my head in the direction of the crowd outside.

"That's too bad," she says disinterestedly, like it's too bad it's just an accident and not something a little more premeditated, and we walk in the opposite direction across the lobby and out into the night.

We traipse along the sensory hellscape that is the Strip, the street crawling with life like a log was rolled away to reveal the wriggling insect city underneath. The sky is already black and bottomless, but everything around us glows, flickers, and gleams, sometimes in gaudy Christmas colors. On all sides, signs compete for our attention and our money, and all around us are idiots who think this is fun. Groups of young people, old people, friends taking selfies, couples holding hands. Dodi studies everything around us like an anthropologist observing a strange cultural phenomenon, and I study her.

Would Dodi snarl in disgust if I reached out and took *her* hand? Or would she squeeze tight, digging her sharp nails into my skin?

Dodi spots the bill for *Murderers at Work* first. She presses ahead, and I follow, showing the tickets to the doorman.

Inside, the stage rises on one side and on the floor are tables. At table sixteen Dodi slings her purse onto a chair and it clunks, but she acts like nothing's amiss, like it's normal to tote bricks around. She orders us cocktails, but she's twitchy all the while, glancing around this way and that, like she expects to see someone she knows. Or be seen by someone she knows.

And then it seems like exactly that happens. A thin, sharp-faced woman at the table just diagonal to us turns and looks directly in Dodi's eyes. Her face flickers in recognition, then slackens into a studied neutral expression. She swivels back around, and next to me, Dodi freezes.

That's when the lights dim. I want to ask her who the woman is, but a clip of familiar music plays, the xylophone jingle at the start of every *Murderers at Work* podcast, and two figures appear onstage in matching shirts that say DEAD IN LAS VEGAS. The room erupts, and one makes a production of casually sipping her cocktail while the other curtseys and smiles bashfully. I don't recognize them until I hear their voices.

"All right, Murderheads," Aya says, and it takes several minutes for the cheering and clapping to die down.

"As you know from reading the giant freaking sign at the door, we're recording tonight, because we're celebrating *five hundred episodes* . . ."

Cheering erupts.

". . . and to kick off, we're going to play Name that Killer!" The room loses it.

Bex continues. "If you've listened to our live event recordings, you know the drill! Each table will send up one representative when called. Send us your best, your funniest, your most dramatic. Act, mime, monologue—whatever you want—and the rest of us . . . will guess the murderer! We can't stop you from using your phones to look up the name, but we hope your sense of self-preservation will compel you to keep that shit in your pocket. After all, we all know about five hundred ways to deal with you if you don't!"

"And," Aya shouts, "look lively! We're going to see how many we can get through in thirty minutes!" She cups her hands around her mouth and hollers, "Table one, GO!"

A woman from table one sprints across the floor toward the stage, and when I glance over, the sharp-faced woman at the table diagonal to us is watching me over her shoulder.

"Who is she?" I ask Dodi. "The woman at that table?"

"No one," Dodi says irritably, and quaffs half her cocktail. I know her well enough to know there's no point in persisting.

"Will you do the Paper Pusher when they call us?" I ask.

Dodi's eyes dart over to the sharp-faced woman, who's no longer watching us. "I can't. They haven't done an episode on her yet."

"'Her'?"

She gives me a look. "It's definitely a woman."

I guess we won't be making jokes about me being the Paper Pusher anymore. But she has no reason to be so certain. The thing is, I know a little more than most about the Paper Pusher urban legend.

A small woman steps up to the mic and the room falls

quiet. She pulls glasses out of her pocket, places them low on the tip of her nose, and says into the mic in a deep, manly voice, "Careful playing Texas Hold'em with me, because my card shark abilities will have you in a *chokehold*—"

"Ed Scully, the Poker Choker!"

The room erupts in cheers and hoots.

"You don't know it's a woman," I tell Dodi.

"I *do* know it's a woman," she says impatiently.

I've been looking forward to revealing that Aunt Laura tidied up four of his "victims," that I temped at three of the offices where the "murders" happened. Her curiosity in me has always been my only angle, and I've been keeping this tidbit in my back pocket to bring out when I needed to.

I lean in to tell her, but she's not paying attention to me. She twitches and huffs, then she pivots, looking at the faces around us, a captivating thought occurring to her. "I wonder how many murderers are in the audience tonight?"

"What?"

"Active ones. Ones that haven't been found out. Ones that got off. Ones that have done their time. They're not all locked up in prison, you know."

"You want to catch one?"

She gives me a disgusted look. "I don't have hero fantasies. I just want to meet one."

"Why?"

"They wouldn't be in a position to pass judgment, would they?" Pass judgment on what? She swivels around, as if looking for one now. "Where else would you go for a bit of appreciation if you were a killer? This podcast glorifies killers, and these people here—they're fans. Wannabes. I could get up there and prove it to you."

There's no need. A man from table two runs up onto the

stage and mimes being trapped in a glass box, to the room's
hooting. These are the people who would have cheered at a
hanging two hundred years ago.

"Jonathan Litsz, the Down-to-Clown Drowner!"

The room bursts into laughter. They're all in on about ten
years' worth of inside jokes. Dodi doesn't laugh.

"Don't you glorify murderers?" I ask. "You marinate your
brain in true crime."

She frowns and drags her elegant fingers down the stem of
her glass, thinking. "Murder is a very difficult thing to do.
Especially when it's the right thing to do. It's easier for people
who are doing it for the wrong reasons."

It's chillingly philosophical in a room full of hooting devi-
ants. Before I can ask her what she means, another man appears onstage. He brandishes an imaginary bag and rings a
doorbell, and instantly, someone yells, "Scott Leipke, the
Door Dash Slasher!"

"What made you think to bring me here?" she asks,
voice low.

"This was the reason you wanted to come to Las Vegas."

Dodi shakes her head, slowly. "I told you the reason why I
needed to come to Las Vegas." She looks me in the eye, like
she's willing me to recall her reason so she doesn't have to repeat herself.

"Right. You need to dispose of a body."

She tips her head to one side, sinuously, exposing her neck
in that Dodi way. I search for a retort, but there's nothing to
work with. She's far too serious.

"You promised you would help me out, if I ever needed."

I wait for a sharp-toothed little smile, but it doesn't come.

"Whose body?" I ask, probing for the other half of her
joke. She's silent, and it doesn't make any sense, but—there's

no way she's just making a joke. She licks her lips and presses them together. She jerks her chin at the room in general.

"My husband would have found this hysterical. He was completely morbid, too. Like you."

I shrink, retract, and freeze at that word: "husband."

"Your . . . husband."

"You've never asked how he died. I wanted to tell you myself, in my own words, but I know you've already figured it out if you brought me here."

I stare at her. I wonder if my face is as expressionless as hers.

"Tell me in your own words," I say. I'm a hand puppet using someone else's voice. "Tell me how he died."

Is that gratitude in her eyes?

"It wasn't natural causes," she says quietly.

The hair on the back of my neck rises.

"Wasn't an accident, either. His death was deliberate. Calculated. Premeditated." Her face is savage as she says this. This is a woman who was wronged. This is a woman who had something stolen from her.

She's a puzzle I've been assembling upside down, feeling pieces out, mashing them together, but now I've flipped one over and finally noticed a picture on the other side that puts them all together.

"Your husband was murdered."

She stares at me with eyes harder than diamonds. "Yes."

In my head a hand reaches out and twists a piece of string around a thumbtack under a photo of a man with blurry, indistinct features.

"And the killer?"

Again, she licks her lips. She's tense. She's a coil wound

tight. Beyond her, the narrow faced woman at the other table glances over again, her gaze sharp and probing.

"Prosecution couldn't pull together a case against her."

The string is pulled taut and the other end is tacked to a Post-it Note—*The killer is a "she"*—

I get a flash of a body falling off a balcony, here, in Las Vegas. The Paper Pusher is a "she." It's something Dodi *knows*. I make eye contact with the strange woman, and she turns away from me.

Dodi continues. "And now she's in Las Vegas, living her best life, in the audience of a true crime podcast live event. What a twisted bitch, right?"

They're not all locked up in prison, you know. Some of them are here tonight, to gloat. The hand scrawls *Paper Pusher* on the Post-it.

Other scraps of paper materialize on the idea board. The bill to the *Murderers at Work* event. The hotel's packed conference calendar, with attendees from all over the continent. We're in Las Vegas to dispose of a body. We're here to take care of the woman who killed Dodi's husband.

"Is the woman at the other table still staring at me?" Dodi asks.

"No."

Dodi lets out a breath.

There are so many questions, but the one that comes out is, "You're capable of murder?"

Relief washes over her face, relief that I've understood her, relief that I made that leap on my own.

"Yes. We all are, Jake. *You're* capable of murder. You just need a big enough reason."

She holds my gaze. I'm in Las Vegas with Dolores dela

Cruz at a *Murderers at Work* event, drinking cocktails, while she asks me to be an accomplice in murder.

"What's a reason big enough for murder?"

Her voice is low, and throaty, and raw. Brittle, and savage, and tender. Her voice is a lot of things. "Love."

The word takes a second to curl up in my ear. It takes a second longer to realize she's called me out. She's seen a shadow inside me that I hadn't even noticed yet, something dark and scary, that twitches from slumber and stretches its limbs and reveals itself to be several times bigger than I thought. She stares at me, and I stare back, and in this noisy, chaotic space, all I see is her. Her face is rimmed with cool light from the stage, ice blue flecks sparkling in her eyes and on her shiny painted lips. She doesn't blink.

I would do anything for her, and she knows it.

"I understand," I say. I understand everything. This twisted flirtation of ours, right from the start—it's been a job interview while she sizes me up, tests my waters, checks to see if I know what I'm doing, and if I can be properly motivated. I'm a body disposal expert, and I've done the job for far lesser reasons. She's wanted something from me all along, and I don't mind. I really don't. She doesn't love me back, and I don't even want her to. I just want her to look at me the way she did when I gave her the doll, when I staged our serial killer playdate, when I made plane tickets to Las Vegas magically appear. I want her to look at me like the boring temp identity is just a disguise, like there's something more to me, something she and I have in common. A secret between the two of us.

"I understand," I repeat.

She sags with relief when I say it. "I thought you would." Her hand materializes over mine under the table, and she squeezes it fiercely, like she's going to wring the blood from it.

"Meeting you was so unexpected, Jake. You knew exactly how to get through to me. You knew I needed to see you're just as strange and twisted as I am. And I still don't know what to make of you. Sometimes I still don't feel ready—you've seen that. And I think I panic or something, and I get so angry. It feels disloyal to him, to move on, and to live my life. But . . ."

She swallows. Painfully, it seems.

"I'm ready now. It took me a long time to get to this point." She presses her lips together. "You made this trip finally happen for me. You snapped your fingers and made it happen. It's time. I'm ready for closure, Jake."

"When?"

"Tonight."

I shiver and nod. "Where?"

"I need some help with that part."

"I'll take care of it for you." I want to say *I'll take care of you.*

"It's something I need to do myself," she says. "But . . . I want you to help me."

"No. You can't. You can't do it," I tell her, and she stares at me, bewildered. "I'll do it. It doesn't matter if I do it."

And then I say it to her. I tell her the secret that's been scratching with splintered claws at the underside of my floorboards. I tell her the secret I haven't told anyone.

"I'm going to be dead soon, anyway."

The room erupts into cheers when I say it, and I startle, but Dodi doesn't even register the noise.

"You're dying," she says. "You're *dying.*"

"Yes."

She pulls her hand back from mine like she's touched fire.

"How long do you have?"

"Table sixteen!" a voice calls out from the stage.

"It doesn't matter," I say. "I'll be around long enough to take care of your husband's murderer."

"'It doesn't matter,'" she echoes. She shakes her head, slowly, stunned. "You're *dying*, and you think . . . you think I want you to kill my husband's murderer."

"TABLE SIXTEEN!" the voice calls again.

Dodi pushes back from the table, and I make to stand, too, but she stops me and slips away in the dark. The woman at the other table watches all this, then leans in and whispers something to her tablemates.

I regret letting her go a second later. I can't see which direction she went in. I don't know if she's coming back. I stand up again, and someone behind me huffs and leans dramatically to one side to let me know I'm an asshole.

"Dodi!" I hiss, and a man shushes me, and—

There she is. Dodi.

I watch her step out of the lip of blue shadow and into the spotlight onstage. She doesn't blink away the light. She scowls into it, clutching her big, heavy purse to her stomach. The woman at the other table goes deathly still.

"Name *this* killer," Dodi breathes into the mic.

The room descends into awed silence. There's something different about this speaker, and everyone feels it in their bones. Faces swivel to her, and in the darkened room, the whites of strangers' eyes glint eerily in the blue light from the stage, like the reflective eyes of night creatures.

"I'm a newlywed, halfway through my MBA, married to a statistician who can count cards. He loves Las Vegas, although I always refuse to go with him for his tournaments. I like to have a few stubborn hills to die on. That's my prerogative. He and I are looking at houses, and thinking about getting a dog, and starting a family, maybe, and life is fucking perfect. There's just one problem: his back hurts."

The people who came before Dodi were comedic, all in, working for their Golden Globe nomination. Dodi on the other hand is a terrible actress, and the room is uncomfortably quiet. No one is standing and pointing. No one is calling out names. It's just Dodi, reciting her piece without inflection. When she stands up there, she's just herself: irritable, bored, vicious. Cruelly beautiful.

"Lung cancer, stage four. We're stubbornly hopeful for a year, even though he's a statistician and he should know better—but then they find brain mets. He feels differently about that. It's different when it's your brain. Your brain is *you*. He gets headaches. He's confused. He can't do numbers anymore. He can't play cards. One day I watch him make a bowl of cereal. He pours the milk first, and then the cereal. I never could get him to pour his cereal first. Weird, right? But no, the really weird part is that he got the bowl down from the shelf last, after pouring the milk and cereal onto the countertop.

"He looks at me and tells me, 'I'm done.' There's going to be too much pain. Too much loss of dignity. Too much loss of control. Too much for me, his wife, who is visibly cracking. He and I are becoming different people. He's turning into a stranger as his brain gets sicker and sicker, and I'm turning into whoever I need to be to get through this. The problem is, he's too weak to do it himself. So he turns to me."

The entire room is holding its breath. It's so quiet I feel like everyone around me must be able to hear my heart knocking in my chest.

"You Murderheads really suck tonight," Dodi breathes into the mic. "Episode sixty-three?"

It's not that no one recognizes the killer from her monologue. It's that they *all* recognize her. The thin-faced woman at the table diagonal to ours stands, and everyone turns to watch as she raises her arm to point at Dodi, specter-like.

She takes a deep breath, and the bottom falls out of my stomach when she says, "Dolores dela Cruz, the Blackjack Widow!"

22

Body Disposal

DODI

I'VE FINALLY HAD A CHANCE TO PLEAD MY CASE. FOR A FULL MINUTE I THINK I've succeeded in ruining their fun, but then a breathless, murmuring chatter breaks out. *A murderer! A murderer amongst us!*

"It's *her*. It's definitely *her*," a voice just below the stage says. "I recognize her from that news article—"

"Holy shit. *Holy shit*."

"Can we get her autograph?"

The room has gone wild, and they all want a piece of me. Twisted degenerates, the lot of them. I pan the crowd, and in the busy, moving mass Jake sticks out, still as a statue. Lips parted, expression blank, the image of a man spun around and dropped in a world where up is down. It's that frozen audience of one that gives me stage fright. He looks at me like he's seeing me for the first time.

I'm rocked, the way I was five years ago when a random email with a link to a podcast fell into my inbox. I'd had a lot of feelings, which was interesting because I'd sworn off feelings—although what else could I do upon discovering the worst moment of my life was entertainment to a bunch of strangers?—but after having been alone for years by then, a social pariah, a hermit, I suddenly had company. I had people. Very sordid, fucked-up people, like me. I listened to podcast after podcast. They were out there, flying under the radar, passing by like sharks swimming in dark water. People who wouldn't judge me. People who would understand. If I could find one single person, I'd settle for that.

I thought I'd found him. Not a murderer, but someone who understood.

I step back into the shadows. There'll be an exit somewhere back here, behind the stage curtains—*there*. One robotic step and another before I pick up my pace. I'm running by the time I reach the exit. The fire alarm triggers when I slam through the door and burst out into the night like a bat out of hell.

"Wait!" A voice follows me as I pelt down the sidewalk. My shoulders knock into tourists, and someone's drink splatters on the ground near my feet.

"Dodi—"

I push at the crowd in front of me and become ensnared in a writhing mass of elderly ladies all wearing pink shirts with flamingos on them, posing for photos in front of the Bellagio Fountains, now frothing and spurting all over the fucking place. I whirl on the spot when a hand touches my elbow.

"*What?*" I shriek.

Jake recoils a step and bends over, hands on his knees, breathless from the pursuit. It occurs to me I'm panting too.

"Dodi—"

"Don't call me that!"

"I didn't know—"

"You knew!" I shout. "You *knew*!"

It comes out sounding feral.

"That day on the roof, you told me I was a ghost. It was like someone finally *saw* me. You *knew* what I was going through. You lost your parents—you know about loss—ever since he died, I've felt like I died too—I'm just—haunting the living—unfinished business—" My breath catches in my chest, and it's a moment before I can speak again. "You *knew*. I told you. I *told* you I was a widow. You told me—you told me you knew about the secret I keep in plain sight on my desk. You got me tickets to their show. You *knew*."

Jake stares at me. He didn't know.

I feel like I've been mugged. Something precious and special I kept clasped in one fist since that day on the rooftop has been stripped from my possession. Another person's understanding. Another person's acceptance.

Another *person*—full stop. He's *dying*. I could fucking kill him.

If he's looking at me like that, I've already lost him. I turn on the spot within the throng of flamingo ladies.

"I'm glad you did it," he says, voice raised over the cackling hubbub of the Flamingo Squad. I freeze, and turn back.

"Not *glad*," Jake amends, voice dropping. He opens and closes his mouth. "I'm dying," he says quietly, and I wouldn't hear the words if I couldn't also see his lips moving. It's almost experimental the way he says it, like he hasn't had practice with the phrase. He holds his hands to show me: ghostly white fingers, like they were during our serial killer date.

"It's a degenerative neurological condition. It's hereditary. There's no cure. No treatment. I'm twenty-nine. If what happened to my dad is anything to go by . . ." He trails off. "It's going to be bad," he says simply.

My chest squeezes into itself like a black hole compressing. This handsome, healthy man. Not so healthy. I really know how to pick them.

"He was lucky to have you help him," Jake says.

I can't speak.

He reaches to touch me, but what's the point? He's dying. I twist and pull away.

"Where are you going?" he asks.

"I have things to do." There was a reason I needed to get to Las Vegas. I wriggle between two women craning their phones to take photos they will never look at again and reach into my bag to make sure the token is still there—yes—but it spins out of my grasp when I pull my hand from the bag. It flips through the air, glinting with reflected light, and lands somewhere on the pavement at my feet. Jake beats me to it. He gets down on one knee and locates it in a crack between the pavers. When he finds it, he holds it up and peers at it.

Around us strangers step back, turn, gasp, and point their phones at us. Jake and I freeze and watch the crowd around us with alarm.

"He's proposing!" a flamingo woman shrieks to her silver-haired friends. "He's *proposing*!"

Jake's mouth falls open and I grow roots. The old girls press close around us, yowling their delight, penning us in as securely as a prison fence with their enormous magenta bosoms, all the while the fountain blaring "Dance of the Sugar Plum Fairy," the silver and blue light flashing gaudily—and I'm convinced this is limbo, and we both died just now, and he and I are probably trapped here in this claustrophobic bubble of sensory torture forever when—

"Say yes!" another woman shrieks in my ear. Her friend jostles me from the other side. *"Say yes!"*

I snatch the token from Jake's hands and the Flamingo Squad claps and squeals and flaps their hands.

"Wait till I show Ruth what she missed!" the original silver-hair gasps from behind her phone, recording the whole thing.

Jake quickly stands and leads me with an icy cold hand to a deserted vantage nook by the fountain. His face is painted in the gaudy lights of the display, the reflections in his glasses obscuring his eyes. We're quiet for a moment. My heart is still pounding in my chest. I wonder what his heart is doing.

"Why did you need to come to Las Vegas?" he says at last.

It's amazing how many times I have to repeat myself. I place my bag on the ground, unzip it, and pull out a square stone vase. The one he's seen on my desk at work. I hand it to him. "Unfinished business."

It takes him a moment to understand what he's holding: the secret I've been keeping in plain sight.

"He wanted his ashes scattered somewhere in Las Vegas," I say.

Jake raises his eyes to mine, understanding everything, finally. He really does see me this time.

I bite my cheek. "You're the body disposal expert, aren't you?"

23

A Vampire in Vegas

DODI

JAKE TWISTS THE URN IN HIS HANDS.

The fountain display has ended and the Flamingo Squad has stampeded off in search of other shenanigans, leaving us quite alone. A warm desert breeze buffets a light mist over us as the lights of the display dim, leaving us lit in a green, phosphorescent glow, and it's eerily, strangely beautiful for a split second as the two timelines of my life touch.

Neil, meet Jake. Jake, this is Neil.

Jake raises his eyes to mine. "How do we do this?" he asks, lifting the urn slightly.

I let out a shaky breath. "I have no fucking clue. That's your wheelhouse. But I have to do something else first."

I show him the silver token still in my fist. I've carried it everywhere with me for the past seven years. "He always brought home a chip from his trips, or a token," I explain. "He'd hang on to it until he could go back, and then he'd pick up at the casino where he left off. He gave it to me to bring back." I look at the fountain next to us. Coins litter the bottom like sparkling fish scales. It would be easy to dispose of it here.

Jake's hand closes around mine before I throw it. "He wanted you to place his last bet for him, then," he says, and I know he's right. He takes it from me and squints to read the tiny words:

CIRCUS
CIRCUS

Jake consults his phone. "Circus Circus is three and a half kilometers from here."

He takes my hand again and leads me to the curb, where he hails a taxi. I squeeze tight. My nails probably bite into the skin on the back of his hand, but he doesn't mind. He shoos me into the cab, and we peel up the Strip, Neil sitting on his knee, the silver token pressed between my palms.

We spill out in front of Circus Circus fifteen minutes later. Inside, the casino is cold and bright and loud. It feels like one of those sleep experiments. Will humans follow a normal circadian rhythm on their own in the absence of diurnal light signals? No. Absolutely not. We will drink and gamble and chase that next burst of dopamine until we drop dead from exhaustion.

Jake takes it all in with a dispassionate glance and looks to me. "What now?"

"I don't know," I say automatically.

"It's just a token for the slots, isn't it?" Jake says.

I know it's for the damn slots. Jake tilts his head, and I follow his line of sight: an old-fashioned machine with a crank handle and real barrels for the reels, with Dolly Parton's busty figure emblazoned on it. As a bonus, it's Dolly from *9 to 5*.

A part of me had thought that maybe I would wander around until I felt drawn to a slot machine—*the* slot machine, the one my husband played. There are only so many of the old-fashioned token slots left here. But instead, Jake's picked out a slot machine that winks at the two of us and our inside jokes.

It's no matter. I have to lose this token and get this part of the evening over with. I slide it into the slot . . . and I don't have to pull the crank, do I? I got rid of it. I've stashed my bad luck away in a game of chance, and someone else is welcome to it. It's the cursed artifact in a horror film, and the bad mojo can go home from Las Vegas with them, not me.

"You forgot to pull the crank," Jake says as I step away from the machine. Before I can stop him, he does it for me.

"I was going to leave it," I say as the reels begin to spin.

"Why?"

"I was never much of a gambler." Not like Neil. If Neil were here, he'd be able to tell me the house odds of every single bet at every single game.

Beyond Jake's shoulder, one Dolly head rolls into place.

"It's just a slot machine," he says. "You put a token in, and if you win—"

Unbelievable. "I know how a slot machine works. I know how to play every game of chance here. Neil made sure of that."

Beyond him, the second reel rolls to a halt. There's something wrong with this machine.

Two Dolly heads.

"Do you?" Jake looks at me like he's spotted a new and glamorous facet in me. He pans around the room, taking in the games around us. "Why don't you like gambling?"

"Because gambling is fucking stupid. The system's rigged.

You can't beat the house," I say. It was all about getting the better of the house, for Neil.

You know how to beat the house, Neil? I said to him once. *By not playing. That's the only way to beat the house.* I didn't win more games than Neil, but I lost fewer at least.

Beyond Jake, the third reel slows. I close my eyes, and I must imagine it, but I feel another warm desert breeze—

The ringing starts, and when I open my eyes, I see three Dolly heads. Tokens spill out like oversized wedding confetti.

I cash out at the cage, robotically, where the cashier counts out the tokens and slides a single greasy hundred-dollar bill across the counter to me, the dirtiest transaction I've ever been involved in. I lead the way outside, and we're off, into the crawling, sparkling night. I breathe deeply, huffing the night air, heart racing.

A little silver token of love from a dead man, carried in purse and pocket for seven years, finally flung out into this noisy, ugly wishing well of a city where the strangest things come true. Definitely not the wish you asked for. I miss the token. But I'm so relieved it's gone. It's the same feeling I had when Neil finally passed. I missed him, more than anything, and I was so *relieved*—nobody ever talks about the relief. All the suspense and dread of an unpromising prognosis gone, and just pure, simple grief ever after.

"What do we do with his ashes?" I ask Jake.

"Not yet," Jake says.

"What do you mean, not yet?"

"It's not time."

It's not time. I stop in the middle of the sidewalk, and the world twists around me and past me on an invisible current of fun and life and pleasure that spat me out years ago. I haven't been able to find my way back to it. I've been twirling in an eddy on the fringes looking in ever since, like a ghost shut out by the living. I could scream at the top of my lungs and no one would hear me. I'm ready to rejoin the living.

It's not time.

"He wanted one last night on the town," Jake says. I can read the subtext. He's protective of a fellow dying person's last wish. He stands there, mirroring me, like he too is a ghost the liquid nightlife slips around and through.

"But he isn't here," I say. That's the tragedy of it. He isn't anywhere anymore.

Jake considers me. "Why did you come all the way to Las Vegas?"

"He wanted me to bring him here."

"I think he wanted to bring you here. He wanted *you* to have his last night on the town," he says.

Around me, people laugh and shriek and take photos. Neil loved all this insanity. *Loved* it. And I know Jake is right. The token, the ashes—this wasn't some gesture Neil wanted for himself. He wanted it for me.

He wanted me to come here when I was ready and lose it all. I have to keep playing until it's all gone—until every penny and every speck of dust has been cleared out. Riches to rags. Rebirth on the Las Vegas Strip.

It won't take long, and Jake's here to help me do it. He holds out his hand experimentally, and when I take it, it feels like we're shaking on something.

Inside the Wynn, Jake says, "What about crabs?" He sounds *so* casual.

"You mean craps?"

Are his cheeks pink, or am I imagining it?

"Yes," he says. "What did you think I said?"

I fucking hate craps, and as it happens, I'm pretty good at

it. Good enough to know how to make a bad bet. When the
dealer flips the marker to OFF, instead of asking for tens or
fives or something I can play for a while, I ask for a single
black chip. I place it on twelve, the worst bet on the table, and
in my head I can hear Neil wailing over house edge.

The stick man pushes the dice over to us, and I let Jake do
the honors.

"Take two!" the stick man shouts when Jake mistakenly
picks up all five, and he drops three back onto the green,
which the stick man hooks back in. Jake rattles the dice like
this is Gambling Clichés 101, and he sends them shooting
across the green. They bounce off the far wall of the table
where I can't see them and settle. People hoot and mutter and
groan, and the stick man and the two dealers throw themselves over the table, scooping away lost bets, moving chips,
stacking fresh chips next to winning bets. *Clack, clack, clack.*
The other players start tossing new chips on the table and calling new bets. I tug Jake's sleeve to go.

"Wait," he says. "Your winnings."

For some incomprehensible reason, the dealer nearest us
groups stacks of chips from his bank together—a few thousand dollars, at least—and then slides it across the green . . .
over to us.

My problem has grown thirty times larger in as many
seconds.

"Take down our bet," I shout. "I want you to take down
our bet."

We cash out again. Outside it's cooling off, and I shiver and
walk faster, and Jake places his coat on my shoulders. My
heart pounds in my chest.

"You have good luck tonight," he says.

"There's no such thing as luck," I say contemptuously.

Whether you're playing dice or fighting cancer or losing the genetic lottery to a neurodegenerative disease. Gamblers are superstitious idiots. They spout maxims and philosophies that sound snappy in a fortune cookie, things like *In order to win, you must be willing to lose everything.* I was willing to lose my husband, for his sake. I won nothing.

Jake shrugs, that small, asymmetrical smile appearing. "Surely we both believe in *bad* luck."

Just inside the door of the Venetian, we stop in our tracks to take in a giant spinning wheel of fortune. Gambling for kindergartners. Neil would have despised this. I hand the cash to the dealer, who does a double take and spares a pitying glance for the idiot tourists blowing their money. He spins the wheel, and it's so big it fills my whole field of vision. I feel nauseous watching it. I close my eyes. Twenty-four percent house edge, I remember. It drifts up out of nowhere. And when I open my eyes, the wheel has stopped, and Jake is staring at me like I'm a magician. The dealer, too.

I watch Jake collect from the dealer, handsome dark head bent, taking the cash with those hands I'd recognize anywhere now. My winning streak won't extend to him. I won't win anything in this game with Jake.

My head throbs. I'm feeling frantic and vicious and hurtful.

At Caesar's Palace, I search out a roulette table with a high minimum bet just in time to hear the ball rattle into its groove. The dealer calls out "Five black even!" and everyone around the table groans or sighs or laughs as he wipes the surface clear. I exchange my cash for several neat stacks of purple chips.

The other players have left yellow, orange, and green chips all over the table. Some sit inside the numbered boxes; some sit on the outlines. There are little heaps in the boxes marked EVEN and ODD.

"Put it on one," I tell Jake without looking at him. It's the best way I know to lose it all in one go. I embrace the terrible odds. I prostrate myself before the house. *Take it all.*

And as I think this, an achingly familiar voice drifts up.

You can't beat the house by not playing, Dodi, Neil had said with a smile—his last smile. We weren't talking about craps or roulette. *We lost this hand, but someday you'll meet someone who will make you want to play again.*

Like I ask him to, Jake takes our chips and slides them all into the box marked 1, the loneliest number, and the spinning starts.

The wheel spins and spins, and an age goes by, and finally the ball starts to skip and hop across the ribs of the wheel, looking for a place to land, and—

I don't know why I need to say it, except that grief latches onto to silly things like numbers to hold its place in your brain, and one is a pet number of mine.

"December first is when my husband died."

24

Jack of Spades

JAKE

DECEMBER FIRST IS ALSO MY BIRTHDAY. I PICTURE MY AUNT AND UNCLE WAIT-ing for me at that restaurant, Dodi seated by herself at a table for two across the way.

I look at Dodi, and there's something on her face as she considers me, like she's calculating a wager. A suspicion blooms.

"You said he was dead to you," I say.

"What?"

"Your date, the one who stood you up at the restaurant. You were having dinner with your husband."

Dodi tilts her head and looks away. "I do it every year."

"One red odd!" the dealer calls out, and the other players and onlookers gasp, but I barely register any of it.

"Sir—" the dealer says, but I cut her off. I know the drill by now.

"We're going to cash out."

A new color chip now—brown. Too many to hold. The dealer gives us a slip of paper instead, and the crowd—the *crowd!— parts as we go.* But the image of Dodi at the restaurant preoccupies me.

I try to imagine if that's something a boyfriend would be okay with. *Sorry, I'm busy that night. Having dinner with my dead husband!*

"How long ago did he die?"

Her stride wavers. "Seven years."

"Have you been alone this whole time?" She doesn't have to tell me. I already know the answer.

Her face shutters. "When did you find out about your diagnosis?" she asks me coolly.

I don't answer.

"Have *you* been alone this whole time, pillow princess?"

I don't need to tell her. She already knows the answer.

"What's next?" I ask.

"We have to keep going. We have to get rid of it."

"Get rid of it?" I echo.

"The money. We have to lose it."

I stop in my tracks. She's been gambling like a shark all night, one win after another. "You've been trying to *lose* it?"

It occurs to me I didn't check to see how much the last win raked in. I fish around in her purse for the slip of paper the dealer gave us.

The number on it doesn't make sense.

I glance behind me. There's still a small crowd of people at the roulette table, watching us, pointing.

I call after her and she turns. "Did you . . . ?" I hold the paper out to Dodi.

"Did I what?"

"Look."

She barely looks at the paper.

"So? We have to keep going."

"Did you actually look at how much—"

She's been in a moody daze since Circus Circus, but now she snaps into focus. "I *know* how much! Thirty-five to one!" It bursts out of her, her finger jabbing at the roulette table behind me. She pulls aside a dour-faced man in a vest and speaks into his ear. He nods and leads the way. I jog to catch up.

"Pitch blackjack," she says to me without looking. "Cards down. Single deck. High stakes."

We travel up a small flight of steps and over to where three men sit hunched at the edge of a table while a woman deals. The game moves slower than the blackjack tables we passed on the way here. These are larger sums of money, and the suspense from having the cards face down is something to be tasted and savored. The players flip their cards over as we watch, and one man chuckles, and another polishes off his drink, and the dealer settles the bets.

Dodi turns to face me, expression hard, and holds out her hand for the slip of paper. I don't give it to her.

She snatches the paper from my hands, crumpling it in her palm, but I refuse to let go—I grab her hand with my own before she does something stupid with it. A few heads from the blackjack table turn our way, and I fire a big easygoing smile at them.

"You should keep the money," I whisper through my teeth. This money doesn't matter to me. Why would it? But it's a life-changing amount for someone like Dodi, someone with her life ahead of her. "You should quit while you're ahead."

Her face hardens. "You think I'm ahead?"

I've accidentally raked a fingernail over a scab.

She takes a half step closer to me and speaks in a low voice. "'If you want to win, you have to be willing to lose everything.' That's what my husband used to say. Smug, happy, healthy—he had everything he wanted in life, *so* much he took for granted, and he actually used to say that, as if he was bravely risking *everything* every time he played one of his stupid fucking card games. Do you know what it's like to actually lose everything?"

Now she's the one who's ripped off a scab.

"No," I say. "I've got nothing to lose."

She blinks, realizing her misstep, and her hand goes slack in mine. She tries to wriggle out of my grasp, but I hold tight.

"I'll give it to you, but this is your last game," I say to her.

Her eyes are glittery and dark. Her body relaxes bit by bit.

"My last game," she agrees.

I hand over the slip of paper. She curls her fist around it and lifts her chin.

"Do you know how to play?" she asks.

I actually do know how to play this one. The goal is to get as close to twenty-one as possible. Face cards are worth ten, everything else its actual value, and aces can be a one or an eleven.

"Yes," I say.

"Then you know this game isn't like the others. I can choose to lose. I don't have to win if I don't want to." Her eyes are dark. "You *always* lose everything eventually, anyway, if you play long enough. The only luck is bad luck, right? So what's the point?"

"Then cash out now before you lose it all."

"I'm not talking about the fucking gambling."

She takes the empty seat at the far right. She places her piece of paper on the table, and the man nearest her looks her over with interest, taking in her dress, shoes, jewelry. These men know wealth and its indicators. Dodi is an impostor in their midst.

The dealer's eyes linger for a split second on the slip of paper, and then she inserts a black plastic card into the deck and deals. One card face down for each player, and then Dodi, and finally herself. And again, until everyone has a second card, and the second card she deals herself is placed face up.

Everyone consults their cards, and in front of me, Dodi peels up the ends closest to her. I watch her spine stiffen, her fingers freeze. I peer over her shoulder, and a metronome in my chest starts up.

Queen of diamonds and an ace of hearts. A natural. She's won.

The dealer deals out one more round of cards.

"Stand."

"Hit."

"Hit."

The dealer turns to Dodi, who says nothing. She spreads her palm on the table and scratches one pointed red nail on the green felt. *Hit.* She's going to fulfill her threat. She's going to intentionally lose, after being dealt a winning hand. I want to reach out and squash her hand flat against the green, but I'm too late.

The dealer sends a card her way, which Dodi doesn't bother to look at, then deals another card face up for herself, flips the original reversed card face up, does the math, and deals herself one more card. Five of clubs, three of hearts, seven of hearts, five of diamonds. Her total comes to twenty. The other players huff and toss back their drinks and flip their own cards over. The dealer takes care of their wagers—every last one of them has lost, of course—and turns to Dodi, who sits there, staring at me, luxuriating in her moment of triumph.

See? I reject the mythology of good luck, kismet, and happy endings.

She flips her cards over, one by one.

Queen of diamonds.

Ace of hearts.

The other players fall silent in confusion. They all stare at the remaining card still face down on the green.

Dodi presses her fingertips to the final card, savoring the moment. I can't look. I can't not look. She slides her thumbnail under the edge of the card, and flips it over.

25

Death Wish

JAKE

LAS VEGAS GLITTERS AT OUR FEET. WE'RE ON THE TOP FLOOR TERRACE OF A hotel, an exclusive little space for people who can afford two-hundred-dollar cocktails served by contortionists who slink around in gold leotards, while a trapeze artist twirls lazily above our heads on a hoop and a tiger prowls moodily on a lead below. The spectacle never ends.

An updraft lifts Dodi's hair as she leans over the wall and peers down, and the bloom of light from the street below catches her beautiful face in strange, underwater colors. Her bag rests on the ledge between us, lumpy and heavy, and next to it, the urn. Another server approaches—liquidly crab-walking and then rising up onto his feet without losing balance of a tray of drinks. He sparks a lighter above them, and they burn blue, and Dodi fishes a wad of hundred-dollar bills out of her purse for him. It's Monopoly money, all of it. It doesn't seem real.

A queen of diamonds, an ace of hearts, and a jack of spades. Twenty-one. She made blackjack twice in one hand. She'd stared long and hard at her cards, like she was reading a Tarot spread, and then she'd wordlessly taken her winnings and led us out onto the Strip again. We'd walked a long time in silence, the palms and lights and tourists all on the other side of a pane of glass, and I'd looked up at the tall buildings brightly lit against the black sky, taken her by the hand, and brought her here.

"What's next for you?" she asks. Her voice is quiet and serious. I don't misunderstand her question.

"Right now it's just my hands. They go numb and I get clumsy. Now that it's started, it'll get worse, quickly."

"Like your dad. What happened to your mom?"

"Car accident when I was nine. She was a teacher. She—" I almost say more, but there's nothing more to say, really. She taught at the same school I went to, and so she was always *there*, all day and night, until one day she wasn't. It's never made me happy to think about her, so I try not to.

"And then your aunt and uncle raised you. Will they be helping you?"

"They don't know I'm sick. My dad wasn't in the picture, and they don't know how he died." It might be the first time I've talked about my dad to anyone.

"What was the name of his illness?" She pulls out her phone as if she's going to look it up.

"It's probably going to be called Markham's disease."

Her brows pinch in confusion. "What do you mean?"

"That's the name of the neurologist I saw." Young and ambitious, he was excited when I walked into his office eight years ago seeking answers.

Without genotyping your parent's illness first, we can't test for it to see if it was passed on to you. We wouldn't know where to start looking. We have to wait until symptoms manifest. Peripheral neuropathy first. Clumsiness—maybe you'll notice it in your hands or when you move around. Everyone's heard about the big ones like ALS or Huntington's, but there are others, too, that pop up in a family line, with so few individuals affected that they haven't been studied properly yet. This might be a brand-new neurodegenerative disease, without a name.

I never went back. Beyond a couple of experimental therapies, there's nothing to be done, and I'm not some fucking guinea pig. I'm not tempted by a slim chance of prolonging this.

The flames have burned off from our drinks, and she hazards a sip and grimaces. "Why are you so alone in the world, Jake?"

"What?"

"No significant other, no friends, no possessions. How many people have you told your diagnosis to?"

None.

In my head I see Aunt Laura's sad eyes and Bill's stooped shoulders. I don't know how to verbalize it all. That it's risky, and dangerous, to let someone in.

I find the words. "I don't want to make any of this harder."

"You let me in," she says.

"You hate me."

She ignores this. "Who's going to take care of you?"

I think of the picture Bill painted for me. *Trapped in his own body. A terrible way to die.* "I'm going to take care of myself."

She looks at me, and I know she knows exactly what I mean. Her husband, sitting there on the ledge between us, knows too.

It's surreal to finally be voicing any of this, the thoughts that knock around in the night. It feels . . . exhilarating to let it all out. A genie escaping its lamp. I might not be able to hide it away again. "I can't control my aunt and uncle stuffing me like a taxidermy raccoon and putting me on display in a casket, or rifling through my personal shit after, but I can control that part. How I die."

"It's legal now," she says quietly. "You can get a doctor to help."

"That's true." I debate telling her the next part, the part that scares me. I think about her husband pouring the milk and cereal onto the counter. "But it will affect me cognitively at some point."

She gets that too, without me needing to explain it. If my ability to make decisions is called into question, no doctor will let me call the shots.

"You need an advocate to make sure you have a dignified death," she says. "And . . . after-death."

I'd never thought about having an advocate. There's no one in my life I could ask. Grant's a narcissist. Andrew's a Catholic. And Laura . . . Laura would understand, but I couldn't do that to her.

I think of how every morning I wake before the alarm goes off. The ceiling materializes above me, the remembrance of what's ahead returns, and for a minute I can't breathe. I start every morning like that. I have no control over my future, how it all plays out. The pain and indignity and uncertainty ahead of me. It's like waking up to find yourself in the seat of a roller coaster at the very top of the biggest peak, already nudging forward inch by inch, and the panic sets in. I haven't slept right in eight years.

This is where Dodi comes in. My shiny, sparkling distraction, from the moment she stepped onto that elevator.

When she looks at me, I'm the serial killer at work, not that other pathetic, sad Jake Ripper. And right now I'm in Las Vegas on a rooftop with a bag full of money and a dead man in a jar. I'm with the most interesting person I've ever met, and she thinks *I'm* interesting. I think us over. A dull lump of a man gray-rocking through life. A sharp blade of a woman like Dodi bent back on herself over and over again like steel, making her tougher and stronger. And when we met, flint struck steel. A spark. Everything became interesting. We created a fantasy world with each other, for each other.

"How are you going to spend your money?" I ask her, my voice different. Suave, charming, politely interested, while I tug on my strangler gloves and measure her neck with my eyes.

She starts, yanked away from whatever thoughts she was immersed in. "My money?"

I jerk my chin at her bag, and her face goes slack for a moment before it tightens back into its neutral setting: bored with a touch of *Fuck you very much.* The snarky Black Widow is online again, stropping her straight razor. She's exactly like that queen of diamonds she was dealt, and all I want to do is keep coming back to slice myself to ribbons on her hard, sharp edges.

"Wouldn't you like to know. I've already spent it," she says. With a thrill, I realize there's another secret here. Another body buried closely to the others.

A dry desert breeze rises out of nowhere and lifts Dodi's hair off her shoulders. She shivers, even though it's warm.

"Why'd you bring me up here?" she asks.

I pass her the urn, and her face goes blank.

"You're right. He would have loved this." She looks out at the city again, glowing, pulsing, alive. She twists the lid off to rest it on the ledge and pulls apart the seal of the liner inside.

"Good-bye, Neil," she whispers, and she sifts him slowly into the warm wind.

Neil.

I give a minute of silence to faceless, intrepid Neil—the statistician, the gambler, the dead man, who Dolores loved and still loves—burned to ash, billowing down the Las Vegas Strip on a desert wind, clinging to the hair and skin and clothes of a thousand strangers, following them back to their hotel rooms, being rinsed off in the shower, rubbed into the bedsheets, taken home on planes all across the continent—the world. That jar of stardust exploding in a supernova across the globe.

What a way to go.

26
Serial Killer Games

DODI

JUST BEFORE DAWN I LIFT MY HEAD AND PEEL A PIECE OF PAPER FROM MY cheek. Benjamin Franklin, lips pursed in disapproval. There's a vase of red roses next to the bed. I toss the flowers on the floor and chug the water.

The room is white. Plush white carpet, white sofa, white everything, and red rose petals everywhere. There are candles burned right down to the base and dripping wax all over the coffee table, where socks and shoes and cards lie in a heap from an abandoned game of strip poker. Condoms blown up into massive balloons roll like lazy tumbleweeds across the carpet under the draft of the AC.

I'm sprawled out on top of a pile of money on the nuptial bed of an extravagant honeymoon suite, an enormous rock sparkling on my left hand. Something else sparkles, too: the rhinestone-bedazzled Elvis romper I won in strip poker. I was serious about getting married by Elvis.

It was an unconventional proposal, perhaps. How many men get down on one knee with a slot machine token while a crowd of Las Vegas tourists cheer? But a few hours later, when I'd had time to think it over, I accepted all the same. Nothing fazes me. I'm a professional. I've seen it all. And this is very much my MO: a marriage of convenience to help a dying man retain his dignity. Sure, we should do the power of attorney stuff too, but this was the reckless, alcohol-fueled start.

He deserves my best work. I knew that, last night, when he explained everything to me. He's given me his best work.

He's dead asleep. Dark eyelashes fanned on his cheeks, stubble dotting his jaw. He lost most of his clothing in the small hours of the morning when I handed his and Elvis's asses to them, and now I get my first look at his pale, lean body, lying next to me, still strong and healthy for now. I wonder how thin he'll get. Neil turned into a bag of bones. It's my last look, too—there won't be any of that nonsense, now. This Black Widow doesn't get attached to her clients.

Loss is the price of entry. Unlike those idiots thronging the casinos, I've always known there's no winning. Just the temporary illusion of winning. The house always has an edge, and everyone loses eventually. Everyone dies eventually.

I watch him as the room slowly fills with light. I close my eyes and I listen to him. His slow, quiet breathing, and underneath, a heartbeat. Maybe it's my own heartbeat, or maybe I'm imagining it. I wriggle closer and I breathe him in. Something warm-blooded and inviting that makes me want to bury my face in his shoulder. The way he looks and sounds and smells right now—and more than that, his kindness, his patience, his dark humor—these are my trophies. I'll keep them in a box under my bed.

There are things Jake needs to do before he dies. A whole list of unfinished business, of loose ends to wrap up, of experiences to have. I've seen it before. But because of real life waiting at home, I can't do them with him. I need to push him off gently. He can't afford to waste any time. I'll be here when he needs me—really needs me—and doesn't just want me. Because it's obvious to me now why he waited to crawl into bed with me, even though I've been scrabbling to get in his pants all along. For him it's never been just a flirtation to stave off the boredom. Jake wants something truly special to happen to him before he dies.

Jake wants to fall in love.

I can't help him with that.

JAKE FUMBLES WITH THE KEY CARD, AND AS THE LOCK FINALLY BLINKS GREEN, the door across the hall opens up. Cynthia grimly takes in his rumpled clothes, my Elvis romper, our bag with stray bills poking out of it. The look in her eyes sends chills down my spine, but she doesn't say a thing. Her door clicks softly shut.

The plane leaves soon. We don't have time to shower. We change our clothes, miserably, with matching hangovers. We check the bathroom, the bedding, the drawers, for things gone astray, just to be safe. *Did we leave anything behind?* Only a whole-ass husband.

Jake compulsively makes the bed and folds the towels, and I leave out a generous tip. We're responsible grown-ups here, in case last night caused any confusion. He gives me the boarding passes and the passports, and he takes the bags. We're so practical and prosaic and—*married.*

A married couple who still haven't made eye contact since we woke up and Jake peered at the ring on his finger. A married couple who still haven't discussed the crazy fact that we are a married couple.

At the airport check-in we find our people—the bleary-eyed,

the greasy-haired, the hungover—all being mentally assaulted by chipper, efficient, bright-eyed airline staff serving up bad news like poisonous hors d'oeuvres on a tray. *Can I tempt you with an overbooked flight? How about a bumped seat?*

"What the fuck do you mean the flight's been canceled?" I ask.

The check-in agent's eyes bug and her painted pink lips freeze in a soulless smile.

"Just, no."

She blinks. "Yes. I can get you on the first flight tomorrow—"

"No."

Jake pulls me out of the line by my elbow. I protest, I dig my heels in, but the agent has turned to the next passenger. I'm so furious, I miss what Jake says next.

"What?" I say.

He presses his lips together for a moment, like he's not sure if he dares to repeat what he said. His eyes coast over my face.

"We don't have to go home. Come with me."

The request knocks the breath out of me.

"Where?"

"Anywhere."

"Guantánamo Bay?"

He smiles, one of his amused, shy smiles, a real one, and my stomach pinches. We're standing in one of the largest airport hubs in North America right now, passports in our pockets. I have my bag filled with enough clothes to last a few days, some toiletries—no. We have *four hundred thousand American dollars.* We don't need anything else. I scan the departure flight displays: Honolulu. Seoul. Amsterdam. Panama City.

I can picture it, a pair of murderers on the lam after their latest rampage in Las Vegas. Or maybe . . . maybe two people finally getting to know each other for a brief while as they see the world together. Getting drunk in first class on sparkling wine. Landing in Guadalajara, where I will casually order our dinner in Spanish, and he will discover that I am conversational after all—certificate in business Spanish, thank you very much. That night in bed he'll want to know how many languages I speak, so I'll take him to Manila next, where he can learn more about me—

I close my eyes and let myself savor the fantasy. He spins the best fantasies.

But real life calls.

"I can't," I tell him. I don't say I don't want to. His smile slips.

"Why not?"

Why not?

A disembodied voice overhead says, *Something-something-terminal.* I hate airports.

"If you want to travel," I say, "I think you should do it."

I worked out my talking points this morning while he slept. I was going to have this conversation with him when we got home—for some reason I pictured us on the roof at work. I was going to tell him that we need to be apart for a while, that he needs to focus on himself for a bit, but that I'll be ready to spring into action when he needs me.

This is better. I can picture him on a tropical beach somewhere, or walking down the streets of some European city. He could even meet someone. There's still time for that special thing to happen to him. I won't be the sort of wife who gets jealous.

"I think you should travel, Jake. And I think you should do it by yourself."

He sighs. "It would be too boring." His voice and manner

have changed. He's putting on the protective mask again: the Serial Killer at Work. Comedic, deadpan, invulnerable. "And boredom's already a chronic problem—"

"Stop with the serial killer games for a minute."

He stares at me from behind the mask, but I learned how to read poker faces from the best.

"Boredom's not just for sociopaths," I say. "You know who else suffers chronic boredom? Really smart people."

He makes an impatient noise, but I push on. There are things that need to be said. There's more to being a good wife than a willingness to shake some pills into your husband's palm and press a pillow over his face.

"You're smart, so I know you're going to understand me. You're bored, and lonely, and depressed. I've always known you're not like this . . ." I gesture broadly at him—at all of him—at the flatness, the friendlessness, his lamprey-like latching onto the dopamine fix our flirtation has given him, the desperation to lose himself in a fantasy world—at everything, basically, I see reflected in myself. "You're not like this because you're a sociopath. You're like this because you're depressed. You need to do something about it."

The mask falls away suddenly and dramatically. It's the first time I've seen anything like anger on his face, and it's a relief to see it. It's human. It's so normal. It's *healthy*.

"I'm not depressed," he says levelly. "This isn't a chemical imbalance. I have a completely valid reason for feeling the way I do. Taking a pill or talking to a therapist isn't going to help me be *happier*."

"I'm not suggesting you 'get happy.' It's your right to feel miserable. You deserve to grieve properly instead of avoiding it. You've been working so hard to convince everyone around you you're fine. The fake smiles, the fake golden retriever, the facade of normalcy. You even used me to lie to your aunt about having a girlfriend."

"*You* told her you were my girlfriend—"

"And she looked so happy, you went along with it. You can't live like this—not if you're dying. Your roommate? Looking after him is a distraction for you. Tell me I've got that wrong."

He stares at me, and I keep going. I *know* I'm right. I've been putting him together in my head since I woke up this morning—and picked his pockets and rifled through his secrets while he was dead to the world.

"You're taking better care of him than of yourself. Is it easier to let yourself get sucked into someone else's crazy and make a whole job for yourself managing their shit instead of dealing with your own?"

He's a statue.

"You want to live in a fantasy—anything to distract you from what's ahead. But you need to work on your real life. You need to cut out the people in your life who make you miserable, like your roommate, and your uncle. You need to tell your aunt you're sick—"

"No—"

"It's obvious she adores you. She would want the chance to help you in any way she can."

"He wouldn't let her, and she's *never* stood up for me against him."

There's so much anger and hurt there below the surface, like a wound that needs to be drained. The kindest thing is to keep digging with my lance.

"You need to figure out what you want to do with the time you have left."

"There isn't *anything* I want to do—"

"You need to figure it out. You need to figure out what makes you happy, at the most basic level, and you need to do that."

I kneel down on the dirty airport floor, unzip my carry-on, and pull out the hotel pillowcase containing half the winnings from last night. I'd divvied it all up when Jake was in the hotel room bathroom folding towels back into swans or whatever he was doing. In the cold, bilious light of day, I feel so grateful to Jake for cutting me off last night. I need the money so badly, but half is enough for what I need to do.

"Here," I say, pressing it into his chest.

"I don't want it."

"It's yours. *Take it.* Hop on a plane and see some of the world. Find something that makes you happy."

"You make me happy."

He reaches up as if to take the pillowcase, but he just holds his hands on top of mine, against his chest, and I can see it coming like a train derailing, one segment after another flying off the tracks, and I want to scream at this shit-for-brains idiot *You can't say—*

"I'm in love with you."

My heart sprints in the worst way, because if he thinks I'm going to say it back—

"I know you don't feel the same way," he says quickly. "I don't want you to."

I unstick my tongue. "What do you want me to do with this information?"

"Print it on a coffee mug."

I try to wriggle my hands out of his grasp, but he doesn't let go.

"I want to be with you. I think you want to be with me too."

I'm flushed and sweaty. My scalp prickles.

"I want to spend the rest of my life with you."

His life has been so unhappy, but there must have been a period in his childhood where someone took very good care of him for him to be able to say exactly what he's feeling like that.

It's not a shabby offer. His love, his attention, his fun—to be at the center of the intense focus of this intelligent, handsome man . . . and he's not asking for anything in return, except my presence. I let him hold my hands, and I let myself picture it one more time.

"We're married," he says quietly, like he's still wrapping his head around it and is afraid to say it too loud. "Let's go on a honeymoon. We'll quit our jobs. No work, no responsibilities, no crazy roommate, and definitely no cat—"

Cat.

Cat.

I'm so glad he says it, because it's there, right *there*, that he goes too far and makes it easy for me to say no. For him to suggest that I ditch her for him—that I leave her in the lurch for a few weeks while I indulge in a dalliance—that I would be the sort of person . . .

This last remaining piece of Neil is the reason I get up in the morning. The reason I stay up half the night on my stupid laptop. The reason I cling to that mind-numbing job. I've done terrible things, but my love for her is the best and most redeeming thing about me—

It hits me that I've been terrible.

I've worked so hard to build a new life, a life I was supposed to have with Neil, a life that honors his memory, and here I've been acting like an idiot, leaving her behind, risking my job, binding myself legally to someone I barely know. I've been completely unhinged these past few weeks.

I make myself sick.

My phone vibrates in my pocket, and I know exactly who it is. I wrench my hands from Jake's. I could throw up. He needs to know where we stand. I need to remind myself where I stand.

"The thing is," I say, "I have a life."

It comes out so much harsher than I mean it to, but it's like I have two settings. Cruel, and even worse. His face goes blank. A thrust, and now a twist:

"I have an actual life. I have love, and a home, and a purpose." I'm so *lucky*, in spite of all the bad luck that came before. I have so much now, even if I lost everything once. Casino bravado has steamed off like a mist in the bright light of day, and I can admit to myself I'd fight till I'm red in tooth and claw to not lose it all again. I'll fight Jake if I have to. "At the end of the day, when we're done playing our stupid serial killer games at the office, I go home and my real life begins."

His face shows utter betrayal. He's been the other man this whole time, the one I cheat on my real life with. But I've decided either I hurt, or he does. Except I still hurt. My phone vibrates again. I plunge my hand in my pocket and squeeze it.

He stares at me, his face turning red. "Is this the same real life you've been escaping from the whole time I've known you?"

I stab him right back. "You don't even have a real life."

"*This* could be real life," he says, and there's a shearing sensation in my chest. Organs twisting until they split.

"For the rest of *your* life, I guess."

It was self-defense, Your Honor. Jake drops my hands.

Buzz.

"Real life calling?" Jake says sarcastically.

I press the phone to my ear and walk to the other side of the newsstand.

"I got the flight cancellation email," my neighbor says without preamble.

"I'm already boarding a different flight," I lie, and my neighbor sighs with relief.

"Good. She misses you. When I woke up this morning she was curled up on the foot of my bed."

I wait until I'm sure my voice won't crack. "Can I say hi?"

"Ha. No. She's far too busy."

"Is that . . ." I strain to hear. "Barking?"

"We're on the roof."

Jesus. "The pet zone?"

"Don't worry. It's just little dogs today."

"It's not safe up there. The walls are too low."

"Either I bring her up or she sneaks up when I'm not looking. She loves the dogs. I think you're going to have to get a little friend for her."

I squeeze my eyes shut. I want to give her a little dog friend so badly. "As soon as we have a place with a yard."

The mythical place with a yard. It's never going to happen. I'm so glad Jake made me keep the money, but I have to use it for something else. Spencer & Sterns. My laptop. My double life.

Across the way, Jake has approached the counter.

"Give her a squeeze from me," I say, and I end the call.

I watch his mask slip on. He flicks on a handsome, charming, serial killer smile, and the agent melts like wax under a flame. She smiles back. He says something, and she titters, and he says something else, and her face fills with concern over whatever lie he's expertly fed her. A moment later, she's printed a boarding pass and handed it to him. A one-way international ticket, first class, for a grand adventure.

He walks back to me and holds out the pass to rub in my face.

"You have a window seat," he says.

I blink and take the pass with numb fingers. "What?"

I stare at it. A seat on the next flight home, later today. "What about you?"

He glances at the departures display. London. Mexico City. Paris.

"I'll catch a different flight." He flashes me a big fake psycho smile, and walks away.

27

Death Rattle

JAKE

I SLURP MY COFFEE AND I PACE, AND TWITCH, AND SWEAT. GRANT'S PENT-house turns dark and then light and now dark again, and the green numbers of my alarm clock are like the eyes of some nocturnal creature come to scavenge. I haven't showered or shaved since getting back from Las Vegas.

You need to figure out what you want to do with the time you have left.

The building sleeps. Grant sleeps. Everyone sleeps, except for me. And now it's Monday again, and I can finally see her, if only on her terms. I shower. I shave. My skin looks pale and shiny in the mirror.

You need to figure out what makes you happy.

I hear the noises of Grant stirring in the next room. He sneezes. He coughs. He mutters to himself—practicing lines he'll use in court today. He pauses to allow the jury to gasp. He slams his hands on the bathroom vanity for emphasis. "Objection . . . *objection* . . ." He tries it a few different ways until he settles on, "Ob*jec*tion, Your Honor!"

He minces into the open living area I keep clean for him, in the suit I collected from the drycleaners for him, and his eyes settle on the breakfast I've prepared for him. He smiles a winsome, toothy grin at me and digs into his egg whites.

You take better care of him than yourself.

"You look like shit," he says conversationally, and I make my mind up in an instant.

"I'm moving out."

Egg whites tumble out of his mouth and back onto his plate. "What? Fuck off. What?"

"I'm getting my own place."

"You can't be this fragile! I just meant you look like you're sick!"

My coffee is cold. I pour myself a fresh cup, and I top up Grant's while I'm at it, but he accidentally knocks it off the table, the black liquid splattering the white floor.

"You *can't*. Who will cook and clean? *I* can't do those things. And you're supposed to get the sauna repaired—"

I stare at the coffee splatter on the floor, and in the pattern, I see a man whiling his short, pathetic life away blending into the walls, letting others be the main character.

"It's my life, Grant."

"You can't do this to me."

"Have a life?"

He loses it. He swipes the plate and cutlery onto the floor with the coffee.

"You're *abandoning* me!" He clutches his head like the pain is incomprehensible. This is why he needs to stick to dolls.

It takes all of ten minutes to pack a bugout bag while Grant disintegrates in the kitchen. I grab a key fob from the drawer and leave. In the basement parking, I click the fob button until

I find the car, get in, and go. But where to go? Work doesn't start for another two hours. I drive up- and downtown. I cross the bridge, and then turn around and drive back again. I feel prickly and sweaty. My hands are white, so I pull my gloves on. I find myself passing the building that houses Spencer & Sterns on autopilot. A block away is an overpass, and underneath, down by the river, a nasty, deserted stretch of urban wasteland littered with traces of tent living. I park the car and watch the river below—brown, sluggish, foamy. It doesn't look like water. It looks like some fluid that would spill out of a sick person, or something Aunt Laura mops up at the end of the day at the funeral home. If I was wrung like a rag, this is what would come out.

28

Terminated

"DOLLY"

MONDAY MORNING. BASEMENT PARKING. BY THE TIME I REGISTER MY FELLOW elevator passenger it's too late.

"Haha, Dolly!"

"Good morning," I say stiffly.

"Not a good morning without a smile from you."

I imagine baring my teeth in a grin, my lips curling back to reveal several rows of fangs, my jaw dislocating to swallow him whole. I'd spit out his brittle, partially digested skeleton a few hours later. If Jake were here, connecting eyes with me across the elevator . . . but he's not. I left him in a Las Vegas airport, and I don't know when I'll see him again. He never gave me a timeline for his illness.

Doug grows uncomfortable under my wordless stare and laughs stupidly one last time before shaking out his free city rag.

HO-HO-HO-MICIDE

Xmas Prank 'Murder' of Dismembered Sex Doll Under Investigation

My insides slip down onto the ground. "I need that," I blurt out.

"What?"

I pinch the top of the paper and yank just as the doors roll open on Ground. I shoulder out before the incoming crowd pens me in and duck into the other elevator, paper held tight against my chest to contain that headline and my pounding heart.

Jake had the right idea. He skipped town. Visions of police officers banging down my door swim in front of my eyes. Cat, roused from sleep, watching me being led away in handcuffs in the middle of the night. Oh yes, Las Vegas bravado has left the house. I'm very much afraid of losing everything.

What the ever-loving fuck. It was just *littering*.

The doors slide open at my floor, and I march with brisk purpose to the annex, avoiding eye contact, far too busy and important to stop for anyone, panicking, panicking, *panicking*, and I'm almost on top of him before I notice him.

Jake.

My ankle rolls and my bag swings off my shoulder and into the crook of my elbow. I stare at him. He's supposed to be dipping his feet in the ocean somewhere, rereading his favorite book, writing letters.

"What are you doing here?"

His eyes flick up briefly from his monitor to take me in. "Data entry for Doug."

I could smack him. *"Why?"*

"It's my job."

His time's ticking out, and he's sitting here under humming fluorescents, straight-jacketed in institutional corporate attire, anesthetizing his brain on spreadsheets.

He notices the paper in my hands. "There's a new sicko on the loose."

His voice is smooth, relaxed, and I feel my shoulders drop. I glance down at the headline. Five minutes ago I thought this was an unmitigated disaster, but with Jake here it seems almost funny.

"I haven't read the article yet," I say.

"You know what I think?" he says, leaning forward conspiratorially.

He wants to go back to our serial killer games. He wants to press the reset button and go right back to where we were. I want to take him by the shoulders. *No.*

"Yes?"

He looks to his right, then to his left, an exaggerated act in this deserted room.

"I think it's two people working together."

I don't think he has any idea how sad it is that he's willing to settle for this, this pathetic game, these pathetic distractions.

"That's an interesting theory. I suppose two heads are better than one."

He leans back, crossing his arms. "Oh, no, not even one head. The head's still missing. What I'm dying to know is, do you think it's a one-off, or . . . will they keep working together?"

I realize what he's doing here in the office today, dinking around with spreadsheets instead of catching a plane to Thailand. He's trying to spend the rest of his life with me.

"I have no idea what these lunatics are thinking," I whisper.

"What do *you* think, though? I know you'd have to really stretch your imagination to put yourself into the mindset of the unhinged psychopaths who did this—"

My chest aches for him, and I can't tell if I'm being generous or selfish for entertaining this. If this is what he truly wants—it *is* small enough that I can give it to him—

We each have a finger on the reset button, bearing down, about to click, when Doug comes panting into the annex like a little dog. He's never tracked me down to my lair like this. He eyes my stolen newspaper and I clutch it tighter.

"Heyyyy, Jack! Dolly," he says with a vacuous chuckle. His face is already pink and shiny, like he's been running laps up and down the halls to escape irate HR people. Jake and I stare at him.

"So, Cynthia's on a bit of a rampage, haha."

My guess was on the nose.

"Oh?" Jake's face is a mask of carefully curated concern.

"Yeah, something about your work trip," he says, and dread pools in the pit of my stomach. The headline pressed against my chest isn't funny anymore. None of this is funny.

Doug stares at us like a nervous child. Jake folds his arms and leans back in his chair again, projecting the entirety of his concerned focus onto Doug. Doug melts right into it with relief.

"What did she say, exactly?" Jake probes.

Doug lets out a big breath. "Something about unprofessionalism and optics and employee fraternization."

Jake connects eyes with me, briefly. Doug should definitely not be talking to us right now.

I knew that my job at Spencer & Sterns would blow up in my face one day, eventually. I just thought I'd get there on my own steam. I thought I'd have time to prepare a safe landing first. Instead, Jake lit the fuse—first with the Ken doll and then this work trip—and it was a very short fuse.

I could be sick.

"You know what they say," Jake says, relaxed and cheerfully conspiratorial. "'HR's not having a good time unless you're not having a good time.' Honestly, Doug, you approved this work trip. Sounds like she's undermining you. Aren't you the supervisor here?"

Doug's eyebrows go up. "Yes. Yes, I am."

"You've been here a long time."

Doug stands a little straighter. "Fifteen years."

"You're a hard worker. Everyone can see that."

Doug puffs right up. "Work is everything to me."

"'Work will set you free,'" I say through my teeth. Jake's eyes flick to mine, big idiot smile pasted on, and there's the subaudible click of the reset button between us.

"Exactly!" says Doug. "Who said that?"

"The Dalai Lama, I think," Jake says. "Look, Doug. I'm just a temp. I don't think my opinion counts for much here. But if someone said to me that Cynthia has it in for you and that she's taking out the general by eliminating his foot soldiers one by one"—here he gestures at the two of us—"I'd believe it. Cynthia is so . . . so . . ."

"Uppity," Doug jumps in.

I wince.

Jake smiles brainlessly at him. It couldn't be easier to play Doug if you put a coin in his ass and cranked his leg. Suddenly Doug flinches, swivels his head around like he's detecting a sound beyond the frequencies accessible to the rest of us, and scurries out of Jake's cubicle like a rat dashing to his hidey-hole.

Jake and I stare at each other.

"Are we about to get fired?" he asks, cocking one eyebrow.
Shit.

Jake trails after me into my office.

"Shit. Shit. *Shit!*" I shriek. I hurl the newspaper, but the pages just slip apart and drift onto the carpet undramatically. I feel nauseated. I locate the wastepaper basket with my eyes in case I need it.

"What's the matter?"

This whole mess is just the next playdate for him. "I can't lose this fucking job!"

"You barely have a job. And they're not going to fire you—"

"They will. If they figure out—" I stop there. I don't know how much *he's* figured out. About being a servant of two masters. About the assignments I've been completing in the desk across from him all this time. About what Cynthia has been sniffing out like a well-trained HR bloodhound.

"If they figure out what?" Jake asks.

I don't answer him. "I thought I had time to come up with a plan." I've been working so hard for us, for her. It was for her. I was so close. And now—

"You don't need a plan. You have money."

"I can't spend that money," I snap. I really am going to be sick.

"We can find a new job someplace else—"

"You think that's my priority? Finding a new job with *you*?" My priority is her. It's always been her—

"We could take temp jobs."

"I need to keep *this* job!"

"You don't—"

I round on him. *"I have to think about my daughter!"*

It's the first time I've brought her out into the open. She's the most precious thing in my life, a treasure I keep safely concealed, and it feels messy and exposing to talk about her here, like pages of a secret diary being scattered to the wind. Jake is equally thrown. He stares at me, face blank, mouth a flat line, still as a statue, like he's internally regretting every decision that led to this moment where he has to have an actual conversation with me about my real life. He's never wanted anything to do with it. He's always made that clear.

My voice is a croak when I speak again. "When you came along, everything started going sideways. People started noticing me." I think of Doug, suddenly taking an interest in me again in the elevator with Jake to help break the ice; Cynthia, drawn to my annex like a harassment-seeking missile; all the random S&S minions peering at me with a frown after the awkward new temp points me out across the break room or down the hall. My voice shakes slightly with my anger. "All of this has been a game to you, but I have worked *so hard* to rebuild my life. For *her* sake."

Jake moves his eyes to a point beyond my shoulder and breaks into a jarring smile. I turn to look, and jump out of my skin when I spot Cynthia stalking down the aisle between deserted cubicles.

"Whatever happens . . ." Jake mutters through his smile, and I turn to look at him. His grin is wide and contagious, but his eyes are serious. "Whatever happens, just throw me under the bus."

Cynthia arrives and raps perfunctorily on my doorjamb. "Both of you, come with me."

She frog-marches us to the elevators and up to the floor that houses the HR department, leading us through the warren-like aisles, this way and that, to a private office at the back that says **Marie Simon** on the door, and below it, on a piece of paper, TEMPORARY OFFICE OF CYNTHIA CUTTS, CONSULTANT.

Inside we find Doug cowering in a chair, looking nervous and sick. Nothing good ever happened in an HR office, as far as Doug's concerned. Sitting against one wall is a small, beaky woman with a sheaf of papers in her lap. She jumps to her feet and hovers awkwardly while Cynthia directs us to take the seats across from the desk.

My stomach flutters and my heart races. I examine my surroundings. A mounted inspirational poster—**PERSISTENCE is the art of turning a "no" into a "yes!"—Robert Spencer, Co-Founder of Spencer & Sterns**—rests on the floor, replaced above by a framed puzzle of a duckling in a watering can. A bag of lumpy, hairy gray yarn spills out on a shelf to one side, knitting needles sticking out at angles, and a row of origami critters made from Post-its lines the edge of her desk.

"Marie?" Cynthia intones.

Marie clears her throat. "Employees on a work trip paid for with company money are ambassadors of the company. Optics are everything. Sharing a room is unprofessional and completely against employee fraternization policies."

For an entire second I let myself think this might be nothing more than a quick HR scolding. Cynthia isn't even watching me. Her eyes are trained on Jake, who is wearing an infuriating smile.

"Of course, the real issue here is even more serious," Cynthia says, and my heart sinks. "Company money was spent on a work trip for a temp who does print room jobs and basic data entry, and"—she gestures at me—"another employee, whose role within the company is obscure to me. What was the purpose of this trip?"

Doug stares at her like a scared little bunny whose instincts tell him that if he doesn't move, he'll be left alone.

Jake answers for him. "To take a lightweight, custom-

tailored, and solution-driven course to equip us with the prac
tical strategies and problem-solving mindset to confidently
implement transformational change in our organization
within a holistic framework."

Cynthia stares at him. We all do. She turns to Doug.

"Doug, what is Dolores dela Cruz's role—"

Jake raises his voice and talks over her. "By the way, why
wouldn't we share a room? We're in a relationship," he says,
placing a hand on my knee. I stiffen and reflexively swipe it
off. I could smack him.

Cynthia watches this with grim interest. She plucks a piece
of paper out of her print tray and writes Jake's name on it. A
couple clicks of her mouse, and she reads off the name of
Jake's temp agency. "That yours?"

"Yes," Jake says, smiling charmingly, and she writes that
down too.

"And your address is 556—"

I realize what Jake is doing. She can't penalize us for workplace fraternization if we're *married*. Jake's nodding along,
but I interrupt with my address, and she writes it down. If she
checks my contact information later, our lie will add up.

But next to me Jake clears his throat, and when I look at
his profile, he gives a tiny shake of his head.

I stop. I've become a passenger, and Jake has taken the wheel.

He slouches rakishly in his chair and squeezes my knee
again. Relationship or no, he doesn't get to paw me in a work
meeting. I shove his hand off my knee again. Now Marie is
eyeing us uncomfortably.

"Relationship disclosures," Marie murmurs to Cynthia.

"Show me where to sign." Jake laughs an excessively
charismatic laugh and crosses his legs, and it's so not like Jake
it's embarrassing . . .

And now he's humming quietly to himself like a jackass. "Flight of the Bumblebee"?

"Doug," Cynthia says levelly, "it doesn't appear that you are able to describe Dolores's official role, despite being her supervisor, and it seems you were either unaware of a workplace relationship, or declined to alert HR about the need for a relationship disclosure, for whatever reason."

Doug fidgets and sweats, but next to him Jake fires up a big fake psycho smile. Employee of the year.

"I want to go on record saying Doug is the best supervisor I've ever had, and I've worked a lot of office jobs."

Doug glances gratefully at Jake, and Jake smiles supportively, and it seems to stoke a fire in Doug. He leans forward, hands on his knees, and starts in on a garbled speech inspired by Jake's pep talk earlier. "I've been working here at SS for fifteen years. My underlings are like SS foot soldiers, and I'm like an SS general—"

Cynthia jumps in like a rabid dog. "It's 'S&S.' You can't say 'SS.'"

" 'SS' is quicker to say," he says.

"It *is* quicker to say." Jake nods thoughtfully.

"You can't say 'SS.' Don't you know what 'SS' stands for?"

"Spencer and Sterns."

Cynthia jabs her index finger into the surface of her desk. "You can't say you're an SS general!"

Something comes loose in Doug. "I take my job seriously. 'Work will set you free.' That's my motto."

Marie squeaks.

"Who have you said that to?" Cynthia hisses, and Doug startles, but Jake gives him a supportive nod. He's still humming. Not "Flight of the Bumblebee" . . . "Flight of the Valkyries." Foot bouncing gently, fingers tapping restlessly—

and all at once I realize whose identity Jake has assumed:
criminal criminal lawyer, gentleman sex doll connoisseur,
tragic romantic—Grant Velazquez, esquire.

"Are you—are you policing what I'm saying now?" Doug
says. "Are you censoring my freedom of speech?"

Cynthia grips the edge of her desk. "This isn't a question of
freedom of speech. Every time you open your mouth, you have
to be mindful of the power imbalance. You are a *manager*.
You are *white*. You are *older*. You are *male*—"

"I didn't ask to be born with a penis!" A fleck of spittle
sticks to Doug's lip. "You people are always like this. You're
jealous of someone else having a good thing."

I don't have time to suss out if Doug's "good thing" is his
position of power or his penis, because he's on a roll. It's one
steaming hot shit falling out of his mouth after another.

"You know what you are? You're a bunch of—a bunch of
feminazis!"

Marie's mouth is a perfect O, and a muscle twitches in
Cynthia's jaw. Jake's wheedling humming is the only sound in
the room for a moment. Not "Flight of the Valkyries" anymore. The tune Jake is humming now is childishly idiotic and
painfully familiar. I've heard my daughter sing this song approximately eleventy million times.

The wheels on the bus go round and round . . .

I look at him, and he looks at me, and I suddenly understand
what he's been doing this whole time. He lifts his hands from
the steering wheel, opens the door, rolls out. I'm at the wheel
now, my daughter safely buckled in the back seat, and it's time
to throw him under. He nods encouragingly. He places his hand
on my knee one more time, and this time I smack it off.

I turn to face Cynthia. "Do you see what I've been dealing with?" My voice is strident and powerful. "I'm not safe here. This company has failed to protect me from workplace harassment and bullying. He speaks Spanish at me and calls me Dolly and tells me to smile, and he—"

I glance at Jake. *He saves my ass.*

"—he plants decapitated Barbies in my office and pretends we're in a romantic relationship. He's been fixated on me from the start."

Next to me Jake laughs. "Dolly. Seriously?" He turns to Marie. "This is what I get for cultivating good old Spencer & Sterns *persistence*, right?" He points to the mounted poster resting on the floor. "I'm going to turn her no into yes."

Marie stares at her poster in horror.

This is an HR shitstorm for them to clean up. All scrutiny apportioned for me has been redirected at Doug and Jake. There will be nothing but placation and false support for me until they can be sure I've been safely talked down from escalating this and engaging a lawyer. Jake has bought me the time I need.

And because I'm an idiot riding my wave of relief, I keep going. "All I've done is try to keep my head down and do my work—"

And Cynthia, dog with a bone, impervious to shit raining from the sky, says, "And what exactly is that work?"

I snap my mouth shut.

"Her little spreadsheet?" Jake chuckles dismissively. Cynthia and I both turn to look at him. "She had me doing data entry for her."

"What spreadsheet?" Cynthia asks.

Jake raises his eyebrows and glances back and forth with a look of mischief. He pulls out his phone and a moment later

Cynthia's desktop computer pings. She clicks around for a moment and then her face slackens in surprise.

"This list . . ." Cynthia says, and I realize Jake has sent her his mysterious list. "Is this what I think it is?"

Jake nods almost imperceptibly.

"Yes," I say. "Obviously."

Marie cranes to look at the monitor, but Cynthia abruptly minimizes the window.

"And . . ." I say, taking a leap and praying for a soft landing, "taking that course in Las Vegas . . . was all part of it. *Transformational change*," I say, and the idiotic words strangle me.

Cynthia creaks back in her chair and considers me with eyes as cold and hard as concrete. The clock on the wall ticks, Doug mouth-breathes, Jake twirls and bounces his foot like a lawyer who bills nine hundred an hour so he can put it right up his nose, and Cynthia weighs my fate.

"You were working on this on your own. A self-directed project. He"—she tips her head to Doug—"wasn't involved, was he?"

I shake my head, and Cynthia makes an expression that could be heartburn or, possibly, a smile.

Next to me Jake pulls out a pack of cigarettes.

"What do you think you're doing?" Cynthia says sharply.

He lights a cigarette.

"Are you smoking? In my *office*?"

Jake shrugs apologetically. "I really should quit," he says around the butt. He stands, shoves the pack back in his pocket, and leaves.

"Did he just quit?" Marie asks hopefully.

I don't linger. I get up and run after him, but he's vanished. I race back to the annex and I catch him just in time, putting on his coat and slinging his bag over his shoulder.

"Jake!"

He turns to look at me, but I don't know what happens next, and neither does he, so we just stand there staring at each other. The circles under his eyes are so dark, and he's clammy and pale. I don't know when that started. I want to reach up and rest my hand against his forehead.

He takes an experimental puff of his cigarette.

"Why the—" He hacks. "These things are disgusting."

"Jake."

He coughs and stubs the cigarette out on his desk. We look at each other and say things without opening our mouths.

I'm sorry.

Thank you.

I do love—

I already have the mug.

He turns on his heel and goes.

29

In Sickness and in Health

JAKE

A LOUD RAP ON THE WINDOW STARTLES ME FROM MY SLEEP. THE SKY HAS turned dark, and the dash clock reads 5:15 p.m. I'm in the car next to the greasy-looking river. I came here after I walked out and . . . fell asleep.

I'm freezing. I ache. I'm soaked in sweat.

Another rap.

It's Dodi.

"What the *fuck*," she says. As usual, there's no question mark at the end of it.

I crack the door.

"What's going on here?" she demands. "Why are you camped out here by tent city like a homeless person?"

"I am homeless. I left Grant's."

"You're homeless," she says flatly. "In a Lamborghini."

"A what?" I glance around me at the interior of the car. I've never understood how people can identify car makes. Cars are the most uninteresting thing in the world to me.

I watch her draw two deep breaths in through her nose. She looks frantic and furious.

"What are you doing here?" I ask.

"It was kind of hard not to notice the giant black supercar lurking one block from work. You're going to get robbed. You need to check yourself into a hotel."

"I don't think I can drive right now."

She peers closer at me. "You look terrible. What's going on? You drunk?"

"No."

"Sick?"

"Sort of."

"I'm not going to keep digging."

"Well, I'm dying, you know."

She narrows her eyes at me, and then, surprisingly, she touches my forehead, my cheek. Her touch is so gentle. "Jesus," she mutters. "Did you pick something up on the plane? You know you're not supposed to lick the tray table."

"I'm fine," I say.

"Idiot," she says without looking at me. "You can't stay here. You could get stabbed."

"It's fine."

"I'll just move up the funeral planning, then. Cremation or mushroom box in the woods?"

I tip my head back against the headrest and look at her face. "Are you still helping me, then?"

"Of course I'm helping you."

I'm so relieved I could lie down and catch up on every hour of missed sleep from the past eight years. "I'd like to be cremated, and I want you to make decorative hand soaps with my ashes and hand them out at the office."

Her lips press into a flat line. "I think you're going to learn to love toadstools." She glances to the left and then the right, like she's searching the environs for inspiration. "Can you follow me?"

I open the car door to step out, but she stops me.

"I meant in the car. You can't just leave the car here."

"Why not?"

"You really don't know a fucking thing about cars, do you?"

"No."

She swears under her breath.

In the end, we leave my car where it is and take hers out toward the freeway. She cranks the heated seat for me and I nod off with the side of my head pressed against the icy glass of the window. The next thing I know, she's shaking me awake. We're in a parking lot surrounded by a familiar mushroom forest of squat apartment blocks. In the elevator, I notice she's holding my bugout bag, and on the third floor she lets me into an apartment that couldn't be more different from Grant's penthouse. It's small and cramped, and it smells like food and Dodi's perfume. The lights are golden and warm, the furniture cheap and worn, and every surface is a petri dish for a living, growing colony of clutter. A special type of brightly colored, predominantly plastic clutter.

Toys. There are toys all over the place. Legos, art supplies, and Barbies—Barbies *everywhere*.

"I know it's a mess," Dodi says defensively. "You try keeping up with a six-year-old."

"Do you have allergy meds?" I ask.

"What? Why?"

"I'm allergic to cats."

She glares at me and stalks off without saying anything. She rustles in the bathroom, knocking cabinet doors open and closed, and I peer around the living room. I circle back to the front door and lean my head into the tiny kitchen. No scratching posts, no food dishes. No cat hair or cat toys.

Was there ever a cat? Did the cat turn into a human child? Because I still feel like we had actual conversations about a fucking *cat*—

I step on something and discover the dismembered Ken doll in a little heap on the floor, his glasses bent out of shape now.

"Cat's been playing Frankenstein with your doll," Dodi says, standing in front of me with a folded towel.

Cat. A little girl named Cat.

Silence, silence yawning wide and deep and endless and . . .

"Her meeting you was never part of the plan, and I don't want her feeling nervous about a strange man staying in our apartment. You can crash here for one night if you stay in my room. If you so much as step a toe outside, you're dead." She undermines this threat by gently pressing the towel into my arms and dropping an aspirin into my hand for my fever.

"Where is she?"

"I have to get her from dance class. You're going to do whatever you need to do, and you better be locked up in that room by the time we get back. You can use the shower and wash your clothes. If there's anything edible in the fridge, you can have it. I think there's a nice bottle of mustard in there. Check the expiration date."

She turns and leaves without looking at me, the door clicking softly shut behind her.

30

Bruce Wayne and Cat Girl

JAKE

I SLEEP THE SLEEP OF THE DEAD, AND WHEN I COME TO, I CAN'T REMEMBER where I am. I'm in a soft bed in a darkened room with bands of brilliant sunlight burning around the edges of the window blinds. As I roll over I get a whiff of a familiar perfume. I'm at Dodi's.

There was no need to threaten my life if I left the room. I fell asleep almost as soon as my head hit the pillow. I open the door and squint against the sunlight. The clock in the kitchen reads ten, which means last night was the longest I've slept in years. I feel . . . light. Rested. I check my phone: five more missed phone calls from Andrew and several voicemails, which I delete. Nothing from Grant. On the kitchen table is a handwritten note with a key resting on top. Her hand is spiky and dark.

Do whatever you need to do, lock up, and give my key to the neighbor. Don't be here when I get back.

I have no one to cook a healthy breakfast for, so I pour myself a bowl of sugary cereal. When I open the fridge I can see she wasn't kidding about the state of affairs. There's an empty milk carton and half a dozen condiments. I check the mustard out of curiosity: expired. I sit at the table in my boxers, blinking stupidly in the bright light, crunching my dry cereal. On the table in front of me is a pile of hair elastics and a hairbrush. A homework sheet with a teacher's bouncy writing at the top that says, *Please call me. Catriona is telling stories about Hades and Persephone again.* A Barbie with her hair shorn off close to her scalp, draped across the chair to my right. On the fridge is a dry-erase calendar crammed full of reminders: Ballet on Tuesdays and Thursdays. Christmas concert this Friday. Pediatrician appointment next Wednesday. It's fascinating. This is Dodi's kitchen. This is Dodi's life.

I put the bowl in the dishwasher when I'm done, and because I'm doing that, I load all the dirty dishes from the sink too, and press start. The bottom of the sink is full of soggy cereal, so I clean it out into the trash, which is overflowing, so I tie that up and set it by the door, where there's a pile of shoes. Once those are organized, I start picking up Barbies, but then I stop myself. There's something very deliberate about the way they've been laid out. On the kitchen counter is an empty granola bar box, which looks like it was torn open from the side by a dog. I collapse it and stuff it in the recycling. I take care of the empty milk carton too, and a knife with peanut butter on it.

They're a pair of pigs.

The morning melts by, shrouded in the fine mist of spray cleaner, prismatic in the bright sunlight. A second bag of trash joins the first. After the first hour, the fridge sparkles, the counters gleam, the dishwasher hums. After the second, the floors shine and the dead bugs in the light fixtures have been liberated directly into the trash. The washing machine burbles as it sloshes around Dodi's dirty laundry from our Las Vegas trip last week—which was left packed in her carry-on in the middle of the bedroom floor, because of course it was. I'm reconstructing the Jonestown Massacre–style arrangement of Barbies as per the photo on my phone after having vacuumed the carpet, when the landline rings. I pick it up without thinking.

"You're still there," Dodi says. I look at the clock and realize it's past noon. I was supposed to leave. I consider hanging up without saying anything, but there's relief in her voice when she says, "I have a problem."

"What do you need me to do?"

There's a pause, like maybe she hadn't anticipated me offering to help so readily.

"My neighbor two doors down is supposed to pick up Cat from school, but her car's broken down again—"

"Where and when?"

Again, the surprised pause at the other end of the line. Then she clears her throat, and her voice is crisp and cool.

"Our Lady of Sorrows. There's a pickup lane. You have to be there by two thirty. I'll call her to let her know."

"What does she look like?"

But there's another voice in the background—several voices—arguing, it sounds like—and then Dodi's voice, far away, like she dropped her phone into her pocket—

And the call disconnects.

I FIND THE CAR WHERE I LEFT IT UNDER THE OVERPASS, NOW ENGRAVED WITH a giant dick on the trunk and *EAT The RiCH* on the side.

Our Lady of Sorrows is a dour little building with a play-ground outside and a bruised, gnarly Christ on a cross at the entrance. I went to a school like this, of course, courtesy of Andrew. An awful little school, where the teachers knew who my uncle was and playground bullies ran rampant. A stress headache creeps up the back of my head just thinking about it. I scan the pickup area as I pull in. The school is like an anthill, the children pouring out, milling in every direction. It's a di-saster. Shrieks, horns honking, and every single child wearing the same uniform. I roll along at a crawl looking at the face of every little girl. And then I see a splash of Dodi red.

It's her, because of course it's her: a sullen little girl in a crimson peacoat who looks like she should be off haunting an abandoned sanatorium. The reason there were no photos of her at the apartment is probably because she doesn't photo-graph. Long, pin-straight dark hair held back with a ribbon headband, she stands with her hands clasped in front of her, her back perfectly straight, staring at something unseen in the distance. Whereas all the other girls her age are wild and be-draggled after a day of play, her tidy hair and neat clothes make it look like she was kept safe pressed between the leaves of a dusty old book. A grimoire.

I come to a halt in front of her and lower the window. "Cat!"

She jerks when she notices me. Her face is a perfect oval, her eyes skeptical and dark like Dodi's. She takes a few curious steps closer to the car.

"Get in."

She frowns at me, thinking, and then—"Ow!"

A grubby little blond girl slugs her in the shoulder as she runs past on her way to the car behind me. "Meow!" the blond girl shouts as she goes. I swivel to look, expecting the man at the wheel to do something about it, but he doesn't. Of course not. He's probably a bully just like his daughter.

"Why?" Cat asks me, rubbing her shoulder.

It hadn't occurred to me that there would be resistance or that Cat would do anything other than hop in the car and sit silently with her hands in her lap as I ferried her home. I probably haven't spoken to a six-year-old since I was one myself.

"Your mom asked me to get you," I say, reassuring smile engaged full force.

She doesn't buy it. "That's what perverts say. Mommy told me."

The car behind me blasts its horn, and I lunge across the car and open the door.

"Get in the car."

"Nope."

The horn blasts again, a sustained wail setting my teeth on edge.

I give Cat a bright, charming smile. "I'll . . . I'll get you a chocolate bar."

A matronly woman in a reflective orange vest with a permanent groove between her penciled eyebrows approaches. A pickup volunteer. I remember pickup volunteers—nosy, self-important—*Is that your dad, Jake? Oh, your* uncle . . .

"Who is this, Catriona?" she asks.

"He said he'll give me candy if I get in his car."

"Oh, for fuck's—" I pinch my mouth shut when the woman's eyes pop out of her head. "My name is Jake Ripper."

No dawning recognition. The pickup volunteer stares at me with suspicion. "Am I supposed to know who you are?"

Behind me the driver taps his horn over and over. *Honk. Honk. Honk* . . . and my shoulders ratchet higher and higher. I have no idea what Dodi told them about me. Am I a coworker?

A friend? And then I remember with a jolt, like I sometimes do about a dozen times a day, that Dodi and I are married.

"I'm Dodi's husband." My throat catches on the suddenly strange and awkward word.

"Catriona doesn't have a stepdad," she says, raising her voice over the honking, and my brain tweaks. I didn't say stepdad. That word is even worse. Cat seems to think so too. She stares at me with a disgusted expression.

The woman uses one broad hand to move Cat behind her body, like she's shielding her from seeing something foul. She edges away with Cat sheltered behind her, but I put my car in reverse and back up two feet alongside her. The car behind me lays on the horn again and I slam the brakes with a few inches to spare between our bumpers.

"Dodi said she'd talk to her teacher about this."

"I have no idea who Dodi is."

"Dolores."

"You keep changing your story. Is it Dodi or Dolores?"

The horn behind me blares again.

"Dodi is her nickname. Do you call your spouse by their full name?"

"I'm not married and neither is she."

Again the horn blares and I see red. I hold up my ring finger to show her. Her mouth falls open and she actually gasps, and I realize too late it looks like I'm flipping her the bird.

Just then the man behind me sticks his head out of his window and yells, "You going to move the Dickmobile, Bruce Wayne?"

I tap the gas so I can pull forward and closer to the curb so the asshole can pass, but I'm still in reverse. I crunch into the front of his car.

I look up and Cat is staring at the smashed front of the

other car with the same malevolently delighted look I've seen on Dodi's face about a half dozen times. Eyes glinting, mouth twitching into a nasty smile at her little nemesis sitting beyond the tinted windows of the back seat. She makes eye contact with me, and I can see one missing tooth in her smile. I'm her champion, and her dramatic exit from her bully's moment of reckoning awaits. The volunteer lunges at her as she slips from her grasp. Cat dodges and twists around her, effortlessly pops open the ridiculous door handle like she was bred to ride in supercars, and slides into the passenger seat as the pickup volunteer raises the alarm.

31

Career Killer

DODI

I GLANCE AT THE CLOCK AND WONDER WITH A KNOT IN MY STOMACH HOW pickup went. I have five missed calls from the school.

"I'm trying to understand. What projects has Dolores been assigned to these past two years?" Cynthia asks Doug.

There's another person present in addition to Cynthia, Marie, and Doug—a higher-up I've seen in the elevator. He watches me thoughtfully while Doug sweats and flails.

"Let's ask Dolores," the man suggests, and my tongue sticks to the roof of my mouth. I have no idea how to describe the "project" Jake showed Cynthia.

"No," Cynthia says quickly and decisively. "This is a management issue. We have a team leader who doesn't know what his star data analyst is doing."

Star data analyst. She means me.

"Cynthia—" the higher-up starts to say.

She rounds on the man and presses her finger into her desktop. "*You* hired *me* as a consultant. I suss out these toxic little workplace dynamics, straighten them out, and hand back a functioning workplace."

The man raises his hands in a conciliatory gesture. Above his head, the minute hand on the clock crawls past the hour. I have to get home.

"We have an underutilized employee whose opportunities for advancement have been thwarted by a dysfunctional management dynamic," Cynthia continues. Doug's eyes bug as he stares at his shoes. "And furthermore—"

The second hand completes one more loop. I can't take it. "It's after five," I say. "I have to go."

"You need to get home to your daughter," Cynthia guesses.

I freeze for a moment. I have no idea how Cynthia knows about Cat. "Yes."

The man raises his eyebrows at me. "We're almost done—"

"Go," Cynthia says to me. "That's another thing," she says, rounding on him again. "The work culture for parents at this organization—"

I bolt from the room, feeling shaky and ill. In my office I pack my things into my bag. Laptop, keys, wallet . . . but no phone. I left it in Cynthia's office.

I disabled the lock last night to let Cat watch cartoons. With a sinking heart, I picture Cynthia snooping through my emails, figuring out what I've been doing this whole time when Doug wasn't keeping his "star data analyst" busy with actual work.

I bolt back to Cynthia's office, but it's empty now, and locked. I peer through the vertical window by the door and spot my phone on the chair. It's a quarter past five already.

Back in the annex I fish two paper clips out of Jake's desk. They've been partially unfolded and bandaged in tape to make them easier to grip. I'm sweaty when I get back to Cynthia's office. I crunch the paper clips into the keyhole and—nothing happens.

I have no idea what I'm doing.

A janitor rounds the corner with a mop, and I stuff the paper clips into the waistband of my skirt. I busy myself plucking a tube of lipstick from my purse. He nears me, passes me—

"Um, excuse me," I blurt out. He turns, and I smile. I scrunch my nose. It feels disgusting and strange, like wearing someone else's underwear.

I tap the door and smile like I'm utterly charmed by my own idiocy. "I'm *such* an airhead. Locked out." I scrunch my nose again. Too many scrunches?

He puffs up with gallantry, pulls a key ring from his pocket, and lets me in. By the time he's turned the corner, he's already forgotten our interaction, and I realize I've learned another trick from Jake.

The door swings open smoothly, silently, and I shut it behind me without turning the light on. It's dim, but I can see enough to collect my phone.

I don't leave right away, though. I examine her office. There's the row of origami animals along the edge of her desk made from Post-it notes. Even in her spare time she's a paper jockey. A tedious, box-checking administrator. She's such a creep. This morning when I arrived she'd been waiting for me, sitting in my office, in my chair, casually folding one of my yellow Post-its into a crane. She'd already logged into my computer and looked through my drawers. She's determined to get me fired.

I've taken a special interest in you, Dolores.

I debate going through her drawers, but this isn't a reconnaissance mission. It's a social visit. I can be a creep, too. I can sneak into her office, sit in her chair, and leave unsettling, indecipherable messages for her to find.

I've taken a special interest in you, Cynthia Cutts.

Tinkle, tinkle, tinkle.

She likes origami. I pluck a piece of scribbled-on paper from her desk and lay it out in front of me.

There's only one pattern I know.

One fold, lengthwise, just to mark the midline for the corners that need to be folded in—twice, I remember. Fold along the midline again, and then fold, flip, and fold. I use the edge of my fingernail to make the creases sharp.

There was a trick to get thrust: I scrabble in her drawers until I find a paper clip. I slide it onto the nose, and it's finished. Sharp, angular, glinting like a knife in the dim room.

I tuck the body of the paper airplane into a crevice of her keyboard and push the roll-away tray back under her desk. She'll find it tomorrow morning: a humble offering to an esteemed colleague, and an invitation to play.

32

After-School Special

JAKE

"ARE YOU KIDNAPPING ME? YOU CAN TELL ME THE TRUTH," CAT SAYS, BLOWING her hair out of her face and righting herself in her seat as I peel out of the loading zone.

"I'm not kidnapping you."

"Oh." She sounds disappointed, but she rallies bravely. She punches buttons at random on the dash and console. Classical music whines from the car speakers, and my seat starts to massage my lower back.

There's an unsettling fearlessness here that needs to be addressed. "You shouldn't be getting in a car with someone if you think they're kidnapping you." I slap at the illuminated buttons until my seat settles on the more manageable vibrate setting. "You shouldn't be going off with strangers."

She looks at me.

"I'm not a stranger," I say quickly.

A curt know-it-all nod. "You're my stepdad." My stomach whomps again at that word. She clicks another button, but unfortunately it's not the James Bond emergency ejection button. Her window glides up.

I'm ready for a subject change. "Who was that kid who meowed at you?"

"That was Charlotte. She has a mom and a dad and a sister and a baby brother and a big house and a pet bunny." I can tell from her tone these facts make Charlotte vile. "I hate her. I hate her so much."

She has a funny, husky little voice. A frog voice. It suits her. It's weird, and not what you expect when you look at her. She snoops in the glove compartment and finds a pair of sunglasses. She puts them on.

"Do you hate anyone?"

I think of Andrew. "Yes."

She sighs happily and leans back in her seat next to me. She's absurdly small. Her little legs stick out straight in front of her. It occurs to me that she should be in some sort of restraint system, in the back seat.

"A booster?" she says when I try to verbalize this. "I don't use a booster anymore," she lies smoothly. "Where are we going?"

"Home?"

"I'm hungry."

I remember the depleted fridge and the empty milk carton, and when I spot a grocery store, I swerve into the parking lot. Another car blares its horn at us.

Inside, Cat hops on the end of my grocery cart and hitches a ride like this is routine.

"Mom lets me have chocolate milk," she says when I pick up a carton of two percent.

I ignore her.

"Mom gets the chocolate ones," she says when I grab the exact same box of oat granola bars off the shelf that Dodi had on her counter.

I ignore her.

"I don't like you," she says.

I ignore her.

An elderly shopper dodges to one side to let us pass and smiles—a full-on, eye-crinkling smile. I glance behind me, but no one's there. This is alarming. No one ever smiles at me like this. "Such a good dad," she coos. "Giving Mom a break?"

Cat shoots her a disgusted look and I hang a sharp right into the deserted bulk section. When we emerge into the meat section, the sight of disarticulated cow and pig and chicken made tidy and presentable in plastic packaging prompts a question.

"What's your mom cooking for dinner?"

Nose in the air, eyes on the far distance, Cat ignores me from her perch at the end of the cart. She's learned from the best.

I pick up a family pack of chicken breasts—I don't think I've ever bought the family pack of anything before—and place it in the cart.

"I hate chicken. I hate it so much."

I ignore her.

But then Cat's attention is snagged. "What's wrong with that chicken?"

She's wrinkling her nose at a packaged critter farther down. It's skinny, and instead of wings, it has front legs.

"That's rabbit."

As soon as I say it, I regret it. Little kids don't like learning that people eat bunnies. Cat's about to have her loss of inno-cence right here under my watch in the meat department and—

"I want to eat it."

Of course she fucking does.

"Why?"

"It looks delicious."

Raw meat does not look delicious. "Does this have anything to do with Charlotte having a pet rabbit?"

"No," she lies.

"Are you going to go to school tomorrow and tell Charlotte you ate rabbit for dinner?"

"No," she lies.

Grant liked rabbit. I know several rabbit recipes. I could do *lapin à l'istrettu*, or *lapin à la moutarde*. Or even just a nice, basic rabbit stew.

"You promise you'll eat it?"

"Yes." She seems to be telling the truth this time. I don't give a rat's ass about Charlotte. I do care about some little twerp turning her nose up at my cooking.

I exchange the chicken for the rabbit, and in the produce section I get mushrooms, shallots, parsley, hearty winter vegetables . . .

"I hate white carrots," Cat says.

"They're parsnips."

"I hate them."

"That's irrelevant."

"*You're* an elephant," she says mutinously. She narrows her eyes at me and slits my throat with a scowl.

At the checkout I throw a chocolate bar on the conveyor belt, and Cat eyes it sidelong. "That's for me getting in the car, isn't it?" she says.

"It's for you getting in the car and doing whatever else I tell you, until your mom gets home." I hold the chocolate bar high over her head. "Do we have a deal?"

Her nostrils flare, but she practically skips back to the car. Inside the car, she scarfs two and a half granola bars, then steps on the remaining half by accident, grinding it into the car's carpet. It's the least of my problems.

"There's rabbit juice," she says when we pull up to the apartment building, pointing at the back seat where the bags of groceries sit. There is, leaking from the meat packaging and pooling on the leather seat.

She leads the way up the stairs, strumming her fingers on the balusters and humming mournfully to herself in a minor key. We drip a trail of rabbit juice right up to Dodi's front door. I let us in and sling the grocery bag into the sink.

"Gross," Cat says, smearing a droplet of blood across the tiles with the toe of her boot.

"Get out of here. Go poke safety pins in your Barbies' eyes or something."

She looks delighted at this suggestion and scampers off without saying another word. In the silent aftermath, it's a minute before I realize my shoulders have been hovering under my ears since driving into the school pickup zone. My muscles relax slowly. I let out a breath and lean against the counter. This is Dodi's evening, day after day. Relentless. I look at the clock. It's not even four.

Plenty of time to cook a proper meal, at least. Dodi has a big Dutch oven, which I set on the stovetop. Her chef's knife is dull, so I sharpen it, and then all the others too, while I have the sharpener out. Everything in this apartment is completely dysfunctional.

I'm not a good enough cook to attempt something complex in a strange kitchen, so I keep it simple. I fry a few slices of thick-cut bacon while I slice the shallots with mechanical precision. When done with that, I fish out the bacon, and into the simmering grease go the shallots and the crushed garlic. When they have become translucent and the kitchen is fragrant, I add the rabbit pieces and sauté until golden. In go the porcini mushrooms and parsnips and carrots, a sprinkle of flour, and a little more browning, and then the broth and red wine. I pour and swirl, then add the sprig of thyme and fresh chopped parsley and bay leaves and, on impulse, a dusting of nutmeg . . . I bring it to a simmer, and on goes the lid, and then it's time for the braised artichokes.

I trim and pare the hearts and stalks, and rub with lemon, and then the artichokes and carrots go into a pot just big enough for them, with the garlic. Rinse, pat dry, and then back in the pot with thyme and a single bay leaf. Wine, water, salt and pepper . . .

And then I rifle through the cabinets, panicked, as it occurs to me too late that someone as apparently undomestic as Dodi might not have baking essentials. I do find it, though: a single package of yeast on the verge of expiry. I mix the dough, knead it, let it rise, punch it down, divide, let it rise again on the pan, and then into the oven.

The hours go by, and then it's just the mess to clean up. I swipe the vegetable trimmings into the compost, wipe down the counters, scour the cutting boards, and pluck the bloody meat packaging out of the sink where I left it. As I turn to place it in the trash, Cat materializes triumphantly brandishing an eyeless Barbie, and I trip over her. She shrieks indignantly, the packaging goes flying out of my hands, bunny juice splatters across the kitchen, and the front door bangs open all at once.

"What—?" Dodi shouts. She stomps into the kitchen, a big paper bag of groceries clutched to her chest, and stops in her tracks at the sight of us. Her hair stuck to her damp forehead, eyeliner wing on one side smudged, clothes rumpled, the bottom of the paper bag apparently giving out, her hand cupping a soup can as it tries to slip through a tear—this is Dodi at the end of a long day, home for the second shift, fighting for her life.

She pans slowly around the kitchen. She takes in Cat with her mutilated Barbie, the knives laid out in a row on the counter, the blood spattered across the cabinets, and me, wearing her absurd, flowery apron.

I'm so relieved to see her.

33

Bunny Boiler

DODI

"YOU'RE HOME," HE SAYS WITH A BIG PSYCHO SMILE.

I drop my disintegrating paper bag of groceries on the bar top with a thud, and the contents spill dramatically across the counter.

"What's going *on* here? Where's my neighbor? And why do I have five missed calls from Cat's school?"

They came in one after another while I was trapped with Cynthia. The school was closed by the time I returned them.

Jake's smile closes up on itself and Cat takes a half step behind him.

"What are you still doing here?" I ask.

"You needed me to pick up Cat," he says slowly and carefully.

"I needed you to drive my *neighbor* to pick up Cat. I told her to expect you."

We stare at each other for a beat. I feel sick. The calls from the school, the cryptic text from my neighbor: Your man friend coming through. I scrabble with my phone now to confirm. Yes. That's what she said.

But I missed the follow-up text a moment later: ?

And I made a pit stop at the grocery store instead of coming straight home to make sure Cat was okay. I stare at her now, assessing for trauma from the experience of school pickup by a strange man. She darts from the kitchen like she thinks she's in trouble.

This is all Jake's fault.

"Why are you wearing my apron?" I snap.

"I'm cooking dinner."

He absolutely is not.

"I had something planned," I say.

He glances at the Kraft Dinner sprawled out incriminatingly on the counter and raises one eyebrow. The snob. He has no idea what it's like trying to cook for a six-year-old who only eats beige.

I lift the lid off the Dutch oven to see what sort of disgusting bachelor special he's whipped up, and an unexpectedly savory aroma steams upward. Stew.

"She's not going to eat it," I say triumphantly.

He gives me a look, as if that's a challenge accepted. He lifts the Dutch oven and carries it into the dining area. I trail after him and stop in my tracks. Place mats, cutlery, trivets—all laid out with geometric correctness. My table has never looked like this. And that's not all. My mouth falls open.

My sofa looks . . . orderly, the cushions smoothed, the blankets folded. The coffee table is cleared and the windowsills, too. Everything feels brighter and fresher. I smell citrus cleaner. I look down. He's *vacuumed*. I bolt across the living room and stick my nose into my bedroom. My bed looks like it was made up by a hotel maid. My suitcase is missing from the floor, and with my heart in my throat I stomp into the laundry nook. It's taken so much work putting together a proper wardrobe on a shoestring budget, cobbling together consignment clothing and sale items, and if that *idiot*—

But he didn't. My hang-dry clothes are hanging and drying exactly as per their care instructions.

I circle back to the dining area.

"What the hell did you do to my apartment?" I hiss, willing myself to feel angry. He overstepped. He definitely overstepped. "I didn't give you permission to clean!"

Jake gives me a blank look. "Did you like the filth?" he asks without inflection.

Fury gives way to mortification and then swings back to fury again. But before I can clap back, Cat materializes and plunks herself audibly into a chair. He ladles stew into her bowl and tosses a roll at her like he's feeding a creature in a zoo, and she digs in.

She actually digs in.

This has never happened. I've never succeeded in creating this tableau of domestic dinnertime bliss. It's always fights and hunger strikes, ending with Cat eating crackers on the floor while I eat directly from the stovetop with a swig of cooking wine to cool my nerves.

I watch Cat in wonder. She chews. She swallows. A physiological miracle.

Jake ladles stew into my bowl and then his. My stomach growls and I cover it with a cough and reluctantly take a seat. We're all dead quiet for a minute, but there's something so hokey and normal about this scene, the actors can't help slipping into their roles. In his apron, Jake the homemaker serves food and mops up Cat's soup splatter and reminds her to try a parsnip. And I, in my rumpled end-of-day business attire, slip into the role of disciplinarian head of household. I clear my throat.

"I spoke to your teacher on the phone this morning," I say to Cat. "She said you and Charlotte got into a tussle."

Cat stiffens.

"She says you apologized very nicely."

Cat stares at her plate, nostrils flaring.

"Cat?"

"The teacher made me apologize! It was Charlotte's fault," Cat says venomously. "She always starts it!"

"Exactly!" I say. "You can't let a teacher strong-arm you into saying you're sorry. Saying you're sorry is an admission of guilt." I'm on her side, but right now she's looking at me like I'm attacking her. Her little claws come out so quickly. I don't know why she's like this.

Cat scowls at me, and I know it's going to be silent treatment for the rest of the evening, but then Jake butts in.

"Legally, it's not actually an admission of guilt in Canada."

The land of people who apologize if you punch them in the face. But that's not the point.

"This isn't a legal matter," I say through gritted teeth. "It's the principle of the thing. I'm not raising my daughter to smile sweetly and play nice and turn the other cheek."

"But Charlotte's an evil little bully, and she's going to figure out that if *she* says sorry and Cat doesn't, Cat will wind up looking like a sociopath to the teachers. Your approach is going to screw her over."

Cat looks up at him with her mouth open. Jake has no idea how to talk in front of a six-year-old.

Jake continues. "If you want her to protect her principles, she can say, 'Are you all right?' It demonstrates concern but doesn't assume responsibility." He butters a bun slowly and carefully and tosses it to Cat. The first bun has already vanished.

"You're overstepping," I say frostily, but next to me, Cat studies him with intelligent eyes.

"And I don't have to actually care if she's all right?" she confirms.

"Of course not," Jake scoffs. "You have to be clever with bullies. Don't let them realize you're fighting back. Study them and outsmart them. Keep notes. Make a list and stay focused."

I balk at him, but Cat glows from the inside. She's been given a mission, a masterplan to follow. A wicked little smile blooms on her face. She stirs her stew thoughtfully.

"Can I take leftovers for lunch tomorrow?" she asks me.

I have no idea what this means. I'm surprised she's even talking to me. Jake stares at her for a beat, then leans forward with his elbows on the table and catches my eye. "She's a future HR nightmare."

I already knew that, but the delighted, twisty smile Jake gives me now makes it sound like a compliment on my parenting. His eyes really are very green. And there's a smudge of flour on his glasses. My face feels warm. I look away.

I still haven't tried the stew. I take a bite, and melt.

"This chicken is delicious," I say begrudgingly. Jake gives me an alarmed look, and Cat grins deviously at him around a knobby leg bone.

CAT POLISHES HER BOWL AND DISAPPEARS, LEAVING THE TWO OF US. UNDER the cover of the table, I unhook my skirt waistband and have a second bowl, an artichoke, and two rolls, all the while avoiding eye contact with him. When I'm done I stand and stack dishes, but Jake firmly takes them from me. I try to scrub a pan, but he silently wrenches it away and elbows me from the sink with one bare arm. I've never seen him in a T-shirt before. It's filthy the way the muscles and tendons tense and flicker just below the surface in his forearms.

"I should clean. You cooked," I say. He ignores me. He rhythmically pumps liquid soap onto a scrubber, then scours the artichoke dish vigorously and thoroughly, using his hands at the end for a careful, deliberate stroke to check for any stubborn bits. He wipes it dry with a sensuous massage through a tea towel and, this tender aftercare complete, places it gently on the drying rack to recover its breath.

I bite my cheek and drag my eyes away from this erotic display of masculine self-sufficiency. I wonder if he owns a pair of sweatpants, too, to go with the T-shirt. It would complete the image of comfortable domesticity. I could buy him a pair. Dress him up like he's my doll. I thought girls were given dolls to play with to prepare them for motherhood, but when I grew up, I realized it had prepared me for babying a series of man-child boyfriends. But Jake isn't a man-child. I watch him carefully wipe out the sink, drape the damp towel over the oven handle, align a wonky magnet on the fridge. He'd probably fold and hang my clothes for me as he took them off.

This is choreplay. This is me on a full belly in a warm, clean house, mind freed up to focus on other physical needs for once. I shake my head. There are knives laid out on the counter with the sharpener. I go to put them away, but he's moved the knife block. I spot it by the stove. It actually makes more sense there, where I keep the cutting boards.

"How was your day?"

I round on him, and he leans back against the counter, eyes

on my hands. I lower the sharp knives. "Are you asking me how my day was?" It comes out as a snarl. I didn't mean it to. Suddenly I feel flushed and angry and confused. His hair is rumpled and sweet. He snooped through my freaking house. I never asked him to cook. Cat *smiled* at him.

"Who do you think you are? Coming in here, cooking, cleaning, getting Cat to actually eat something that's not a freaking Pop-Tart or a granola bar? I guess you're trying to show me how it's done? Show me how easy it is?"

But Jake is Jake: cool, unflappable, like my moods don't mean a thing. The unblinking serial killer watching his victim flail and shout. "I wasn't doing anything else today. And it looks like you've been busy." He tilts his head toward the calendar on my fridge, and I'm exhausted just looking at it. I'm so tired. I fell asleep on Cat's bed last night. It's the only time she lets me cuddle her.

"I wanted to say thank you for putting me up," he says quietly.

With fury I realize if I blink a tear will probably shake loose. I have no idea why. I'm not sad. I glare at him, a staring contest.

"That, and you're a pair of filthy animals and I can't resist a good mess." He twists the knives out of my grasp and slides them into the block.

"It's *my* job to cook and clean. I'm her mother. I've always done it all. On my own."

Jake ignores me and sweeps the floor, corralling approximately ten specks of dust into the pan.

"How was your day?" he repeats.

I ball up a paper towel in my hands and start ripping it to shreds.

"I walked in this morning to find Cynthia parked at my desk, waiting for me."

Jake watches me thoughtfully as he taps the dustpan on the edge of the garbage bin. He doesn't jump in with advice.

"She's fixated on that list."

"She would be," Jake says mildly, mysteriously. He takes the paper towel pulp from my hands.

"The list that my name is on. At the very top."

"Is it?" Jake says disinterestedly. I frown. Did he remove it?

"She's fixated on me."

"In a bad way?" he asks, and I almost laugh at the absurdity of the question. "She's protective of you."

I scoff. "You don't know anything about her."

Jake's expression has turned thoughtful.

"What?"

He shrugs. "I recognize her from somewhere. Somewhere I used to work. She was like that. Weirdly protective. Maybe after decades of being persona non grata to worker bees and higher-ups alike, she's set her sights on a mentee before she retires."

He's always been one for spinning fantasies. He sprinkles the macerated paper towel in the trash.

"Go relax or something," he says, and I deflate suddenly like an air mattress splitting open at the seam, all the pressure inside belching out in a breath of stale air. "I can't clean the place with you shedding messes everywhere you go."

I peer around the corner at Cat, who is sitting on the living room floor surrounded by her dolls. She makes dialogue, bouncing her Barbies on their toes as they talk to each other.

I creep slowly out of the kitchen and across the carpet. Three feet from her, I stop. Slowly, awkwardly, I kneel on the carpet just behind her. Her hair is tangled. She needs to let me brush it. That will be another fight, later, but for now it's nice to just sit near her and listen to her play with the toys I pinched and saved to buy her.

But then Cat looks over her shoulder at me, surprised, like the sight of her mother getting down on the floor is alien to her. I suppose it is. There aren't enough hours in a day to be a good mother and a fun one. I quail under that look, but then Cat slithers over to me and slides into my lap—soft and warm, claws tucked away, well fed and at ease in this tidy, nice-smelling apartment—and hands me a Barbie.

"You can be Charlotte," she says in her funny, furry little voice. "Your bunny's missing."

34

Black Widow

JAKE

I TIP MY HEAD BACK ON THE SOFA AND CLOSE MY EYES. I CAN HEAR THE MUR-muring of Dodi's and Cat's voices getting ready for bed in the other room, the splashing of water, the TVs of neighboring apartments, the elevator going up and down. I tune out. I hover in that space between consciousness and sleep. Then . . . the hairs on the back of my neck rise. I open my eyes and Dodi is leaning against the corner of the wall where the hallway opens onto the living room, considering me. She's changed into her nightclothes, a long-sleeved black nightshirt just short enough that I can see the tattoo dangling down one side of her thigh—a dagger, right where a woman would tuck one into her garter. I try not to stare at it.

"Did you figure out someplace to go?" she asks.

"No."

She doesn't point out that I have a pillowcase full of money and could easily explore hotel options. Instead she glides to the kitchen and returns with a pair of wineglasses and a half-full bottle. She flicks on the TV, and the crime scene photo of a chalk outline on a downtown sidewalk fills the screen. She watches, and sips her wine, and I watch her. If I'm perfectly quiet and she forgets I'm here, I can stay another night. I could turn into a closet squatter, creeping out during the day to use her shower and kitchen, vacuum her carpet, cook her meals, and scurry back Gollum-like to the crawl space when she comes home. It would be a good life.

"You going to stare at me all night, you weirdo?" she says without looking at me.

"Yes."

She mutes the TV and twists to face me, coiling her bare legs up on the cushion next to her.

"Are you going to tell me what your list is about?"

"No."

"Why not?"

"Because you want me to."

"I'll need to know if I want to keep my job."

"Why would you want to? You don't have to work a soulless corporate job ever again. Use your winnings to start fresh."

She frowns at me. "I *want* a soulless corporate job."

"Why?"

"I *like* working downtown. I like the glitz, and the money, and the rush. I like stomping around in high heels and pencil skirts. I want to earn shitloads of money and have a corner office with a view and go shopping on my lunch break for overpriced silk scarves that I never wear and wind up in a tangled mess in a drawer. I want an assistant and a nice car, and I want to send my kid to a posh little artsy private school where I can pay the teachers to back off and just let her blossom into the spooky little goth girl she's meant to be."

I suppose it's good for Cat that she has someone in her corner.

"You're not like that, though," Dodi says.

"Like what?"

Dodi places one arm on the back of the sofa, her fingertips coming to rest six inches from my shoulder. "You don't care about shiny, expensive things. You don't like tall buildings and fast cars, or world travel and penthouse apartments."

I don't. I don't like *any* of that shit.

"What do you like?" she asks quietly.

I like you, I could say like a paste-eating child.

Apart from that, I have no idea what I like. There was a while there when I was younger when I was trying to figure that all out, before I realized it didn't really matter in the long run, because there would be no long run. She doesn't press me. She looks at me like I'm mysterious and fascinating. I've done and said such ridiculous things to get her to look at me like that, and here she is, giving me that look for slouching on her sofa after a day of playing homemaker. I wonder . . . I wonder if this evening was *real life* enough for her. What she thinks about me being a part of her real life. She takes a sip of wine and I do too.

"You have two hundred thousand dollars and a terminal illness. Some people would buy themselves a sports car and start driving across the country, or throw a massive party in the most expensive hotel room they can book, or hop on a plane and see the world. But here you are—in my crappy little apartment that smells like stale apple juice and dirty socks—cooking meals and folding throw blankets."

Maybe not mysterious and fascinating after all. I'm the boring temp who blends into the walls at work. But Dodi melts across the sofa cushions toward me, and the hair on the back of my neck does its thing again.

"I've figured out what your MO would be," she says, her voice lower now that she's so close to me. She props her elbow on the back of the sofa near my shoulder and leans her face into her hand, and the line from under her ear to the curve of her bare shoulder where her shirt has fallen to the side is one long, sinuous stroke.

"Yeah?"

"You would be known as 'The Caretaker.' I'm imagining a job interview mix-up: you're hired by the mob to 'take care' of some people, so you do just that—you break into their houses one by one and *take care of them*. You clean, fold laundry, and feed them up." As she says all this she's not smiling, but she's not *not* smiling. I'm meant to crack first.

"How would I kill them?"

She sighs loftily. "Haven't figured that part out yet. All I know is by the time they get to the dinner table with the good china laid out, they realize they're goners. They know something terrible is waiting for them."

"Cleanliness, nutrition, and evening leisure time."

She glances around the room self-consciously, any prospect of a smile gone. I've insulted her. She's like a porcupine, always curling up tight around her tender underbelly at the first sign of a threat.

Backtrack, backtrack, backtrack . . .

"But you always have to do it all yourself," I say. "You don't get any help."

She considers my attempt to rectify. "This is not the way I pictured it, you know," she says.

"The way you pictured what?"

"My life."

"How did you picture it?"

Against all odds, she uncurls for me. "There was supposed to be a house near a good school. We were going to have a dog—something fluffy and stupid. There was supposed to be a pair of grandparents helping out. *I* grew up with my grandparents in the house with us. Cat was supposed to have a dad. I was supposed to have a husband."

One for six. We sit in silence for a minute.

"What happened?"

"You know that old saying—'When you off your husband, you find out who your friends are.'" She scratches the stem of her glass with her thumbnail. "We had a down payment for a house saved, but I ended up living on that for a few years after Cat was born. No life insurance, of course. Neil had lots to say about the house odds of life insurance. And I wouldn't have been able to cash in, anyway."

"You didn't do time," I conclude.

She considers me. "You didn't look it up?"

I haven't searched online. It felt like cheating. I like her the way she is, a hazy question mark, revealing herself to me in shocking flashes. The way she looks at me right now tells me I did right.

"The laws around medically assisted suicide were changing even as the DA was forming his case," she says in a low voice, eyes on her glass. "And the prosecution of a young widow—a *pregnant* young widow, as it turns out—was poised to become . . . how do I put it? A full-blown media circus and emphatically not a good look. I'm lucky. The media coverage died down almost before it began."

She swirls her wineglass. She's ready for a subject change.

"Why was Cat playing with a pair of Dolce & Gabbana sunglasses?"

"She found them in the car."

"Can I have them?"

"I already gave them to Cat."

"I thought you were allergic to kids," she says.

I wonder how big of an idiot I'd be in her eyes if she knew I thought Cat was an actual cat all along.

"I'm allergic to people."

"Relatable. And I guess she's not really a kid, is she?"

"Not like any kid I ever met. Does she float when you give her a bath?"

Her lips twitch. "I do sometimes wonder if I shouldn't burn her at the stake to be safe."

"Couldn't hurt."

Dodi's face goes serious. "Most nights it's not like this. It's not easy. *She's* not easy. She's so . . . prickly."

"It can crop up randomly in a family."

Another lip twitch. "She's impossible."

"Have you tried an exorcism?"

The lip twitching is outright dangerous now. "I don't have any credit with the priesthood."

"I think you're doing great with her."

She's rendered silent for a moment.

"I want better for her than this," she says quietly.

I look around the cozy little apartment. I like it better than Grant's. I like it better than the cold, immaculate house I spent my teen years in with Andrew and Laura. A memory has been slowly surfacing all day.

"I lived in an apartment like this with my mom. Just the two of us. I never thought twice about the things we didn't have. I had a good childhood." I think of that calendar on the fridge. "You're giving her a good childhood." Another memory rears up. "I fucking *loved* Kraft Dinner."

My words land somewhere in Dodi's psyche where I can't see them. She watches me for a beat.

I'm still trying to wrap my head around this new Dodi who is a mother. There's something about the very idea that changes everything about her. It's that cliché of a vase giving way to the two profiles on either side. A framed picture on a wall turns out to be a window to an entire world upon closer inspection. All the softness and tender care in this messy little apartment— the basket of folded laundry, the cozy furniture, the snack food, the toys—all of this is Dodi seen from a different angle, Dodi keeping something behind her and out of view. The dark side of Dodi's mysterious, remote moon.

Mostly it's been fascinating listening to her go a whole three hours without dropping an f-bomb.

"I'm a bit older than you," she says suddenly and randomly. Her voice is quiet and serious.

"I already knew that."

Dodi is the sort of person who spends their twenties looking ten years older than they are and their thirties looking ten years younger. She's a mystery. But she's been married and widowed, and she has a six-year-old kid.

"You're *a lot* older than me," I point out.

She frowns and sits up straighter.

"What are you, five . . . six hundred years old?"

The corners of her lips spasm and she takes a quick sip from her glass to cover. "Are you done with the vampire jokes?"

"I have a few in reserve."

She creeps closer, until I can practically feel the warmth radiating from her. I never drink, but it's not the wine that's making me feel flushed and weird. My understanding of the moment shifts, and this time I realize in advance where we're heading.

She studies me. "You've been so strange with me. Sometimes you look at me like . . . I don't know. Like Jeffrey Dahmer doing some meal planning in his head. But then I throw myself at you, and you're the nerdy kid who flinches and turns his back to the football. I can't tell what you want from me."

I never knew what I wanted from her. I just *wanted*. Maybe it is hunger. From the moment she stepped into that elevator, it was like not realizing you were starving until you were offered something to eat.

She leans closer. "Is it your illness? Does that—?"

"No," I say quickly. "It's not like that."

She cocks her head to one side. "You need zip ties and duct tape to get turned on."

"No."

She presses her lips together. "So it's me."

"Yes."

"I don't do it for you." Her tone has already changed. Lofty, could give a fuck. She pulls away, picks up the remote, eyes back on the TV, where there's a vista from the top of a downtown skyscraper.

It came out wrong, but the idea that Dolores could think she doesn't do it for me after literally all of *everything* is a brand-new, previously unlocked level of head-assery.

"I know it's been a while since you've been able to see your own reflection. You do it for me so well you scare the shit out of me," I clarify, and it's true. I'm running on stress hormones whenever I'm around her. I never know how an interaction with her is going to go. Her cheeks turn faintly pink, her eyes still on the screen, where there's the image of a paper airplane.

"This is probably a shocking twist, but I haven't been married that many times before."

The corners of her lips move again.

"And obviously you have several centuries' worth more notches on the lip of your coffin than I do."

"Fuck off."

"What *was* sex like before showers?"

She tosses the remote onto the coffee table with a clatter and turns to face me.

"Go long, nerd," she whispers, and then she bites my neck.

My brain blinks out, all color contracting into a dot before vanishing, like an old TV turning off. My mouth finds hers, and it's pure brain stem action after that. Touch and taste and basic functions, like breathing and pulse and, beyond that, nothing except a mayfly's instinct to at least check this off my list before the clock's done ticking.

I like her on top, like she's going to take care of the important decisions, so I hook her behind one knee and pull until she's straddling me, her long hair spilling onto me, and she runs her hands over my shoulders, my chest, my throat. My hands find her knees. I don't remember ever noticing a woman's knees before, but when a woman dresses the way Dodi does, like her body is privileged information, the bits you can see take on significance. Her neck. Her knees. And now above her knees, up the sides of her thighs, under the fabric of her nightshirt . . . on the right I can feel bumps. Lines. Scars in the skin from a part of her tattoo that went too deep. I want her to show me all her tattoos.

She bends her face to mine and kisses me like an animal licking its wounds. Brain activity completely flatlines, and if I were in a hospital bed plugged into a monitor, the only humane thing to do would be to remove the feeding tube. Not give me a shot of adrenaline directly into the heart, which is what it feels like right now. I could run a minute mile. She kisses me harder, and one of us makes a sound, or maybe it's both of us, and it feels for a moment like she's everywhere, and there's nothing else, and then she takes my hands and puts them where she wants them—which is also where I want them—and she's soft and warm—

"Your hands," she says suddenly, and the moment skips and stumbles and crashes.

My fingers are completely white. Cadaverous. They look awful. I shove them between my thighs and the sofa cushions.

"Do they hurt?"

I shake my head. "They just go numb."

I feel stupid for ruining the moment again. I try to slow my breathing. I look everywhere but at her.

"Jake."

She pries one hand out from where I've hidden it and holds it between her own hands, warming it. I finally look up at her. Her face is serious and stoic, and the mood is completely gone, I know it. How could it not be?

She licks her lips. "How much time *do* you have?"

My dad was dead by thirty-four, but for the first time it occurs to me I don't know when his symptoms started, or at what point life became unbearable for him. Only one person in the world has that information. I open my mouth to explain all this, but—

"Hey, what about my chocolate bar?"

It's Cat, glaring at me from the end of the sofa in an old-fashioned nightgown that makes her look like a Victorian ghost. Dodi leaps off me and straightens her nightshirt, and I burn with gratitude that my hands were somewhere G-rated.

"You have to leave," Dodi says abruptly.

She doesn't need to tell me twice. I throw on my coat and go, down the stairwell, out the fire exit. As the door snicks shut behind me, I realize I forgot my bag. I step out into the street, no idea what happens next.

The car is half a block away. I click the key fob, and the entire city blinks out into darkness.

35

Blackout

JAKE

THE INTERIOR LIGHT OF THE CAR IS THE ONLY POINT OF ILLUMINATION IN THE vast, dark night. Streetlights, house lights, everything else has winked out.

I shiver, as if somewhere in the future someone has stepped over my grave. When I get in the car the light flicks off, and I'm in a darkness so thick you could lie flat like a starfish and float on it. My eyes adjust. Stars materialize in the sky. Have I ever seen stars in the city? Then an eerie glow blooms in the window of the house nearest me. A gaunt face illuminated from below appears, and disappears after setting a candle on the sill.

Power outage. Of course.

In my head I see a space heater with no power to run it, in a dusty, cluttered room getting colder and colder. I start the car and pull a U-turn onto the road.

When I arrive, Bill's neighborhood is full of dark-eyed houses too. The door swings open under my tenth knock and a flashlight shines in my face.

"Come back to kill me?" Bill says. "Good night for it, and just in time. I would have frozen to death before morning."

It's why I came. I follow him inside. It's chilly, my breath clouding the air in front of me.

"Do you have a fireplace?"

He frowns. "Of course."

"And firewood?"

He thinks. "I haven't had a fire in years. There must be some in the garage."

There is, and it's dry as bone. Bill watches with suspicion as I kneel at the living room hearth.

"You're doing it wrong," he says. He can't get down on his knees, so he starts poking and knocking my handiwork with his cane. "Balance that one on top, like that, or it won't draw."

He has a great, ancient box of matches, mostly gone. I strike one, and it gives a delicious *schwick* as a tongue of fire licks up. Bill and I watch the flames curl around the paper and set to work on the edges of the wood. The firelight peels back some of the darkness in the room, and when I examine Bill, I can see he's still wearing his thin terry cloth robe. The idiot.

"Your dad never teach you to build a fire?"

"My dad's dead," I tell Bill. "So no."

Bill peers at me. He looks even more confused when I settle him back into his easy chair and drape a blanket over him. I pull the ottoman close and sit on it. It's time to confess. It's time for an exchange of information held hostage. Sitting on Dodi's sofa, I realized there are things I want to know from Bill. I want to know how this is going to go. I want to know how long from onset to game over. I want to know how long until that tipping point where loss of quality of life matters. I want to make the most of this.

"I'm not casing you out. I check your mailbox to make sure

you came out. If you miss a couple of days, I look in the windows to make sure you're not sprawled out at the bottom of the stairs or something."

"Who are you?"

I've imagined many times how this might play out. It's hard not to think of the way Aunt Laura looked when I suddenly appeared in her life: stricken, confused. Or Andrew's immediate resentment, or the way his conservative family still looks at me like a slimy, disturbing secret slithered out from a crevice—the fatherless son of Laura's estranged, unwed sister. It's tempting to imagine Bill's craggy face softening into surprise—*joy*, even—but how long would that last? He would see I've got my dad's hazel eyes, the myopia; how many seconds would tick by before his mind went to the other goodies in my genetic grab bag?

I'm about to find out.

"My name is Jacob."

He raises his eyebrows, face soft all of a sudden. "That was my son's name."

"I know."

He frowns. "What is your last name?"

"Ripper." He narrows his eyes at me. "Ripper" is being turned this way and that in his head, held up to the light, tapped against the heel of his palm while he thinks.

"My mother's name was Elizabeth Ripper," I add.

Something shifts deep in the sublayers of Bill's memories, and his face collapses in shock.

I WAS EIGHTEEN WHEN I GOT MY HANDS ON MY BIRTH CERTIFICATE FOR THE first time and saw for myself the blank line where my father's name was supposed to go. It was a dead end until Laura smuggled me a small folder of my mother's papers from Andrew's office right before I moved out. Amongst them was a photo of a man—glasses, wide smile—and a letter. A breakup letter, to be precise, dated nine months before I was born and signed *Love always, Jake*. It was a project I picked away at, uncovering first his obituary, then a distant cousin or two on social media, and finally an old friend still living in the city. It was from him I learned about my father's illness. He was the one who told me where to find my grandfather, Bill.

BILL'S RANGE IS GAS, AND IT MAKES SHORT WORK OF BOILING WATER. HE SITS in his armchair, cupping a mug of tea in his hands, warm water bottles wedged under his feet and in his lap.

"Elizabeth Ripper," he says, and it has all the effect of someone unlocking the door to a dusty, forgotten room to hear my mother's name said aloud after all these years. "Sweet, shy thing. I remember her. They were going to be married. And then he didn't answer his phone for two weeks, and when I was good and worried, he showed up on my doorstep. He'd figured out he was dying. He'd decided to let her go—give her a chance to be happy. He didn't even tell her why, the idiot. Didn't want her to argue with him. The poor girl must have been so hurt."

I nod, slowly. I think of Dodi holding my hand, asking me how much time I have, like maybe it almost matters to her.

"He was only thirty-one when it started," Bill continues. "His decline was pretty quick after that. He turned into a hermit. He let his friendships go. He just gave up. He was housebound after about a year, and after that, things got really miserable. He was confused. Not himself anymore. It wasn't pretty."

"Did anyone else in the family have it?"

Bill's face collapses. "His mother."

My grandmother. I already knew this from my sleuthing.

"She went so quick—I felt like we didn't know what hit us. And then Jacob, twenty years later—"

"Hereditary."

He looks at me with an expression so anguished, my stomach twists. This right here is the reason I never introduced myself before. It seemed selfish to satisfy my curiosity at the expense of this lonely old man's equilibrium.

But there's no need for any of that. One year until I'll want to check out. Less time than I thought, but I might outlive Bill, at any rate. I slip on a fake smile, as easy and habitual as tying my shoes.

"I hope you're not worried about me. I've seen a neurologist. I'm going to live to a hundred," I say.

THE POWER FLICKS BACK ON THE NEXT DAY, BUT I STAY WITH BILL. I COOK AND bring his meals to his easy chair, and when he nods off sitting upright, I clean. I scrub grime out of crevices, I dust, I consolidate piles of trash, sort them, and dispose of them. I throw out hundreds of dollars of expired pantry items and replace them with food he can actually prepare himself. I run loads of laundry, I scrub toilets, I shampoo rugs. I organize the mess of pill bottles by the sink, then fill up his pill box for him. I make arrangements for the boiler to be fixed and fiddle with the ancient radiators until the whole house is warm.

"What in the hell are you doing?" Bill asks. "No. Don't touch those glasses," he says, one day after lunch. "I can do some dishes for once."

What I'm doing is not thinking about Dodi on the sofa,

asking me what I like. Dodi in the airport, telling me I need to figure out what makes me happy. Other people have lists, and it never occurred to me to compile my own. Every day I imagine going back to Dodi's and buzzing her apartment. Every day, I think about my dad leaving my mom alone, trying to let her be happy.

I keep busy. There's so much to do, and each job creates another. It's like yanking on the loose thread of a sweater to snap it off, only to unravel an entire row of stitching and wind up with more thread to deal with. When Bill notices me wearing the same shirt for the third day in a row, he tells me to help myself to whatever I find in the bedroom closets. It's the permission to snoop upstairs I was waiting for.

What I find is a bedroom. A man's clothes hang in the closet: button-ups and slacks, a few silly ties. He was a teacher, like my mom. The bed is stripped, but an old-fashioned alarm clock still sits on the side table, and next to it a pair of thick-framed glasses. I remove my own and place them on the bridge of my nose. Our prescription is almost the same, his a little stronger. He was a bit older than me when he died, but only a bit.

I leave everything as I find it and close the door.

THE MORNING OF CHRISTMAS EVE, I FIND BILL WATCHING TV IN FRONT OF HIS fire—the fire is lit every day now, even with the power back on.

". . . a citywide turkey shortage in grocery stores thanks to a turkey pileup on Highway 1 . . ." a news reporter with reindeer earmuffs says on TV. Behind her is a semi rolled over onto its side, little white lumps of vacuum-wrapped Butterballs pimpling the highway.

Bill taps the mute on the remote control I uncovered under the sofa to give me his full attention. I hand him his mail: a hydro bill, a package from a law firm, and an envelope from a lab. Bill's health is a full-time job to manage. I don't know how he's supposed to do it on his own. He rips open the envelope from the lab first and stares at the contents for a long minute. It can't be good news, but he doesn't share it with me. I understand the preference for privacy. He folds it up and stuffs it in his pocket without looking at me.

"I'm going to my aunt's for Christmas," I tell him.

He gazes at me long and hard. I feel like he's looking at my eyes, my glasses, my hair. I don't know what he's looking for. He nods his head. "All right."

I have the impulse to invite him, but I don't. Andrew is a corrosive substance, and I wouldn't inflict him on anyone.

"Will you be all right here?"

"I've been all right here on my own for almost thirty years," he reminds me gruffly. "Is this it?"

"What do you mean?"

"Will you be coming back?"

I've been waiting for him to ask. I want to say yes. It's not like there's anywhere else for me to go. But there's a change in the air, a difference in Bill's mood all of a sudden.

"Do you want me to?"

Bill shrugs without looking at me, diffident. "I don't see why you'd bother. You're young. You have better things to do."

The room is awkwardly silent apart from the babble of the TV. I've been carving out a little nook for myself in someone else's life these past weeks, trying to be useful, essential, and once again it hasn't worked. Bill and I have been dancing around our connection this whole time. He hasn't uttered the word "grandson." I haven't called him anything other than "Bill." Blood connection doesn't equate a relationship, after all. He's a tired old man who was grateful for some help, and that is all.

I leave him there by the fire with his stack of mail.

36

Christmas Killjoy

JAKE

I PARK GRANT'S CAR THREE BLOCKS FROM ANDREW'S PRYING EYES AND NOSY questions and walk the rest of the way, until I stand in front of the two-story white polyp of suburban architecture I first washed up at twenty years ago almost to the day with nothing but a bag of clothes and my dog. A sunburst window over the front door, sheer white curtains in the windows, hedges trimmed and fiddled within an inch of their life, manicured lawn on display even now thanks to this green Christmas. Conventional. Unchanging. Eternal.

I haven't been back in three years, but last night Laura's name came up on my phone, and for some reason I answered it.

"It would be so nice to see you," she said. "You and . . . anyone else you want to bring."

She meant Dodi, and since all my Dodi thoughts are linked chaotically like a barrel of plastic monkeys, I immediately heard Dodi saying, *You need to tell your aunt you're sick.* I'd pictured them all assembled around that long, shining dining room table, the extended family that has always looked at me like something embarrassing that has crept out into the open, as I dropped my bombshell. They would finish chewing and dab their lips with their napkins. *Sounds neat, Jake. Can you pass the potatoes?*

I accepted the invitation alone and here we are. I wonder if the bichon frisé is still kicking. And as if he reads my mind, he comes snuffle-trotting down the walkway, his tongue hanging out one side of his underbite, his eyes in business for themselves. Princess. He's delighted to see me. A former cellmate back in the clink.

I stand there for a good minute on the welcome mat, reminding myself the nausea is just Pavlovian conditioning. Princess is a dog, so he's knows all about it. He shivers and stinks and leans against my leg. His nails need a trim. The hair in front of his eyes, too. I press the doorbell. Footsteps, and the door swings open, and I paste a big smile on my face, quick as lightning.

"Jake!"

Laura wears a Rudolph apron dusted with flour, and just like the house and yard, she's unchanging and eternal, except in her case I'm grateful for it. I don't really know what comes over me. Without thinking, I reach in and hug her. She freezes, then puts her arms around me in a fierce squeeze.

"Where's your bag?" she asks, blinking rapidly with misty eyes and not looking at me. She peers out the door, like she hopes to see another person coming up the walkway.

"I didn't bring one." It's still at Dodi's. Laura's face falls, and I change the subject before she can ask if I'm spending the night. Depending on Andrew, I might prefer to sleep in my car. "How many people will there be at Christmas dinner tomorrow?"

"Fifteen," she says, closing the door. "Andrew's parents will be shuttled over from the home. Ninety-five and ninety-

 twin this year, and still gallivanting around for the holidays. Can you believe it? Of course, they want to spend Christmas with their great-grandkids." At the mention of Andrew's sister's grandkids, her smile flicks back on in full force: "*Three* little ones this year. June and Molly are five now, and there's the baby of course—Oliver." Laura beams at me. It's all about the kids, for Laura.

Andrew's voice emanates from somewhere in the house. It's a one-sided conversation, or argument. Laura twists her head to listen in on this half of the phone call, her smile slipping again, and I reflexively leap into distraction mode, like I always did when I lived here.

"Is the tree all decorated?"

In answer, she swans ahead of me into the vaulted living room where a ten-foot Christmas tree flaunts itself in sparkling, twinkling glory. Garland is threaded through the banister, silver stars dangle from light fixtures, holly and cedar swags hang on the doors, Christmas ornaments clutter every surface— Santa throw pillows, snow globes, snowman nesting dolls.

Christmas *belongs* to Laura. She practically invented it. It's always been that way—at least, after that first awful Christmas when a car crash landed me in this strange house with a pair of strangers. There hadn't been a single holiday decoration of any sort in the entire place that year, and I'd wandered the house silently at night while they slept, wondering what sort of aliens I found myself living with. But now it's all perfect, the entire house. The pile of gifts under the tree is obscene, the biggest one left unwrapped: a deluxe Barbie house festooned with ribbons. Laura has a tendency to go garbanzo beans over the girls.

Andrew's voice gets louder, and it's clear now that it's his sister he's arguing with. Laura drifts to the foot of the stairs and listens, still, her hand like a claw gripped around the banister.

Distraction mode. "What needs to be done in the kitchen?"

Laura swivels and fires a bright, strained smile at me and leads me to the kitchen. The oven is on, all stovetop burners firing, and every inch of counter and tabletop has been assigned to a job. Crystallized cranberries dry on a baking sheet, candy cane brittle cools on a rack, peeled potatoes lurk in a big pot in the sink . . . it's endless. More has always been more for Aunt Laura. She's spent days working on this. I take an apron off the pantry door, tie it tight around me, and when I turn around, she's smiling for real.

There's a bang upstairs, and I redirect quickly with our favorite game.

"The mixer," I say.

Laura glances at the mixer. "How?"

"He'd have to be wearing a tie."

"Oh, grisly!" she says appreciatively. "Asphyxiation or broken neck? Either one, I suppose. Now, tell me what you think of this." She fishes a kitchen gadget out of a drawer. "I saw it and bought it just to show you. Right through the orbital socket and into the prefrontal cortex."

She engages the plunger and little claws come out of the hollow shaft and click together. *Clack clack clack.* Princess twitches on the mat at her feet.

"You win," I say, and she glows, the yelling and the banging forgotten. That's the magic of I Spy a Murder Weapon.

Laura tugs a dish towel off the counter to make room for a cutting board—and a chef's knife lurking underneath goes spinning through the air. She yelps. It twirls in slow motion, glinting with Christmas colors as it pirouettes through space above Princess where he lies on the kitchen mat, and my hand reaches out all on its own to catch it.

I make contact.

"Jake!" my aunt shrieks.

I hear her plop down onto the floor next to me—because I'm already hunched on the floor myself—and she squeezes my shoulder.

"Jake," she says softly. "It's okay, honey. Open your eyes. You can look."

It's not okay. I've got it clenched into a fist now, but I got a glimpse of my hand—of the *inside* of my hand—the split second before I closed it.

Slow footsteps come down the hall, and the kitchen door swings open.

"What's the shrieking about?" Andrew says coldly. He eyes me dispassionately.

"Jake's cut his hand."

Andrew's eyes are skeptical slits. "There's no blood."

"He's stanching it."

"Why are you sitting on the floor? What's wrong with you?"

That's when Princess sticks his face in it. Snuffling, dirty white, with rust stains coming from his eyes, he presses his stubby, arthritic paws into my lap and wafts his foul breath into my face—

"Get up," Andrew says.

Princess tries to stick his wet nose to my hand, and I jerk it away.

"Shoo, Princess!" my aunt says, but Princess becomes more committed.

"There's nothing wrong with you," Andrew says. "You're always like this. You always think you have something wrong with you."

"He cut his hand—"

"I don't see a cut."

"His palm—"

"Open your hand, Jake," Andrew says.

Everyone's talking at once, and Princess keeps at it, sticking his fucking damp face—

"Open your damned hand, Jake!"

I open my hand, releasing the pressure on the cut, and pain suddenly blooms through my hand, up my arm—

The *blood*. Oh, the blood.

Laura squawks and bundles my hand in a dishcloth with vegetable trimmings still clinging to it. "Stitches!" she cries.

"He doesn't need stitches," Andrew says. He yanks me to my feet by my wrist and sticks my hand under the sink, then runs the cold water. The bottom of the basin swirls pink and red. I close my eyes and gag. I'm not good with blood.

"Unbelievable," Andrew says, dropping my wrist. I clench my hand back into a fist and the bleeding stops, and I lean heavily against the counter. Andrew plucks up a clean holly-patterned napkin from a stack folded neatly for dinner tomorrow and wipes his hands. I've been sorted. He's ready to move on to more important things.

"They're not coming," he announces.

"What?" Laura says blankly. She's still wearing her apron, but she's slipped on a coat and has her car keys clutched in one hand.

"Judith is doing her own Christmas," he says with the air of injured royalty, as if he didn't intentionally pick a fight with his sister and then hold Christmas hostage. I've seen him use this move a dozen times over the years. Good old Judith finally called his bluff.

Laura's face falls. The food. The decorations. The Barbie mansion—

"But I spoke to her this morning—"

Andrew says the most Andrew thing possible. "You know what she's like." Then he turns and walks out.

Laura stares after him, stunned, as the kitchen door rocks on its hinges behind him, the scuffling noise of Princess licking his balls the only sound in the room.

When I see Laura's face, I know I Spy can't touch this. I sometimes wonder if there's an evolutionary advantage to being an asshole. Maybe it's calorically more efficient.

"I don't need stitches. I'll bandage this up." I wrap my hand in a clean dish towel and flick the radio on to Christmas tunes on my way out.

In the bathroom I find a roll of gauze, which I wind tightly around my hand across the sliced webbing between my thumb and index finger. Princess follows and watches the proceedings. When I finish, he and I stare at each other.

Princess's villain origin story is that he is the replacement dog my uncle brought home after he put down the senior golden retriever I arrived with. I named him Princess to piss off my uncle and never forgave him. Uncle, that is. Maybe this is *my* villain origin story.

"Who's a good boy," I grunt in the flattest, deadest voice I can summon, and he wags his tail, delighted. I trim his bangs with the bandage scissors while he licks my knuckles in ecstatic supplication. Maybe he'll spend the night with me in the car.

WHILE LAURA GETS LUNCH ON THE TABLE, I INSPECT THE PICTURE-PERFECT Christmas tree, resplendent in winking fairy lights and old-fashioned, kitschy ornaments. With my good hand, I try to adjust a Santa perched too close to the end of a branch, but his body detaches from his head and falls to the floor. The severed head bounces on the springy branch, and it makes me think of Cat. She would like that ornament. Laura is still busy in the dining room, so I snap the body off a snowman hanging nearby. An angel next. A reindeer. And finally a drummer boy, before Laura calls me to lunch.

Andrew sits at the head of the table, as usual, with Laura to his right and a space for me at his left. He allows Laura to serve him, and then he rubs his hands slowly, like he's wiping something nasty off his skin. He finally looks at me.

"I wasn't sure if we'd ever hear from you again, Jacob," he says lightly.

Laura keeps her head down and slices through her quiche slowly and deliberately. If he's been hounding me for three weeks about that dinner, I wonder what it's been like for Laura.

"Any new developments in the world of 'temping'?"

Needle, needle, needle. It's what he does best.

"No," I say pleasantly.

"Any new developments at all?"

"No." I put on my happy idiot smile, the one he hates.

"It didn't last long with that woman," Andrew says, forking quiche into his mouth. Maybe if I shocked him, he'd choke.

"It's lasting just fine. We got married," I announce.

"What?" Laura says incredulously, her fork pinging off the edge of her plate as it falls from her hand.

"We eloped."

Laura's face goes still. "What . . . ?" Her mouth forms several other words, but no sound comes out. Andrew continues shoveling quiche like nothing in his universe has changed.

"Dodi and I got married."

"Her name's Dodi?" Laura says. I never even told her her

name. She'd asked me to call her after that dinner, and I never did. Laura stares at me, and I realize with a sinking feeling that I've hurt her. I've hurt her very badly.

I want to tell Laura everything—well, almost everything—but not with Andrew there twisting and distorting all the facts in his narrow, disagreeable mind.

"Where is she now? Why isn't she here for Christmas?" Laura asks.

Andrew scoffs. "He's not serious. He spouted this nonsense about getting married by Elvis at the restaurant." But as he reaches for the salt near my setting, his eyes fall on the band on my left hand.

"*Is* that a wedding ring?"

I say nothing.

Andrew stares me down with gunmetal eyes. "Are you going to answer me?"

It's funny how certain phrases punch dusty old buttons in our psyche. I was a twenty-nine-year-old adult male until that sentence was uttered, and now I'm a nine-year-old child just arrived on the doorstep of these two strangers, frozen, sick to my stomach. The moment passes.

"I can see how much respect you have for your family," Andrew says.

Under the table I cross my fingers for another ice spell. All I want for Christmas is a few days of stonewalling. Andrew stands up and tosses his napkin onto the table next to his unfinished plate, and Laura and I go still.

He's like an ice-capped, dormant volcano. We feel the tremors beneath our feet, and every time we wonder if today's the day—

"Disappointing, but not surprising," he says quietly, ice cap glacially cold and intact. Christmas comes early: he leaves.

From the dining room we hear him put on his coat and shoes and let himself out of the house. Somehow in twenty years he hasn't realized that flouncing out isn't quite the punishment he thinks it is.

It takes several minutes for the temperature of the room to go back to normal. When I look at Laura, she's pale and faded, like a bit of paper bleached by the sun.

"I don't blame you for eloping," she says.

"I'm sorry."

"I would have liked to get to know her. I mean, I *would* like to get to know her. *You're married.*" She flaps her hands weakly. "You met someone, and fell in love, and *got married.* And I had no idea."

"I'm sorry."

She waves her hands at me exasperatedly. "This is *good* news. Where is she?"

"She's at her place. She . . ." I cast about for a way to not lie too much. "Eloping was an impulse. We haven't been together very long. We decided to stick to our original Christmas plans."

"Her place? You don't live together?"

"No. She—" And then I get my stroke of genius, the thing that will distract her completely from the snags in my story and absolve me of my sins. I'm manipulative and terrible.

"We're not going to rush that because she has a daughter."

The result is instantaneous: Laura melts. "A daughter?"

I am forgiven.

"She's six."

Laura clasps her hands over her heart. "Oh, Jake."

It's a tropical paradise in this room now with Laura's sunny smile, and even Andrew wouldn't be able to touch it. If he came back, he'd melt and vanish into the cracks between the floorboards, and that would be the last we ever saw of him.

"Her name is Catriona, but we call her Cat, and . . . she . . . likes Barbies."

Straight to hell. Do not pass go. Do not collect two hundred dollars. This is my birthday dinner with a fake girlfriend for Laura to get emotionally invested in and break her heart over all over again. I feel queasy, but Laura is levitating. There's no way either of us is finishing our quiche now.

"Can I see photos?"

"I . . . don't have any on my phone."

It's been a very long time since I've seen a smile like this on Laura's face. Normally she has to borrow her sister-in-law's grandbabies, but this shiny new Catriona? Her very own proprietary grandniece.

I throw in one last tidbit. "She doesn't have any living grandparents."

Laura is deceased. Toes up, flat on her back, ready for the embalming fluids. She flutters off in the direction of the kitchen, and I follow, bringing dishes with me in my good hand. Some deep programming has her plugging in the mixer, pulling out the flour, the butter, the sugar . . .

"You can't meet her just yet," I remind her.

"I know," Laura says frantically. She wrestles the mixer attachment in place and starts churning the butter and sugar together. There's no stopping her. An offering of cookies to this absent child is a done deal. I will be leaving with a pound of them tomorrow.

I try to load the dishwasher, but my hand throbs. A speck of blood has been slowly spreading across the gauze bandage all lunch, and soon my whole palm will be soaked.

"I'm going out," I say, and Laura whirls around on me. "Just to get a new knife," I clarify. The one I dropped snapped across the middle of the blade. "There are good deals right now."

I leave her there with her cookie dough and Christmas radio.

I GET FIVE STITCHES AT THE EMERGENCY ROOM FROM A DOCTOR WEARING A Santa hat and whistling "All I Want For Christmas Is You." I can't watch. I keep my eyes glued on an empty wheelchair across the room. If Dodi were here, I'd tell her about Tari. I left her in a wheelchair just like that.

"Never much of a wait on Christmas Eve," the doctor says when she finishes. "Most people having accidents today are too busy to come in." She bundles me up with gauze, then flips my hand over to look at my white fingers. "Do you need me to look at that too?"

"No." I yank my hand away.

When I step outside it's already getting dark. I go to the mall and buy a new knife from an upscale kitchenware store, where the sales team eyes my blood-freckled shirt with wide-eyed concern. If Dodi were here, we would have some fun with them. I pay up, but I'm not ready to go back, although I don't want to stay at the mall, either. There isn't a single square inch of space on this planet where I'd like to be right now. Although maybe that's not true. It's hard not to think of Dodi's apartment, specifically the left seat cushion on her lumpy old sofa, while she watches true crime next to me. I wouldn't mind being there right now.

I pass clothing stores and toy stores, a hair salon, a makeup outlet, a pet store. There are three yellow puppies tussling in one of those vile pet store window display boxes. I slow down and linger. If Dodi were here, I'd tell her I like dogs, but dogs live a long time.

And then I feel something unfamiliar, something I've never felt in my life: a tiny, warm hand slipping into mine.

37

Missing Cat

DODI

"NO, HER *NAME* IS CAT. I DIDN'T LOSE A FUCKING PET CAT. I DIDN'T BRING MY cat with me to try on shoes at the mall."

"*Ma'am.*"

"Is that a thing that happens? People bringing their cats to the mall?"

The skinny young mall cop rocks back and forth with his moist lips pressed to his walkie-talkie. He absently picks a mole on his neck, his eyes fixed forlornly on the Cinnabon to our right closing up for the day. He'd been waiting in line when I'd approached him.

I scan the crowd milling around us. There's a reason her coat is bright stop-sign red. Cat wandering off, head in the clouds? All of this has happened before; all of this will happen again. A glowing, hard-to-miss jacket has always been my hack, but at this time of year, there are so many false alarms. My eyes snag on a flash of crimson—someone's Christmas gift bag. Another splash of vermilion—just a giant fucking bow tied around a pillar.

The handles of my bags are cutting right through my fin
gers. They're as bloodless as Jake's. He's a dimple in my brain
where my thoughts gather a hundred times a day. I brush him
away irritably. I've been feeling like an idiot ever since the
night of the blackout. After I put Cat to bed, I sat up in the
dark waiting for him. What had I blurted out at him when Cat
appeared? I *told* him to come back, didn't I? We were supposed to have a real conversation about where things stood.

It's been two weeks since I've heard from him. He probably
ended up hopping on a plane, after all. Awkward, chaste making out on a rickety sofa with a single mom while her daughter
interrupts is not how any man would choose to spend his remaining time on this planet.

"How many exits are there?"

The mall cop's eyes rotate slowly in his head to connect
with mine.

"You can't tell me you don't know how many exits there
are," I say in disbelief. "What if you and your little mall cop
buddies needed to secure the building?"

He's looking everywhere but at me. Mentally he's licking
his thumb and flicking through all one and a half pages of the
work training manual.

"Or, random hypothetical, what if a little girl got separated
from her mother on one of the busiest days of the year and was
abducted from the building by a stranger and lured out to the
parking lot—"

"Abductions by strangers are very uncommon," the mall
cop says defensively.

"I bet that's a real consolation to the families of abducted
children."

"Does your daughter know your phone number? Would
she be able to ask a grown-up to call it?"

Of course. My phone number has been drilled into her ever since she could speak. I'd already thought of all this on my own, but at his reminder, I want to hurt someone. Myself. I let my phone die.

She was just trying on shoes. She's old enough now to be by herself in busy spaces for a few minutes. We've been practicing. It's an essential skill for an only child–single parent dyad. I was just outside throwing out her empty hot chocolate cup, and when I came back, she was gone.

It's the perfect opening for a *Murderers at Work* episode. Someone will listen to it and be relieved they're not like those other *stupider* mothers. No, they'll always have a charged phone. They'll make sure their child's sense of stranger danger isn't compromised by sending strange men to take care of school pickup. They certainly won't be a single mom, trying to make Christmas happen on their own. They'll have a spouse to take the kid to do Christmas stuff instead of dragging the kid along to see the unglamorous, unmagical behind-the-scenes work.

"Would this grown-up be willing to do that for her, or is he too busy luring her into a windowless van with the promise of a litter of puppies—" All of the fear and tension abruptly leave my body. I know where Cat is.

A second mall cop arrives, and Mall Cop One radiates relief.

"The cat has a red coat?" she asks me. "Do you mean to say its fur is orange—?"

"Is there a pet store here?"

"You think it's gone looking for food?" she asks, and I bite my tongue. She frowns and walks me over to the glass railing rimming the second floor of the open atrium, the food court below. She pans the view thoughtfully. "There."

I follow her outstretched finger and spot a pet store across the way, on the same floor as us, but on the far side. Another flash of red—and *this* one, this one is a little red peacoat.

I could expire from relief. I peel away from the rail.

"Ma'am?"

"Thank you," I throw over my shoulder, and for once I mean it from the bottom of my cold, dead heart.

I keep my eyes on Cat as I start the circuit around the atrium. I bump into a man and get spun around on the spot, but she's still there when I look again. Still there. Still there. I round a fat pillar . . . and she's gone.

No, she's just moved. She's walking away from me now, and—my heart sickens—

Her hand is held tight in that of a strange man.

Sound cuts out, the universe rolls to a standstill, and that sickening, paralyzing chemical bath suffuses my brain, my heart, every fiber of my body from my hair follicles to my toes. Adrenaline.

And I think of Jake.

For a single, self-indulgent moment I imagine him here, saving the day again, solving my problems, keeping Cat safe for me.

Jake? I need your help. Yes, another body. No, an actual murder this time.

But he's not here, and I don't have time to throw up or hyperventilate. Those can happen later in an order pleasing to me behind the locked door of my bathroom after I've put Cat to bed tonight. I'm on my own—I've always been on my own—and my options are fight, flight, or freeze. I choose fight. I *always* choose fight.

I drop my bags and pull out the sport shop purchase I made just before Cat disappeared—a children's baseball bat. I keep my eyes on her as I break into a sprint. I don't even try to side-step the outraged shoppers in my path. I slam into people's shoulders. I twist past a throng of idiots blocking the corner rounding the atrium and jam myself through a narrow gap between a pillar and the glass railing to detour a hot chocolate pop-up. It's a clear run across the bridge and around the far pillar—and now I can't see her anymore—

I sprint down the crowded thruway leading off to the upper outdoor parking level. I jump up onto a bench and strain, try-ing to spot a blip of red in the darkening evening beyond the tiny glass doors leading outside. Then I work backward, scan-ning the crowd for a splash of red, a splash of red, a splash of red—there's going to be so much red splashed all over the place by the time I'm done—and then my eyes do catch on something red: Santa.

38

Christmas Orphan

JAKE

I PRACTICALLY STARTLE OUT OF MY SKIN. CAT STANDS NEXT TO ME, STARING AT the puppies with me.

"Mommy said she'll get me a puppy when we have a house," she says.

I notice she's not wearing any shoes. It's bewildering. It's like a bad dream—not a nightmare; just something excessively weird that will make me feel uncomfortable for the rest of the day.

"Where *is* your mom, Cat?"

She shrugs. "Dunno."

I pan the busy atrium for a glossy black head or a pop of red. Nothing.

"Why'd you go away?" she asks.

I wonder how much she knows about terminal illness, medically assisted suicide, and complicated grief.

"Your place is too small. Not enough room for me."

She nods like this is reasonable.

I stare at Cat's socked feet, trying to figure this out. "Were you trying on shoes?"

"Yes."

The mall map nearby shows two shoe stores. There's no way she went barefoot on an escalator, so I steer her to the one on our current floor. We turn a corner, and there it is. Dodi is nowhere in sight, but Cat's winter boots are. She pulls them on.

"What's your mom's phone number?"

She narrows her eyes at me. "I'm not telling you."

"Why not?"

"It's only for if I get lost."

"You *are* lost."

She gifts me with a withering look and flounces disdainfully out of the store, but abruptly stops, eyes trained on something beyond. I follow and spot Santa's workshop, replete with fleecy blankets of glittery white snow, fake trees laden with gaudy plastic orbs, and Santa himself on a golden throne like a despot of Christmas cheer.

"It's Satan," Cat whispers, pointing at the sign.

Satan. Santa. She's just starting to read.

"That's mall Santa."

"No. Satan's all red."

"Are you for real?"

"He brings you gifts if you're good and sends you to hell if you're bad."

It occurs to me that I should keep Cat right here, for when Dodi circles back.

"Do you want to ask him for something?"

She shakes her head. "I haven't been good," she explains.

"Give him someone else's name when you talk to him."

She considers this.

"If you sit on his lap, you can get a picture."

"Can I take your knife?"

"What?"

She points at the kitchen knife I purchased, forgotten in my hand.

"No. You can't take my knife, you weirdo. Go."

I pay the elf a ridiculous sum, and Cat trots up to the dais and stands in front of Santa, hands clasped, feet together, the picture of innocence. More innocent than the last "person" I took to be photographed with Santa. That had been . . . David. A brief, failed experiment for Grant. I'd assured Santa he was just a clothing store mannequin and it was a gag photo. And then I'd promptly run off.

"I'm Charlotte," says Cat. "I love spiders. Please bring lots and lots of spiders to my house on Christmas."

"Ho ho ho, little girl," Santa booms. He hoists her up onto his knee, and she goes rigid and glowers at the unexpected contact. She looks just like Dodi when she's been cornered by Doug in an elevator. When Cat catches sight of my grin, her glare is deathly.

"Get up there with your daughter," a surly elf says to me, and that's enough to wipe the smile off my face.

"What? No, she's not my—" The words die in my throat. It's hard not to think of every single time Andrew went out of his way to correct anyone who mistook me for his son.

"It's required. An adult has to be present with all minors."

I skulk up onto the dais and sidle up next to Santa and Cat, and she shoots me a nasty look from Santa's viselike grip. I connect eyes with Santa, and he frowns at me. I frown at him. He looks—well, all Santas look familiar. I took David to a completely different mall.

"Cheeeeeese," the surly elf says, and I grimace for the camera, but before he presses the shutter button, an outraged voice rings out, and there she is: Dodi.

She stands by the gate leading to Santa's little workshop of horrors with a child's baseball bat wrapped in Christmas ribbons cranked high over her shoulder. She's frantic and sweaty and *furious*.

39

Satan's Workshop

DODI

CAT IS INEXPLICABLY PERCHED ON SANTA'S KNEE, AND NEXT TO HER—CRAZY smile pasted to his face, red paint spattering his shirt—is Jake.

Jake, who is supposed to be anywhere but here.

"What are you *doing*?" I snarl at him.

He takes me in, baseball bat and all. His big smile collapses down to that small, asymmetrical twist, the real one, and my stomach flutters and I feel foolish and sweaty. "What are *you* doing?" he says.

"I want Mommy," Cat says sullenly from Santa's knee.

"Come," the grand old gentleman says in a stentorian voice, beckoning to me with one white glove. An elf grabs me by the coat sleeve and hustles me along, impatient to process this special holiday moment. I stumble up onto the dais to stand on Santa's other side, and the surly elf grunts directions.

"Happy birthday, baby Jeeeeeeeeeeeeeeeeeesus."

"Smile," Jake says through gritted teeth, and I force one out at the last second. The flash blooms and my vision goes for a moment. Cat rubs her eyes and Santa unceremoniously dumps her from his lap.

"All right, move along," the elf says. Cat hops off the dais with me, chattering.

"He's a pervert. He made me sit in his lap, and then took a *picture*," she says.

The elf tries to hand me a photo, but I didn't pay for a stupid photo. A voice rings out.

"I recognize you!" Santa shouts, and I turn to look. He's frozen on the dais, eyes locked with Jake.

"You're in the business of giving gifts, too, aren't you?" Santa says in a different voice, his normal voice, which carries quite clearly, nevertheless. "What have you got for me this year? Another sex doll?"

There's a split second's pause before Santa jumps to his feet and shouts for security. Jake glances at me.

How many dolls *were* there?

"Jesus freaking *kidding* me." I grab Cat's hand, Jake takes her other, and the three of us *run*—down the thruway, across the mezzanine, down the escalator, across the food court— Cat shrieking and holiday shoppers dodging out of our way with outraged expressions—and we don't stop until we reach the deserted cinema at the far end of the mall. Cat lets go of Jake's hand and melts onto the floor, spread-eagle.

"What happened?"

He pretends to misunderstand my question. He holds up a bandaged hand. "Knife accident," he says breathlessly. The paint on his shirt is *blood*. He waves the knife in his other hand. "Had to get a new one."

There's a sigh from the floor. "I *hated* that," Cat says rapturously. "I *hate* Mall Satan."

There's a flicker of that twinty smile when he looks at her, but he's serious again when he looks at me.

I break eye contact immediately. "I don't do Santa stuff with Cat."

"You can't teach her it's acceptable for a strange man to keep tabs on her and break into her house and leave her gifts."

"Exactly! I—" I can't tell if he's agreeing with me or making fun of me. I look at his face, and he's definitely making fun of me. I feel pissed and traitorously delighted, but before I can come up with a retort, it hits me all of a sudden: *gifts.* The bags of presents I dropped to pursue Cat.

"Come on, Cat," I say urgently, taking her hand. I leave him there and half jog back across the food court, up an escalator, Cat trailing with her sweaty hand in mine. The crowd has mostly left and half the shops have already been shut for the night. Upstairs, I scan for the bags I dropped. I spot a trampled bag kicked under a bench and pull it out. Empty. The presents were all beautifully wrapped . . .

I stand and pan around, feeling about an inch tall. There's no trace of the other bag. Cat watches me with wide dark eyes.

"What are you looking for?"

I startle and turn to find Jake behind me, standing next to Cat. He followed us. I lift my chin. "Nothing." I'm not going to say it in front of Cat. I have a few other presents at home. A few.

I head toward the exit and Jake falls into step next to me, Cat trailing after us singing "Jingle Bells" in a mournful key to herself.

I wonder where he's been this whole time. I don't know how to ask him without sounding pathetic.

"You really do look like Ted Bundy now," I say.

He glances down. A polyester button-up with a deep pointed collar, pants that almost suggest a flare, and a knife.

"I had to borrow some clothes from someone."

"A time traveler?"

"No."

"The blood's a nice touch. Somehow you can pull it off. Who's getting the knife, and are they going to live long enough to enjoy it?"

"Me, I guess. I'm making Christmas dinner."

"At the homeless shelter? Or is there a little kitchenette in the back of your supercar?"

"Nothing fancy. Just a burn barrel under the bridge. Are you doing turkey?"

I bite my cheek. I didn't have room in my freezer for a turkey because there was a sex doll's head taking up real estate, so I left it to the last minute to buy one.

"No. We're victims of the Great Turkey Shortage this year. We'll be heating a tin of beans for Christmas dinner."

"You could do a roast," he says oh so helpfully.

"I'm a garbage cook."

"That's fine. You—"

"I've lost most of her presents," I snap. I glance over my shoulder to make sure Cat's out of earshot. "Our Christmas tree's broken," I hiss. "I had to duct-tape the fucking thing together. I haven't had time to make cookies with Cat, either, and someone stole some boxes from our basement storage and now we don't have any Christmas ornaments. I don't need advice on how to salvage Christmas because it's already completely fucked."

I can't look at him. I'm furious. I'm pathetic. If I look at him right now he'll see right past the anger in my voice, and he'll say something helpful and supportive, swinging a mallet at the weak point in my architecture. Everything will come down and I really will have to kill him.

At the exit I wait for Cat to catch up, and finally notice she's lost a boot. I have no idea when. For all I know, I took her on an escalator without a boot. Outside the glass doors the rain is picking up again. I can't look at Jake. I wish he would sink through the floor and disappear and I could get on with my shitty parenting and my shitty Christmas. *You're giving her a good childhood,* indeed.

I turn back to Cat in time to find her strangling Jake from behind as he crouches on the floor. He hoists her up in a piggyback ride and waits for me to open the door. My throat closes and my eyes burn.

At the car he swings Cat into the back seat, and I stash the baseball bat on the floor.

"You play baseball, Cat?" he asks.

"No. Mommy got it to keep by the door."

I shrivel a little. Jake doesn't even react. "Maybe you can get a turkey if you call around," he says to me.

"Whatever," I mutter. "I hate Christmas."

"Me too," he says.

"Me more," Cat says from the back seat. "I like Halloween."

That twisty little smile again. "Halloween is objectively better by every metric." He looks at me, and his eyes are so green. This time the smile stays in place, uncertain, but still there. He's wondering if he'll get some sort of smile back. There's no danger of that. It's taking everything I've got to keep my face from collapsing right now.

I climb into my car, shut the door, and pull out.

40

The Grinch

JAKE

ANDREW'S CAR IS STILL GONE WHEN I GET BACK. MAUDLIN CHRIST-BABY MU-sic plays inside, and I find Laura wrapping up a batch of sugar cookie dough in the kitchen. It doesn't make sense that she's only just finishing up now, all these hours later, but when she goes to place it in the fridge, there are several other batches of dough already bagged and waiting inside. She's been busy.

She pours hot chocolate into matching snowman mugs and we settle on the living room sofa. My aunt stares balefully at the Christmas tree. All this work, for what?

But I know for what, don't I?

"Are you still putting on a Christmas show for me?" I ask.

"Yes."

"I'm almost thirty."

She shrugs. "I've never really forgiven myself for that first Christmas."

"I thought I was putting on a Christmas show for you."

"Does that explain the decapitated ornaments?" she says, and I go still, a misbehaving child found out. But she's not an-cry at me and my anxious little boy antics. "I think they really capture the festive spirit. I added a few myself."

She smiles a big, brave, fake smile at me. I flick on a matching fake smile. I learned from the best. I will see her Christmas spirit and raise her. I lean forward, elbows on knees, and catch her eye.

"The Christmas tree star."

She glances up. Sharp edges, metal and glass. "Sure," she concedes. "If it went straight into an artery."

She doesn't seem too excited.

"Strangulation by string lights."

"Oh, I like that," she says, cocking her head to one side while she pictures it. "That would be . . . dazzling."

We both picture it for a moment.

She eventually sighs. "Nope. I don't think either would work. I think both are too good for him."

It's been twenty years, and we still haven't figured out the perfect way to off Andrew.

"Do you want me to check your phone?" I ask. Now and then he installs something nefarious. A tracking app. A spy app.

"It doesn't matter. I never go anywhere exciting."

I brace myself. I had this conversation once with her, years ago, when I left for university, but she shut me down. I don't know if I'll get another chance, so I try it out again. "I wish you'd leave him."

The statement lands like a Christmas ornament exploding on the floor. Her face goes slack for a moment, and the glimmer of unease that follows is scarier than any expression I've ever seen Andrew make. That look right there is the reason I would never ask her to help me at the end, to do something that would be in defiance of Andrew.

She clears it away rapidly and squeezes my hand.

"You know I don't stay for him," she says, frankly this time. "I have no living family—Andrew's family has always been my family. I don't want to lose that. Family is so important to me." She smiles at me, willing me to understand. This little dysfunctional family is everything to her, for some reason. I don't tell her that we could have been a family, just the two of us. When I was younger, I fantasized about us packing up and riding off into the sunset. I'd lost my mother, and she'd lost her estranged sister, but Laura and I—we hit it off immediately, despite the grief. Maybe because of it. Together we could have been happy.

"And . . . how would I, anyway?" Laura continues. "He's outmaneuvered me. He's a majority partner in my business. He's got our money all squirreled away. I'd say we're going to wait and see who dies first, but he's never going to die. His parents are in their nineties and they still do the couples dance classes at the home. He's going to gradually . . . *desiccate*, like one of those monks." She lets out a shivery breath and bravely perks up. "Did I tell you about the mummy that came in last year—?"

"Yes."

She smiles ruefully and stops her retelling.

"I have money, Laura."

She waves me to shut up. "No."

"I do. I have a lot of money."

She looks at me like I'm a child offering all the buttons and bottle caps in my piggy bank to her. "Hush. I'm not asking you to solve my problems. I was going to leave him when I was younger, but at the last minute, I couldn't."

This is brand-new intelligence.

"When?"

"Twenty years ago. But I would never have done that to you, Jake. After everything you'd been through, I decided you needed an extra parent figure on hand to help. I couldn't take you away from Andrew, could I? I stayed for your sake."

I stare at her in horror. She stayed because of *me*. Because of some misguided, traditional notion that I needed a father figure. How many times did Andrew make pointed comments within my earshot about *unwed mothers* and *boys being raised without fathers*, and how *at least now Jake could be raised in an environment with proper family values*. The whole time I lived here, she tried so hard to facilitate that relationship. *He does care about you in his own way, Jake.*

She looks my way, a smile in place, but it drops from her face when she sees my expression. I hoist my own smile into place, too late.

She watches my face for a moment with a regretful air, then sets her empty mug down and stands.

"I'm going to bed, Jake."

She drifts up the stairs, leaving dissatisfaction and disappointment suspended in the atmosphere like a scented holiday candle. I remain downstairs, alone with the Christ-child music and the blinking Christmas lights. It's the perfect Christmas tableau: tree, stockings, nativity scene perched on the coffee table—all perfectly coordinated like a homeware catalog—and it's all an elaborate facade to a deeply rotten family. I always wanted a different sort of family.

I pull the creased Santa photo from my pocket. Santa's in the center, of course, wholesome and jolly, with red cheeks and a white, whiskery smile, but Dodi and I aren't smiling so much as baring our teeth in big, fake, psycho smiles that don't reach our eyes. I'm spattered in my own blood, clutching that kitchen knife in such a way that my hand is positioned over the handle, the clear plastic housing vanishing against my coat and leaving just the blade visible, and Dodi is holding that aluminum baseball bat. Santa looks like he's about to get his head caved in and his joints disarticulated. And Cat—Cat sits primly on his lap, ankles crossed, hands folded, her hair ribbon in a perfect bow above one ear, as she gazes solemnly at the camera with eyes deader than blown-out candles.

I think of Cat with her duct-taped tree and tin of beans. She deserves something like what Laura's put together. Not me, a cynical old person army-crawling my way through another holiday season. The song on the radio changes to "Silent Night," sung by Elvis of course, and I don't think of Dodi. I definitely don't think of the way her face twisted strangely when she saw Cat garroting me in a piggyback ride, before it abruptly settled out again, like a rumpled blanket yanked straight. I've been leaving her alone so she can be happy, but she didn't seem very happy.

I pick up the mugs to take into the kitchen, and now I think of Laura, and how alone she is. She'll be even more alone soon, with me gone, although I don't kid myself I've ever been much of a consolation to her. On the way I stoop to pick up a wrapped gift and prop it up higher onto the pile, out of the way of foot traffic, when my thumb rips right through the paper and into the squishy contents. I flip the present over to read the card: *For Jake, Love, Andrew*, written in Laura's loopy handwriting. I rip open the package and inside I find an expensive robe of bamboo silk, soft and warm-looking.

Bill needs something like this.

Fuck Andrew. Fuck Andrew, and fuck Christmas, and fuck—

Elvis trills his last, and a stupidly familiar song comes on. Horns flare, strings skip jauntily up the scale, a percussive burst, and—

You're a mean, one, Mr. Grinch

You really are a heeeel . . .

I'm instantly calm.

In the kitchen I pull a yellow glove over my bandaged hand and wash and dry the mugs, whistling along to the tune, and then, instead of putting them in the cupboard, I wrap them up in paper and set them in their original box, the one they're stored in every year between Christmases. I locate the other six in the set and pack those too. I pack up the Christmas dishes and cutlery in their boxes, the tablecloth and table settings, and then I remove the prepped ingredients and the cookie dough from the fridge, everything already neatly stored in Tupperware and Ziploc bags.

In the living room I take down the severed head ornaments and all the others one by one, pack up the garland, the presents, the throw pillows, and Christmas blankets. Everything goes into the front hallway in a big pile, and from there it goes to the car. Andrew keeps an old spool of nylon rope in the garage. It takes a blundering half hour, but I manage to hoist the tree on top of Grant's car—the branches making some interesting grating noises against the paint job—and tie it in place with rope fed through the cracked windows.

My final move is to creep up the stairs and shake Laura awake.

"Come."

41

The Nightmare Before Christmas

JAKE

I SMILE AT THE LITTLE OLD LADY TUGGING HER SHOPPING CART UP THE WALK to Dodi's apartment building, and she narrows her eyes at me suspiciously, as if she, out on an icy walkway at midnight on Christmas Eve, isn't ten orders of magnitude more out of place than I am. Her wheel catches on the lip of the step and I reach down to pick it up before she can stop me.

"*Thank you,*" she says pointedly, but I don't let go. I continue to blast my pure-of-heart church-boy smile at her, and she flounders for a moment before reluctantly letting me into the poinsettia-infested lobby. She stabs me with her eyes in the elevator and shoots several wary glances behind her when she leaves me on the second floor. I beam at her and carry on to the third.

The lights of Dodi's apartment were on when I stood in the street below, but she doesn't hear the first knock or the second. I've raised my hand to rap again when the door jerks open to rest against the full length of its chain.

"What—" Dodi says, and stops and scowls.

I smile. *Merry fucking Christmas!*

"You always look unhinged when you smile like that." She's fully dressed, but there are creases in her cheek from whatever surface she fell asleep on. Her hair is mussed and her eyeliner smudged.

"Open the door."

Her response is to make the opening narrower, until she peers at me with one eye. "No. This is exactly what these bolt-and-chain locks are for: creeps knocking in the middle of the night. What do you want?"

What do you want? What do you like? What makes you happy?

Her. It's always been her. *Dolores dela Cruz* at the top of my list.

"What are your plans for Christmas dinner?" I ask.

"None of your business."

"We *are* married."

"You're really hung up on that detail."

"Not to brag, but I have a turkey," I say. "And a tree."

"Well, look at this overachiever. Must be a really nice little cardboard box under the overpass."

"It's a house."

"I'm not coming over," she says flatly.

She's completely wrong about that. She's coming over if I have to toss her over my shoulder and carry Cat under one arm like a piece of luggage. I'm here on her doorstep channeling a higher power: Christmas spirit. It's Baby Jesus's birthday wish. It's Mall Satan's will that we spend the holiday together.

I should have brought bolt cutters for the chain.

There's a pause, and then she speaks in a scratchy voice I've never heard before. "I can't. A complete *asshole* slid into me at an intersection on the way home. I had to get my car towed."

She shuts the door in my face abruptly, and I stand there, staring at it. But then it reopens, chain dropped.

"Here," Dodi says, thrusting my bag at me. "You could have warned me there was two hundred thousand dollars cash in there. I could have been fucking robbed. And *by the way*," she says, her scratchy voice pitching higher, "I just got a cryptic email from Cynthia about how she's putting my name forward for a promotion over that list, and I still have no fucking idea what it is."

Her little fingers are biting into the edge of the door, the tips white from the pressure. I reach up and touch them with my own. She doesn't pull away. The door swings wider by an inch, and another. One more.

"I'll tell you over Christmas dinner."

I push through the gap, a burglar insinuating himself inside. It takes me a second to make sense of what I've stumbled into. A dilapidated fake Christmas tree with one measly string of lights and no ornaments leans drunkenly in one corner, but that's about it for Christmas decor. A life-sized skeleton sits in one armchair, and bats dangle from the light fixtures. There's a ghost hanging in one corner, lit up with green light, and plastic pumpkins flickering with fake candlelight are perched on the side tables. Stretched out in every nook and corner conceivable, fake cobwebs. Fake cobwebs *everywhere*.

Dodi twitches and crosses and uncrosses her arms beside me.

"I still had the Halloween decorations."

Scattered on the floor is a jumble of ratty, half-used wrapping paper tubes and a pile of presents needing to be wrapped, an open bottle of wine and a half-full glass, scissors, and—

"No tape," I point out. Dodi crosses her arms again and stares stonily at the floor.

"Tell me about this Christmas dinner," she says quietly,

majestically, her normal voice restored. She tips her chin and manages to stare down at me despite being half a foot shorter. "Where is it? What time?"

"Now," I say.

"Now?"

"Pack an overnight bag. Everything is ready."

"What do you mean?"

"You hate Christmas. You said so. I took care of it."

She blinks at me and waits for more of an explanation, but we stand there in a stalemate because that's all I'm telling her. She has to see the rest in person.

And maybe she recalls a serial killer date, and a night in Las Vegas, and the magical transformation of a disgraceful termination into a promotion. Maybe she trusts me just a little, because after a minute, without saying anything, she uncoils her crossed arms and pads off to her bedroom to pack.

The beat-up bankers boxes labeled HALLOWEEN DECORATIONS are stacked in one corner. In it all goes—pumpkins, ghost, bats. Down come the cobwebs, the spiders. It's faster coming down than going up, is what I've learned tonight. I stack the full boxes by the door. The unwrapped gifts and the wrapping paper, too. It's all coming with us.

"What are you doing with my stuff?" Dodi barks when she reappears with an overnight bag and a Barbie backpack stuffed to bursting.

"I'm bringing it. Cat's going to love it."

Her mouth twists, and she stares hard and unblinking at the crappy tree. She doesn't say anything as I take the first load down and then the second. I take everything—even the half-full bottle of wine and the skeleton. Finally, the apartment is bare except for the pathetic tree, and Dodi stands waiting for me with Cat in her arms, her sleeping face smooshed on her shoulder, her winter coat draped around her. I take the overnight bags and we go.

There's one decoration I missed, and in the elevator, I notice it swinging from Dodi's fingertips by its hair. Fake blood is smeared across her silicone face and there's a spider glued to her forehead, but I'd know Verity's glassy gaze anywhere. Dodi feels my eyes on her, and after a minute, she makes eye contact with me over Cat's head. She shrugs, and I spot the tiniest glimmer of a smile.

It all goes in the trunk in a heap. The snow is coming down now, finally, in big downy flakes that fall slowly like they're drifting through syrup. I open the back door for Dodi to deposit Cat, and she freezes.

"This car stinks. It *reeks*." She coughs and swallows.

Unfortunately, there was a week of above-freezing weather while I was at Bill's and the bunny juice on the back seat had time to thaw and really come into its own. This is the clean side of the back seat, at least.

"We'll drive with the windows open."

But open windows in the middle of a cold winter night during holiday season is a very interesting thing to patrol cars, and my busted taillight from front-ending Charlotte's dad is a legitimate excuse for a traffic stop.

A police car flashes its lights behind us as we turn onto the Christmas light–festooned Main Street, and I pull off to the side, right beneath an enormous Christmas tree all done up by the local business association. The cop slams his door and strolls up under the golden streetlights, his breath steaming in the cold air, fat snowflakes landing on his shoulders. He looks like he's fresh out of the academy. I roll down my window and he bends down, leaning right into the car to catch a surreptitious whiff of my breath.

"Your taillight is smashed. License and registration." He sniffs, then coughs and gags. "What the fucking—" He pulls back and gags again, and a ribbon of spit dangles from his chin. "Fucking Jesus *shit*. What is that smell?"

"It's nothing."

He stares at me in disbelief. I pass him my license and the car's registration, and he frowns at it.

"This isn't your vehicle." He peers at my license and then my face.

"I have permission—"

"I'm going to ask you to step out of the vehicle, sir." The cop paces a few feet away and pulls his radio off his belt.

Next to me, Dodi's eyes are wide, her jaw clenched. She turns to look at me. "Is this car stolen?"

I balk. "No. Grant lets me—"

"Did your ex-roommate *report* this car as stolen?" Her nostrils flare. "I'm practically an *acquitted murderer*, you fucking idiot!" she whisper-hisses out of the side of her mouth. "I have to toe the fucking line! I can't be driving around in the middle of the night in a stolen supercar!"

"Sir!" Baby Cop shouts.

I unbuckle my belt and open my door. My fingers are clumsy.

"Don't let him look in the trunk," she hisses without moving her lips.

"Why not?"

"Are you—Jesus *Christ*, Jake," she says, turning to me and dropping the ventriloquism act. "There's a mutilated sex doll, a real human skeleton, an open bottle of wine—*two hundred thousand American dollars*—"

"The skeleton's real?"

"I don't know, okay! It was Facebook Marketplace—"

"Out of the vehicle, *sir*!" the police officer says.

Dodi lunges for my jacket front. "Zip your fucking coat! You still have blood on your shirt!" she hisses. "Can you try not to act like a fucking serial killer for once?"

I snatch my zip up to my chin and step out onto the road.

"Stand right there," the cop says, pointing. He speaks into his radio some more, and I make out the words "canine" and "backup" and not much else. When he turns back to me, he's revved up. He's floating a foot off the ground. This right here is why he went to the police academy. It's all been building to this moment.

"It smells like a dead body in there." He's delighted. Christmas has come . . . exactly on schedule.

"It's rotten food," I explain. "Some packaged meat leaked."

He peers in the tinted rear passenger window and startles when he notices Cat slumped in the back seat.

"Why is there a minor in the back seat?"

Dodi stares at him in confusion. The sleeping kid is the most normal thing in my vehicle. Maybe he thinks he's busted a human trafficking ring.

"That's . . . our daughter." It's possibly the most awkward sentence I've ever uttered. I smile at him and channel happy family.

"I'm going to take a look in your trunk."

"No!" Dodi calls out, and if the cop had a tail, he'd wag it.

"I don't have to consent to that," I say.

The gears whirl rapidly in the officer's brain. He tips his head to the smashed taillight. "I'm thinking your car might need to be towed," he says, standing in a plastic muscle man action figure stance with his arms bulldogged and his feet apart. He's loving every second of this. He's in control. He is God. He probably practices this pose in front of the full-length

mirror of his closet every night, reciting his lines. Naked. *Li*
cense and registration. *License and* registration. License *and—*

"I would have to do an inventory of contents, if that's the
case," he continues. "*Including* whatever's in the trunk." It's
clear this moment of power will be an erotic memory for
weeks.

Another patrol car pulls up behind his, "Santa Baby" blast-
ing for a split second before the engine cuts. A man and a
woman step out, and when Starsky sees their faces, it's like
someone shoved a pin into a plastic inflatable. He visibly deflates.

"Hiya, Pete," the woman calls out.

Pete stiffens at the use of his given name. "Officer Stubbs,"
he says pointedly. "Where's the K9?" I can hear him using the
letter and number shorthand in his head.

The other two officers exchange looks and Stubbs's lips
twitch. They're older than Pete, and if Pete is a baby cop, this
pair is smoking cigarettes behind the school bleachers. Stubbs
beckons Pete, and Pete stiffens. She does it again, crooking her
gloved fingers, and Pete dies a little. He glances at me and
straightens up, hands on his belt, and swaggers over to them
like he was headed that direction anyway.

"You're not on patrol tonight," Stubbs says conversationally, voice low in a bid to keep things private, but it's a silent,
holy night in this snow-dampered winter wonderland and I
can make out every word. From where she's sitting, Dodi has
her ear craned to them through her open window too.

Baby Cop puffs up. "I don't stop being an officer of the law
at clock-out."

"No, of course not. You just restlessly patrol the city,
guarding the innocents from the lurking danger of busted tail-
lights."

"*Suspected foul play,*" Pete hisses.

Stubbs snaps her fingers. "Right! You wanted the dog." She turns to her partner. "What could that mean, Amir? Drugs? Is someone having a *white* Christmas?"

My stomach drops out. Would Grant keep a baggy of nose candy stashed somewhere in one of his cars? He would. He fucking would—

"Dunno, Stubbs. Maybe . . . human remains?" Amir experiences an exaggerated lightbulb moment. "A . . . decapitated head? Wrapped up in Christmas paper?"

I glance at Dodi at the exact moment she glances at me.

"We *are* still waiting for the head to turn up," Officer Stubbs agrees. She claps her hands. "Let's call it in. Get the whole Homicide Department out to the scene in the middle of the night. *Again.*"

Pete is practically vibrating with frustration. "For fuck's sake, why am I the only one taking what's clearly a Secret Santa copycat act seriously?"

Dodi's mouth falls open.

"Whoever was behind that is a psychopath," Baby Cop continues. "It was a *practice* murder. It's going to be a real body next—"

The reason for Baby Cop's vigilante patrol duty on Christmas Eve comes out. Stubbs adopts an exaggerated, hard-boiled movie cop voice. "Whoever it is, he's methodical, disciplined, and worst of all, he's *learning*."

Amir matches her voice. "Perfecting his approach. *Tweaking* it. And watching us scramble to catch up in time for Christmas morning gift opening."

Pete raises his voice to talk over them. "It's the same creep who's been leaving the sex dolls around town, and his fantasies are escalating!"

A hacking cough comes from Dodi's direction, and I can't look at her. I haven't told her about the others. Only Anastasia and Una.

"I've entered the coordinates of every location where a doll was found into a map, and this street right here is part of his normal circuit! He's clever, he's meticulous, he's always one step ahead—"

Stubbs carries on, dead serious, her TV cop voice gravelly from sleepless stakeouts and stale coffee. "You're too close to this, sergeant! I'm taking you off the case!"

"Take some personal time! That's an order!" says Amir.

Pete talks louder. "He has multiple vehicles—*that's* why we can't pin down the make and model—but there's always a luxury car around when a doll appears. I've tracked down eyewitnesses and interviewed them on my own time—"

He's *obsessed* with me. I risk a look and find Dodi staring at me with wide eyes, and I almost think . . . I *want* her to know about the others. It was so much work. It feels . . . flattering to know Baby Cop was watching. No one ever pays attention to me.

Stubbs's eyebrows ratchet up. "You've gone rogue!" she snarls in pretend outrage, imaginary doughnut crumbs puffing out of her mouth.

Amir shakes his head in disgust. "He's a loose cannon! He's going to bring this whole detachment down with him!"

"Badge and gun, now!" Stubbs shouts.

"Oh, fuck you!" Pete hisses. He shoves my license and registration into Officer Stubbs's hands and skulks back to his vehicle without a backward glance. Amir and Stubbs shake with suppressed laughter.

"This isn't going to bring her back!" she calls out to Pete's retreating form, and Amir doubles over.

Pete sits behind his wheel, sulking.

Officer Stubbs comes to stand about a dozen feet from me, feet apart, like we're Wild West cowboys about to duel. I match her stance. She lifts one leg. I lift one leg. We stand balanced like a pair of flamingos.

"Nine steps, straight line, heel toe."

I comply, coming to a stop in front of her. She lifts one finger, and I lift one finger too, and she rolls her eyes at my stupidity. I quickly drop my hand, and she drags her finger side to side in front of my face, watching my eye movements. She glances in the back seat and her grim face crinkles at the sight of Cat.

"Cutie," she says, handing over my license and registration. "Can't wait to break up her house party in ten years. Fix your damn taillight, and have a good holiday."

She stumps back to her partner and mutters in her wisecracking movie cop voice, "I'm too old for this shit!"

When I slide back into the driver's seat, Dodi is hyperventilating, tears pouring down her face. It takes me a second to realize she's laughing.

42
Naughty List

JAKE

"WHAT IS THIS PLACE?" DODI ASKS.

What this place is, is old and decrepit and dusty. I turn to see Dodi frozen in the foyer, eyes wide, and it's impossible not to feel embarrassed. Laura and I did the best we could—garland woven through the curved banister, tinsel stars dangling in doorways—but there was only so much a Band-Aid treatment could accomplish.

She sways a little on the spot with Cat asleep in her arms and examines the crimson wallpaper and the old, dark floors, shining now from my polishing. She peers around the doorway into the music room, where a ponderous old piano sits quietly and thinks on its youth. A tarnished chandelier twists perpetually overhead, disturbed by a draft that never stops, and old bookcases line the walls.

At Grant's, all the surfaces were new and smooth, and easy to clean, but here at Bill's, it's impossible. Carved wood collects dust, rugs sponge up dirt and smells. When Dodi looks up at the plaster molding around the light fixture above us, I notice cobwebs. I don't know how I missed those. Her eyes track the stairs to the halfway landing, where a grandfather clock mutters darkly.

And then she says something that surprises me: "This place is beautiful. Who lives here?"

I try the words out for the first time. "My grandfather." Laura hadn't asked. She's been conditioned not to pry.

Dodi peers at the photos of the smiling young man with the glasses hanging in the hallway, understanding on her face.

"This way," I say, and she follows me upstairs over creaking steps to a room with a four-poster bed.

She deposits Cat between the fresh sheets, and I leave her there, tucking the old satin coverlet around Cat. I go to my room and finally change into fresh clothes from the bag I left at Dodi's.

She's hovering in the hallway, waiting for me. She follows me back downstairs, and we swig directly from the half-full bottle of wine together while I unpack the Halloween decorations.

"What are you doing?" Dodi asks peevishly, but I ignore her.

I spread fake cobwebs all over the tree and hang her ghost over the mantel.

"That looks stupid," she says self-consciously when I put the skeleton in an armchair by the fire, and "You're an idiot," when I place Verity's head on the mantelpiece.

But when I finish and return to her where she sits on the rug in front of the crackling fire, the ratty rolls of Christmas paper and her unwrapped gifts piled up beside her, the wine bottle cradled in her lap, she looks at me with an expression in her eyes that makes me feel warm to my very fingertips.

"I just know you have tape somewhere," she says.

I do

We've done this before, but it goes a little faster when you're wrapping boxes instead of limbs. She's still trash at wrapping presents, so I let her do the taping. The firelight rims her cheeks and glints in her hair while we work, and no one else will ever see her as she looks right now, privately, secretly beautiful for an audience of one, in the middle of the night, while the house sleeps and the snow drifts up against the mullioned windows.

"What's the list about?" she asks quietly without looking up.

"What are you doing at work on your laptop?"

A small, bitter smile twists her lips, and she hesitates. "I'm afraid to tell you what I've been doing," she says at last.

"Why?"

"Because it's probably a lot less interesting than you think." She raises her eyes to mine, dark and deep like twin wells. "You always look at me like I'm . . . I don't know. Mysterious. Fascinating. Not just a tired single mom with no life. You're going to be so disappointed to know the truth." She presses a piece of tape over the edge of paper I hold in place for her.

"After—*everything*—I didn't work for a while. I couldn't. I had Cat and . . ." She stares into the fire. "Well, what do you think came up anytime a prospective employer googled my name? It was a hard time. And finally, when Cat was ready to start school, an old friend reached out and told me they'd help me get a job. I moved here to start fresh. My friend was in HR, and I managed to get in without anyone doing that Google search. But then"—she purses her lips and shrugs—"one week in, the layoffs started. My department was gutted. My supervisor got axed. *Her* supervisor got axed. My friend in HR was let go. I think I wasn't laid off because I was still being added to the system—I don't know. She told me to lie low and see if I could get another paycheck or two, and to line up my exit plan. I had no job prospects, and I had so much debt already. All I could come up with was to go back to school and live off student loans. So I got my application in. I was accepted. The loans came through. Except . . . the termination never came. Then the pandemic happened and we all started working from home.

"Another paycheck came in, and another, and another. An entire year went by. I kept getting cc'd to meeting invitations, so I kept making appearances on Zoom. I kept my camera off. I was never given any work to do, so I worked on my school assignments. And then one day I got an email telling me work from home was over and that I had to report to Doug. I walked into his office, and he said something about how nice it was to be back at work where the pretty girls are, and I just . . . I couldn't. I turned around and walked right back out again."

I can picture Doug sitting at his desk, damp, pink-faced, realizing he'd just created another HR mess for himself, panicking.

"And . . . he just gave me a wide berth after that. I got myself a cubicle, but then I stumbled upon my old annex. They were still on the hook for the lease, even though they didn't have the bodies to fill it. I stole an office, and continued with my online studies, and now I've almost finished my MBA." She straightens a little, reaching the part of the story she's proud of.

"I won't have to worry about finding an understanding employer anymore because I'm going to start my own consulting business. Isn't that what everyone wants? To be their own boss, picking and choosing their own clients, working their own hours? I would have more time for Cat."

Nothing about this confession is surprising. Dodi is re-
sourceful and self-protective and used to figuring things out
on her own. I can picture her, a one-woman show, swirling in
and out of boardrooms in all black, aloof, sharp, sexy—and
all those qualities only making clients want her more. She's a
natural-born shark. Hardworking, driven. Any enterprise she
put her mind to would go fuckbusters.

"What will you consult on?"

She scowls like I'm an idiot. But I'm learning to speak
Dodi, and I realize I've embarrassed her. She wanted to im-
press me, but instead I poked a finger right into the gaping
hole in her plan: she hasn't had time to figure out her angle yet.

She licks her lips. "Transformational change within a holistic framework, obviously."

"Or maybe they can hire you to sniff out plainclothes serial
killers on payroll."

Her dark eyes flick up to mine, strange, mysterious. She
doesn't smile at my joke.

"And the Las Vegas winnings are seed money?"

"No. My problem all along has been how to leave my job
at Spencer & Sterns without making them aware of my existence. Once they realize I've been taking a paycheck all this
time . . . but I have the money now. I can pay them back."

"But the promotion—"

She shakes her head. "I can't stay there. I need a fresh
start." She clears her throat primly. "I've revealed my boring
secret to you. Your 'Terminate' list better be equally boring. Is
it a list of people who stole your lunch from the break room
fridge?"

It's even more boring.

Long before I started playing serial killer games with Dodi,
I'd invented an elaborate spy game of my own. Something to

make me feel like my life was more exciting than it was. Something to distract me, a mental exercise to get through the boredom and loneliness. The alternative was to stick a Bic pen up my nose and swirl.

Dodi looks at me expectantly.

"It's literally just a list of people to be terminated," I admit. "I do this everywhere I work. I calculate how much money the worst employees are costing the company."

She blinks.

"And?" she prompts.

"That's it. I compare their value to their cost—their salary and everything else—and I put them on my list."

She leans back. "What?" She frowns. "How do you know their salaries?"

Well, this is the less boring, slightly more illegal part. "I look at payroll." I have the urge to brag. "I also look at emails and HR records."

She stares at me.

"I can usually get into a company's systems pretty quick. People are idiots."

It's not just getting into the systems. It's eavesdropping on watercooler gossip while colleagues complain about one another. It's keeping my head down in the elevator at the end of the day while the C-suite assistants vent to each other about top floor perverts. It's taking advantage of my ability to blend into the gray corporate decor to stalk the people on my list as they go about their day. It was fun, in its own way.

"You're a recreational bean counter," she says after a long pause. "Cool beans." She stacks a present under the tree. "So it's a list of unprofitable employees. Cynthia saw all that in the spreadsheet and got a massive hard-on."

It's the first time I've shared my list with someone who could implement it.

"But what's the point?" Dodi says irritably. "Why do you care about making Spencer & Sterns more profitable?"

"I don't."

"Last I checked, Doug and I are on there. But maybe he and I are living the dream, pulling a salary for doing dick all, sticking it to the man—"

"It's not a list of freeloaders and incompetents."

She narrows her eyes at me. "So what is it?"

"It's the bullies."

She raises her eyebrows.

"The perverts. The predators. They're impossible to fire in these big companies. Instead, their victims get fired, or resign."

I hate bullies. *I* grew up with a bully.

"But companies care about the bottom line," I continue. "It's all they care about. So I make these spreadsheets to show how expensive they are to the company. Assholes are *very* expensive." If they seem valuable and essential on the surface, it's an illusion. They waste people's time. They terrorize their colleagues. They cause turnover and intensive HR investigations and lawsuits. They steal. I add it all up: HR salaries, the cost of losing a client, the cost of training a new secretary, the cost of sick days when a colleague is too stressed to come in. The cost of stolen paper clips.

She stares at me.

I always fantasized about handing in my list when I left each office. Although sometimes the bullies took care of themselves. Three of the worst offenders on my lists were suicides. Jumpers. Usually after a failed HR investigation. They weren't fired, but the stress from the investigation must have gotten to them. Alleged Paper Pusher victims—fuel for the urban legend, I suppose.

"I was at the top of your list," she says, her voice low and menacing.

"Yes."

She narrows her eyes at me. "Why?"

Why, she asks. I take her in, her aggressive red lips, her sharp claws, the tension in her body even now, curled up on the floor beneath a Christmas tree I procured for her.

"Because you were being a nasty little bully to me."

Her cheeks turn dark.

"I'm sorry."

"I know."

She bites her lip. "I'm not a very nice person."

I've always respected that about her. There are so many other more important qualities. Integrity. Bravery. Kindness— which is completely different from being nice. And it's dangerous for a woman to be nice to the wrong man. I knew that even before listening to her murder podcasts.

"The thing is," she continues, tilting her head to one side in that way she does, her voice dropping to a whisper, "you've always scared the shit out of me."

It's a dark little secret she's been clutching tight. This is Dodi finally lying down and exposing her belly to me.

"My serial killer vibes."

"Sure. The serial killer vibes." There are twin flames in her eyes from the fireplace. Her voice is soft. "You're not afraid of me, though."

Not even a little. The thing about Dodi's hardness is it's brittle. Her sharpness is from all the jagged edges left from every time she's been bumped and dropped and knocked around, when each trauma sprouted protective shards, poking out like spines. Glass like, glittering, cold as ice, or diamonds, or some substance that will cut and freeze you at the same time, the softness inside protected from thin-skinned idiots who make a clumsy grab for it. But I've never been afraid of her sharp edges. When I lean into them, my own jagged edges line up with hers. I give way where she needs me to, and the gaps missing from her contour draw me out into my own authentic shape, too.

"Am I still on that list?" she asks, leaning in close.

I shake my head, and my voice is a whisper. "I took you off ages ago."

"I'm glad," Dodi says, her breath on my lips.

She kisses me, while the clock on the mantel ticks sedately past four in the morning and the fire crackles, Bill snores in the sitting room next to the kitchen, Laura sleeps upstairs in the room next to Cat's, and the house is as still as a tomb. With the sort of confidence I wish I could summon at will, Dodi rests her head on my shoulder and takes my hand in hers, and it's settled: I'm not moving an inch until my flesh peels from my skeleton and my bones turn to dust. We fall asleep.

43

Christmas Spirit

DODI

I WAKE SLOWLY TO A HEARTBEAT TICKING UNDER MY EAR. WHEN I PEEL MY face from Jake's shirt front, he blinks blearily and rubs his eyes, leaving his glasses askew on his nose, and I have the stupidest, half-asleep instinct to reach up and straighten them, to touch his stubbly cheek, to scritch my fingernails against his scalp as I smooth his hair. Snow still falls outside, although it's early morning now. The last embers smolder in the grate, and the tree twinkles.

I start when I realize we're not alone. Jake's aunt stands in the doorway to a grand old dining room, decked out in outrageous Christmas pajamas, an old-fashioned silver coffee service in her hands and a huge, sunny smile on her face. In the doorway opposite stoops an old man I don't recognize, with tufty white hair and a ratty robe. He gazes dumbfounded at the scene before him, like he was a recipient of Jake's Christmas surprise too. Jake and I shuffle upright on the old velvet sofa, bones cracking, sensation shooting painfully back into our numb limbs, and then there's a creak on the stairs. We all turn to look.

Cat drifts down in her odd Victorian nightgown, dragging her fingers along the carved wood banister, singing a weird, dirgelike tune, and I'm not certain, but I think I can make out the words to "Frosty the Snowman." She's always been my weird little Wednesday Addams, and I love her that way, I *do*, but in this moment, I just want her to be the sort of happy Christmas child that claps her hands in wonder at the tree. I tried my absolute hardest for her, failed catastrophically, swallowed my pride, accepted help, tried again—and I just want to know I did it right. I *never* know if I'm doing it right.

She glides into the room and mutely takes in the tree, the holiday homeware aisle exploded all over the room, the smattering of Halloween interspersed throughout, the grown-ups she knows and the two she doesn't, and gazes at all of us with that solemn wise-child expression that always sets off all my alarm bells when we're out trying to pass for a normal mother and daughter, and says, "This house is haunted."

I shrivel for one second, but then Jake's aunt sighs like that's the sweetest thing she ever heard, and the old man, who has apparently already adapted to the upside-down world he woke up in, says with a twinkle, "Anyone can see that." She does look like a little ghost or spirit in that gown. He directs a crinkly old smile at Cat, and Jake's aunt beams at her too, like they both already had little Cat-shaped holes in their hearts and she's popped right into place.

We settle down to unwrap the presents under the tree. Most of the gifts are addressed to people who aren't here. Cat unwraps each one and passes it to whichever adult claims it. Bill makes a bid for a luxurious bathrobe. Laura helps herself to a wool blanket she'd apparently bought for her sister-in-law. I take a black Chanel handbag—*this* season's—and bundle it back up in its tissue paper and cradle it in my lap like a little baby while Jake gives me a look. I'm a materialistic monster. And there's more, so much more. Cat takes a Barbie mansion and a dozen more gifts besides—two of everything, for some reason—but she seems happy enough about it. Throughout it all, we drink coffee and chitchat and joke, like this isn't strange at all. No one asks for an explanation for the sudden appearance of Christmas, or for waking up in a strange house, or for the relationships linking us together. We all just narrowly escaped a dreadful Christmas by the skin of our teeth.

"It's a lovely old place," Jake's aunt—*Laura*—says to Jake's grandfather—*Bill*. "It would make a lovely funeral home."

I get the feeling this is Laura's highest praise.

Bill scratches his hairy ear with a skeptical look and points at the grunting mass of straggly white fur on the rug in front of him. "I pulled something like that from my shower drain once. You're not supposed to name it and feed it."

"She's mine now," Cat says rapturously, tugging the dog into her lap. The old bichon frisé whines in ecstasy as she pulls a freshly unwrapped baby onesie over his head.

I jump in quickly. "It's not our dog."

"Oh, a family dog is everyone's dog!" Laura says. "We can share him."

This is quickly getting out of hand. I glance at Jake, but he just watches me, inscrutable. Amused?

"But you said we would get a dog," Cat reminds me. "We have a dog roof."

Cat unwraps another present and another. Now she passes them all to Jake, but he just gives her a small smile and passes them on. He won't keep any of the presents for himself. It's impossible not to think of that bare bedroom at Grant's, the Swedish death cleaning he's already done. He drinks coffee like he's breathing air and observes us all like a scientist watching an experiment unfold. He's placed himself on the outside again. He did this all for us, and not for himself.

AT SOME POINT JAKE DISAPPEARS, AND THEN SUDDENLY THERE ARE PANCAKES on the dining room table, and more coffee, and hot chocolate for Cat. Bill eats and eats, and Jake surreptitiously taps some pills from a box out onto the table next to his plate. I follow him with my eyes as Jake stokes the fire and cleans the mess of wrapping paper. More pancakes appear, and dirty dishes disappear, and then Christmas music is playing. Bill nods off in an armchair with his chin on his chest, and after Cat finishes cutting about a hundred sugar cookies with Laura, I melt onto the floor in front of the warm fire and play haunted Barbie manor with her. It's something I never get to do. Or maybe it's something my hamster brain never *lets* me do. There's always so *much*—always, always go go go—studying, cleaning, cooking, driving, worrying, fretting, rushing. I don't know when she got so big. She has a whole inner world I don't know anything about. We both do. Fantasy worlds in our heads that we retreat to.

And then, suddenly, Christmas dinner. Norman fucking Rockwell. We sit around the table for hours, and I think of the life I told Jake I had planned. The old house, the fluffy, stupid dog, and the grandparents there to help. Laura smiles and compliments me on Cat, my strange, uncanny girl who never gets compliments, and her sweetness gives me a toothache; Bill shows Cat the pictures in a dusty old copy of *Peter Rabbit* with gnarled, trembling hands, and Cat tells him that she *loves* rabbit; Princess farts blissfully on the Persian rug in his third outfit change. My eyes finally connect with Jake's.

He's been watching me this whole time—all day—to see what I think of his latest gift. Every time I look his way his eyes are on me. And for some reason it's impossible to hold his gaze for more than a few seconds. I feel like he'll read my mind if I do, and I don't know why I don't want that—I don't even know what thoughts I'm trying to keep hidden from him. But I look at him now. He's tired and pale, and he never got around to shaving, but he smiles a shy, twisty smile at me—a real one—and my heart stutters, and who am I kidding? It's obvious what thoughts I don't want him to see.

He's an agent of chaos. An opportunist and a manipulator of Machiavellian proportions. A magician who pulls coins from my ears and rabbits from hats, makes my problems vanish behind a false wall, cuts me in half and puts me back together again. My jack of spades with his shovel slung over his shoulder, who knows where all the bodies are buried, and can take care of a few more for me if I need.

44
Hag Dream

JAKE

ALL EVENING THERE ARE LITTLE SIGNALS, LITTLE SIGNS. AS WE WASH THE dishes at the sink, she stands close; her elbow touches mine. When I sweep the floor, she waits for me to finish, then takes the dustpan from me, our fingers brushing. When I pick up Cat for her from the sofa where she's fallen asleep, she trails after me up the stairs and watches as I lay her down on her bed. She twitches the covers over her and flicks off the lamp beside the bed. Outside Cat's room, we look at each other in the dark hallway for a moment.

I shouldn't be surprised when she creeps into my room later and slides on top of me in the dark. The mattress dips as she slings her leg over me, straddling me, her hands on my chest pressing the breath out of me.

"Dodi?" I whisper. I'd been half asleep.

"Who else?"

I can smell her perfume and, underneath that, the smell of skin as her hair brushes my chest in the dark. My fingertips find her knees on either side of me.

"I thought I was having a hag dream."

"Fuck you." She laughs against my lips as she begins a kiss.

My breath catches in my chest, and I just lie there, afraid to breathe, afraid to move, afraid to fuck this up. She kisses me slowly, intensely, her soft inky-black hair spilling around us, her sharp nails digging into my skin through the fabric of my shirt. She drags her lips across mine one last time as I almost suffocate.

"I really hate you," she whispers with a sharp smile. And because she lies to me, it's easy to lie to myself. *She hates me.* This isn't going to hurt her one bit.

The belt of her robe is cinched tight like the ribbon of a beautifully wrapped gift, and I take a chance and tug it loose. In retaliation she shoves my shirt up and over my head, and it's such a relief—we're doing this—it's actually—

Her hand slithers down from my shoulder, across my torso, down my belly, and doesn't stop until—

I bite my lip, but her lip's in the way and I bite her by accident. She doesn't mind. She comes back for more, and even though I feel like I'm smothering, I let her. Air is for chumps. I'm sinking into the mattress, stars behind my eyelids—

45

Our Lady of Sorrows

DODI

I PULL AWAY. "YOU'RE NOT WEARING YOUR TIE," I WHISPER AGAINST HIS CHEEK. "It's kind of a problem."

"Why?"

"I had plans for it."

I've imagined two dozen scenarios involving Jake's tie and not much else. Leading him to the bed like a leash before I push him backward and climb on. Cinched tight around my wrists. Cinched tight around *his* wrists. Blindfolding his eyes—

I press my nails into his chest and his breath hitches. I rake my nail tips downward, and his rib cage spasms, then his stomach clenches, and he curls up slightly as I spread one hand over the warm, bare skin of his belly. Slowly, he relaxes back into his pillow, watching me in the dim light, waiting for whatever comes next. A reprise of cat and mouse, and the mouse has been dying for it.

He lets out a little moan when I slip my hand down and wrap my fingers around him. I never actually said I disliked a good pillow princess, did I? I touch him while he lies back, helpless, eyelids fluttering, and then he rolls his hips involuntarily, his hands creeping up my thighs, his fingertips digging in—

"You said we'd follow my MO," I remind him. I pry his hands from my hips and shrug my robe off.

It's embarrassing how many times I've snuck this exact condom around with me, tucked in my purse or bra, just in case, since our trip to Las Vegas.

"What's your MO?" he whispers, barely breathing.

So I tell him. I whisper it into his ear as I bite his earlobe, and he shudders. I whisper it against the skin of his neck and his chest, the muscles flickering in his sides as he convulses against the tickle of my breath. He smells so good. And then I whisper the final part against his lower belly. I'm silent after that for a little while, and I make sure he's not. He twitches and trembles, and when his fingertips trace frantic nonsense patterns on my face and scalp, I pull away and climb up his body. He pants like he's run a minute mile, and I don't give him a chance to catch his breath. I drape myself over him, slide myself onto him, and devour his little moans with my mouth.

I hold his face between my hands—his jaw, his throat. I scratch my nails slowly across his scalp, through his thick hair, and he lets out another stifled sigh. I want to get more than a sigh out of him. I press myself against him more firmly and he kisses *me* then, blindly, hungrily—

And then slowly, languorously—and then he pulls away.

He licks his lips and strokes my knee with one thumb, hesitating. His breath is careful and shallow, like he's being mindful of disturbing the poor dust motes suspended in the air.

He cups the side of my face and his thumb ghosts over my eyebrow, my nose, my lips.

I'm trying to force an MO. The texture of this moment is different from what I'd imagined a few weeks ago.

How many more times will we get to do this?

I kiss him again, slowly, deliberately, the stubble under his lower lip scratching my skin, and now I'm filing away details, itemizing memories, vacuum-packing them and numbering them already for the twisted little museum in my heart. I'm an archivist, and I want to document everything—I want to know everything—I want to rifle around until I've found all his hidden clasps and latches and undone them all. I want to luxuriate in all his details. He lets out another stuttering sigh, like he'd been holding his breath for too long, and even his breath tastes right. We move against each other—skin, sinew, bone, beating hearts—two fragile, perishable structures safe enough for a moment to be vulnerable with each other.

I sit up to survey him—I need to document a bird's-eye view—but Jake's not having any of my shit. It's not my MO anymore. He pulls me down on top of him again, his arms roped around me tightly, possessively. Wanting me, even as he has me.

He's always wanted me, prickly little monster that I am. I'm one of those pin impression toys, and Jake is the soft hand pressing me down. I don't know if he has any idea how faithfully I'll keep his imprint after he goes.

46
Last Words

JAKE

"I'VE BEEN THINKING ABOUT THAT SECRET SANTA COPYCAT ACT THAT WAS IN the news . . ." she says in the dark.

I open my eyes, but I don't see that much more than I did when they were closed. What little light there is comes from beyond her darkened head next to me on my pillow.

"I think they should keep working together. Two heads are better than one."

I watch the outline of her profile against the dim gray wall, a shape I know well. She's spent so much time half turned away from me. She turns to me now and it vanishes.

"Have you figured out what you want to do with the rest of your life?" she whispers across the pillow. She threads her fingers through mine, and they begin to tingle.

"I was thinking," she continues, "you seem to like . . . normal, everyday things. Boring, real life." She squeezes my hand. "Nights in, and messes to clean, and cooking to do. And if that's what you want to do instead of jet-setting around the world and ticking off a bucket list . . . you could move in with me. I'd like that."

I can't feel her hand in mine anymore. It's completely numb. She wasn't supposed to actually want any of this.

For a moment I'm so tempted. I try to math it in my head, knock it all into an equation that doesn't produce zero-sum in my favor. I throw in my two hundred thousand from Las Vegas . . . but there's nothing else, really. It's a laughable offering when what Dodi deserves is an entire living, breathing person for the rest of her life. I can't tidy up this equation because it's all a fucking mess, and I hate messes.

I think of all those sharp edges left by the last bump in her life. It'll keep happening—every time a blow happens, another crack, another row of shards to prick other people with, and herself too. Keeping people out, keeping her locked in, alone.

"I don't care if we can only do this for a little while," Dodi says, as if reading my mind. "I want to be with you. You want that too. That's all most people want at the end, to be with family. I know how much that sucks to not have family."

I think of that night on her sofa, drinking wine. Laura gazing with hearts in her eyes at the two of us clasping hands. Bill gruffly teaching me to light a fire.

I can't help but think of Cat slipping her hand into mine at the mall.

"I'd like to have you with me . . . because I—"

I cut her off before she can say it. "How would that be good for her?"

I'm asking how it would be good for Cat because I can't ask how it would be good for Dodi. She wouldn't put up with that. But their life isn't some Jenga tower I can smoothly slip out of. I was counting on a year, maybe, but what if I turned selfish and decided to milk as much time as I could? What if I really deteriorated, and changed, Cat watching from her place on the rug as I slowly faded away, Dodi watching Cat watching me, and regretting this choice she made to see me through to the end. I know I'm capable of it. I've already been so selfish. I should have carried on as I had been, loner temp gray-rocking through the world.

I can hear her lick her lips. "Maybe when she's older, she'll remember a relationship where two people looked after each other. I don't know how else she's going to get an example of a healthy relationship. Jake, I—"

"We'd have to pretend to have a healthy relationship?"

Dodi doesn't laugh. I didn't expect her to. I don't feel like laughing either.

"I think I've only said this out loud to a few people in my life, but I—"

"The thing is . . ." I say, cutting her off again. She hesitates, waiting for me to finish. "I've got everything figured out on my own," I lie. "I don't need your help after all."

She inhales deeply, like she's about to plunge into cold water. "Jake, I lo—"

It's going to feel so much worse if she says it out loud. "I think we should get an annulment."

I imagine a hairline crack added to all the rest, but a tiny one, with no sharp edges sticking out. Neatly and mercifully done.

She doesn't speak again, but she doesn't leave, either. She knows why I'm doing this. She has the mug. We both lie there, fingers threaded, so still and quiet, I don't know which one of us falls asleep first.

47

The Skeletons

JAKE

IT'S THE DEATHLY QUIET OF EARLY MORNING AFTER CHRISTMAS. I SPOT AN Uber through the front door's side windows, idling outside.

She emerges from the dark hallway, her steps slowing for a moment, just a moment, as she notices me come down the stairs into the dim foyer. Maybe she thought she could sneak off before I caught her.

"I was just saying good-bye to Bill and Laura," she explains.

"Were you going to say good-bye to me?"

"No."

"Will you now?"

"No."

She stares at me, and I look at her. Lips the color of holly berries, her hair spilling around her shoulders, rumpled and unbrushed. I don't want to say good-bye to her either, and we don't have to. This won't be the last time we see each other. We'll cross paths, randomly, when we least expect it. We'll connect eyes across a parking lot. We'll find ourselves walking toward each other on a downtown sidewalk. She'll shank me with a sarcastic smile and say, *Still stalking me?* and I'll say, *Until the sweet grip of death takes me*, and she'll say, *Something to look forward to, then*, and we'll stand there for a few seconds, our eyes saying something completely different. She'll keep spotting me, until one day the sightings stop. I wonder how long she'll hold out for another.

Cat appears from behind her, Princess lumbering along at the end of a flimsy leash, snorting and puffing enthusiastically.

"Shoes, Cat."

Cat scrabbles with her Mary Janes and Dodi slips on her boots. She passes the little red peacoat to Cat, who takes it.

"Shoes, Jake," Cat says around the collar of her coat in the same bossy tone as her mother.

"I still have some cleaning up to do," I say.

Dodi and I exchange one last look. The Uber honks. The door opens, and all the warmth of the house swirls out into the cold morning with them.

The house is dead and empty now. A floorboard creaks, and I turn to see Laura.

"Did you two quarrel?" she asks sympathetically. "I won't pry. You'll work it out. It's obvious you two love each other very much." She fiddles with her snowman necklace for a minute. "Or . . . you *could* go after her. I'll hold down the fort . . ."

I prop up a fake smile and try to look confused—*Dodi and me, fighting?*—but Laura sees through me. I learned all my fake smiles from her, after all. She gracefully drops it.

We gravitate to the kitchen, our default, and she pours coffee and restlessly picks up crumbs off the surface of the kitchen table with the pad of her finger.

"I'm going to have to turn my phone on at some point." She

laughs hollowly. "How many missed calls do you think there are?"

Andrew would have come home to an empty house yesterday, expecting us to be cowed and conciliatory. I can picture him now, checking that tracking app, useless with Laura's data turned off. Firing off text after text, calling over and over, face getting grimmer and grimmer.

I want to reach across the table and place my hand on Laura's. *Don't go back.*

She twists her hands, and her face twists too.

"I need to talk to you, Jake. It's been eating me up inside, what I said the other night. I should never have worded it like that, like I stayed because I *had* to. Because I could have left. I had my bags packed when you showed up—there was a reason I hadn't bothered with Christmas that year. But I *chose* to stay. I *chose* it. I would choose it again. It was all worth it. *You* were worth it."

I freeze. "What do you mean?"

She places her hands on mine and squeezes, and the pins and needles in the tips of my fingers start.

"I finally had my proof of the affair—well, *one* of the affairs—and I had my exit plan figured out, but then the social worker showed up with walking, talking proof of a completely separate affair, and his dog in tow, and—"

She stops for one second, emotion catching up with her. It catches up with me, too. I remember that day clearly, this strange woman standing in her front door, staring at me like she'd seen a ghost.

"You weren't anything like Andrew. I could tell that at a glance. You would never have survived growing up with that sociopath—I knew that *instantly*. And then after what he did to that poor old dog—" Laura cuts out again for a second. "Jake. I was never going *anywhere*."

My fingers are blocks of ice.

I stare at Laura—the large, dark doe eyes, the heart-shaped face—so much like my mom, who I look like—my mom, the youngest, prettiest teacher at school—a little public school, because she'd left the Catholic school system after having me out of wedlock—who had never in my entire childhood spoken of her estranged sister, Laura. Never had so much as a photo of her in our apartment.

Because they're not sisters. They're not sisters, but Andrew has a *type*.

Laura squeezes my hands and her mouth moves, but I don't hear a word. My mind is skipping like a stone over still water from ifs and thats to thens. It was easy to fabricate a redirection of the public's speculation—I look like my *aunt*. An easy, sleazy lie. A way to keep squeaky clean the reputation of my uncle, the Catholic school superintendent—my uncle, who always bristled when anyone mistook me for his son. My uncle—

My *father*. I could be sick.

I remember that dinner on my birthday. *How dare you tell her I'm your father . . .*

Laura thought I knew. Of course she did. What normal person wouldn't have put it all together? Andrew's family did. Those wary, disapproving stares at family dinners, those probing, uncomfortable questions about my parentage in those early years—

Laura's been talking this whole time—saying what, who knows—and now she pulls her hands back from mine for a moment, and my fingers aren't just white, they're blue at the tips. This is a new symptom. I'm getting sicker. My nerve cells falling apart, myelin disintegrating. I feel nauseous—my heart starts thudding—the well-trodden physiological circuit of an anxiety attack starting—

And it's the missing step on the stairs at night. I lurch as I find my mental footing.

I'm not dying.

In my mind's eye, Andrew's parents—*my grandparents*— doing their ridiculous dance classes at their retirement home, rudely spry and physically able. Disgustingly healthy. Showing no signs of slowing down as they close in on a century on this planet.

"When did this start? Poor thing," Laura says, taking my blue fingers into her warm hands. "Raynaud's syndrome. Capillary spasm. Looks *so* much scarier than it is. Andrew gets that too, in his feet. That's why you never see him without a pair of socks. Triggered by cold or stress. Have you been stressed?"

Have I been stressed. My heart's been eating itself in my chest for eight years. It's empty now—quiet and still inside.

Laura comes into focus in front of me, her lips moving, words forming, but I'm in my own head. Of course she didn't take me away with her. Of course we didn't leave Andrew in the dust. I wasn't hers. I was *his.*

I always thought she was weak, but she was so strong. Not the sort of strength that stood up to force, but the sort that quietly bore great pressure. What was that like, always rolling over, giving way, placating, placating, placating your psycho husband so you could stay put in a horrible marriage and keep an eye on his kid? The kid you had no legal right to?

"Oh, honey," Laura says, squeezing my arm, seeing something on my face I can't tuck away and hide. "Don't be stressed. Talk to her. It's normal for new relationships—"

This is peak Laura right here, calming, soothing, a steady drip of encouragement. She's always been the best. The absolute best aunt a lonely, grief-stricken boy could ask for.

She's not my aunt, though.

I look her in the eyes, finally. She smiles. "It's going to be okay." She consults her watch. "I have to go soon."

"Where?" I ask.

Her face is cheerful again, and it's not all forced. "I'm baby-sitting Cat. I offered. Dodi has to wrap up that school assignment." *As you know, of course,* her tone suggests. "Cat and I are going to give that horrible white monster a bath."

She pulls out her phone and turns on the data, all her message notifications and missed phone calls populating the screen. Andrew, Andrew, Andrew. She swipes it all away, taps out a text to Dodi, and sends it. She already has her in her contacts.

She squeezes my hands one last time, but I hold on when she tries to pull away. She smiles at me, eyes misty.

"I'm glad we got to have this Christmas together. I think you should keep the decorations here. No point in taking them back. Where would I keep them?" And then she drops her bombshell. "I've decided to leave him." She ducks and pecks me quickly on the cheek before she leaves.

Alone in the kitchen, I stare at the obituary photo of the handsome man with the glasses, the man my mother named me after. Maybe because that's who she wished my father was. I look around the room, at all the things, all the clues about who I am and where I come from, and none of it connects to me after all. I spot two empty water glasses on the counter, one of them with Dodi's bright red lipstick on the rim, and it calls something to mind. The water glasses Bill wouldn't let me wash.

I find Bill on the collapsed old velvet sofa Dodi and I slept on the other night. He grips the top of his cane with both hands and rests his chin on top of them, gazing at the tree.

"It's been a while since you've had a Christmas tree," I surmise.

"Longer than you think," he says humorously. "I'm Jewish."

I notice it in his hand, the envelope from the lab that came in the mail before I left for Laura's Christmas lunch. He sees me looking at it. He touches the cushion next to him, and I sit. Across from us, Dodi's skeleton slouches in his armchair, grinning toothily. We're silent, all three of us.

"There's been . . ." He trails off, and starts over. "I did a DNA test . . ." He falters again.

There's a hollow in my chest, deep and bottomless. If you stuck a hand inside, you'd lose your watch. My sentence has been commuted, but at the cost of a kind-faced father who loved my mother; a wise old grandfather, sardonic and gruff; and the gentlest, kindest aunt anyone ever had. None of them belong to me. I'm no one to any of them. I'm a stray. All I got out of this was Andrew, the one person on this planet I would happily fire into the sun, and if Laura is leaving him, she won't be around to sweeten the bargain.

I don't know how I'll ever get up from this sofa.

Bill clears his throat, opens his mouth, and then abruptly folds the envelope in half and tucks it into the pocket of his robe. "Just so you know, I've got a liver enzyme problem," he says at last. He clears his throat and frowns. "You'll have to watch out when you get older, since it runs in the family."

He avoids my eye as I stare at him. I can't think why he's lying to me. *Don't you know I thought I was dying?* He didn't. I told him the neurologist said I was in the clear. He has no idea how this misunderstanding has affected me.

"I have a great-granddaughter," he says suddenly, and I

start. He spent two weeks telling me stories about all the dead, broken-off branches on our—*his* family tree. There is no great-granddaughter.

"Two weeks ago I had no one," Bill continues, "and now I have a great-granddaughter. And a grandson and a granddaughter-in-law—are you married? I didn't ask. I didn't want to sound like some old idiot. It's fine to not be married."

It's the first time he's uttered the word "grandson." I don't know what to say to any of this, so I just say, "We're married."

"And Laura?"

"She's—" I swallow, mind whirling. "She's not related to me by blood, but she's always been like an aunt."

"You don't need to be related by blood to be family," Bill argues gallantly on Laura's behalf.

"Cat isn't related to me by blood, either," I say numbly. "She's Dodi's daughter, by her first husband."

"And she's ours now."

Ours. Bill's and mine. How has that letter from the lab not burst into flames in his pocket already?

"You don't need blood relation to justify a family," Bill repeats. He hasn't looked me in the eye this whole time. We're silent for a beat.

"This is a big house," he says unexpectedly. "My granddaughter-in-law seemed to like it. That little waif seemed to like it, too." He lets it hang there.

I can't make any sense of this.

"And there's that school, just down the street."

The weird, artsy little private school, the sort of place that would probably let Cat bring mutilated Barbies for show-and-tell. I don't follow.

"There's no reason for me to be living here all alone, with

all this space going to waste," Bill continues, and I finally get his meaning.

I look around. It's a huge old house, and Bill doesn't even step foot in the entire upstairs. The two weeks I spent here were the easiest living arrangement I've ever had. Bill and I get on together. He likes my cooking and my help, and more than that, he likes talking to me. I like listening to him.

"I could use the company—and the help," he says with dignity. "I don't want to get moved into some facility by a social worker. I'd like to die in my own home."

I answer automatically, without thinking. "Of course I'll help." If there's one thing I understand, it's the desire to be in control of the end. It's all spun around so quickly, and now here I am, offering the advocacy I always wanted.

Next to me Bill's shoulders relax a little. I hadn't realized how tense he was. He's been barely hanging on to independence for so long.

That secret in his pocket—his lie by omission—his motive for concealing the results—

He thinks he's *conning* me.

The sneaky, daft bastard. I don't even mind.

He continues. "And you may as well make use of the place now as later. You don't need to wait to cash in on your inheritance before moving in."

This takes a minute to process. "My inheritance?"

"It has to go to someone."

I look at it all—the old wood and the discolored curtains that need to be replaced, the abundance of molding and carving ripe for collecting dust, the floors that need to be waxed— my fingers twitch. I love messes. I love taking care of things—and people. It's my MO.

There's an offer here: be my grandson, and I'll be your grandfather.

Dodi's skeleton still slouches by the fire, staring at us with empty eye sockets, grinning humorously at his skeleton friends tumbling out of closets, attempting to crawl back in. I'm used to living in a family full of lies, and I'm over it. Bill and I will come clean with each other. Later. And I think I'll accept his offer.

Right now, it's Dodi I need to talk to.

48

The Mad Dash

JAKE

MY PHONE VIBRATES AS I SLAM BILL'S FRONT DOOR BEHIND ME. IT SLIPS OUT of my fingertips and onto the ground, screen cracking, bouncing into a shallow puddle. The snow is melting already, spiky green grass peeking through all over Bill's lawn.

The screen says LARS.

"What?" I snarl into the dripping phone.

"Where's the Lambo?" says Grant's friendly, curious voice.

"The what?"

"Black, um, sleek . . ."

"Did you check your closet?"

"It's a car."

"It's right in front of me." Its lone taillight pulses as I unlock it remotely.

"Oh, that's a relief," he says with an indulgent chuckle. "Just, uh, borrowed it?"

"Yeah." I throw myself into the driver's seat and pull the belt across my body.

"That's fine, that's fine. And where's the Brunello Cuci-nelli?"

I crank into reverse and run through my mental inventory of his cars. One has the Italian flag incorporated into its crest, I think?

"Is that the green one with the racing stripe?"

"It's blue wool . . ."

"Dry cleaners."

"And the espresso machine—"

"You have to twist it all the way."

"And the sauna repair company—"

"They're not coming back because you left a sex doll in there last time."

"I don't have *sex* with them," Grant says primly.

There's a pregnant pause while Grant takes a deep breath, and I ram the rear end of the Dickmobile onto the sidewalk and into an elm sapling encased in a protective plastic tube.

"I've been a bad friend."

"You're not even a friend. You're a bag of dicks, Grant." I'm swiveling madly, ripping the wheel around with one hand, trying to twelve-point turn my way out of this parking job while holding the phone in my other. The back right wheel goes over the curb again and again.

"I know," he says sadly. "I know."

"Do you? The bag of dicks has sentience and self-awareness? This is really fascinating." I'm coasting down the street now with one hand on the wheel. The Bluetooth connects suddenly and Grant's voice fills the car.

"When are you coming home?"

"I've got a new place."

His breath catches. I toss my phone on the passenger seat and hang a right.

"I respect that," he says sorrowfully. And It's . . . surprising. "I didn't really deserve your friendship. I see that now. But I want . . . Can I make a gesture of amends?"

His new therapist must be good.

"I want to . . . I should have been paying you. For your help. Can I . . . Well, I want to know what would make your efforts feel acknowledged."

The car's been warming up and it fucking stinks. I roll a window down, and I think of Dodi's hair blowing ragged in the night wind on the way to Las Vegas. I remember her smashed-up car. She belongs in something fast and expensive and . . . fast.

"I want one of your cars."

His breath catches. "The Lambo?"

I think of the smashed rear, the pine sap, and the rabbit juice. The giant dick on the trunk. "No." I clear my throat. "I know this one's sentimental to you. You can give me a different one." I remember the car I drove Dodi to the airport in. She'd stopped in her tracks and hissed, "Fucking *kidding me*," under her breath. I think that meant she liked it. "The red one with the black leather interior."

His breath comes out in a whoosh. Relief.

"The Hellcat. I'll leave the deed on the kitchen counter here. Are we still friends, Jake?"

Were we ever?

"Of course. Grant?"

"Yes?"

"Legal question: if someone was hired for a job, and then she was supposed to be laid off, but she wasn't, and the company forgot about her and kept paying her for years because of a clerical error—"

"Not really my wheelhouse, but was there a letter or email of termination?"

"No."

"Then she wasn't terminated and she was owed that pay-check."

"Even if she wasn't being given any work, and no one was supervising her and it was obvious that—"

"Jake," Grant says, his voice persuasive and smooth. "Work-for-hire is a fixture in today's highly competitive corporate world. It's a strategy to sequester talent away from the competition. Even if your company doesn't *need* another top-tier analyst or software engineer—or what have you—at least you can keep her away from assisting the competition, right? Do you see what I'm saying?" Essence of suave criminal defense lawyer condenses on the windows and drips all over the expensive leather upholstery. "She was given no reason to think her situation was anything other than that. And she showed up, didn't she? She was available for work every day. Professional. Ready. Willing. We have character references and testimonials notarized and ready for submission at discovery—" He sketches in the details, falling in love with his own story.

"Got it, thanks," I say.

His voice abruptly returns to normal. "I'll always have your back. If you ever need a criminal defense lawyer—"

"I don't plan on it."

"I'm here when you need me. Oh, and Jake?"

"Yes?"

He clears his throat, and I know what's coming. No. No, no, no.

"I was wondering if—"

We're on W now. "Wendy? Wanda? What did you call this one?"

He sighs. "Willow."

"No."

"I need her out of here—Jake—*please*. I've been journaling. *Everyone* needs to journal, Jake. And I'm realizing things about myself. I'm afraid of rejection. I'm afraid of disappointing someone and failing in a relationship. I work *so* much. And the sex thing"—disgust and anguish enter his voice now—"it's so hard to date when everyone expects that." He sighs. "I just wanted to love someone. I wanted to have a person. I wanted to feel *normal*."

Twenty-three sex dolls in the pursuit of normalcy.

"I get it," I say slowly. And I kind of do. Dodi did, right from the start. Being afraid someone won't accept you as you are, being afraid of hurting other people, being afraid to share your secrets. And if you get past all that, being afraid of losing them.

"So can you throw her out for me when you come by for the car? I've got a full bag of compost under the sink too."

I end the call.

There's an accident on the bridge, which means I have to go north and take the other bridge, which takes me past Grant's. On the other side, it's going to be gridlocked all the way from the bridge to Dodi's . . . I grit my teeth. I slam my brakes for a red light and another caller is announced by the dashboard screen: SPENCER & STERNS.

"What?"

Cynthia's cool HR voice is on the other end. "I've been trying to get in touch with you. I have a piece of paperwork here on my desk with your name on it."

"I don't work for Spencer & Sterns. I'm a *temp*—"

"I make a point of wrapping up all unfinished business myself before my contracts expire," she says firmly.

"—and it's the day after Christmas."

"I'm not sure I follow? If you are not an employee of

Spencer & Sterns, you are not enjoying paid time off right now. And I work on contract. I never stop working."

She's truly remarkable.

"If you have a moment to meet . . . ?"

"Sure thing, Cynthia," I spit at the dashboard screen. "But it's the *holidays*. Come over now for some fruitcake and do an in-person exit interview. You have my address in your system. Come right up to the top floor."

I imagine her showing up at Grant's penthouse. I'm going to leave the door unlocked and the sex doll right there on the couch for when she walks in.

There's a pause and then, "All right," and the call ends abruptly.

Immediately my phone vibrates again: ANDREW. I throw it out the window.

AT GRANT'S BUILDING, I FISHTAIL INTO A RESERVED PARKING SPOT IN THE basement and leave the Dickmobile straddling a white line. The elevator is waiting, and I go up and let myself in, holding my breath—

Grant is gone. The deed is there on the counter with a pair of key fobs. I shove it all in my pockets. In my room, I get the box of papers from under my bed. I reach for the coat hangers with my shirts and slacks, and I stop. I don't need any of that shit. I take my box and go. I have to get out of here before Cynthia shows up. But as I pass through the living room, I finally notice her.

Long black hair, dark eyes, tan skin. At some point they started making them with tattoos.

Sometimes it's necessary to compartmentalize, because I'm not fucking thinking about this right now.

At least he never treated an actual woman like an object, never tried to control or possess a real one. Unlike some men. Dangerous men. Men who shouldn't be anywhere near a real woman, because that's when they *really* get nasty—when the women refuse to be possessed. When they try to leave.

My guts fold in on themselves.

Through the window I can see the bridge and the commuter highway beyond, bumper to bumper with traffic. Somewhere beyond that are Dodi, Cat, Princess, and Laura. Kind, gentle Laura. Has she already called Andrew? Why didn't I tell her to coordinate a plan with me? Because Andrew's out there somewhere too, stewing, furious to be coming home after ruining Christmas to discover he didn't ruin anyone's Christmas after all. To discover his wife left with a suitcase, humiliating *him*. Did Laura turn off her data again after texting Dodi? Is he looking up her location right now? I pat for my phone to call Laura, but I don't have it.

I need to get to them, now.

49
On the Roof

DODI

I PEER OVER THE LOW WALL AND THERE IT IS, THE CALL OF THE VOID, THAT IN-trusive impulse gusting up the side of the building like a breeze. The unsummoned visual of my own body on the ground below winks in and out. Thrilling and terrible. It wouldn't hurt one bit. Nothing hurts right now, although I know from experience all that means is that it will really hurt later. The longer the lag between injury and sensation, the worse the hurt. And yet, it's better this way. I'm grateful to Jake for that. Mighty high-handed of a man to tell a grown woman how she gets to break her heart, but he's seen how reckless I can be. I've always needed him to cut me off. This is no different than that night in Las Vegas.

My body on the ground below morphs into a man in busi-ness attire. A woman screams on a balcony between us, and the lights of Vegas twinkle and glare . . .

"This rooftop is Paper Pusher bait," Laura says next to me with her elbows resting on the dangerously low parapet, and I return with a start to my apartment building's rooftop dog park.

"It's just an urban legend," I say without thinking.

She shakes her head. "Did Jake not tell you I tidied up four of her victims? All came to me from the coroner's office, and they're not *supposed* to say anything . . ." There's a flicker of mischief on her face. "But it's what they *don't* say, if that makes sense."

"Her?" I ask.

"Didn't you watch the documentary? It's obviously a woman. Sometimes I wonder . . . You hear stories about falls in other cities, and I think to myself, 'Is she on vacation?'" Laura laughs. "One time I even called up a funeral home in another city to dig."

She's into this shit, too. I suppose she would be. Maybe Jake turned her onto it. Or maybe she got him started.

I stare at the parking lot asphalt below. The idea of the Paper Pusher on a working vacation is delicious. That fall victim in Las Vegas didn't necessarily fall off that balcony. Why did I assume that? Perhaps that woman witnessed the fall as he fell from the roof—

"I'm going to call her Tinkerbell," Cat announces, and I'm back on the rooftop of my apartment building again. She's standing in front of me, eyes sparkling, cheeks flushed. She looks like a normal child for once.

"But the dog's a boy," I say weakly. "See?" I point to his back end, where it's clear as day the thing was never neutered.

"Girls can have balls," Cat says matter-of-factly, conflating actual balls and metaphoric ones. I flinch and look at Laura. She seems like the sort of soft, sweet older woman to care about language, but there's no disapproving side-eye.

"Girls can have anything boys can have," Laura agrees.

Cat peels off and Laura smiles after her like she wishes she could jot down this Cat one-liner.

Something in the way Laura looks at Cat makes my chest ache. I push myself off the wall. I have to get back to the apartment to submit that assignment.

"Thanks again," I say to Laura without making eye contact. I'm using her, unfortunately. I know she wouldn't be here if she knew Jake and I were over, so it's unfair what I'm doing: accepting the help of an aspiring grandma who will not be getting the permanent position. She practically threw herself at me with an offer of free babysitting. Perfect timing since my neighbor has stopped answering my texts.

"It's my pleasure," Laura says warmly, and she really does exude pleasure. I've never seen anyone this happy to spend time with my odd, uncanny little girl.

It's hard not to worry just a little that Laura doesn't quite know what she's in for. "She can be very . . ." I have a list of words I don't mind Cat overhearing me use. Persistent. Tough. Independent. Outspoken. "Assertive."

"You know, when I was a girl, our mothers made a point of bringing us up to be polite and gentle and *nice*," Laura says, skewering me and my mothering neatly and knocking the breath out of me with the shock of it. She manages to say it so sweetly, too, with a smile like a day in June. My heart scales over in an instant, and my eyes snap to Cat.

"But it's such a relief to see you're smarter than that," Laura continues. "You and Jake aren't going to have to worry about her, are you? She'll be tough enough to handle the world herself."

My eyes stay trained on Cat as my heart softens again and a fresh ache twists through it. I want to keep Laura, even if I can't have Jake, and I wonder if I can, if this is a friendship worth the risk. I would be able to keep tabs on Jake, at least.

In seven years I've never made a genuine attempt at a friendship. But for Cat's sake, I think I would try.

There's a whole dance that we do. Mirroring, sharing, meeting for coffees, reading each other's book recommendations, and slowly, slowly friendship takes root and sprouts and blossoms. But I'm shit at plants. I cut to the meat.

"Can we be friends?" I wouldn't have said anything if I had known my voice would sound this strangled.

"We're *family*." She smiles fondly at Cat, who loops close before peeling off again. "Jake adored dogs when he was little. He'll have to teach Cat how to train Princess to do tricks. They'll have so much fun with that."

My heart twists again, an uglier pain this time. Every other sentence has been "Cat and Jake" this, "you and Jake" that. It's high time I set her straight. I summon all the flat matter-of-factness I can and push past the knot in my throat.

"Jake and I aren't going to stay together."

Her face slips. "But Jake says you haven't even tried living together yet. Jake is very easy to live with."

My eyes swim until Cat is just a red blur. Laura's so sweet my teeth hurt. I'm not like that. I've always been an acquired taste. People like Laura don't usually take to it. I give her a taste of it now. "We would end up killing each other if we stayed together." It's half true.

"At least you would be merciful about it. Oxycodone overdose in your own bed isn't such a bad way to go."

My skin prickles and my organs slide out of my body.

"Jake, on the other hand, he's very creative with his murder weapons. I'm not sure how you'd make your home a weapon-free zone."

I find my voice. "What?"

"Strangulation by Christmas lights was his most recent brainwave." She shakes her head. *That Jake!*

I stare at her, dumbstruck. Does she know about Neil? Either Jake told her, or she googled me, or she listens to *Murderers at Work*—

And yet this woman, who stuffs cotton batting into corpses and spray-paints their cheeks or whatever it is she does, just told me I'm family. We *would* make the perfect little family.

Laura's face changes suddenly and dramatically, and she steps back from the wall. I follow her line of sight to a silver-haired man standing five stories below in the parking lot, staring up at us, his body tense.

"Is that . . . ?"

"Andrew."

Jake's uncle.

"What's he doing here?" I ask.

Laura doesn't answer. A strange alchemy is occurring. This sweet, warm woman is turning cold and withdrawn right before my eyes.

"He sees me," she says. "I should go down."

"Why?"

"If he comes up, he'll cause a scene." Her eyes dart to Cat, playing with Princess on the Astroturf.

"He can't just come up. Someone has to let him in."

She shakes her head, face pale.

This is all pretty new to me, but friendship for me must be like a breaker switch, because I feel myself moving, realigning to enclose Laura within my own invisible armor. I put my hand on her arm. "Stay. If he comes up, we'll send him on his way."

"I'm sure Jake's told you about him," she says, her voice

dropping, like she's about to say something dirty. "It's not very nice."

She smiles at me again—a warm, fake smile—and I get a dreadful inkling of where Jake learned his fake smiles and why.

This is why I don't teach my daughter to be polite and gentle and nice. Listen to enough murder podcasts and you'll eventually learn about fight, flight, and freeze's lesser-known baby sister, fawn.

"I'll just go down and smooth things over," she says.

"No," I say. "Absolutely not."

I lean over the wall to look again, and he's gone.

The bulkhead door groans open next to us and Laura flinches, even though it would be impossible for Andrew to be joining us so soon. A woman stomps onto the roof in practical thermal galoshes and a puffy purple straightjacket of a coat.

"Cynthia?"

Cynthia blinks through her owllike glasses, misted up from her own breath forced upward by her scarf. She stares at me, expressionless, and I notice she's holding . . . a paper airplane? I recognize the paper clip I shoved onto the nose.

The fucking creep. I didn't invite myself to her house when she left a paper crane on my desk. This is my *home*. That's my *daughter* over there.

Two dozen steps and I'm toe-to-toe with her, blocking her advance, before I've even thought of what to say.

"Dolores," she intones. She looks past me at Laura and Cat, and scans the rooftop for anyone else. Just one other neighbor with a Chihuahua in a Christmas sweater. Her ice-pick eyes bore into mine. "I hadn't realized you would be here too."

"What do you mean?"

"Although perhaps I should have expected it," she continues

in her carefully enunciated monotone. "You remind me of my-self in that way. You take initiative. You like to identify problems and fix them yourself. I knew that when I saw the list."

That fucking list. "You don't know anything about me," I snap. "Who do you think you are?"

Her face is an impenetrable wall when she says, "I know who *you* are, Dolores. You're an ethical person. Someone who isn't afraid to do the right thing, even if the right thing is difficult. And the right thing is always difficult."

Another person who knows all about me. There's the same sensation of my stomach dropping out that I felt just a moment ago with Laura, but more than that, a familiar feeling up and down my spine. Little mallets tickling a xylophone tune from my bones.

"I think we understand each other. I knew that when you left this for me," Cynthia continues, and I notice the paper airplane again. What did I do when I left this paper airplane on her keyboard? What message did I send?

With dead fingers I take it from her hands and unfold it. Inside I find the notes she made during our HR dressing-down. Jake's name. My address.

Tinkle. Tinkle. Tinkle.

My stomach feels acidic.

"Why are you here?" I whisper.

Cynthia's eyes are as cold and hard as pavement.

"Jacob Ripper's exit interview."

And then the door swings open again.

50

The Paper Pusher

JAKE

IT'S THE SAME LITTLE OLD LADY WITH HER PULL CART. I SLIP INTO THE BUILD-
ing behind her.

"*Excuse me—*" she says.

I try to press past her, but she steps into me.

"I'm going to report you to the building manager for waltz-
ing in like this! I recognize you, too. I'm going to tell them I
saw you sneak in like this the other night—"

"And I'll tell them I saw you at one a.m. on December
twenty-fifth pulling that exact cart, except it weighed about
fifty pounds that night, and I heard something clanking inside," I blurt out over my shoulder before I've had a chance to
hear myself think. Dodi's true crime paranoia has ruined me.

I stop in my tracks. Hopefully I'm going to be coming here
a lot, for a while yet, unless Cat and Dodi want to move in
right away—my thoughts are all over the place. I turn around
to apologize to my new neighbor, but her face has gone hard.
She stands taller and straighter than a second ago, her hand
firm and strong on the pull handle. Her other hand shoots out

to smooth the little blanket draped over the top of her pull cart, concealing the contents, and she swirls on the spot and marches quickly away, the bumbling limp from a moment ago gone.

Definitely a serial killer, Dodi's voice drawls in my ear as I watch her go. They'll be moving in right away.

Dodi's not in her apartment. I bang on her door until a girl steps out from the elevator with a Chihuahua in a Christmas sweater in her arms. "I saw them up on the roof," she says, flustered. "I'm calling the cops."

"What?"

But she doesn't answer. She bolts down the hall and disappears.

The elevator takes me to the roof and spits me out into a little vestibule with a metal door. On the other side is a miserable patch of Astroturf living its worst life, a few passive-aggressive signs about leashing and pickup, and across the way—

Chaos.

Screaming, yelling, a man and a woman flailing at each other, a small dog running in frantic circles, his yapping echoing off nearby buildings—

"Get your hands off her, you son of a *bitch*!" A figure in a puffy purple coat lunges at a man, who lurches backward— Andrew, I realize with a jolt. I reflexively search out Laura— there, cowering behind Dodi, who has her arms spread wide and a ferocious expression on her face. Andrew dodges, and Purple Coat stumbles and catches herself on the low parapet, and when she turns, I see it's . . . *Cynthia*?

"Cat!" Dodi shrieks as the little red peacoat bolts from behind Laura to grab Princess.

Andrew lunges for the dog at the same moment. "He's

mine!" he snarls, red faced, explosive. Behind him Cynthia reclaims her footing, and she's just as deranged. This cool, inhuman HR robot with the icicle eyes lunges and flails at him from behind, hammering his arms with her fists, her chunky homemade scarf swinging madly.

I'm across the soggy Astroturf in a moment to tug Cat back as Andrew snatches Princess from her arms.

"He took my puppy!" Cat yowls venomously.

Cynthia hollers, "Give back that little girl's dog, or so help me god—"

"He's my dog!" Andrew shouts, twisting in disgust as Princess licks his face frantically, joyously. He's never received this much attention from Andrew in his life.

I swing Cat over to Dodi and she crumples with relief around her daughter. Her hair is mussed and the shoulder seam of her coat is ripped. I look at Laura, and the side of her face is red. My stomach twists in half. I missed something very terrible. Laura shakes like a leaf behind Dodi, and I realize I'm shaking too. It's finally happening. The volcano is finally blowing.

"You've always been like this!" Cynthia shrieks at Andrew. "Always taking what you want! And as soon as you get it, you discard it! People too! Throwing away people like they're garbage!"

"You're a meddling shrew, Cynthia! An HR busybody! Always sticking your nose in, thinking you have everyone's number. You don't know a damn thing! This is none of your business! It's never any of your business! This is *my* dog!"

"This isn't about the fucking dog!" Cynthia rages. "You always were a creep, Andrew! You were my formative creep—everyone in Human Resources has a formative creep! 'Never again,' we say to ourselves." Cynthia finally notices me.

"There!" she yells. "There's another one! Another formative creep! *Your* formative creep, Dolores. Right? Jacob Ripper! He's just like you, Andrew. I saw that the moment I laid eyes on him—a handsy, narcissistic egomaniac on a power trip, manipulating vulnerable women—the very spit of his father!" she cries, and a drop of spit flies out with her words.

For a second I wonder how she knows anything about Jacob, Bill's son, my mistaken father with the glasses and the hazel eyes and the kind smile. How does she know I'm the spit of my father? And then I realize she's not talking about him, of course. She's talking about my real father—Andrew. She knows. She knows this thing about me that only two other people know.

Of course she does.

Cynthia fucking Cutts. I didn't cross paths with her at one of my temp jobs. I realize now why she's always looked down at me like some disgusting, misbehaving child. I *was* a child when I met her. She was someone my mom knew, someone from her years teaching in the Catholic school system. She used to come around and drink coffee at my mom's kitchen table, speaking in euphemisms and spelling words out letter by letter to make sure I didn't understand what they were talking about. Mom used to watch her warily, wearily, and then sag with relief when her rants about bullies and revenge and playing the long game came to an end. She'd close the door behind Cynthia, serve me a giant bowl of ice cream, and remind me, apropos of nothing, that I was the best thing that ever happened to her. *Jacob* Ripper? Cynthia had asked that day back in the annex, on the prowl for workplace harassment. *Jacob fucking* Ripper? *Spit of his father.* She must have been there when it happened, the workplace affair that led to me.

"He's a monster just like you!" Cynthia continues, jabbing her finger in my direction.

"No!" Dodi shouts, her face horrified. "Not Jake! We really are in a relationship!"

"Really?" Laura murmurs with absurd hope. Dodi presses Cat into Laura's arms and bolts to me.

"Jake, listen to me—" She pulls my arm, but wild horses and all that.

"Keeping your pecker in your pants these days, at least?" Cynthia says, prowling menacingly side to side as Andrew backs away, step by step, until his back is against the low wall. "Not messing around with any young, naive schoolteachers rendered vulnerable in the midst of personal crisis? You swooped in so fast after Jacob left. Definitely not fathering little babies, either, and getting the mothers stealth-fired for having a child out of wedlock—oh, my pearls!" Cynthia snarls, reaching for an imaginary necklace. "What about Catholic values in Catholic schools? The institution of marriage? Blah fucking blah, you fucking hypocrite! I still have copies of the letters from my Catholic school board days—everyone's statements, including Beth's. The times have changed and people actually give a shit about how women are treated in the workplace now! I can bring them out anytime!"

I'm finally getting the whole story after all these fucking years. My origin story, hollered from the rooftops. Andrew looks at me with poison in his eyes. A vein throbs in his forehead and his expression turns violent. He's a monster backed into a corner, ready to lash out and take us all down with him for our part in his humiliation—this public viewing of his nasty little secret, cracked open, wind whistling through its innards, all of us peering in.

"How *dare* you!" Andrew snarls at Cynthia. Princess yips excitedly and his legs run tractionless on the air in front of him.

"Did you know I went out on my own and started my own consulting business, Andrew?" Cynthia continues. "HR departments hire me to push out assholes and creeps and *bullies*, and now I've found someone to mentor, someone to pass the torch to—"

Dodi's arms tighten around my waist from behind. "Don't go near her," she says in my ear. "Jake, are you listening to me?"

I'm not. I'm listening to Cynthia, who's sounding more and more like my twisted fairy godmother with every word falling out of her mouth.

There are different ways to handle bullies. Unplug, block, gray-rock, smile blandly. Be the most unsatisfying bear to poke. Fawn, if you can stomach it, if it's something you have to do to survive. Slink away in the night if you can manage it. Do what you have to do to get on with your life, your job, your social circle, your godawful family. Your escape is to lie awake at night fantasizing about the retribution you would dole out if only you could. Because my lived experience has taught me there's no beating bullies like my uncle. They operate by a different rulebook. They'll always be willing to go further than you, break more rules than you, suffer more social sanctions than you. They'll hurt the people you care about if you try to make them think they can't hurt you. Your righteous anger will give them life and fuel their self-victimization. They will always have the last word. There's no winning. I've always had to pinch my nose and eat shit.

But the thing is, if I've got another fifty or sixty years, that's an awfully long time to be eating shit.

I glance at my aunt's scared face—my *stepmother*, I realize for the first time. Laura, who always picked me—how could I think otherwise—

There's Dodi, behind me—that rip in her shoulder—

And Cat, wriggling out of Laura's arms, grunting about her dog, watching and learning how to deal with bullies in real time—

They're my people, my ragtag family. Not this creep who fathered me. He doesn't get to terrorize them. And for some reason, it feels easier to stand up for them than it ever did to stand up for myself.

"Give me that fucking dog!"

Cynthia stops midmonologue and Andrew's mouth falls open like he sat on his balls. He's never heard me raise my voice.

I lunge at him, dragging Dodi in my wake, her fingers digging into my sides like some tree-climbing marsupial while she hisses a whisper in my ear about Cynthia being dangerous, a paper pusher who's going to come after me, which is ridiculous, because I don't even work there anymore.

Laura shrieks "Cat!" as she breaks from her grip, and Cynthia rounds on Andrew with renewed demands to turn over Princess—powerful, snarling, menacing as a pit bull—

Andrew retreats, his back against the low wall, and Cynthia lifts one hand—to admonish him? To hit him? To . . . *push* him?

And now I'm level with them both, and Cynthia's hand is reaching to me instead—

"He made the list, Cynthia!" Dodi shrieks. "Get away from the wall, Jake!"

I don't listen. I reach out to grab Princess from Andrew's arms—

And then the world buckles—or at least this small part of

the Cascadia Subduction Zone. The earth rumbles and movement comes from the left, like someone has picked up the roof by one corner and shaken it, sending a broad, shallow ripple across the whole thing, like they're trying to flick sand off a beach towel. The ripple reaches us, and Dodi topples into me, sending me forward like a domino. My hand collides with Andrew's chest and the wall catches him about three inches below his center of gravity, sending him backward in slow motion, the only sound to break the horrified silence on the roof coming from Princess, still yipping joyfully in his arms—

"Tinkerballs!" Cat shrieks, running to the wall.

"Cat!" Dodi cries.

I don't even think. I intercept Cat before she hurls herself over the edge. I hoist her up into my arms and safety, but she shoves one hand right in my face for leverage so she can crane backward and peer over the edge.

"He's all right!" she hollers. "Look! He's all right!"

I shake her hand out of my face and glance over. Andrew is emphatically not all right. If Laura wants to do an open casket, she has her work cut out for her. But Princess landed on a squishy body, and he's fine. He twirls in a tight circle, panting, tongue hanging out, ass wagging, wondering where on earth we all disappeared to.

When I turn around, Laura stands frozen by the parapet, her hands clasped over her mouth. She doesn't scream. She doesn't cry. Dodi is on all fours on the Astroturf behind me, dog urine and thawed snow seeping into the knees of her pants. And Cynthia stands still as a column, her eyes on me.

We're all silent for a minute, our breath ragged, our hearts beating in our ears. Shaky, wild-eyed, shell-shocked. I stare at my hand. I spy a murder weapon.

In the distance a siren wails, and I see a flash of police of-

ficers, handcuffs, courtrooms. *Voluntary manslaughter.*
Grant's idiotic voice chirps excitedly in my ear. But there was
an altercation beforehand. I'd been screaming at him—I'd
backed him up against the parapet. Third degree murder—
Second, depending on witness testimony, Grant says again,
and I stare at Cynthia. This woman who looks at me like I'm
the worst sort of monster—it comes down to what she has
to say.

And I watch as Cynthia and Laura and Dodi exchange long
glances, and there's something there . . . a space, a silence, an
understanding between three women on a roof after a close
call with a dangerous psycho, the sort of psycho women have
to deal with all the time—at home, at work—by smiling and
turning the other cheek, or fleeing, or—if you're fierce and
strong like Dodi and Cynthia—standing your ground, taking
matters into your own hands, pushing back—*pushing*—

Dodi called her a paper pusher. But no, she didn't say *a* paper pusher—

I realize something awful about Cynthia, the same moment
she sees something redeeming in me.

"What a horrible accident," Cynthia says without inflection.

I'm like a parade inflatable snagged on a lamppost. I deflate, go limp. Cat wriggles from my lax arms, and Dodi takes
her, mutely, clumsily. She squeezes Cat so tight I hear joints
pop. I drop to my knees and reach out for Laura, who falls to
the turf next to us, and I put my arms around them all.

51

Arrested

JAKE

WITHIN MINUTES, AN EMERGENCY RESPONSE TEAM SPILLS OUT OF THE ELEVA-tor bulkhead and onto the roof.

"It was all a horrible accident," Cynthia says levelly over the bustle and din of the EMTs and police officers in her trade-mark unnerving monotone.

"You're going to be okay. You're in shock," the paramedic says, fluffing a big silver emergency blanket and spreading it around Cynthia's shoulders. A police officer writes her state-ment on a pad while Cynthia gazes at me with emotionless eyes.

The hand that touched Andrew's chest tingles and turns white.

"It wasn't your fault," Laura reassures me. We wrap our arms around each other, and I watch Dodi pace back and forth restlessly, distractedly, like a caged tiger, Cat still curled into a ball in her arms, watching Cynthia all the while.

My father is dead. That was a lie for most of my life; now it really is true, but I feel nothing about the loss. Everyone who matters to me is safe.

Eventually, Laura given a statement to the police too—cool, calm, collected.

"It was all a horrible accident," she says firmly, squeezing my hand with both of hers.

She seems taller, straighter, like she fills space differently somehow. She hands a business card to the officer and takes one of his. Next is Dodi's statement.

"It was all a horrible accident," she says without blinking, leaning into my side.

I feel like I'm watching myself when I give my own statement. "It was a horrible accident." I'm not lying.

The building manager arrives, carrying Princess in a grubby baby onesie. He scrabbles out of her arms and pelts over to Cat.

"Yes, there's a security camera, right there," the building manager says to the inquiring police officer, "but it's directed at the dog park, not the wall. Jesus. What a horrible accident."

At last they don't need us anymore, and we can go. With one final look at Cynthia still swathed in foil across the roof, perched on the parapet like it's the best seat in the house, I take Cat by the hand, and Dodi slips a protective arm around Laura—one widow supporting another—and we go, passing a pair of police officers as they step onto the roof.

"God," one mutters, "what a horrible accident."

"JAKE," DODI SAYS IN THE ELEVATOR. "WE NEED—TO TALK."

I look at her. I think what she needs is a change of clothes and a shower, but Laura is in agreement.

"You two go for a walk," she says, eyes darting between us. She wants a reconciliation. A happily ever after. She wants to keep Cat so badly. "I'll take Cat back to the apartment."

She darts out on the third floor with Cat and Princess in tow and leaves us.

In a whisper, Dodi says, "Cynthia—"

"Cynthia," I agree.

She lets out a breath. "She's covering for you. What are we going to do about her?"

"She can wait."

She nods, eyes wide, feet apart in a fighting pose. "Table the discussion of this paradigm shift for now?"

"Put a pin in it and circle back later for a proper face time, because we have other things to discuss."

Dodi stares at me. I stare at her. I press G, the doors close slowly, and there's the fairground feeling as we watch each other in that small, falling space, my entire future life flashing before my eyes. I have time—so much time now—and yet I've never felt so pressured in my life to get something done as quickly as possible. It can't wait.

"I'm walking it all back. I love you, and I want to spend the rest of my life with you."

I'm dropping clichés like a Hallmark ghostwriter, but what else are you supposed to do when there's no other way to say it? The message lands. I see her feelings on her face for once. Surprise. Relief. Regret. Sadness. So much sadness. She winds her arms tight around her midsection instead of around me.

"And I love you," she says bravely. "I wish I could spend the rest of my life with you, too."

And I knew, theoretically, Dodi was capable of crying, but it's something else to see it happen. Her face doesn't wind up or turn red. She just calmly, quietly sheds tears, like a placid stone statue performing a miracle in a deserted transept for her one true believer.

I completely fucked up my delivery.

"You can."

"What?"

"My real grandparents are almost a hundred. Can you put up with me that long?"

She smears her tears across her face with her coat sleeve. "What?"

She didn't understand a word of what Cynthia said on the roof about my parents. "Bill did a DNA test—"

And I don't need to explain anything else, not this second, because "DNA test" are the magic words that make a hereditary disease vanish in a puff of smoke. Dodi's mouth falls open and a shuddering breath comes out. She shivers as a secondary earthquake ripples through her mental landscape and shifts *everything*, and she needs a minute to assess the lay of the land in the aftermath. I can give her as many as she needs because I have a *lot* of minutes now.

"Fuck's sake, Jake!" she says, swiping at her eyes. She's furious and relieved and trying so hard to turn the tears off. "That's the sort of thing you lead with!"

The movies say this ends in a dramatic kiss. I step close, and she reaches for me—

The elevator doors heave open and three firemen shoulder in. I grab Dodi by the hand and pull her outside into the circus of ground zero. Lights flash, people shout. It's insane to watch any of this. His body is there—right *there*. I watch the paramedics zip the body bag and lug him onto the stretcher like a sack of potatoes.

This isn't the place for that kiss, either. "Let's go for a drive."

Dodi wrinkles her nose in disgust at the thought of the stinky Lambo, but I fish the key fob out of my pocket and place it in her palm. She stares at it.

"I didn't steal this one," I say. "It's yours."

She rotates the fob slowly in her hand and stares at the logo, then presses the lock button. A beep sounds behind us. She turns and stares at the sleek red car, her mouth hanging open.

"What? *How?*"

But the beep also startles a police officer standing half a dozen feet away. He spins around and our eyes meet.

It's Baby Cop.

His nostrils flare, and he's about to duck his head and walk in the other direction, but then he freezes. His eyes bulge and his mouth falls open.

"Jesus shit!" he yells, staring at something inside Dodi's new car.

It's Willow, still sitting shotgun after helping me meet the required passenger number for the carpool lane during holiday gridlock, her uncomfortably round, open mouth pressed to the glass like a tank-cleaning fish.

Another cop jogs over to assist Baby Cop. "What the fucking hell—what's wrong with her?" The new cop slaps the glass. "Lady? *Lady!*"

A paramedic sprints over and shines a flashlight in her eyes. "She's not responsive!"

A second paramedic, two more cops, and a fireman—we've got fucking firemen now—swarm the car, and another fireman runs over with a window breaker—

"Stop!" Dodi shrieks, clicking the fob buttons madly. She punches the panic button, the lock button, and finally the unlock button. A cop yanks open the door and Willow topples out onto the asphalt. The paramedics pounce.

"She's cold and clammy! I can't find a pulse!"

All hell breaks loose, but to one side, Baby Cop hasn't moved an inch.

"You," he says, looking right at me. "You sick *pervert.*"

His voice rings out and heads turn to look. He takes one step toward me and another, arms bulldogged around his vest and hands hovering near his belt. "Where were you going to leave this one, huh? Sitting on a swing making daisy chains?" He jerks his chin toward the playground behind Dodi's complex.

Preposterous. It's the middle of winter.

"Or on the steps over there, scattering bread for the pigeons?" I sigh.

"Or maybe sitting on that bench there," Baby Cop continues, pointing, "a white hot chocolate in her hands, her skates in a bag on the ground and two tickets to the Santa Skate for Tots in her pocket, waiting for her date to pick her up."

My mouth falls open. He *gets it.*

He gets the happy stories I was trying to create, the Life After Grant I was giving his emancipated prisoners. Una down by the river, bundled warm and perched on a rug to admire the view of the glittering downtown, with a bottle of champagne, a bouquet of red roses, and an engagement ring sparkling on her finger, waiting for her new fiancé to come back from his phone call to announce the news to his parents.

Tari, perched in a wheelchair, a tensor bandage around her ankle, a pair of dance shoes in her lap and a nightclub's stamp on the back of her hand.

Katrin, waiting in arrivals with a printed itinerary in her pocket and a big sparkling sign saying *WELCOME HOME.*

David, perched on Santa's knee, Christmas movie tickets in one pocket and a wrapped present in another, a gift for his significant other—an apartment key—

And so many others. Rich, interesting lives for all of them, from A to V. Well, from B to U. Poor Anastasia. And Verity— Dodi was a *terrible* influence.

Everyone's staring at me. The paramedics have abandoned the doll, the firemen form a ring, and half a dozen cops creep close like a pack of wolves circling.

And there's Dodi, eyes wide, mouth as round as Willow's.

When I look at her, I know I have my own rich, interesting life waiting for me.

I summon my best serial killer smile. "Get out of my head."

He pounces. I'm pinned to a cruiser in an instant, being patted down and mashed against the metal body of the car. I taste blood on my lip.

"Pete. Pete!"

It's a familiar voice. Officer Stubbs? I can't move my head. Handcuffs ratchet tight around my wrists.

"What— No! That's *my* car!" Dodi is shrieking at the same fireman who tried to smash a window. A cop hears this and now Dodi is pinned to the hood of the cruiser next to me.

"A bit extreme, Pete," Stubbs's voice rings out.

"It's *him*!" Pete snarls.

"Public mischief, Pete! That's the best-case scenario!"

"He's going to have fucking decapitated heads in his freezer. Skeletons buried under his patio. I *know it!*"

"Jesus . . . the Homicide Department thought it was *funny* . . . no one was laughing *at* you, but then you started—"

He presses his big paw on top of my head and ducks me down and into the back of the cruiser. My face collides with the sticky vinyl of the back seat, and the door slams behind me. I wriggle around and sit up. Outside, Pete's yelling, spittle flying out of his mouth, and Officer Stubbs watches him, coolly, eyebrows raised. She catches my eye.

I think I see the slightest flicker of a smile.

The opposite door opens and Dodi tumbles in like a rag doll.

"We need a lawyer," Dodi grunts into the seat. She rolls over and looks up at me, panting.

"We've got the best one in town, and he's taking us on pro bono."

She frowns in confusion and then gasps. "Shit!"

I follow her line of sight through my window to Laura perched on Dodi's balcony on the third floor, Cat's little face peeking up over the railing.

"Shit, shit, *shit*!" Dodi snarls. This affects *Cat*.

But for the first time in years, I'm not afraid of anything. No background noise of anxiety and dread. Nothing.

"Trust me," I tell her.

By now she's learned to. She falls still and waits patiently for my lead.

I peer out the window and mouth, *We'll call!* I don't know if Laura sees that, but she waves and takes Cat by the shoulders, doting grandma on babysitting duty for the night while Mom and Dad go on a proper date. It's so hard to make time for date night, but *so* important.

Dodi catches my eye.

I lean forward and whisper in her ear. "You wanted to play serial killer games with me," I remind her.

She bites her lip. "I don't mind the handcuffs," she says in a low voice, slipping into the fantasy with me. "I prefer zip ties, but in a pinch . . ." She's . . . turned on, the little freak. Her lipstick is smudged, her eyeliner smeared, her hair tousled, spilling all over the seat where she lies.

I still haven't explained everything to her. I haven't told her about the house with the built-in grandparents, or the school down the street, or the fact that she gets to keep our Las Vegas winnings for our consulting business seed money—I've got twelve clients lined up for us out of the gate, all of whom have

HR departments that will be interested to learn how my spreadsheets can help them remove expensive assholes from payroll. There's so much to tell her. We're set.

It's time for that kiss.

Officer Stubbs climbs in behind the wheel and, after one long look in the rearview mirror at me, presses a button on the dash. "Jailhouse Rock" fills the cruiser at full blast. We round a corner and Dodi slides across the slippery seat and into me. We can't hold each other, but we don't need to. She wriggles up and latches her mouth onto mine in a wet slide, a warm twist—and another sudden corner topples us into an even better position. Baby Cop can slap the fucking shatterproof plastic window between us all he fucking wants, I'm never coming up for air.

This is it: happily ever fucking after.

EPILOGUE
Serial Killers Ever After

DODI

I HAVE A TOP-FLOOR MEETING.

The executive worries her pen elegantly with the blunt tips of her white manicure as she considers the papers spread out in front of her.

"I can't argue with the bottom line," she says thoughtfully. She leans back in her chair and considers me with an expensive, veneered smile. "And who would say no to the offer of *transformational change.*"

Next to her a woman who could be her clone, but several decades younger, nods her head and flashes an identical smile at me. The executive bows her blond head over the contract, slashes her signature in four places, and engages me to cut problem employees from payroll and transform her organization into a healthier and more productive workplace. My consulting business has a growing reputation. No one knows quite how I get the numbers.

She has no idea her name is going to be at the top of the list when I hand it over to the company's directors. She's the biggest psycho here.

A door swings open, and both blond heads swivel to take in the new arrival: a man in standard-issue office attire, gray slacks, white shirt, thick-framed glasses. I narrow my eyes at him. I *think* I recognize him. A temp I run into from time to time as I circulate through the downtown office core. Funny how we keep crossing paths. He's three steps in before he stops in his tracks and adopts a rueful smile.

"I'm interrupting."

"Never, Jonathan," the executive says, extending her hand to take her coffee from him. He passes a tea to the younger woman, and then he holds out the tray with the last coffee to me.

"I always get an extra," he says. "Black, no sugar." He shrugs apologetically.

"Exactly the way I take it." I twist it free and look at the name on the side: DOLLY. It always says that.

I raise one eyebrow at him, and he shoves his glasses up his nose with his middle finger.

The executive watches him lazily as he leaves, then turns to me. "When you start gathering your data . . ."

I let her blather importantly as I sweep up the contract and sample documents. The data has already been harvested, processed, and sorted into a comprehensive report. For the next month I will take over a cushy corner office in her headquarters with a temporary sign bearing my name taped to the door while I listen to podcasts on my earbuds and sexually harass the poor office temp. I shake the executive's cool, limp hand, and then her daughter's, and tell them I'll see them on Monday.

In the hall outside I look to my left, then right. A near-identical stretch of hall extends to either side. I go still as a big cat about to pounce and sniff the breeze.

To the right

I prowl down the hall, my heels clacking on the hard white floor. I round a corner and drag my fingernail along the wall until it catches on the frame of a door. I scratch my nails down the outside of the door, twist the handle, and step inside.

I guessed right.

He clicks the door shut, and all we can see in the dark is the band of light at the bottom of the door illuminating the edges of our shoes. The two lunatics are still working together.

"When are you going to quit temping and get a real job?" I whisper against his jaw.

"Never. It's the perfect cover while I pursue my real interests." His mouth drifts near my ear, and then down to my neck.

"Stalking?" I twist his tie around my hand.

"Yes," he mutters.

"Casing your next victim." I pull.

"That too." The door thuds gently in the frame behind me as he presses me against it.

"And . . . perfecting your MO." His stubble is rough under my fingertips. He needs a shave.

"Of course." His fingertips are on my jaw, too. They drift down, and now they're around my neck.

"Still a creep," I breathe against his lips. "Show me?"

NOW OUR LIFE IS LIKE THIS:

There's a living, breathing man in my bed when I wake up. Sometimes his eyes are already open and on me; sometimes I get to watch his thick eyelashes flutter in his sleep. Mornings are slow. We never rush. There's time—so much time. All the work I used to have to do, split between two adults. He makes breakfast, he packs our lunches—our daughter's and mine—he pours coffee into a thermos for me. By now are you seeing a pattern here? An MO taking shape? Don't worry. I'll circle back.

I drop my kid at school and commute downtown to meet with clients. I have a succession of corner offices I don't pay rent for, with views of the bustling, writhing masses below, my kingdom for the conquering. I'm good at my job. I get results. I'm in demand.

If I finish early, I might do a speck of window-shopping. I'm materialistic. I like things. I like to acquire little . . . *trophies* to mark successes and important events. A heavy paperweight that fits just right in my palm, that I can keep on my desk near my right hand. Or maybe a tie, a dark green one—silk, so that the knot slides easily when pulled tight around the neck. I have someone to shop for now.

At the end of the day I go home, where it's clean and smells like dinner, kick off my very expensive shoes, and play with Barbies on the floor like the card-carrying adult that I am. My family life is acutely wholesome, which is exactly what you'd expect of a murderer. We even have a new golden retriever puppy.

Jake's slipped into a convincing facade of wholesomeness with me. He's lost the dark circles under his eyes. I'll never trust his big lunatic asylum smiles, even though they go all the way to the eyes now, but the twisty, shy half smiles, like he's embarrassed at how happy he is? I know they're real, because I do them too. And when the kid is in bed, and Grandpa too, and the house gets broody and dark, the wholesome family ruse slips away and we're a pair of night creatures again. A glass of wine, a true crime show . . . or maybe date night, if Grandma is free.

The other day was our one year anniversary: paper. In our case, in a neat little stack, which he pushed across the breakfast table to me. An itinerary for a belated honeymoon in a castle-infested forest while the grandparents watch the kid.

"Transylvania?"

"Antarctica's a zoo this time of year," he said apologetically. "And Cuba's out, since vampires have to stay out of the sun."

"There will be other anniversaries."

"Maybe a few more," he agreed.

"Maybe," I said. And we'd looked at each other, shrewdly, suspiciously.

Because after all this time, I think we've figured out each other's MO. I can see it when he looks at me, his expression dangerous and cunning. I know he sees it in my eyes, too—the dark motive behind every smile, every kiss, every *I love you*. We're both playing the long game. We're each waiting for the moment the other lets their guard down. But in the meantime we're going to take care of each other, play games with each other, love each other tender and love each other true, for better or worse, through sickness and in health, until eventually, after a few decades, we finally, *finally* succeed, in loving each other to death.

ACKNOWLEDGMENTS

Thank you, in order of appearance, to—

My parents, whose love and support are behind everything I do, for figuring out I was writing a book, respecting my veil of secrecy, and never once asking me a single question about it. Legendary.

My sister, who was my first reader when she read my diary and told me it was really good, and she wanted to read what happens next. You're the best.

My husband, the real doll in all this, even though you're not supposed to marry your stalker. It's a long list and getting longer, but I'm pretty amazing too, so we're even.

David. We've come a long way from writing absolute trash on my living room floor. We now . . . *(consults notes)* . . . never mind. Your support has been everything, and I hope I'll always be there for you the way you've been here for me.

The fan fiction fanatics, especially Finn. It was a real slice.

Tari, the baddest good cop, the goodest bad cop, and the best storyteller; you are such a good friend.

Katrin, because every angry swamp witch needs her coven. Thank you for your wisdom, for your snark, and for your *discerning* taste in books.

Chelsey, for taking the biggest risk, for teaching me how to be a better writer, and for about a thousand hidden agent things you do when I'm not looking.

And Sareer, for volunteering to be the final sequence in this Rube Goldberg machine of family, cheerleaders, and friends that helped launch this book into the world. I can't wait to see where you take it.

SERIAL KILLER GAMES

Kate Posey

READERS GUIDE

QUESTIONS FOR DISCUSSION

1. What's the appeal of serial killers?

2. How would you dispose of a sex doll? How would you dispose of a sex doll if you knew you wouldn't get caught?

3. Do we want to see Grant find true love? Or should he just carry on with the dolls?

4. Favorite pet: Cat, dog, or rabbit? Discuss. Favorite stew meat? Discuss.

5. What genre would you classify this book as?

6. There are two types of plot twists: the ones you don't see coming, and the ones you gleefully anticipate. Which twists fell into each category for you?

7. I wanted to find a romance novel with all my favorite tropes in one place: Marriage of Convenience. One Year to Live. Enemies to Lovers. Secret Baby. Secret Parentage. Main Character Inherits a Fucking Amazing House. Found Family. Obligatory Food Porn. Holiday Orphans . . . My list of demands was *extensive*. So I wrote it. What are your favorite genre tropes? What tropes would have to be in your perfect book? Are you writing that book now? Why not?

8. What genre of book are you living in? How so?

9. What are the tropes of your own life?

10. What do you want your HEA to look like?

ABOUT THE AUTHOR

Kate Posey lives in Canada with her family. *Serial Killer Games* is her debut novel.

Ready to find
your next great read?

Let us help.

Visit prh.com/nextread

Penguin
Random
House